THAW OF SPRING
KNIFE'S EDGE, ALASKA
BOOK TWO

REBECCA ZANETTI

Copyright © 2025 by Rebecca Zanetti

All rights reserved.

No part of this book may be reproduced in any form or by any electronic or mechanical means, including information storage and retrieval systems, without written permission from the author, except for the use of brief quotations in a book review.

To the Mah Jong Girls—One by one, your stories will find their way into this series. Thankfully, real life comes with fewer plot twists and way more snacks. (At least so far.)

*To Debbie Smith—my sister, my friend, and the only person I know who can sink a birdie and a vodka soda with equal precision. From epic laughs in Vegas to your killer golf game, you've shown me that life's better when you play it bold, swing big, and never bet against yourself. Your kindness, wit, and sense of adventure light up every room, and every fairway.
This one's for you, with all my love, and a silent nod to our next round —on the course or at the slots.*

CHAPTER 1

Knife's Edge didn't thaw quietly—it cracked, hissed, and burned its way into spring. Every year, without fail, more visitors showed up in the small Alaskan town once the mountain passes and tumultuous sky cleared. Not even the drilling rain could keep them away.

Christian Osprey skirted a purple-haired female standing beneath an eave and in front of some lit circle contraption holding a phone, her eyes animated. What the hell? He kept walking, noting the Green Plate restaurant was open for the day. In the winter, Gus and Janet only opened for dinner.

He sighed. Apparently spring had arrived. Damn it. He'd have to gather supplies and head into the mountains sooner rather than later. Glancing at Sam's Tavern across the muddy street, he felt a tug in his chest he didn't appreciate. Not at all. He would not go in there. Nobody really knew who Sam had been, but the name had stuck throughout the ages. The current owner was a sweetheart, and one he needed to leave alone.

Hunching his shoulders, he allowed the rain to fall on his thick hair and stood for a moment on the torn and winter-damaged sidewalk, staring at Sam's and the small storage building between the tavern and the grocery store.

"Hey. Excuse me?" The gal with the purple hair tugged on his arm, her pink sweatshirt damp from the rain.

He glanced down and smoothly stepped away, freeing himself.

Her eyes widened as her gaze dropped to Tika, by Christian's side. "Is that a baby wolf?"

For crap's sake. "No." Christian gave an imperceptible jerk of his chin, and the wolf-husky puppy immediately moved forward, in front of him and to the side. Away from the woman. He turned to do the same and she grabbed his worn T-shirt sleeve. Again.

"Wait. It's so cool that both you and the wolf have two different colored eyes. Can I interview you?" She stepped closer, bringing the scent of lavender with her.

"Absolutely not." Christian's eyes were green and black, while Tika's were blue and bluish-brown.

The woman didn't seem put off and instead switched topics. "Why does this town have the only sheriff in Alaska?" Still unfortunately holding the material above his wrist, she pointed to the banners strung across the main street of town. One announced the spring fishing derby next week, and the other announced that Knife's Edge claimed to have the only Alaskan sheriff.

At the sight of the bigger one, he felt his lips twitch. Brock would fucking hate that. Served him right for becoming the sheriff.

"Well?" The woman turned her attention back on him, looking up many inches to his face. She was cute. About five foot six. Blue eyes, nice bone structure, girl-next-door grin. Too young to be alone in the Alaskan wilderness.

"You eighteen?" he grunted. If not, he'd take her to Brock's office. As the sheriff, his brother would have to deal with her.

Her smile brightened. "Not anymore. I'm old enough to drink, handsome. Want me to prove it to you?"

He heard the side door to the tavern open across the street and then he felt her move through it. *Her.* His gaze slid to the opening between the rough wooden building housing the bar and the one-story storage building, catching a glimpse of Amka. Just one second glimpse before she disappeared inside.

At all times, he could feel her location. Her energy. Somehow.

In that instant of seeing her, he'd noted her black hair up in a ponytail, her blue flannel shirt open to show a black cami over full breasts, and tight slim jeans that hugged every delectable inch of her legs. His own energy flowed through him, pushing him to cross the street.

The female finally released his arm. "Dude? You okay?"

Still remaining motionless, he cut his gaze to her. "Yes."

She swallowed and finally had the good sense to step away from him. "You've got such an intense vibe, man. It's both kinda hot and kinda scary." Squinting, she studied him from the top of his dark hair to his well-worn boots. "More hot than scary." Her grin returned. "I'm Nixi Halliday. From Halliday's Adventures and Holidays?"

He had no clue what that meant. Grunting, he jerked his head at Tika and turned away from Nixi.

"Wait." Now exasperation filled her tone, but she didn't grab him again. "Seriously. You've never heard of me? Aren't you on social media at all?"

He needed to get to the damn store for provisions, yet his boots remained on the muddy sidewalk. It wasn't the woman demanding his attention that kept him rooted to the spot. It was the woman he couldn't see right now. Having Amka out of sight left him unsettled in a way that hadn't even caught him while he'd remained motionless in a perch for hours on end worlds away...waiting for his mark. That's why he had to escape into the wilderness.

Now.

"Please let me interview you really quickly about the town. About you and your cute puppy. Please." Nixi fluttered her eyelashes, somehow making her look even younger and cuter.

He had no interest in cute...or so young. While he might be in his late twenties or even early thirties—who knew—he felt eons older. Knew it showed in his eyes. "No."

Now she put out her bottom lip in a look that no doubt helped get her way with most people. "Come on. One of the requirements for the traveling challenge is to interview a local at each small town, which is something I usually do for my channel, anyway. So, please? I'll even buy you a drink afterward."

He'd hate himself later for asking. Just knew he would. "Challenge?"

"Yeah." She hopped once, splashing up a bit of mud over her brown boots and the bottom of her faded jeans. "The Nowhere USA Challenge sponsored by Rusty Spoke Jerky? They listed twenty towns, tiny ones, where their jerky is found for creators to visit and explore. We have to spend at least a week in the town, but most people like to shoot footage over a couple of weeks, then we upload our content to our social media channels. At the end of June, a winner will be chosen. The pot is fifty thousand dollars." Her eyes gleamed. "I already get paid for my content, but this would be a huge boost. So what do you say?"

Oh, fuck no. What in the world was a creator, anyway? How many of them would be descending upon his town? He had to get out of here.

The rain fizzled. Somewhat. He turned his body this time, facing that building across the street.

Silence overcame the downpour. Just inside his head.

Something—

Fire flashed and the front window of the storage building blew out in an explosion that tore through the spring day.

Amka.

THE BLAST BLEW Amka away from the table and into the side wall. Pain slashed down her back as she fell to the floor. What had happened?

Her ears rang. Heat flashed against her face. The room wavered around her. Provisions clattered on the cement floor as smoke filled the air. She couldn't see.

"Amka!" That voice. She knew that voice.

A rush of cool air swirled through the room. She blinked, on her side, fire coming for her. Flames licked from the front of the building through the middle, right toward the door. In every direction. Fast. Way too fast.

Smoke filled her lungs as the fire flowed toward her. She had to move. Why was everything fuzzy? She couldn't think.

A form filled the doorway. Solid and strong. Male.

Christian?

He came through the flames and smoke with a rough grace. A burning slat of wood fell from the ceiling, bouncing off his shoulder. He reached her, ignoring the fire trying to swallow him. "Amka." He crouched, soot already across his forehead as one strong hand cupped her face. "Are you hurt?"

His words came from very far away, his voice deep but too distant.

She swallowed and shook her head, trying to focus. "I'm okay." Pain tore through her side, but she forced herself to sit.

More boards rained down around them. "There's propane," she coughed out, looking wildly toward the front window at the one cylinder beneath what had been a counter. She used it for her outside barbecue. The tank hissed and started to glow red.

Propane vented like a demon exhaling gas. She had to get it out of there.

Pushing away from Christian, she started to crawl toward it. Embers burned her palms. She should take it outside.

Strong hands grabbed her hips and she was suddenly sailing through the air to impact a chest harder than rock. The air whooshed out of her lungs and she sucked in a breath, inhaling heated smoke.

She yelped, cradled against Christian as embers dropped onto her shoulders.

He huddled over her, protecting her from the burns, and turned to barrel through fire and smoke to the rain outside. Fast. Sure. Safe. She closed her eyes, coughing out smoke. "We have to get the propane," she whispered.

"Too late," he said grimly, tearing around the building toward the street. "Everyone run," he bellowed. "Take cover."

The few people on the sidewalks immediately launched into obedience, running away. No cars were driving their way. He kept moving, holding her tight, pounding down the muddy sidewalk to the other side of the tavern.

A blast boomed through the rain, and she looked up to see debris blowing into the sky, even above the tavern.

Then, the crackle of fire.

He lowered her to her feet as rain pummeled them both. The fire hissed loudly from the other side of the building, fighting the rain. "How badly are you hurt?"

She coughed several times. "Not bad." Her throat was on fire. "Bruised my side, I think." Her left arm felt odd. She looked down.

He did as well, running both hands down her arms. "Nothing broken." Obviously concentrating, he felt along her ribcage and down her hips to both legs, bending to look up. "We'll have Doc look at the bruises."

She stared at him, noting a burn on his cheek. "You're hurt."

Ignoring the concern in his dual-colored eyes, she brushed the slight wound.

He closed his eyes for just a moment before reopening them. One green and one black. Something flashed in them. An expression she couldn't read but felt deep. "I'm fine." He stood then, towering over her. "Stay here." He gave her one hard look and then crossed to the front of the bar, angling his head and then disappearing from sight.

Something about his tone made her stay in place. Until her brain caught up. Wait a minute. Her storage building just blew up, and her bar could be on fire next. Gathering her strength and ignoring the pain in her side, she limped to the front of the building and to her front door, noting the town's one water tanker screeching to a stop with Lucas Landom, their tanker chief, hopping out. Sheriff Brock Osprey was right behind him in his truck, and he leaped out, running toward Christian and the tanker. The three men worked quickly, yanking out the hose and attaching it to the truck valve to spray at the fire.

The rain was already winning.

Amka hurried to help and stopped cold when Christian turned his gaze on her. "Move back," he mouthed.

She obeyed.

Why, she'd never understand. Nobody told her what to do.

But she leaned against her door as several other townspeople emerged from buildings and arriving cars to watch the fire being beat. Lucas rapidly unfolded the hose as Brock and Christian moved in. She watched the Osprey brothers. Both tall with dark hair and Inuit features, both ex-Navy, they moved in tandem and won the battle. Christian had a shadow across his rugged jaw and was the picture of raw male muscle as he worked.

He'd probably saved her life.

She wanted to thank him, to make him dinner, to buy him drinks, to just spend more time with him. While he wasn't a keeper, who also didn't want to be tied down, he was still her friend. Kind of. She raised a hand to brush soot off her chin, and her engagement ring caught her attention.

For a moment, she'd forgotten her fiancé. Completely. Jarod hadn't come to the bar today, and she'd forgotten all about him.

Brock rolled up the hose while Christian and Lucas disappeared into the debris.

Enough of this. She didn't follow orders. Ignoring the pain in her arm, she moved forward as most of the people around her did the same, noting the demolished and still smoldering building. The structures on either side showed damage and some burn marks, but both had remained standing. She reached Christian the same time as Brock.

"The fire moved too fast," Christian said to his brother, kicking over a couple of smoking boards.

Lucas crouched to look closer at the floor. In his early thirties, he had short brown hair and serious brown eyes. He'd been a smokejumper before moving to the small town to write several novels and had been elected the tanker chief two years previous when he'd missed the annual town meeting. "Way too fast."

Brock lifted one dark eyebrow. "Accelerant?"

"Affirmative. I could smell it when I kicked open the door." Christian scrutinized the floor. "The explosion was supposed to start a fire that engulfed this entire building." His already hard jawline hardened even more as he turned his formidable focus on her. "We need to get you to the doctor. Now."

She gulped. "Somebody did this on purpose? How?"

"We'll figure that out later," Brock said grimly. "Right now, go get checked out."

She started to shake her head, but Christian picked her up, strode outside, and started moving down the street toward Brock's truck. She should've protested. Should've kicked and screamed and reminded him she could walk just fine. But her arm throbbed, her chest ached, and something worse than smoke was clawing at her lungs. So instead, she let herself be carried—cradled like a woman who could somehow be saved— by the man who *wasn't* her fiancé.

Behind them, the rubble didn't crackle anymore. It hissed. As the wreckage faded, a new thought burned hotter than the fire.

Had somebody known she was in there?

CHAPTER 2

Amka couldn't let herself get too comfortable as Christian easily balanced her in one arm and opened the door to the older black truck as the rain punished them both. How was he so strong? "We can't just take Brock's rig," she protested rather weakly.

Christian grunted, like that was sufficient, and placed her gently on the seat. The upholstery chilled her butt. She shivered.

He opened the back door, and Tika jumped in, stretching out and yawning.

Christian shut the rear door and returned his attention to Amka, reaching across her for the seatbelt, his arm brushing her collarbone. "Let me know if this hurts," he said in a low and calm voice with that faint growl at the edges. His head dipped close as he leaned in, crossing her chest to snap the belt into place. The motion sent a wave of heat across her skin.

He paused just a moment too long before pulling back. His eyes held hers. "Does the belt hurt?"

Everything hurt. Her ribs ached like they'd been used for target practice. Her arm throbbed in a dull rhythm. Even her scalp felt scorched. She forced a shrug and looked down at his soot covered T-shirt. "No. I'm fine."

His knuckle slid beneath her chin, and the contact made her breath catch. He tilted her face up toward his, gentle but insistent. "Don't lie to me."

She blinked once, then again, her lashes brushing her skin before she dropped her gaze to his mouth. She'd noticed it long before today. Christian Osprey had a great mouth. Firm. Serious. Sexy. "I'm not lying."

His expression didn't change. "You are."

She sighed, the breath shaky. "I'm a little bruised, Christian. The seatbelt doesn't hurt me. But I don't think we should just steal the sheriff's truck."

Christian didn't argue. He stepped back, shut the door quietly, and walked around the front of the truck.

She adjusted the seatbelt with her good hand. Her body didn't like the angle.

He climbed in, shut his door, reached beneath the driver's seat, and pulled out the keys to twist in the ignition. The engine roared to life. Without hesitation, he flipped a hard U-turn in the middle of the street, the tires bumping over wet and muddied pavement.

"I can get myself to the doc's. I think I'm fine," she said again.

Christian barely grunted in response.

This time, she had the odd urge to hit him. Which was ridiculous, considering he'd just saved her life. Probably. Still, the grunt was obnoxious.

He drove carefully down Main Street, one hand loose on the wheel, gaze sharp through the windshield. At Dalika River Drive, he turned right, heading toward First Street and the long, flat building that served as the town's only medical hub—doctor's office, dentist, and hospital all mashed into one.

Before he could fully stop at the curb, she reached for the

seatbelt and winced as she released it. Her ribs were not fans of movement.

"Hey," she said. "You didn't wear your seatbelt."

Unsurprisingly, he didn't answer. Just opened the door and stepped out.

Fine. She didn't mind quiet. It was better than forced chatter. She opened her door, but he was already there. Before she could swing her legs out, he leaned in and lifted her again, placing her gently on her feet.

"Do you need me to carry you?" he asked.

"No." The word came out too fast. Her body wasn't on board, but her pride was louder. Being carried by Christian Osprey was a strangely addictive feeling. Solid arms, complete control. Like gravity didn't apply.

What would it be like to have that kind of strength? She couldn't imagine it. She was barely five foot three, and even though she tended bar and waitressed most nights, hauling trays and dodging drunks, her strength was lean and wiry. Functional, but not especially impressive. Usually it worked just fine. Just not right now. "I think I'm good," she added, more to convince herself than him. "Christian, you don't have to come inside with me."

He shut the door. "Tika, stay in the truck."

She knew he didn't like being indoors longer than absolutely necessary. He'd been several years ahead of her in school, so they hadn't exactly hung out. But she remembered watching him play football and hockey from the bleachers.

Back then, she couldn't recall ever seeing him inside unless he was at school. He was always outside—working on his family's boat, running drills, disappearing into the woods outside of town.

That hadn't changed, not even since he'd come home from the Navy. He walked with her to the front door of the clinic and opened it.

"Thank you," she said, then hesitated. "I mean, for everything."

He gave her a short nod, chin tilted toward the entrance.

Typical. She couldn't help rolling her eyes as she walked into the waiting room, and the door clicked shut behind her.

Lance Fredrickson looked up from behind the reception desk, earbuds in, phone in hand as he scrolled. The young man worked around his remote-learning college classes. He set the phone down and pulled the earbuds free. "Whoa. What happened?"

"You haven't heard?" Amka asked.

Lance frowned, his dark hair around his shoulders and his brown eyes somber. "No. Should I have?"

"There was a fire," she said. "Actually, more of an explosion."

Christian stood beside her, arms crossed. He didn't move, didn't speak, but somehow still managed to dominate the room.

Amka rubbed her arm. "My storage building. The one I share with Friday's Grocery? It blew up."

Lance stood so fast his rolling chair squeaked. "Wait—seriously? Is everyone okay?"

"I think so." She tried to keep her voice even, but her throat felt like she'd swallowed embers. "I was inside when it happened. The blast threw me across the room." Her arm throbbed. Her ribs pulsed. Her hip had developed a slow, annoying ache. A headache, low and steady, was just settling in. "But really," she said, forcing a small shrug, "I think I'm fine."

Lance just stared at her. "Wow. An explosion."

She shifted on her feet. "Christian, you don't have to stay with me."

"I want to make sure you're okay." He looked out of place in the soft light, all hard edges and quiet intensity.

"You're throwing off the cozy clinic vibe," she muttered.

Dr. May Smirnov strode into the room wearing her usual aqua scrubs, blonde hair pulled back in a high ponytail, a half-eaten sandwich in one hand. "What's going on?" She halted. "I smell smoke. Was there a fire?"

"I can't believe you haven't heard yet," Amka said.

Lance's phone buzzed. Then again. And again. He glanced down at the screen. "Ah. There we go. Texts are rolling in now. Apparently your storage building blew up."

"No kidding," Amka said dryly.

May's eyes narrowed. She handed her sandwich to Lance and moved toward Amka, already shifting into assessment mode. "Were you inside the building when the explosion occurred?"

"She was," Christian said, his voice grim.

"I'm okay," Amka added quickly. "Just sore. My ears are ringing a little."

May squinted at her eyes. "Any loss of consciousness? Blurred vision? Nausea? Headache?"

"Not really. A tiny headache and some pain in my arm."

May's gaze swept over her. "Let's check your vitals and get a better look at that arm. Blast trauma doesn't always show up right away." She turned slightly toward Christian. "You have soot all over you. Were you in the blast?"

"No," Christian said shortly.

Amka wanted to help him get outside where he could find comfort. "He ran into the building and saved me."

May squinted. "Are you experiencing any symptoms? Burns? Respiratory issues?"

"I inhaled some smoke. A couple of minor burns." He glanced toward the door. "Nothing that needs treatment. I'll wait outside."

"I can find another ride home," Amka said, a little louder than she meant to.

He looked at her again. Calm. Quiet. Watchful. "Where's Jarod?" It was the first time he'd said the name.

"Um, he mentioned doing some spring fishin' up at Rugged

Creek, so I'm not sure when he'll be back." Well, he had mentioned it the other day, so that's probably where he'd gone.

Christian nodded. "Then I'll wait for you." He turned and walked out without another word.

May watched him go. "Those Osprey brothers are kind of bossy, right?"

The chuckle came before Amka could stop it. Pain followed. She winced, pressing a hand gently to her ribs.

May noticed immediately. "Right. Holding your side like that tells me we could be dealing with more than bruising. Let's take a look at those ribs and then check for any signs of concussion or soft tissue damage. If your ears are ringing, I want to do a tympanic check, too."

"Thanks." Before following, Amka glanced through the front door.

With his broad back to her, Christian stood outside in the rain, arms crossed, head slightly tilted as he stared off into the distance. The mountains loomed ahead of him, all jagged peaks and resilient strength. He didn't flinch from the cold. He looked like he belonged in it.

She sighed and turned to follow May down the hallway.

Now was not the time to dream about Christian Osprey. *Never* would be a good time, for tons of reasons. She rubbed her chest.

May glanced at her. "Are you having chest pains?"

"No." Not the kind the doctor could fix, anyway.

AFTER AN EXTREMELY THOROUGH—WAY too thorough— examination, Amka strode out of May's office, ears still ringing. "I really am all right," she said, half to herself, half to May trailing behind her.

"I know," May replied, arms folded across her chest, "but

you're bruised. You need to take it easy for at least a week, and if you have any nausea or dizziness, you have to let me know."

Lance looked up from his desk in the corner, his eyes wide. "It's all over town now. Christian carried you out of there like some hero in a war movie."

Amka closed her eyes for a beat and fought the urge to smack her forehead. "Oh crap," she muttered. "He's going to hate that."

May and Lance nodded at the same time in perfect sync.

The door banged open.

Wyland Friday and his son, Sheldon, bustled in, both of them dripping wet and smelling faintly of river water. Wyland had owned Friday's Grocery for decades upon decades with his wife, whom he'd lost to kidney disease seven years ago. The men still wore fishing waders and hats, hooks and lures bobbing with every step.

"Our building burned down," Wyland said, voice hoarse. He shook his head like he still couldn't believe it. "Heard you were inside. You all right?"

Amka stepped forward and touched the older man's hand. Wyland was around seventy, though arthritis had been chewing at him for years. He had grizzled gray hair, kind blue eyes, and always the same outfit: flannel shirt, jeans, fishing waders—rain or shine. "I'm fine. With just a little headache."

Sheldon gave her a short nod. In his thirties, he had the same piercing blue eyes as his father, though his brown hair was still untouched by gray. "Do you have any idea what caused the explosion?"

Amka shook her head. "No, but the sheriff thought it was set on purpose."

The silence that followed felt heavy.

"We'll need to file an insurance claim," Sheldon said, glancing up at his dad like he was waiting for permission.

Amka gave him a look. That was fast.

Wyland's frown deepened. "It's a little early for that, don't you think? Let's make sure everyone's safe before we start counting inventory."

"Dad, we had a lot of provisions in that storage unit."

That wasn't exactly true. Amka shifted her weight, noting a new pain in her right ankle. "Your spring shipment hasn't even arrived yet. There wasn't much in there. You'll be fine."

"There was more than you think," Sheldon said quickly. "I'll call the insurance company today."

Wyland shook his head. "We don't even know what exactly happened."

"There was an explosion and accelerant on the floor," Amka said.

Wyland's eyes narrowed slightly. "Why would someone burn down our storage building?"

Amka couldn't figure it out. "Who knows? We own it together, and there wasn't a whole lot inside at this time of year."

"Except you," Wyland said grimly.

Amka's stomach turned over. Why would anybody want to hurt her? Nobody, at this time, would benefit from her death. She didn't have family and wasn't married yet. Should she get a will?

Sheldon cleared his throat. "It's too early to talk about any of this, but you're right—it's not a great place for storage anymore. Someone's going to want to build there eventually."

Build there? The property was probably worth a lot more than it had been just five years ago, considering Knife's Edge was gaining more popularity.

Wyland's hand landed lightly on her arm. "It's way too soon. We're just glad you're okay."

"Where's Jarod?" Sheldon asked.

Amka had forgotten about Jarod again. "Fishing, I think. I guess I should've called him."

"I'll give him a call." Sheldon pulled out his phone and walked toward the far wall.

Wyland rubbed at his brown-spotted jaw. "Sorry about that. Sometimes he gets ahead of himself."

Amka couldn't think about insurance right now. Plus, if the fire had been arson, didn't insurance people conduct an investigation? She'd worry about that later. "It's nice you two were fishing together today."

"Oh, we weren't." Wyland almost smiled. "He was up on the North Fork, I was further down. We had a little competition going. I called him when I heard."

"You want a ride home?" Sheldon asked from across the room.

She paused and could've said yes. But Christian was outside. He'd pulled her out of that building without hesitation. She hadn't figured out what to say to him yet, but she wasn't a coward. "No, thanks. Christian already offered."

"All right," Wyland said with a sigh. "I'll let Sheldon handle the insurance. He's been taking over more and more of the finances for Friday's Groceries anyway. I'm getting old."

"No, you're not," Amka said quietly. The words came out before she could think too hard about them. He moved slower now, sure. But old? No. Not the way he still showed up for people. "Why don't you come by the tavern tonight?" she added. "It's not clam chowder day, but I can make one of your favorites."

Wyland straightened. "You're a sweetheart, but you need to go home and sleep."

"Exactly," May said adamantly. "Listen to your doctor and your friends. Get some rest, Amka."

Amka didn't have time to rest. "Of course."

"Why don't I walk you out to Christian?" Wyland asked, moving toward the door.

Amka turned and gave May a quick hug. They'd become

friends almost instantly when May had moved to town last year.

"Thank you. I'm feeling better."

"I'm not kidding," May replied, her voice low and firm. "You need to take it easy. Don't make me pull rank as your doctor."

"All right, all right," Amka said, a dry chuckle slipping out. Not that May could actually stop her from doing anything.

May's eyes twinkled. "Say hi to Christian for me, would you?"

Amka didn't answer and just followed Wyland out the door.

CHAPTER 3

Christian turned off the paved road and onto the gravel stretch winding along the river. His knuckles flexed once on the steering wheel before relaxing again. Behind them, the hospital faded into memory. Ahead, the late Alaskan spring unfolded—barren and waking, the kind of in-between season that never really promised safety.

Snow still lingered in the shadows of the tree line, like the last remnants of a threat not quite done with them. Bare birch trunks reached into a sky the color of wet slate, and the Dalika River ran swollen and fast beside the road. He eased the truck through a muddy bend and cut left, tires crunching against frozen gravel and away from the main river. Another half mile brought them to Amka's land.

Tika snored happily in the back seat, spreading out like he owned the vehicle.

Amka's cabin rose out of the ground like it belonged there in two stories of weathered log and green metal roofing, tucked at the edge of a thicket where the forest would someday reclaim everything. The place had a comfortable vibe. Welcoming.

However, it was way too exposed and would be easy to infiltrate.

He killed the engine.

Amka shifted beside him. Even that small movement made her wince.

He didn't like the wince. "You said that Doc May cleared you except for the bruises and that your rib might be cracked." He spoke without looking at her, his gaze still pinned to the cabin where a small curl of chimney smoke drifted above the roof.

"I think I'll be fine," Amka said, her voice hoarse but steady. Her fingers brushed a streak of soot from her thigh. "I got ash all over the truck." She shivered as if unable to warm up. It was probably the shock setting in. "I'm sorry. I smell like a firepit."

He turned his head slowly. "No. You don't."

She blinked at him.

"You smell like cloudberry." The second the statement left his mouth, he wanted to take it back and bury it under the permafrost. What was that?

Amka tilted her face toward him. Eyes dark, rimmed with red from smoke or emotion. Her hair was pulled back in a messy ponytail that had mostly come loose. "Cloudberry?"

Hell. He was already in. Might as well commit. "Yeah. Like apricot, amber, and rose. Sort of wild. A little sharp." He cleared his throat. "Even after the fire." Why was he still talking?

She watched him. Not blinking. Not smiling. "I think that's sweet."

Sweet? No. He didn't know how to even think about being sweet. Even to someone like her. He huffed out a breath, half a laugh, more a self-directed curse. "Don't misread me or see anything that isn't here."

A silence settled between them, heavy but not awkward. More like the land itself had leaned in to listen. He shifted in his seat, trying not to think about how she'd taste if she really did smell like that fruit. Bright, tart. Maybe sweet around the edges.

Jesus, he had to stop.

"Christian?" Her voice barely reached him. Tentative.

He hated that. The hesitation. The uncertainty that curled around his name like she was afraid of him. Which, honestly, made sense. Most people were.

He was a damn menace—tall enough to block out sunlight and with a face that looked like it had seen one too many nights without rest. He didn't talk much, didn't care to be seen, didn't trust easy. Crowds made his skin itch. Noise made him leave. And people? Most of them weren't worth the oxygen they burned.

Still, he tried. Plastered on something neutral and turned to face her, aware that he took up more than his share of space in the cab. His voice came out rougher than he meant. "What is it?"

Her long lashes, pure and natural black, fluttered against the pale skin beneath her eyes. "Thank you. For saving my life."

That caught him off guard. Not the words because he'd been thanked before. But not like that. Not quiet. Not raw.

Something about her saying *thank you* tugged at him. Not quite enough to pull a smile, but his mouth twitched, traitorous. "You probably could've saved yourself, darlin'."

She stilled. "You do that a lot."

He paused. "Do what?"

"Use endearments." She tilted her head, studying him. Really studying him. "But not as a compliment. More like to distance yourself. You very rarely call me by my name."

He kept control of his body, like usual, and didn't shift in the seat. Nobody got beneath his skin and saw the real him. They'd go running, screaming if they did. But Amka had always had a way about her. Intuitive. If he believed in magic, she'd have it.

He couldn't figure out what it was about her that got past his armor. Maybe it was the way their drive from town had been filled with silence, and not the awkward kind. The good kind.

Like she understood that not every second needed noise. That sometimes, silence was its own language.

She let out a breath, easy, like she wasn't going to press him. "Would you like to come in for an early supper? It's the least I can do."

His gut tightened. Food sounded good. Her cooking even better. But it wasn't hunger pulling at him, it was the invitation. The warmth behind it. The door she was cracking open. Being in her presence, just around her, somehow provided a quiet peace. One he couldn't figure out.

He looked at the cabin, sharp-eyed. Everyone knew that she and her fiancé didn't live together, which was another thing he didn't understand. If she were his woman, he'd never leave her alone out here. Not with wild animals around, not with unstable terrain, and definitely not with men like him on the prowl. He'd be protective, possessive, and probably a complete pain in the ass.

Which, yeah, probably explained why he didn't have a woman.

Or shouldn't.

Her front door opened, and Jarod Teller stepped out.

Whatever Christian had meant to say dried up before the words got anywhere near his mouth.

"Oh." Amka started. "Jarod's here."

Why did she sound surprised to find Jarod at her place? They were engaged.

Christian opened his door. Amka scrambled out fast, hopping down and slamming hers like she was afraid he'd try to carry her again.

Jarod's eyes scanned her up and down as he walked toward them, his boots leaving imprints in the light mud. "What happened to you?"

Christian moved without thinking, rounding the front of the

truck and planting himself just slightly closer to her side. Not protective. Just...close by.

She hesitated a beat. "The building we used for storage blew up. I was in it and Christian helped me get out."

Jarod's gaze cut to Christian. "What were you doing in there?"

Christian didn't answer right away and let the silence do some of the work. He watched Amka's fiancé—six feet tall, maybe—shift under the weight of it. The guy had brown hair and wore a white button-down shirt that still had creases from a hanger. His eyes never quite landed on anything for long. "I wasn't in the explosion," Christian said. "You don't look like you went fishing today."

Jarod glanced down at his pressed shirt. "No. I had several Zoom meetings." He stepped closer to Amka and reached for her arm. "Are you all right?"

Pink crept into her cheeks. "Yes. I'm fine," she said, then hesitated. "There was an accelerant used, we're pretty sure."

Jarod's eyebrows lifted. "Seriously? Someone deliberately set your building on fire?"

She gave a small shrug. "I guess. I don't know. But it spread fast."

Jarod looked over at Christian. "And you...what? Helped put it out?"

Amka shifted her weight, eyes flicking between them. "Christian saved me."

Jarod slid an arm around Amka's shoulders and tugged her close.

She breathed in sharply.

Christian's jaw locked.

"Thank you for that," Jarod said. "I guess I owe you one."

They didn't look right together. Or maybe Christian just didn't want them to, although he didn't want any part of a relationship, so why did he care? "You're hurting her arm."

Jarod stared at him.

Amka gave a soft cough, then angled her body slightly away from the pressure, though Jarod didn't drop his arm. "Yeah," she murmured. "I think I landed on it. Doc says I'm just bruised."

"Oh. Sorry." Jarod didn't move. His brown gaze stayed locked on Christian. "Well then, thanks for bringing her home."

Amka looked at the ground, then back up at Christian. "Thanks for saving my life."

He gave a small nod, unsure what to do with the words now that she'd said them again—with him standing here, and Jarod's arm still draped over her like a claim. The air between them thickened.

"I'll check in with Brock and see what he knows," Christian said. "There were enough folks in town earlier today that somebody had to have seen something." Maybe. Hopefully whoever had set the explosive hadn't wanted to hurt Amka specifically. Either way, Christian would figure it out.

"Oh, don't you worry. I've got her." Jarod tugged Amka closer again like he couldn't help himself.

She stiffened and tried not to show it. But her face went pale at the pressure.

Christian kept his gaze on her. "If you need anything, call me."

"You got a phone now?" Jarod asked.

"Yeah," Christian muttered. "I've got a phone." His brothers had made sure of that. He kept it off most of the time. Not because he was hiding anything, but because he didn't want people knowing where he was every second of the day. GPS, Bluetooth, cell tower triangulation—Christian wasn't paranoid, just experienced.

Amka had the number. He'd given it to her weeks ago, just in case.

Not that she was his business.

Still.

"Well, that's good," Jarod drawled. "One of my Zoom meetings was with investors. Thinking about rebuilding the motel now that tourism's picking up. Since you're unemployed, I'm willing to hire you as a day laborer. You could handle construction, right?"

"Jarod." Amka pressed a hand to his ribs as if trying to create space.

Jarod just smiled like she'd said something cute. "What? I'm trying to help."

Christian's skin heated at the base of his neck. Yeah, if she were his, he'd be possessive, too, but he wouldn't hurt her. Of course, he'd try to cover her in bubble wrap and probably drive her crazy, which also wouldn't work. "I don't need your job."

Jarod chuckled. "Come on, Christian. You're unemployed, and you must be tired of sleeping in the forest. With a little extra money, you could rent a room somewhere. Live like a human."

Christian forced a smile. Not a real one because he didn't feel that. But he knew how to flash his teeth when necessary. Satisfaction that he'd regret later rolled through him from the sudden awareness in Jarod's eyes. The same look prey caught when a hunter came near.

Amka's chin lifted. "I'm sure Christian will seek employment if and when he wants. For now, I assume it's nice to be back home and living with such freedom."

Jarod lost his smirk.

Something warmed in Christian's chest. How could any one person be so fucking sweet? Jarod sure as shit didn't deserve her. Neither did Christian. There probably wasn't anyone on the planet who deserved such an angel. Yeah, if rose-colored glasses existed, he was wearing them.

Then, because he couldn't help himself, Christian gave Amka the faintest wink. Not playful. Just...a reminder. That she had options. Temporary ones, anyway. "Call me if you need anything." He turned, boots crunching the gravel as he moved around the front of the truck. Then he climbed in without looking back.

Tika stared at him from the back seat. The pup's head tilted, ears half-cocked.

"I know," Christian muttered, pulling the door shut. "I know."

CHAPTER 4

Everything hurt as Amka worked the dinner shift at the tavern. She'd forced Jarod to get out of her place the night before, and for once, he hadn't argued or tried to kiss her. She'd like to think it was because she was hurt and he wasn't as big of a jerk as she suspected, but that was doubtful. He probably had a date somewhere.

Not that she cared in the slightest.

She'd slept in but had headed to the tavern upon awakening. For now, she didn't let the discomfort show. She bent slowly behind the bar, fingers curling around the water pitcher with her non-dominant hand, and filled three glasses she'd already lined up on a tray. Moving carefully, she placed the pitcher on the counter and straightened. Her side pulled tight where the bruising ran deepest, but she ignored it.

Smoke from the fire earlier hung in the air, even inside the tavern.

The tourists sat near the back fireplace, leaning in toward each other and laughing with the free sound of people on vacation. They wore loud T-shirts covered in fish jokes, and one of them wore a foam trout hat. Fishing derby types. They came through every June hoping to catch a good trophy and were good for the local businesses.

She approached their table, balancing the tray with both hands. It helped keep her from limping too much. "Here you go." She placed a glass in front of each of them.

"Thanks," the first man said, smiling up at her. Like his friends, he looked to be in his mid-thirties or so. "What's good here?"

"Everything," she answered, the line coming out smooth from repetition.

They ordered burgers and a pitcher of beer. She smiled and made her way back to the bar with her spine stiff and her pace measured.

It was late, and the place was about half full. Locals lined the counter, boots scuffed and heavy from long days. A few newcomers leaned close to the jukebox as if they hadn't seen a real one in ages. They probably hadn't.

Daisy blew in from the kitchen, cheeks flushed, red curls frizzing out like she'd been fighting with the fryer again. "I told you that I'll handle the floor," she said, pushing the swinging door open with her hip. "You got blown up yesterday. You shouldn't even be upright."

Amka waved her off with her good hand. "We don't have anyone else," she said simply.

Daisy scowled, tugging off an apron and tossing it onto the back counter. She was in her early thirties and had left a big city law firm to return to Knife's Edge, where she'd spent her first ten years. "Seriously. Take it easy."

"I will," Amka said. "As soon as I can. Weren't you going to hang your shingle this spring?"

Daisy grinned. "Yep. I'm saving up to rent a place. Truth be told, I can do both jobs. I don't think there's a lot of lawyer work to do around here. I'll probably draft some wills and deeds."

Thank goodness, because Amka needed her at least through the summer. She moved to make coffee. "I appreciate it, but don't want you to give up on your dreams just to help me."

Daisy snorted. "My dream was to move here and live. I'm doing so. Like I said, I can work half days in the office and half nights here. Besides, if you want to actually talk to people around here, you've got to either pour their drinks or feed them. Otherwise, they don't say a word." She nodded toward the trio in the back. "What's their story?"

"I didn't ask," Amka said. "They're here for the derby. Obvious enough."

"The blond one's kind of cute." Daisy craned her neck to get a better look.

Amka turned her head. She hadn't really noticed when she'd taken their water to them. One of them wore mirrored sunglasses on the back of his head like he thought it was still 1997. But the blond one wasn't bad-looking. "They ordered burgers and a pitcher of beer."

"Gotcha." Gracefully turning, Daisy went to fill the pitcher.

Amka glanced into the kitchen. The grill was popping, and the smell of seared beef filled the air. Rudolph was at the flattop, flipping patties with the same efficiency he'd used since she was a kid. "You doing okay?" she called.

"Always." His always gruff voice held a warmth in it. Rudolph had been with Sam's Tavern longer than any of the names above the liquor license. He didn't want to own the place, never had. Just wanted to cook, then go home to his land where he could hunt elk and pretend to ignore his doctor's advice. "Start pushing the Cobb salad, would you?" He flipped two more patties with perfect formation.

Amka nodded and immediately regretted the action. The headache morphed into a sharp ache behind her eyes. She needed Advil. Or bourbon. Or both.

"You shouldn't even be here," Rudolph said, echoing Daisy without knowing it.

"I know," Amka replied. "But I'm here anyway." She winked at him.

He flushed, muttering as he turned back to the burgers. "Don't flirt with me, young lady. I'm what they call a confirmed bachelor, and no woman is gonna change that. Ever."

"I'd never want to change you." She grinned. He was massive —a broad-chested, mountain-shaped man, still hauling around more than three hundred pounds, a lot of it muscle. His black hair had gone gray at the temples, but his eyes were sharp and bright, usually twinkling. She'd been trying to put him on a diet for two years, and he still snuck in fried bread and moose sausage every morning like she couldn't smell it.

But he never called in sick, and he never let her down.

"How about a salad tonight?" Amka asked.

"Sure. I'd love one with my burger."

She didn't bother arguing considering her head wanted to explode like the storage building had earlier. "Let me know when the burgers are up."

"I think you need to go sit down and make sure you're okay," he muttered, not looking up from the grill.

She stepped out from the kitchen and crossed the room, checking that everyone had what they needed, spotting a few empty pint glasses on one table, a napkin on the floor, but nothing out of control. She tucked her hair back and made a mental note to grab a fresh pitcher for the table against the far wall.

The front door creaked open.

Widow Flossy stepped inside wearing her bright purple coat and a pale pink knit hat pulled low over her short gray curls. She stood just over five feet tall, even wearing new black boots she'd purchased for the spring. Her gloves stayed in one hand, pinched tight together as she scanned the bar. "I came to help."

She walked toward the counter, pushing her gloves into her pockets. "Heard you got blown up yesterday."

"There was a small fire." Amka poured a mug of coffee for the elderly woman. "Besides a headache and a few bruises, I'm fine."

Flossy pulled out a stool and sat, wobbling before steadying. "You sure?"

"I am, and I figured you'd be busy at your place."

Flossy ran the only bed-and-breakfast in town. The place was old, solid, and booked out most of tourist season. She took a sip of the coffee. "We're family, Amka." She leaned in, her gaze softening. "I owe you. Besides, the McGregor girls are covering the desk tonight. Loud, but they can fold towels."

From the kitchen, the sound of the spatula hitting the grill picked up. Rudolph was moving fast, but steady.

"Would you like anything to eat? The Cobb is the special, but I'm sure Rudy will make you one of those cheese crepes you like," Amka said. Flossy loved the fancier dishes.

Flossy cupped both hands around the mug. "I already ate, but thank you. I heard Christian pulled you out of the fire."

An inappropriate heat flushed through Amka. "He came through the flames to get me."

Flossy smiled, showing perfect dentures. "It's always the quiet ones. You can count on them."

To be heroic, sure. But not to be stable.

Jarod walked over from the dartboard, beer in hand. "What are we talking about?"

Flossy didn't look at him. "I was wondering why Amka is working so hard while being injured and you're over there playing pool?" She sniffed.

Amka bit back a wince.

Jarod looked at her, then shook his head and walked around the bar to the till. "Hey, I just lost twenty bucks to Rocco playing darts." He opened the drawer and pulled a bill from the stack.

Flossy turned slightly on her stool, watching him.

"Write it down in the register," Amka said, already regretting not making a bank run earlier. The till was too full.

Jarod reached in again and removed two more twenties. "You write it down." He nudged the drawer closed with his hip and grabbed a magazine from the end of the bar to slide in front of her. "Have you picked a dress yet?"

It was one of those heavy bridal magazines, glossy and unread. She hadn't opened it once. Why in the world would she pick out a dress? "No," she said.

"We might want to get on it," he said.

The front door opened, and cold air slipped inside along with presence. Definite presence. Amka didn't need to look up to know who'd entered.

Christian walked in with his brothers, Brock and Ace, heading for their usual table by the fireplace. Christian gave her a nod as he passed. They were just missing Damian, and it would've been all four Osprey brothers in one place.

"Where's Olly?" Flossy yelled after them.

Brock looked over and smiled. "Still at the station. She'll be here soon."

Ophelia Spilazi had come up from New York as an FBI agent on a case and ended up staying for the sheriff. From the way things looked, she and Brock weren't far from setting a date for their own wedding.

Amka liked her. She was tough, didn't waste time, and treated people straight. Having her around made things better.

Daisy hurried up to put dishes in the sink. "I'll get the Osprey brothers," she said, already turning toward their table with a little bounce in her step.

Amka watched her go, not sure if the woman was looking for a steady man or just chasing a good time. "Sometimes I wonder what she wants." She'd flirted with the tourists for a while and now was leaning close to Christian, pointing at something on the menu. Way too close to him.

Flossy blew out a breath. "Oh, who cares? As long as she has a good time."

Several more tourists came through the door and took seats at a table near the window. Amka went to work, grabbing menus and taking orders while collecting dirty dishes on her way back to the kitchen.

When she returned, Flossy was clearing plates at one of the tables.

Amka hustled over as fast as her ribs would let her. "Flossy, come on. You're a guest," she said, trying to take the tray from her hands.

Flossy held onto it. "Amka. We're family." She said it quietly, already walking the dishes toward the back. She was surprisingly quick for her age, and Amka had to sidestep to get around her and wipe down the table before Flossy could.

They were busier than expected with the locals mixing with derby tourists, filling every table.

A young woman with bright purple hair came in and walked straight to the bar.

Amka met her there, already circling behind the counter. "Hi. What can I get you?"

"I'd love a dirty martini."

Amka studied her for a second. "Can I see some ID?"

The woman laughed and pulled a wallet from her back pocket. "Yeah, no problem."

Amka checked the date. The woman was twenty-five, and her name was Nixi Halliday. Cool name. "Oh, sorry."

"That's okay. I don't mind looking young." Nixi glanced over her shoulder, scanned the room, then focused in on the table by the fireplace. "Hey, the guy in the dark green T-shirt—what's his name?"

Why was she asking about Christian? "Why?" Amka asked, reaching for the vermouth.

"I saw him save you yesterday. He burst out of the flames, surrounded by smoke, with you in his arms. Serious hero material there." Nixi slid onto a barstool. "I filmed it. The video already has two hundred thousand likes."

Amka winced. "People are pretty private around here. He's not going to like that."

"What's his name?" Nixi asked again.

Amka's chest tightened. Christian would hate being on the internet. "You should take down the video." He didn't even like being looked at too long, let alone going viral. "Seriously. He wouldn't want that."

"Not a chance." Nixi reached for a menu. "Do you have a special tonight?"

"We do. The Cobb salad is excellent." Amka finished the drink and placed it on a cocktail napkin. She didn't wait for a thank-you and just moved back down the bar to refill two beers and check a soda at the pass-through.

The crowd didn't let up for another hour. Somewhere around ten-thirty, things finally started to slow. Amka took a glass of water and slipped two Advil into her mouth, swallowing hard. Her arm still ached and the pain in her side had sharpened.

Daisy came up beside her. "I can finish out."

Amka looked around. Most of the crowd had drinks, and plates were mostly cleared, but the tavern was still too full for comfort. "I'm really fine." Except she wasn't. Her arm throbbed, her legs burned, and even her back ached from the constant movement. Her ribs were the worst. Something was definitely cracked.

A sharp clinking cut through the room.

"Excuse me, everybody," Jarod called out, smacking a knife against his glass.

Amka bit back a groan. His voice had that slight slur she recognized. She hadn't been watching his intake. He served himself, and that made it hard to track.

He walked around the bar and slung an arm over her shoulder, pulling her tight to his side. Pain shot through her ribs and down her arm. She smiled through it and definitely had to figure a way out of this mess.

Across the room, Christian stood. Not fast, not loud. But she felt the shift in the air like a wire pulled taut. Her spine went rigid.

Jarod didn't notice. He raised his glass. "I wanted to tell everybody—since you're all here—that Amka and I have set a date." He grinned. "We're getting married. June eighteenth."

A few people clapped. The murmur rolled through the crowd like a light breeze, one mostly of excitement.

Flossy, seated across the bar flipping through the bridal magazine, looked up. "That's only three weeks away."

"Yes," Jarod said, leaning in and pressing a kiss against Amka's cheek. "We couldn't wait any longer."

Her stomach twisted, and the pain along her ribs deepened. She smiled, or tried to, but her lips trembled. "We didn't talk about this, Jarod," she said under her breath.

"It doesn't matter. It's going to happen." He kissed her on the temple again.

Her body went still. She kept the smile on her face, or something close to it, and tried to hold it steady. Even so, her eyes drifted across the room.

Christian was staring. Not just him—Brock and Ace too. All three Osprey brothers watched her with the same expression. Confusion, maybe. Something close to anger. Definitely suspicion.

She shifted slightly and caught Flossy's face across the bar. She had the same look with maybe a bit more bewilderment. Amka forced her smile wider.

"Drinks are on the house!" Jarod yelled.

A cheer went up from half the tavern. A few claps, a couple whistles. Someone slammed a hand on a table.

"Just great," Amka muttered, finally pushing away from Jarod as he began lining up shot glasses on the bar.

The door opened and Doc May walked inside with a box in her hands. "Hey. I told you to go home and rest." She pushed the box across the bar. "You should be home in bed binge-watching something good."

Amka would need to work late just to pay for the drinks Jarod was already spilling. "What's in the box?"

May sat on the stool next to Flossy. "No clue. It was right outside."

Amka leaned over to see her name scrawled on top in black marker. She swallowed. "That's weird." Reaching beneath the counter, she found a knife and quickly opened the top, looking in.

May leaned over. "What is that?"

Amka pulled out a can of lighter fluid, dropping a note on the bar. Her breath quickening, she turned it over to read: *That was just the beginning. The whole world needs to burn.*

CHAPTER 5

After midnight, Christian leaned against the rough wood siding of the Kattuk family mercantile, arms crossed, boots set firm in the gravel. Across the narrow road, the sheriff's office sat quiet under a mist that curled and lifted with the breeze, too thin to be rain, too thick to ignore. The silence had weight to it, like the town was holding its breath.

Tika sat to his side, the wolf-pup's ears flattened in what looked like ease. He yawned wide, jaw splitting with the slow, lazy stretch of a creature comfortable in the night. Christian reached down and scratched behind one of those ears, fingers moving in the familiar rhythm. It grounded him more than he'd ever admit.

The door to the station creaked open. Ophelia Spilazi stepped out, gaze sweeping the street. She found him instantly and came down the stairs to cross the road on a pair of very fashionable boots.

Brock's woman loved her boots.

Tall, all angles and confidence, with long black hair pulled back and eyes that saw more than most people wanted her to, Ophelia was a force. The scent hit him halfway across the street

—strawberries. Not strong, but deliberate. Brock's favorite. Of course.

Christian hadn't expected his brother's happiness to come wrapped in a city girl with a badge who looked like a model with a gun. But she'd shown up and stayed, and more than once she'd proved she belonged in a place like this.

"Hey," she said, slipping her hands into the pockets of her black leather jacket.

"Hey."

Another thing he liked about her—she didn't press. Didn't ask why he hadn't walked into the station. Didn't try to fix whatever she might see wrong in him. She let people be who they were. Just like Amka did.

"Brock's sending the box, lighter fluid, and note to Anchorage along with the small bits of shrapnel from the device," Ophelia said. "There's an FBI agent there. We'll see if we can get fingerprints."

That was way too much of a longshot. "I'm not counting on it."

"Neither am I." She looked up at the station, jaw set. "But it's arson, and Amka might be the target."

Christian's hand stilled on Tika's head. His spine straightened, barely. "Maybe."

Ophelia stretched up on her calves as if breaking in the boots. "I offered to drive her home after she gave her statement, but she insisted on driving herself."

"I followed her home and made sure she got inside safely." His voice was quiet now, the kind that came after a long time not talking. "Teller's rig was in the driveway." Although the asshat should've gone to the station with her and then driven her home.

"At least Jarod's keeping an eye on her," Ophelia said. "Who do you think would want to hurt Amka?"

Christian shook his head. "Absolutely nobody in the world."

Ophelia nodded. "That's my feeling as well. But somebody's obviously taken an interest. We have to assume they waited until she was inside that building before igniting the explosion."

"I took another look at it," Christian said. "It was rigged so when the door opened, the flame lit. They couldn't have known it'd be Amka. It's shared with Friday's Grocery—they keep overflow in there."

"I know," Ophelia said. "But the note was left outside the tavern."

Irritation and heat flared up inside him, crawling under his skin and sharpening every nerve. "I know. But the grocery store had already closed for the day."

Ophelia sighed and pushed a strand of hair out of her face, only for the wind to slap it right back. "The town's been open for two weeks, and we've had tons of tourists coming through. Plus, a lot of the mountain people have been down. We need to get some security cameras in place."

Christian winced. "The topic was brought up at the town meeting a few years ago and it was a shit show, or so I've heard. I was still in the Navy, halfway across the world at the time, but news gets around. People live here because they like their privacy. Nobody wants cameras."

Ophelia shifted her stance. "I know, but come on. At some point the town has to join the modern times, at least a little."

He shook his head, his jaw aching. He had to stop clenching it. "I hate the thought of cameras all around, but I would like to know if somebody is watching Amka or the Fridays."

Ophelia looked up at him from under lowered lashes. "What's your interest in her, Christian? Is there something—"

"No." He cut her off before she could expand the question. "We're friends, and she's in my town. Sometimes I drop by the bar and help out, and she always feeds me. That's it. There's nothing more."

Ophelia arched a brow. "If you say so."

"I do," he said, firm and flat.

"Okay." She backed off without pressing. No smirk, no challenge, just a clean shift of energy. "Well, it's probably a good thing since apparently she's getting married in June. What do you know about Jarod Teller?"

Christian cocked his head to the side. He'd smile if he remembered how. "Are you interviewing me?"

Ophelia's lips ticked up. "Maybe. I don't think this is an FBI case, but who knows? The local law can always request FBI assistance."

Christian snorted. "Yeah, but we've got a problem with the whole local law situation, don't we?"

She winced. "Yes, but no one seems to care about it, including my boss in DC." Her gaze drifted to the sign stretched across the street declaring that Knife's Edge had the only sheriff in Alaska. "I'm surprised no one's challenged that."

Christian lifted a shoulder. "There's never been a need. I thought maybe Brock would at one point, just to get out of the job."

The town had come up with its own sheriff system decades ago, back when they were too far out for anyone to respond in time. It was unofficial, but nobody cared. State troopers still handled the major cases in most of Alaska. A few larger towns had their own police departments, but even they didn't have sheriffs. Knife's Edge clung to the title like it was part of the landscape.

Ophelia chuckled. "If Brock gets tired of the job, he might try to change it."

That wasn't going to happen. "People like tradition here," Christian said. "Whether we've got the only sheriff or not, no one's looking to change that."

"I understand," she said. "I'm not getting involved in any

jurisdictional issues, but arson and attempted murder are serious crimes."

"I'm aware." Christian's jaw tightened again. At this point, he was going to deserve the migraine he was giving himself. "As for Jarod Teller, he moved to Anchorage when he was around twenty and worked one of the fishing outfits for a few years. Then he bought the local motel."

Ophelia scanned the area. "The one that burned down."

"Two years ago," Christian said. "An inspector from Anchorage confirmed that faulty wiring caused the fire."

Ophelia didn't speak right away, just watched him, her expression unreadable. Then she gave a slow nod. "Still…two fires in a small town."

"They were two years apart," he said. "So maybe it's nothing. But I've thought about it too." He nudged her with a shoulder, careful to keep from being too rough. "Why are you still an FBI agent? We could use an assistant sheriff around here."

She snorted. "An assistant sheriff? I don't think so. Right now I'm solid in my job. There are several missing persons in Alaska, as you know, plus a couple of cases I'm still working." She wiped dew off her forehead. "Word came in earlier. The district attorney decided not to prosecute Flossy for Hank's death."

Relief slammed through Christian. He'd loved Hank, who'd been his guardian, and understood why Flossy helped him die in December after his cancer had progressed so horribly. When she'd confessed, so had most of the town, so there wasn't enough evidence to prosecute anybody. "That's a relief."

Ophelia frowned. "I know, but still. I don't like going around the law."

There wasn't much of a choice, and the district attorney had the final say. Christian focused on Ophelia. "Are you happy here?"

"Yes." She blinked as if caught a little off guard by her own answer. "Yes, because of Brock. Definitely." Her eyes sparked, softening. "But I also like the town. I like the people. Plus, the pace of life doesn't suck."

"Good." He didn't want her deciding Knife's Edge was too remote and packing it in. Brock had enough weight on his shoulders in the form of demons from their childhood and from the service. Seeing him content for once? That mattered.

"I'm not going to hurt your brother," Ophelia said, dead-on reading him without needing an invitation.

Christian relaxed. That was all he needed. While he might never find peace, he intended for each of his brothers to do so. Whether they liked it or not.

AMKA PEELED off rain gear inside the narrow vestibule of her quaint home, the fabric cold and slick in her hands. Water dripped onto the mat, the steady rhythm of it loud in the stillness. Her shoulder ached from hauling stock all day, and her fingers were numb. She wanted a shower. Maybe tea. A moment to breathe.

She stepped into the cabin and stopped cold.

Jarod was passed out on the sofa again. One arm dangled toward the floor, and his boot hung half-off, mud crusted along the sole.

At least he wasn't in her bed this time.

She crossed the room and kicked his foot. Harder than she meant to. A shock of pain ricocheted up her leg.

"Ouch," she hissed under her breath.

Jarod groaned, rolled onto his back, and looked at the ceiling. "Oh. Hey. You're finally home." He sat up, squinting. "Did they find out who sent that note to you?"

"As much as I appreciate your concern, they have not." Her

voice stayed even. "You don't need to be here, Jarod. Go back to your place."

He scrubbed his face with both hands, the bleariness fading just enough to show behind-the-eyes calculation. "No, I think I'm gonna move in. You know, since I'm your fiancé. I don't want you to get hurt."

"Cut the crap." Her jaw locked. "You're not moving in. We are never living together."

He stood, sudden and unsteady, and she stepped back before she realized it. The room shrank around her. Sometimes she forgot how big he was until he pushed into her space.

"I am moving in," he said. "My lease is up at the end of the month. So get used to it."

"Absolutely not." Her voice came out flat. He could continue living out at the Willows, a depressing landscape of run-down duplexes, and away from her tidy home. She kept her feet planted.

He looked at her, head tilted just slightly, like he was trying to decide how far he could push it. "Wrong."

She wasn't fighting about this. "We've been engaged because you said you needed it for respectability or whatever bullshit reason. I agreed to a temporary arrangement. I've said that since day one."

Jarod smiled then, showing too many teeth. The smile he used at barbecues and fundraisers. The one that used to fool people. "Well, I decided we are getting married."

"No." Her tone sharpened. "I've gone along with this because I haven't had a better option. That's it."

"You don't have a choice," he said, and the way he said it chilled her more than the weather ever could.

Her pulse thudded in her throat. "Enough is enough. You have to be respectable by now. I can't do anything else for you."

He leaned in and grabbed her arms with both hands. "You just don't get it. Why I want this."

Pain ripped through her so fast she gasped.

"It's you. It's been you. I want you. Yeah, the respectability of being engaged and then married to the town's golden girl is definitely appealing, but we're in this together. You and me, and you're not going anywhere." He jerked her toward him and pressed a hard kiss against her lips.

She struggled and nearly dropped as more pain slashed through her ribs.

He kissed her harder, reaching for the hem of her shirt. She struggled, panicking. He'd tried this once before, and she'd shut him down. "Stop."

"No." He yanked her closer.

She shifted to the side and brought up her knee, nailing him in the groin.

He coughed and released her, shoving her. "Damn it. Bitch. All women want it and just don't realize it. You will." He stepped back, his face an angry red. "I'm moving in this weekend, so get used to it." He turned and walked to the door, opened it, then looked over his shoulder. "We are going to be married in every possible way." He slammed the door.

As he left, she sank onto the sofa and wiped her mouth with the back of her hand.

What was she going to do? He was getting more and more sexually violent.

As hard as it was to admit, she had thought about dropping his ass in a creek. She probably couldn't kill anybody, but it was tempting. Still, the blackmail he had on her was real, and if she made the wrong move, it would get out. Somewhere, somehow, it was waiting to be released.

She picked up her phone, needing to talk to somebody. The problem was, she didn't know who.

The line clicked. "Hello?" A very sleepy Doc May answered.

"Hi, May. Do you have a minute?" Amka asked.

"Of course. Are you hurt?"

"My ribs are killing me," she admitted, pressing a palm against her side like it might help.

May's voice sharpened. "Okay, I'll meet you down at my office—"

"No. I'll come to you." Amka was already headed back for her raincoat and her green knit hat. It was cold out there. "I need to talk."

CHAPTER 6

The cocking of a pistol stopped Christian as he slipped halfway into his brother's cabin. He grinned. "You heard me?"

"No. Felt a disturbance," Ace mumbled.

Christian moved all the way inside to see his brother sprawled on the threadbare sofa, gun in hand. A fire roared in the wood stove behind him, warming the entire cabin. "You're slurring a bit too much to be holding a gun on me."

Ace snorted and placed the weapon on the crumbling sofa table next to him. A nearly empty bottle of Jack, no glass, also took residence there. "I figured you'd be by one of these days." His light green eyes were bloodshot and his brown hair stood on end. But he'd shaved, and his newest scar showed from his jawline down to his collarbone. A scar he had yet to explain.

Chances were it came from crashing that military jet a year or so ago, but who the hell knew? "I thought you quit drinking."

Ace snorted and stretched his legs onto the dusty coffee table, knocking over several empty beer cans. "I only stop when the bottle goes dry, brother."

"All right," Christian said amiably.

Ace's gaze narrowed. "All right?"

"Yep. If you're going to be a total dumbass, I guess it's time to drag your ass to Smitty." The guy was the closest thing they had to a shrink in Knife's Edge, considering he'd worked as a bartender for sixty years. "Let's go." He flexed his hands, ready to start throwing punches.

Anticipation quirked Ace's full lips. "Much as I'd like to go a couple of rounds, Smitty went to visit a friend in Anchorage. He left earlier this morning."

Christian stilled. "Two questions. How do you know that, and who's flying the plane?"

"Smitty dropped by on the way to town to bring me a pie, and I guess the Thombley brothers are flying the routes around here."

Ah. Smitty baked great pies. "Did he shrink your head?"

"Tried to, but he was swearing up a storm when he left, so I think he failed." Ace slowly grinned when Christian looked toward the messy kitchen. When had he cleaned this place last? Hank would hate the mess. "I already ate the pie."

Asshole. "You know the Thombley brothers are jackasses who don't take enough safety precautions. Come on, Ace. We need you back up in the air." Would it make sense to just force his brother into a plane? Christian could do it, although he might need Brock's help. Would Brock go along with that idea?

"No." Ace reached for the bottle.

Christian kicked out, nailing the glass. It flew behind the sofa and crashed. Glass splintered loudly across the wooden floor. "No more," he growled.

Ace dropped his bare feet to the floor. "That just wasn't nice, C." He crossed his arms. "You gonna break all of my bottles?"

"If I have to." The heat from the fire roared through the room, burning Christian's ears. The walls started to close in. He wished he could be outside with Tika running through the trees.

Ace groaned. "Go concentrate on Damian and not me. We all know he's probably in trouble working at EVE, and frankly, he hasn't dated anybody since he got divorced. You should figure that out."

The Electromagnetic Vibrational Experiment, or EVE, was a facility through the pass that included many satellite dishes, a massive antenna field, and grids of transmitters sprawling over fifty acres. Supposedly they studied the ionosphere there, but nobody really knew. Damian had recently become the head of security for the place, which did not make sense.

Christian lifted his chin. "Damian got married for a job, probably during some spook spying shit, and then ended it. That's not real."

Ace shrugged. "I don't know. He bunked with me last time he came home, before he went to work at EVE, and yelled out the name Stella. His ex-wife."

That was news. "Fine. We'll figure out Damian next. For now, I'm here to give you a heads-up. Somebody set fire via an explosive device to the storage building between Sam's and Friday's, and Amka was inside. She's okay, but I wouldn't mind a few of us keeping an eye on the tavern for a while."

Ace stared at him.

Christian stared back, confident his face betrayed nothing.

"Why?" Ace asked.

"If we have somebody in town trying to burn it down, we should find out who. Don't you think?"

Ace leaned his head back. "Fine. I'll come to town more often."

Christian relaxed. Ace might be killing his liver with booze, but he could fight if necessary. Brutally. "All right. We'll talk more about drinking later." Christian had to get out of there.

"Can't wait," Ace drawled.

∼

Dr. May Smirnov slid out of bed and pulled on leggings and a sweatshirt. She moved quietly through the hallway into the main room of her cabin, flipping on the lights as she passed. The fire had burned low, so she added two more logs and stirred the embers until they caught. She reached behind the stacked wood where two guns were partially visible, shifting them into better cover. The others were already stored—one in the locked drawer beneath the sink, the rest where no one would find them unless they had a key and time.

She went to the door and unlocked the two middle bolts, leaving the top and bottom in place. She nudged down the floor bolt she always engaged at night to keep the door from being kicked open and checked the windows out of habit. Everything was still covered. No gaps.

In the kitchen, she opened a bottle of sparkling water and paused. Wine crossed her mind, but that was out. If Amka had a head injury, alcohol was a bad idea.

A knock came. Soft.

May still flinched.

She exhaled, shook it off, and went to the door to unlock the remaining bolts. She opened it just far enough to confirm it was Amka and then let her in. "Come on," she said. "You're pale. Are you hurt?"

"I'm all right. I took some Advil." Amka stepped inside.

That wouldn't be enough if there were cracked ribs. May bit back the impulse to ask for a pain scale rating and helped her out of her jacket. "Do you want me to prescribe something stronger?"

Amka kicked off her boots and hung her hat on a hook. "No, thanks. I need to keep my wits these days."

"Sit." May resisted the habit to check her friend's vitals. She noted Amka's pallor and the guarded way she moved while favoring one side. That bruised rib must be hurting her. "I have sparkling water and some hot chocolate somewhere. Are you hungry?"

"No, thank you. Sparkling water is good." Amka walked into the main room and sat back in the corner of the couch, arms wrapped around herself.

May poured the water and brought it to her. "Here."

Amka took it with both hands, her fingers shaking.

May sat across from her, cataloging her friend's breath rates and composure. She tucked one leg beneath her. "All right. What's going on?"

Amka stared at the glass for a moment. Then she looked up. "I needed to talk to someone. Since you're my doctor, that means this stays here, right? Confidential?"

May gave a short nod. "It does."

Amka stared at her, face unreadable, eyes sharp in the low light. "No matter what?"

May took a sip of her drink. "Of course. Always, Amka. If not by friendship, then definitely by doctor-patient confidentiality."

"So you can't tell anyone what I'm about to say?"

Awareness crawled up May's spine. "I promise I won't say anything unless you're in danger. Or someone else is. If that's the case, I have to speak up."

"The danger is in letting this get out," Amka said. Her mouth curved into something that might have been a smile but looked more like a pained grimace.

May tilted her head, trying to read more in the expression than Amka was offering. What in the world was going on? She was missing something and couldn't catch a thought. "Do you know who planted the explosive device?"

"No." Amka waved a hand. "Of course not. I have no clue." She blinked, then looked away. "That's just one more thing to deal with later."

May sat forward slightly. Wait a minute. Somebody might've

tried to kill the woman, and that wasn't her biggest concern right now? "What is going on?"

Amka took a breath, held it, then let it out slow. "Okay. I'm not sure if you heard, but the district attorney decided not to prosecute Flossy for shooting Hank."

"I heard," May said. The relief hit faster than expected. "I'm glad. I like Flossy, and honestly, from the medical records I read, Hank was close to dying already. He had to be in so much pain."

Amka flattened a bruised hand on one of her jean clad legs. "Yes, he was."

May nodded. "That's good news, though, right? I mean, I get that the whole town confessed—including me—but she only did what Hank asked. That's not what's bothering you?"

Amka shook her head. Her grip on the glass tightened. "No. Not at all, and nobody knows this." Amka looked up at May, her voice lower now, more raw. "I helped her."

May's eyebrows drew together. Wait. What? "You helped Flossy?"

Amka wiped her eyes. "She didn't have the strength. I was on my way to work on the snowmobile, heading to open the tavern. I came up on them by the river. Hank was all but begging her to do it. She was holding the shotgun, but she could barely lift it. Her hands were shaking."

May stared, silent for a beat.

"I didn't pull the trigger," Amka added quickly. "I just steadied her. Helped her hold the gun. That's it. The recoil knocked both of us over when it went off, and then Hank…he fell into the river."

"Oh my God." May sat back, stunned. "I read that he did have water in his lungs but not a lot. The shot killed him."

"Yeah, they said he died seconds later. Might've already been gone when he hit the water. Either way, he didn't make it. We left. I was late getting to work, and no one asked questions."

May's voice was quieter now. "Amka, I understand. I really

do. So would most people in town. But I don't see what this has to do with the explosion."

Amka threw up a hand. "Nothing. It doesn't. That's the point. This has nothing to do with the fire."

May pressed her fingers to the bridge of her nose. "Okay. I'm lost."

Amka hesitated. "Jarod was coming back from a fishing trip that morning, or from staying with some tourist, or from getting drunk and passing out somewhere. I don't know and it doesn't matter."

May sat up straighter. A cold spike of recognition lit through her. "And he caught you?"

"He filmed it." Amka's voice went flat. "He had his phone and filmed the whole thing."

May didn't speak right away. Her chest tightened. "That's why you're engaged to him."

Amka gave a short laugh. "You were surprised?"

May shook her head. "He's such a dick. I'm sorry, but no one can figure it out. I mean, sure, he's good-looking. He knows how to be charming when he wants to be. But still. He's a…dick."

"Yeah." Amka exhaled. "He's blackmailing me. Jarod said if I didn't go along with the engagement, he'd turn over the video to the authorities." Her shoulders dropped.

What a terrible burden to keep to herself. "I'm so sorry," May whispered.

"They'd have no choice but to charge Flossy. And probably me." Amka let out a slow breath. "I wouldn't mind going to trial and fighting it. I'd stand up there and tell the truth. But Flossy is elderly. She wouldn't make it through something like that. It'd wreck her."

May sat back, arms folded. "You're not actually going to marry him."

"No," Amka said. "I agreed to be his fiancée for a few months so he could clean up his image and get financing for one of the businesses he's always chasing. That's all it was supposed to be. But now he says he wants to actually get married. That I don't have a choice." She paused. "I don't know. I don't trust him."

"I don't trust him either," May said. "You've got to go to Brock with this."

"Why? What can the sheriff do?" Amka asked. "Jarod holds the cards. If he turns in that video, we're screwed." She pulled at a loose thread from the blanket tossed over the couch. "Honestly, I was thinking maybe I could just stay engaged until Flossy passes on."

May didn't react right away. "You mean even if it took years?"

Amka flushed. "Yeah. I don't mean that in a bad way. Just... she's old."

"No, no. I get it," May said. "You're just trying to make a plan." Although that one wouldn't work. "Let me be honest with you. Flossy's in great shape. She's sharp. Still hunts. Still gardens. She could last another twenty years."

"I hope she does," Amka said quietly. "But that doesn't help me."

"You have no idea where the video is?" May asked.

Amka shook her head. "No, and it gets worse. Jarod said if anything happens to him, the video automatically gets sent to the district attorney's office."

May froze. "Automatically?"

"He has someone ready to email it for him if he dies or disappears or whatever." Amka lifted a hand, expression tight. "Not that I'm planning on killing him or anything."

"Well," May muttered, chewing the inside of her lip. "The thought would've crossed my mind."

Amka cracked a dry smile. "You and me both."

"Do you know who this friend is?"

"No." Amka's posture sagged. Her voice had lost its edge, and her focus slipped, gaze dropping to the floor. "I know most of his friends. Even the ones in Anchorage. I've gone through his contacts more than once, but none of them fit. It's probably someone I wouldn't expect."

That was a pisser, if he was telling the truth. "What about the video itself? Is it on his phone?"

"Yeah," Amka said. "Who knows where else. He could've backed it up. Copies could be in the cloud or on a flash drive buried in a shoebox. I can't trust that it's only in one place."

That so completely sucked. "Can you get into his computer?"

"I don't know. Maybe. But even if I did, I have no idea what I'd be looking for or where to start. He's not dumb, May. He's careful."

May sat back slowly, the weight of it sinking in. "Why are you telling me all of this now?"

"I need someone to know the truth." Amka's voice quieted. "In case something happens." There was a flicker in her expression that made May stop. Not just stress. Not exhaustion. Real fear.

"Are you afraid of him?" May asked.

Amka didn't look away. "He's a blackmailer and an asshole. I'd be stupid not to be afraid of him, but I can take care of myself."

May swallowed hard. She knew what it felt like to be cornered, to believe there wasn't a way out. "You shouldn't have to worry about him, and you're not going to do it alone." She reached over and took Amka's hand, trying to ground them both.

"I appreciate it," Amka said, finishing her drink. "I just… don't know what to do."

"We'll figure it out." May meant every word. She didn't have a plan yet, but she wasn't about to let her friend walk into the fire alone. "Do you want to stay here tonight?"

Amka looked around, her shoulders hunched. "I do. If that's okay with you."

"Of course. I'll make up the sofa for you." May stood, trying to remember where she'd put the spare sheets. "You're not going back there tonight, and you're not marrying that prick, no matter what he thinks he's got."

May had survived something once that nearly ended her. She'd built a life after it. She knew what it looked like when someone was sliding toward that edge. She wasn't going to let Amka go over.

At least not alone.

CHAPTER 7

After a night with very little sleep, Christian moved quietly through the brush, the thaw-softened ground muting his steps as he followed a faint ridgeline above the creek. Snow still clung in the shaded hollows, but most of the trail was open now. He crouched near a broken spruce and ran gloved fingers along the gouges in the bark. Not fresh. But recent enough. The spring had come late and messy, and that meant bears would be hungry, out early, and unpredictable.

He considered and quickly discarded the idea of leading a hunting party or two in the autumn, when the season opened. He didn't want to have the wilds to himself, but sometimes he wanted the wilds left alone. Completely.

The air smelled of thawing spruce, wet moss, and distant musk. The ground was soft and torn by fresh tracks. Water trickled nearby, a slow melt through stone. Wind moved through the trees, not loud but just enough to remind him how far he was from anything that talked. The light was flat, gray, pushing through low clouds.

The hair on the back of his neck rose, and he partially

turned, his shotgun cradled in the crook of his arm. He caught wind of the man before he strode between two fir trees.

Dutch Reddick squinted in the early light. "Mornin', Christian."

"Dutch."

Dutch's bushy eyebrows rose. "When did you catch my scent?"

"Not soon enough." Not true. Christian would've had plenty of time to either shoot or take cover should Dutch have been an enemy. "You here on a job?"

"Always." Dutch loped closer, his Alaska Wildlife Trooper badge scuffed on his olive green parka, matching in age and wear to his shoulder patch. "Been meaning to look you up for a while, since I heard you returned home."

Christian noted the man favoring his left leg. "Why you limping?"

"Got shot a few months back. Poacher." Dutch shrugged, the deep lines in his face showing more wear than his patch. "Took him down. Won't poach again."

The AWT members were almost mystical in the state of Alaska, and this one was legendary. Rumor had it he was a ghost in the woods until he wanted to be seen. Or heard. He'd been friends with Hank, and Christian had known him his entire life since Hank took the brothers in after the rest of their village had perished in an avalanche.

"You really Dutch?" Christian asked, surprising himself.

Dutch paused as well, running a hand through his grizzly gray hair. "I dunno. Probably not. My daddy might've been, but my mama was Inuit, like yours. Probably. Not that we ever figured out about you four. You ever consider doing a DNA test?"

"No." They all looked alike, and Christian figured they were biologically all four related. "We're brothers." Period.

Dutch nodded. "Yeah, that's what Hank said. I'm glad he

finally gave you names. It was irritating as hell when he called you A, B, C, and D."

Christian didn't really remember that time. "Why are you here, Dutch?"

"I was lookin' for you." Dutch kicked an icy pinecone out of the way. "I'm getting old, Christian. Want to leave my territory to somebody who'll take care of her."

Christian barely kept himself from taking a step back. "Ask Ace."

"Ace belongs in the sky, and you know it." Dutch lowered his gray stubble covered chin. "Brock's keeping the town safe as sheriff, and who knows where Damian is right now."

So Dutch wasn't in the loop. "Damian was honorably discharged and has taken over as the head of security for EVE."

"No shit?" Dutch scratched his neck. "That can't be good. What is he doing? You sure he was discharged? The guy worked in intelligence, you know."

"I know." Christian had yet to decide what to do about Damian. He'd gotten Brock all settled in, and right now, Ace required more of his attention. Well, when he wasn't saving Amka from an arsonist. "That's an issue for another day. Damian could take over for you."

Dutch snorted. "Right. Like he'd give up his three-piece suits to scramble around in the brush. No. It's you, Christian. Either that, or somebody from one of the cities, who won't love this place like you do. Right now, the town needs cover."

Christian's chin lifted. "Meaning?"

"A possible killer in the mountains. Hank's murder. Flossy's confession. The entire town covering for her so the prosecutor can't charge anybody. Anchorage is pissed, and while I get it, Knife's Edge is under scrutiny now. Especially since now we got someone setting buildings on fuckin' fire. You want an ally out in these mountains, and right now, I'm all you got."

"I'm not lookin' for a job."

"Why not?" Dutch took a granola bar out of his pocket and slowly unwrapped it. "You plannin' on livin' on your thrift pension plan forever? You weren't in the Navy long enough to get a retirement pension, but rumor has it, you did your job well those twelve years."

Christian didn't want to talk about being a sniper. Ever. "You think I need money?"

Dutch took a bite and chewed thoughtfully. "No, but you might wanna get married, and women like money. So do kids."

Christian shook his head. "I ain't ever getting married."

Dutch ate half of the remaining bar and then swallowed. "Famous last words. Just because Hank never married doesn't mean you won't. You might fall for some sweet blonde gal who wants security."

His type was not blonde. "You never married."

"Who says?" Dutch finished the bar and shoved the wrapper in his pocket.

Christian stiffened. "You're married?"

"Was. For ten years."

Christian cocked his head. How had he never known that fact? That was huge.

Dutch sighed. "It was a good ten years. Cancer got her. There never was another one like her, so I didn't do it again. But maybe you'll find the one for you."

"No." He'd never looked twice at a woman for anything beyond a night—except Amka. Not that they'd ever had a night, because if they did, he knew he'd never let her go. *That* guy didn't live in him. She was too kind, too soft, too feminine for a killer like him. Even if she didn't have a fiancé, which she did. "Not gonna happen."

"Well, then? I guess the reason you take the job is to protect Knife's Edge. It's up to you, C." Dutch glanced down at a series of deer tracks. "Besides, Hank would want you to have purpose. You know that. He wouldn't like you living on the mountain, away from people, just eating off the land and wandering around when you're not looking for game. You gotta protect your brothers and your town. Your home."

Christian shifted his shoulders. Hank had always been big on purpose. What was Christian's? He'd needed to get his head on right after leaving the service, and he'd wandered the mountains enough to do that. He hadn't given much thought to employment, but being an elusive AWT fit better than anything else. "Are you offering me a job?"

Dutch cracked his neck. "Close enough. You missed the application deadline for the fall session of the Alaska Law Enforcement Training, but I can get that waived once you fill out the public safety written test. Then you can shadow me, work as a consultant, until you have to attend ALET in the fall. The training is for only sixteen weeks, and you'll ace it all, Christian. But you gotta do it to wear the badge."

Great. More training. "When?"

"Mid-July to September. It's worth it. Then I can turn the territory over to you." Dutch rolled his shoulders. "I'm eighty-two. The cold digs deep into my bones these days, and I'd like to retire on a beach somewhere. One with sun and not wind."

Christian narrowed his gaze. "Bullshit."

Dutch grinned, wide and unapologetic, flashing the gap beside his right molars. "All right, maybe not. But it'd sure be nice to work with you until I can't move any longer. I really could use some help. Starting with the recent explosion in Knife's Edge. The state sent me in, and there are Alaska state troopers on the way as well. I don't want to piss off Brock, but I don't have a choice. Sure could use another set of eyes, especially if they see a lot better than my old ones do."

The explosion and fire that had almost harmed Amka. "I would like to investigate that with you. The note sent with the lighter fluid promised more fires or attacks." Christian intended to be involved. He noted the sound of birds in the distance. Maybe eagles.

"Great. I've got that and the dead body your brother found that disappeared in December. We still got nothin' on that one." Dutch lifted his head as if also looking for the birds.

Ah. The body. Brock and Ophelia had found a dead male, probably in his fifties, wearing a sweatshirt with EVE embroidered on it. His eyes had been brutally scratched out. Then the body had disappeared, and the folks at EVE had no clue as to the identity of the victim. "Brock is still trying to figure that one out as well."

"The FBI agent in town. Is she gonna be a nuisance?"

Christian smiled. Slowly. "Probably."

"Huh. Why is she still here, anyway? The office in Anchorage told me to liaise with her, whatever the hell that means. I know the body was found on federal land, but still, shouldn't she be gone by now?"

"You haven't heard." Christian shook his head. "She's with Brock. In for the long haul."

Now both of Dutch's eyebrows rose. Bushy and full. "No kidding? I always figured Ace would be the first to fall."

"Oh, he's fallin' lately," Christian muttered. "Drinkin' too much. I've given him enough time to get his head on right." There were probably two people outside of his brothers that he'd share such information with, and Dutch was one of them. Maybe the only one.

"I saw him in January and he seemed okay," Dutch noted.

Christian had thought so, too. "Yeah, he got his act together for a couple months, but the closer we got to spring season and decent flying weather, the more he started drinking again." Ace had crashed an F/A-18 Super Hornet before being honorably discharged, and he hadn't been up in the air since. Hadn't even flown commercial to get home.

Dutch turned his head and coughed several times, the sound wet.

Christian studied him. "You good?"

"Yeah. Just old."

"Where are you staying in town? Flossy's B&B has to be full up."

Dutch wiped off his mouth with the back of his gnarled hand. "I thought I'd hit up Brock since he built that nice cabin, but not if he has a female there. Even if she is FBI, I don't want to be around a couple of lovebirds. Makes me lonely." He brightened. "Amka will take pity on me and let me stay in the room at the tavern. That way I'll get fed while I'm here."

Christian shook his head. Amka had a back room where drunks often slept it off. He'd slept there a few times during the years, in fact. Best sleep of his life. The entire room smelled like her. "You're a smart one, Dutch."

"Yeah, I am. I've stayed with her before, and it's the best. For now, you takin' the job?"

Christian studied the man he'd known his entire life. "I guess I am."

Dutch held out a hand and they shook. Hard. "Good. Because it's not one murder and missing body up in the mountains."

Caution whispered through Christian. "Excuse me?"

"Yep. We've got at least three murdered victims with their eyes removed, and we can't identify even one of them."

Well, shit.

CHAPTER 8

After staying the night with May, back at the tavern, Amka took two ibuprofen from the drawer below the register and swallowed them dry. She nodded at Lucas Landom as he took his normal to-go order of two breakfast burritos and headed out the door. The tanker chief was predictable, if nothing else.

The breakfast rush had wrapped, and the place had settled into its usual mid-morning rhythm. Down the street, Janet and Gus had the diner open all day now, drawing the early regulars with pancakes and chatter, which meant fewer greasy orders on Amka's grill in the morning and more time to breathe. It was good. She liked the tavern better in the off-hours, when she could hear herself think and wipe down counters that didn't need it yet.

The door opened. A man stepped inside wearing a sun-worn pack and trail dust on his jeans. He had tan skin, was clean-shaven, and moved with a calm, steady way that held grace. He glanced around, gave her a small nod with his blond head, and headed to the bar. "Hi there. Could I get a Bloody Mary?" He slid onto a stool and rested his arms on the counter.

"You've got it." She pulled the vodka and mix from the cooler and reached for a glass.

"My name's Steve Coldtrap. I'm doing the challenge." He watched her make the drink.

She added olives, lemon, and celery, not rushing. She'd been hearing about the beef jerky contest all morning. "The fifty grand thing?"

He smiled. "That's the one. I need to interview one person from Knife's Edge to enter the contest. Would you be willing to answer a few questions?"

She placed the drink in front of him. "No thanks. You're the fourth influencer to ask today." It was doubtful many locals were agreeing to that part of the contest. "Also, I'd appreciate it if you didn't film in here. Even though it's public, most folks don't like that."

He lifted his hands. "No problem. My phone's in my pocket." He took a sip and gave her an approving nod. "That's solid. You don't skimp on the heat."

She wiped the counter and gave a half smile without looking up.

"You'd look good on camera," he murmured.

"I appreciate that," she replied.

He looked her over again, slow but not creepy, like he was cataloging something interesting. "Whole picture's working, if I'm being honest."

She let out a quiet laugh. "You might want to slow down."

"I'm just making observations."

The door opened again, and Jarod strolled in with his sunglasses hooked in the collar of his T-shirt, his sleeves pushed up, a faint sunburn across his nose. He walked with ease, wearing what looked like new boots. He stepped up beside Steve and leaned against the bar, casually, like he owned a stake in it. "What's going on?" he asked, not taking his eyes off Amka.

"Nothing," she said, reaching for the rag again. Did he know she'd spent the night at May's? Why would he?

"I'm Steve," the other man said, holding out his hand.

"Jarod." He shook it, firm and fast. "Are you here for the fishing derby?"

Steve shook his head. "No. I'm working on the jerky contest and am trying to talk to folks who actually live here. It's one of the requirements for each small town we hit. I just asked the pretty bartender if she'd be up for a quick interview."

Jarod glanced at her. "Don't tell me. She said no?"

"Yup, but I haven't poured on the charm yet," Steve said.

Amka chuckled. The man had charm, that was for sure. But who made a living chasing contests around the world by making social media videos? Of course, maybe most people wanted to travel. She'd always liked it right here in Knife's Edge.

Jarod snorted. "Amka is no fun, but I am. How about you interview me? I'm a local."

Steve turned toward him. "That would be fantastic." He glanced back at Amka. "But I'm sure you're wrong about her. She's too pretty to be boring."

Now Amka had to roll her eyes.

"She's pretty and she knows it." Jarod shifted his stance and looked at Steve. "However, since we're friends now, I'd like to take you out to where I'll be building the next motel and maybe get some early interest in the place."

Steve straightened. "So long as I get the interview, finally, I'll go anywhere you want."

"Excellent. Give me a few minutes." Jarod clapped him on the back and moved on, scanning his phone as he walked down the bar.

Amka took the coffee pot and made a slow pass through the room, topping off mugs, clearing a plate, wiping down a small ring of syrup left on one table. She returned to the bar as Steve set his glass down. "Hey, could I get a water?"

"Sure." She filled a clean glass from the tap and passed it to him.

"Thanks." He drank half of it without stopping and plunked it back on the bar.

The door opened. She looked over, and warmth hit her straight in the chest. Dutch came in first, boots solid on the floor, coat open, his limp heavier than last time. Christian walked in behind him, taller, quieter, his gaze scanning the entire tavern and then returning to her.

Delight tickled through her. "Dutch," she said, already coming out from behind the bar.

His grin revealed the gap in his teeth. "There's the prettiest girl in the wilderness."

She hugged him hard, arms around his wide frame, careful of his bad leg. "I didn't know you were coming to town." She stepped back and motioned toward the bar. "Come on up. We've still got some of the egg casserole left."

"I'll take it." Dutch followed her to the bar. "And a seat." He eased himself onto the stool next to Steve, set his hat down, and stretched out his leg with a quiet grunt. "Oh, and a Bloody Mary wouldn't hurt. I'm off duty."

Steve leaned forward, grinning. "Hey, pretty lady. How do I get a hug like that?"

The air cooled. Not the room. Not the temperature. Just the mood.

Steve glanced to his right and then took a small sip of water.

Amka followed his look. Christian stood just inside the door, not moving. His face gave nothing away, not even a twitch. Her heartbeat increased, fluttering against her ribs for some reason that didn't make any sense. The guy had…presence. She held his green and black gaze for a second and then started making the drink for Dutch.

"Dutch'll want the back table," Christian said, giving Steve a look that didn't linger but still carried weight. He turned, nodding once to Dutch, who slid rather gracefully off the stool. The two made their way to the back, and the slow, even sound of their boots crossing the floor was the only noise for several seconds.

Steve leaned slightly across the bar, voice dropping to a whisper. "Hey. That's the guy from the fire and the video, right?"

Amka gave a small nod. "I heard about that but haven't seen it." She hadn't had time to scroll through social media yet.

"Oh, man. You need to." Steve pulled out his phone, thumbs moving fast until he found what he wanted. "That damn Nixi got it. She's always in the right place at the right time. The chick is a witch, I'm telling you. Here."

The video opened in full screen. Fire licked at the walls of a wooden structure already collapsing in the back. Smoke curled past the lens like a living thing. For a second, it was chaos—no clear subject, just burning timber and motion.

Then Christian came through the flames.

He moved fast, shoulders squared, arms locked tight around the person he carried. Her. Amka didn't breathe as she watched. Her head had been tucked against his chest, arms folded tight, legs swinging as he stepped over debris and smoke. Her flannel was scorched on one side. His T-shirt was covered in soot, catching sparks, his expression hard and locked in place.

An epic swell of music rose under the footage, edited in, clearly, but timed perfectly to the moment Christian cleared the threshold.

"That's you," Steve said, looking up, his eyes widening. "I mean, you can't see your face, but it's you. And that's him."

Amka didn't respond at first. The video looped again, showing the same heroic scene. "He would not like that video of him out there."

Steve shook his head. "Yeah, that's too bad. This guy's a hero, and you wouldn't believe some of the comments. I think there are at least three hundred, if not more, marriage proposals."

Amka wrinkled her nose. Christian really wouldn't like that. At least Nixi hadn't included his name. "This will die down, right?"

Steve nodded. "Sure, but it also might bring a cache of available young women, or men, straight to your town. This is video gold." He frowned, flicking the volume down. "I wish I'd caught that. I was across the road and didn't even think to pull out my phone until it was over. Nixi could get millions of views on this."

Amka hoped Nixi didn't post their names.

Steve cleared his throat. "Are you sure I can't interview you? I'd love to ask you about that moment."

"Not a chance." She looked toward the back of the bar. "I wouldn't ask him, either."

Steve chuckled and leaned back in his seat. "Oh, I got that. I got more than that from him." He tapped the phone screen to pause the video.

She cocked her head. "I don't know what that means."

Steve tapped his fingers on his phone. "Seriously? That vibe? It was touch-her-and-die vibe. Are you his?"

The archaic language zinged through her faster than a shot of bourbon, sizzling sharp. "What? No. Of course not."

"Huh. I'm usually on track better." Steve shrugged. "Guess I misread him."

Jarod came up the back of the bar to the till, his voice already too loud for the quiet between breakfast and lunch. "I've already reserved the diner for our reception," he said, grinning. "And we need to talk about construction for the motel when I get back."

Amka moved toward him, wiping down the mahogany as she walked. The guy had lost his mind. "Why's that?"

"Because we'll probably need to mortgage this place to help pay for it."

She started sorting through a few receipts left from the early morning tabs. "That's not going to happen, Jarod."

He stepped closer, his voice dipping. "The fuck it isn't. I need money. I'm flying to Anchorage later today to meet with the contractors. Our future is tied together, and we might need to use the equity here for part of the motel."

Her hand stilled on the edge of the register. "You have the insurance from when the motel burned down."

"Yeah." He leaned on the bar. "I need more. We're going to do it right this time. I don't want some hole-in-the-wall motel. This is going to be high-end, and we're going to get more tourists here than ever before."

She opened the drawer and started pulling change for a half-paid ticket someone had left. "I don't think the town wants that."

He slapped the drawer shut with the heel of his hand. She yanked her fingers free just in time.

"Too bad. That's the plan." He grabbed her arm.

"Let go of me, or I swear to God, I'm going to kick your balls out." She didn't flinch or raise her voice, but she was done. Just done with him.

She also felt the shift. Across the tavern, Christian looked up. At them. She didn't need to see it to know it was happening. The air changed.

Jarod lowered his head. "That asshole's way too interested in you."

"You might want to let go of my arm," she said.

He did. After a beat. Then he reached past her, popped the drawer back open, and glanced inside. "There should be enough for a plane ticket here." He took what he needed, counted it without apology, and stuffed the bills into his coat. "I'm not stealing. I'm investing in our future."

Amka stared at the bar, at the smudges left behind from the breakfast rush. "It's a good thing you have that video secured in case you die," she whispered tersely, meaning every word.

He didn't appear scared. "It's too late for you to get tough." Then he leaned in to kiss her.

She reacted without thought, putting both hands on his chest and shoving. Hard.

He fell back a step.

Everyone in the tavern—at the tables, at the bar—paused and stared.

Jarod forced a smile. "Man, you're in a mood. All right. We'll have fish and not chicken at the reception." He rolled his eyes and looked at Steve. "My chick is turning into a bridezilla, right? Let's go." He stepped away and walked around the bar, shoving the door open with more force than was necessary.

Steve gulped, frowned, and put a ten on the bar. "Thank you." He spun off the stool and followed Jarod, glancing back once before disappearing into the spring day.

Amka took the money and put it into the till, ignoring all of the questioning expressions on the familiar faces around her. What in the world had she just done?

CHAPTER 9

"What's going on here?" Christian asked as he stepped into the room, the rear door of what he thought was Puck's Bar closing behind him with a dull thud. Tika had taken off from his place earlier that day, and he didn't expect to see the wolf for a few days. The animal seemed to be stretching his legs and boundaries a bit.

Dutch snorted. "Ah, the AWT has rented this back room for as long as I can remember."

Puck's was a street over and south of Sam's Tavern and served as the only other bar in town. Owned by one of the Puck family through the years, it was as old as Sam's and had been a fixture in town since before anyone bothered keeping records. A rough mash of logs and river stone, it served cheap, burning liquor and not much else. No food, no snacks, and definitely no wine. It was the kind of place built for drinking and fighting. Sometimes both, often in that order.

But this room—this back room—had been updated. Someone had paneled it in light oak that still smelled faintly of fresh-cut wood and industrial varnish. A small stove sat tucked in the corner, right now silent but with logs already piled perfectly inside.

The rectangular space held a long, heavy table made from a carefully cut and polished slab of cedar. Three folding chairs, none of them matching, were pushed up to one side like someone had lost interest mid-arrangement. The tile floor was cracked and worn smooth in spots. There were no windows. Two massive corkboards blanketed the far wall covered in pinholes and ragged tape ghosts, with a monstrous map of Alaska spreading across the entire adjacent wall.

"I've never been in here." Christian pulled out one of the chairs to sit.

"Yeah, most people haven't," Dutch said. "We only use it if we have cases in the area. And every once in a while, if I have to crash somewhere and can't find a bed." He glanced down at the tile. "Believe me, I always try to find a bed."

The cracked floor looked less inviting than a pine needle covered trail for sleeping. "Why don't you just use the sheriff's office?"

"Because Alaska doesn't really have sheriffs." Dutch coughed into his hand, his shoulders shuddering. "Just because we let Knife's Edge have its idiosyncrasies doesn't mean the rest of us don't follow the law. Plus, I like my own space."

The air smelled faintly of old cleaner and warm dust. As a space, Christian didn't figure it was too bad. He'd lived in worse.

Movement sounded outside and the door opened. "Hi." Ophelia crossed inside, today dressed in dark jeans, black boots, and a black leather jacket. Even after months in Knife's Edge, she still looked like a city girl. She held out a hand. "I'm Agent Spilazi. My boss called yours, and they told me to meet you here."

Ah, Dutch wasn't going to like this. Christian moved to intercede and then caught the look in Dutch's eyes.

The gnarled trooper stood taller and smoothed back his wild gray hair before taking her hand in both of his. "I, ah, I should've called you myself, and I apologize for that."

Christian snapped his mouth shut. Had Dutch just said he was sorry? What was happening?

Ophelia smiled, looking like a movie star. "That's all right. I'm so happy to meet you. Brock says such fine things about you."

Pink wound beneath Dutch's weathered cheeks. "Ah, now, that's nice."

Was he fucking blushing? Christian just watched, unable to do anything else.

Dutch drew Ophelia over to one of the chairs. "This is the best we have right now, but I'll find better ones, I promise." He brushed off the seat with his bare hand.

"Oh, it's fine." Ophelia sat. "Thank you for working with me on this. One of the bodies was found on federal land."

"Of course. I'm so happy to have your help." Dutch reached into his jacket, pulled out three folded papers, and pinned them to the corkboard with silver thumbtacks. Each page showed a location. Two had photos. The kind that didn't need captions.

Christian stood, walked closer, and looked them over. He pointed at the third page. "This is where the body Brock and Ophelia found disappeared." They'd found the middle-aged man, wearing an EVE sweatshirt, with his eyes gouged out, but had to find shelter from a storm. When they returned, the body was gone.

Ophelia crossed her long legs. "Yeah, that looks like the place. We were freezing, so my memory isn't great. I can't believe the body disappeared."

"We'll figure it out. We have the two other victims to study as well." Dutch tapped the first picture. "The first victim was a woman, around forty. Dressed in black, she was found on her back with her eyes removed."

Christian frowned. "When?"

"Six months ago." Dutch motioned to the next photo. "The next vic was a male in his seventies or early eighties. Same thing. Eyes missing."

Ophelia studied the photos. "How did they die?"

"They were stabbed. Each sustained multiple wounds, but it was hard to tell exactly how many."

Christian stepped back. "What about the eyes? Gouged out how?"

Dutch sighed. "Some kind of tool. We haven't identified it. Lab hasn't either."

Christian dragged his hands down his face. "So you have both bodies. These at least didn't disappear."

Dutch nodded. "Yes. They were autopsied up in Anchorage, and the cause of both deaths was from stabbings. The eye removal happened after."

All right. So the monster walked on two feet. "A person did this. Not animals."

Dutch coughed. "Sorry. I'm fighting something. The coroner won't say that outright. He can't rule out scavenging, but the marks don't match anything usual."

Christian glanced at the board. "Three bodies in a year. All missing eyes."

"Four," Dutch said. "If you count Tamara Randsom."

Christian exhaled slowly. "She was killed by Monica. I found the body, remember?" He had been sorry to find the mother dead in that warming hut. He turned to check on Ophelia. Monica had shot her and nearly killed her.

"I'm fine," Ophelia said, her jaw hardening. "Monica swears she didn't touch Tamara's eyes."

"But they were taken out." Dutch pulled a fourth photo from his back pocket, flattened it against his leg, and tacked it to the board beside the others.

Christian looked at the picture of Tamara in that warming

hut. Monica had been obsessed with Brock. She'd killed Tamara because she believed Tamara and Brock had spent the night together. The reality was different. Tamara had been with Ace. By the time Monica learned the truth, it didn't matter. Tamara was already dead. Monica still claimed she left the body in a warming hut, ensuring it would be found. She also swore she hadn't touched the eyes. "Is there any way Monica killed the other three victims?"

"No. I've already verified her alibi for all three, or I wouldn't be here still looking," Dutch said.

Fair enough. "So you think we have a serial killer?" Christian asked.

"We've got something," Dutch said. "Unfortunately, this is all we've got. We searched the areas around both bodies. Found nothing. And the worst part is, they haven't been identified to this day."

Ophelia frowned. "These days you can identify just about anybody."

Dutch tapped the board. "Not these two. There aren't any matches in any system."

Christian stepped back, arms crossed. "Where were they found?"

Dutch moved to the opposite wall, where a map of the territory was mounted. He reached for the bottom of the board, grabbed purple pushpins, and pressed them into the board one at a time. "The bodies were found all within a hundred miles of Knife's Edge, which is the closest town to all of the scenes. Coincidence? Maybe. Maybe not."

Christian studied the spread. "Are we sure this is one killer? Rumors in a place like this...they get carried on fumes. Somebody might know to kill and then take out the eyes to make it all look related."

"That's possible, except for two things." Dutch turned back toward him. "The coroner in Anchorage still hasn't identified the tool that took out the eyes, and we can't ID three of the victims, counting the one we can't find."

Christian couldn't put the pieces into a reasonable puzzle. "That's weird."

Dutch's jaw tightened. "If it were scavengers, we'd usually know the signs. If it were a specific tool, same thing."

"I agree." Christian cleared his throat. "I'm more of a shoot-him or beat-him-up kind of guy. I stalk, track, or hunt and then take care of threats. I don't know what to do in an investigation like this."

Dutch pulled out one of the folding chairs and dropped his weight into it. The metal legs creaked but didn't collapse. "I know, but think of it like hunting in a different way. I've got the reports and case files from these two, plus Tamara's, coming in on the supply plane tomorrow."

Made sense. There was at least one daily plane arriving now that spring had arrived, usually carrying supplies and now tourists. So much for Christian heading up into the mountains until tourist season ended.

"We'll start here in Knife's Edge." Dutch tapped the table once. "We'll ask around and see if anyone recognizes any of the victims. The town is the closest to all of the crime scenes, so hopefully somebody will know something to send us in the right direction."

"I'm not great with talking to people," Christian said.

Dutch snorted. "I've noticed." He leaned back in the chair, arms crossed. "Now that you're on the payroll, we've got more than just dead bodies to worry about. Be on the lookout for contraband flights. With the skies open again, someone's bound to get creative. We also need to keep an eye on poachers."

"I'm on board with that," Christian said. Tracking a person wasn't all that different from tracking game. But interviews and evidence? None of that landed right. "The investigation stuff," he added. "I'm better at ground work."

"Don't worry," Ophelia said. "I'm sure there'll be plenty of that as well. Plus, come on. You like solving problems. Think of this as a mystery that needs to be solved." She smiled at him. "We're a task force of three. I like this."

Christian liked being able to keep an eye on her. She was trained and tough, but she held his brother's heart in her hands. Or whatever the expression was. If anything happened to her, Brock would be destroyed. Christian's thoughts drifted back to the bar and another mystery that wouldn't leave him alone. The way Amka had shoved Jarod had shocked him. Not because Jarod wasn't a jerk, but more like, Amka didn't have a violent bone in her body. But, it wasn't his business. Still, the moment stuck in his head.

Something was off. He just didn't know what yet. Apparently he needed to solve more than one mystery in town.

CHAPTER 10

Amka's headache continued throughout the day, but she kept a smile in place and gratitude in her heart. At least she tried. The smile was easier than the gratitude. But there was so much. She had friends and a somewhat successful business. Times weren't exactly easy in Knife's Edge, but the tourist season helped.

"You good?" Daisy asked, bussing a couple of pitchers from some social media folks in the corner.

"Yeah." Amka looked up at the man and two women. "This is a new development."

Daisy rinsed the beer glasses before plucking them into the dishwasher. "Might bring some business in, but I'm not sure anybody local wants that."

Yeah. There was a fine line between wanting new folks in town and enjoying the solitude of the middle of wintery nowhere.

Wyland and Sheldon Friday sat at the bar, finishing burgers. Sheldon had a new sports watch. He smiled when he caught her glance. "I bought it the other day, and it came in on the plane."

Wyland shook his head. "You can't be spending insurance

money we don't have. Plus, once we have the money, we need to rebuild."

Sheldon rolled his eyes. "Why? We have enough storage area on the bottom floor. It's a basement we don't use. Amka? What do you think about you taking over that land? We can use our part of the insurance for something else."

"If we get insurance," Wyland said, wearing his going out clothes of a nice red flannel and brown slacks. "Sometimes when there's arson, the insurance people don't pay out."

Sheldon sucked in air. "None of us set the fire or the explosion, so the insurance company has to give us the money." His eyes gleamed. "I'm tired of working for scraps, and we both need a vacation somewhere warm."

Wyland frowned. "Warm? It's spring and will soon be summer. I ain't going anywhere, and neither are you."

Sheldon winked at Amka. "You could use a fun vacation. Amka, how about you ditch your fiancé and date me?"

Amka's jaw nearly dropped open. Sheldon had asked her out quite a few times the last couple of years, but as soon as she'd become engaged to Jarod, he'd stopped. This was new. "Um, that's a kind offer, but I don't think so. Thanks, though."

"Any time," Sheldon murmured quietly.

That was odd, but Amka had enough to worry about. She walked to the other end of the bar, where Daisy was wiping down an area where one of the social media influencers had spilled a margarita. "Daisy? I need to make an appointment. With you as a lawyer."

Daisy's green eyes lit. "Really? Awesome. You're my first client. Do you mind if I take over that dark corner with the one table? It's away from the bar, pool tables, and dart boards."

Amka craned her neck to see that far corner, where she tried to keep a candle to make the dark space appear romantic. "Sure. In fact, there's an entire wall behind that main chair." She'd always meant to put a light or poster on that wall since it was far from the windows but had never found the time. "You can hang your shingle there. What is a shingle, anyway?"

Daisy snorted and shut the dishwasher door. "I'm pretty sure that means your diploma, or maybe your acceptance from the state bar, but I'm not totally sure. Is it really okay for me to take over that corner?"

"Sure." The last time someone had commandeered that corner table as their own, Bussy Mosten and Bert Knob had been having an affair. Of course, they had both been widowed and were in their nineties, but still, they considered it an affair. Amka hadn't wanted to know anything more than that. She looked around the mostly vacant tavern. "I'm available now."

Daisy hopped once. "This is so exciting." She removed her apron and placed the logo covered material on the bar. Amka had been proud to start selling Sam's Tavern shirts and hats just a year before. Daisy plucked a high-end looking briefcase from beneath the counter. "Ms. Amaruq, please follow me to my office."

Amusement and a hint of hope flowed through Amka as she followed, not hiding her chuckle. Who knew? Maybe this would be the perfect place for Daisy to practice law. Of course, they could always build a room or office where the storage building had burned down. She took a seat across from Daisy, who all of a sudden wore a serious expression. "What now?"

Daisy pulled out a yellow legal notebook and a pen. "So, I'm assuming this has to do with the destroyed storage building?"

Amka paused. "No." She glanced around to verify that nobody was paying them any attention. "I need a will."

Daisy's eyes lit. "Cool. Excellent. I love drafting wills." She started scratching notes on the pad. "What are your assets?"

Amka could answer that easily. "The bar, my house, the Jeep, and my snowmobile."

Daisy kept writing. "Anything else? Jewelry, family heirlooms, weapons?"

Amka kicked out her legs. It had been a long day, and her calves were protesting. "Just two shotguns and a nine millimeter. No jewelry or heirlooms." She hadn't known her father, and her mother hadn't had time for baubles.

"All right." Daisy looked up and smiled. "I assume you want to leave everything to Jarod?"

Amka's stomach ached. "No. I, ah, want to leave Sam's Tavern to you and Rudolph with equal shares. You get my snowmobile and handgun, and Rudolph gets my shotguns. As for the cabin and my Jeep, I'd like to leave them to Christian Osprey."

Daisy sat back, blinking once. Then twice. "Um—"

"He needs a place to live, and both you and Rudolph have nice places." Heat filled Amka's cheeks. She and Christian weren't close, had never been, but she wanted him to have a home of his own. Why not take hers? "Nobody else in my life needs a place to live."

Daisy sat back, her face clearing. "All right. I need a dollar."

Amka reached into her apron for a bill and slid it across the table.

"I didn't need that to be your lawyer, but it helps. I'll draft up a letter of engagement tonight for you to sign. For now. You can't leave me part of the bar."

"Sure I can."

Daisy pushed her wild hair away from her face. "That's sweet, but I don't get it. Tell me why you are trying to disinherit your soon-to-be husband."

"No."

Daisy quirked her lips. "All right. Well, since you're engaged, I need to know if you plan on changing this will once you are married?"

Amka cleared her throat. "I'm not planning on getting married, but if something happens to me beforehand, I'd like my stuff to go to people I care about."

Daisey's eyes widened. "You think the arson attack was meant specifically for you?"

"I don't know." That was the truth. But just in case, she wanted her life organized.

"All right. So, as your attorney who is bound by client confidentiality and total discretion, why aren't you planning to be married, and why don't you want your estate left to your fiancé?"

Amka glanced around again. Nobody was paying a titch of attention to them. "I don't love Jarod, don't want to get married, and definitely don't want him to end up with my cabin or my bar."

Daisy paled. "Well. I don't like the guy, but I figured he rocked in bed, which explained everything."

Amka exhaled. "I wouldn't know. I've never slept with that asshole." Although he kept making moves. He was becoming more daring, and she tried not to be alone with him often.

Daisy coughed and just stared at her. "Um."

"I don't want to talk about it." Amka could barely breathe. The less people who knew about Hank's death, the better.

"All right." Curiosity glowed bright in Daisy's eyes. "That's fair. But I'm your lawyer now, so you can tell me anything."

Amka had already shared with May, and that was enough for now. She couldn't take another friend looking at her with a mixture of pity and fury. Although, if she needed a posse, she might be able to put one together. "So what's the plan?"

Daisy studied her for a moment. "The will as you've specified will be valid until you say *I Do*, and then Jarod would have a spousal election in your estate in case you die. A spousal election in Alaska depends on how long you've been married, so the longer the marriage, the more of a cut he'd get. But he'd get something, no matter what. Unless you both sign a prenuptial agreement before getting married."

"Draw it up." Amka had no intention of actually going

through with the marriage ceremony, but maybe seeing a prenup would get Jarod to think twice. He'd already mentioned using the tavern as collateral for his big new touristy hotel. "Is there a way you can gift part of this tavern now to people without letting them know?"

"Including me?" Daisy frowned.

Yeah, that didn't make much sense. "Jarod wants to use my collateral in Sam's Tavern to get a loan for the motel. How do I make it unavailable to him?"

Daisy scrunched up her nose, showcasing a myriad of freckles. "Let me think. I guess you could leverage it yourself? Like use the tavern as collateral for another project?"

That made sense, but what project? "I don't want to risk the bar, but I would like to take any financial incentive away from Jarod."

Daisy bit her lip. "As your attorney, I'd really like to know what's going on."

"I'm not ready to talk about it." Amka glanced around the room to make sure the few remaining patrons didn't need refills.

Daisy coughed. "All right. Are you in danger?"

Was she? Somebody had planted an explosive device in her storage building that had detonated when she'd been inside. "I'm not sure."

"From Jarod?" Daisy asked.

"No." It didn't make sense for Jarod to hurt her when they weren't married. He wouldn't automatically inherit anything. "He's a jerk, but I don't think he's too dangerous." Except when he'd tried to rip off her clothes. She'd handled him each time, though. Her stomach ached. What if she couldn't handle him next time?

Daisy jotted down a couple more notes. "All right. I don't like being in the dark here, but I can draft both the prenup and the will as your lawyer." She placed the pen by the notepad. "As your friend, I can help you bury his body where it can't be found."

Amka burst out laughing. "I appreciate it."

"Are you frightened of him? Is that why you're marrying him?"

"No." Amka stood.

Daisy tapped a finger on her lips and leaned in. "Is it because of Christian? He's so hot, and he always watches you."

"No." Amka sighed. "I admit that Christian's good looking, but I want someone who takes care of me once in a while. He did save me from the fire, but I always bring him soup, have done his laundry and stuff like that. He needs taking care of."

Daisy smirked. "I think you're wrong. If that man goes all in with a woman, he'll take care of her. In every way." She wriggled her eyebrows.

Amka laughed. She'd been on her own for so long, she didn't want to feel like that forever. Was it possible? Christian was a lone wolf except for his brothers and for hero moments. He sacked out wherever he could find a bed, didn't have a car, and wasn't looking for work. While he was a much better person than Jarod, he wasn't exactly stable. She most certainly needed stable and constant. Somebody she could count on at all times. "Thank you for being my lawyer, and you're welcome to use this corner of the tavern as your office as long as you want, but I do expect to be billed for the work."

Daisy sat back. "How about we exchange my work for use of the bar as my office?"

"It's not the same. You have to bill me something." Amka turned to head back to work, her body aching. It was going to be a long night.

CHAPTER 11

The rain came down hard, drilling and punishing, pounding the roof in a steady rhythm that masked most other sounds. Water gushed from the eaves in thick sheets, pooling along the gravel alley and soaking everything that wasn't under cover. Christian stood tucked beneath the narrow overhang on the side of the tavern, one boot braced against the wall, his arms crossed tight to stay warm. His jacket collar was damp, and water still tracked down the back of his neck.

He felt like a fucking idiot, but he wasn't leaving.

The sky was pitch black, the clouds thick and low enough to feel like a lid. No stars, no moon—just rain and the constant hum of runoff sliding through the gutters and hitting the earth with dull splashes.

The smoke lingered in the air, though the rain had drowned most of the smell. He looked over at the remains of the storage building. The fire had gutted it completely, leaving nothing but a heap of blackened wood and collapsed metal sheeting. Someone should clean that up. He wasn't sure what they were waiting for. Then again, he hadn't asked.

The door to Sam's Tavern opened with a sharp creak, spilling weak yellow light onto the wet ground. Amka stepped out first, followed by Doc May and Wyland Friday.

Christian pushed away from the wall. It was two in the morning. Nobody had any business being out, least of all Amka. Of course, he was there waiting to make sure she made it home safely. What was wrong with him? He didn't have room in his life for a woman, and that one was taken.

May stopped short when she saw him. "Are you guarding the place?"

"I was just walking by." His voice sounded rough in the storm, even to him.

May stood close to Amka and Wyland, and the way her shoulders stayed tense made him think she expected one of them to collapse. The doctor clearly appeared exasperated. "I've been telling Amka to go home for hours, but she wouldn't listen. I swear, the patients in this town are the worst."

Wyland snorted, then hiccupped. "I totally agree."

May rounded on him. "You have arthritis. You need your sleep. It's too late for you to be out, and you should not be drinking doubles like that."

"You sound like a cranky schoolmarm," Wyland muttered.

"I'm your doctor. That's my job," May grumbled, the rain matting her blonde hair to her head.

Amka glanced back inside the window, where a trio of fisherman could be seen still drinking beer. "I should close up and not leave Daisy to do it."

May waved a hand. "Daisy's happy to do it, and they're tipping like drunks. Stop worrying about it."

Christian studied his three charges. May looked pissed yet solid. Wyland was running on pride and stubbornness. But Amka swayed slightly, not from the wind. Her face had gone pale, and the dark circles under her eyes showed a woman pushing herself way too hard.

"I'll drive you home," he said, looking at her.

May slid her shoulder beneath Wyland's arm, taking some of his weight. Rain tracked down both of their faces. "I was planning to give them both a ride, but if you don't mind taking Amka, that would be great. We're headed the other direction."

Christian nodded once. The Fridays lived upriver, past the last gravel turnoff. Their land had been there longer than the town. "Sounds good."

Amka made a noise and opened her mouth as if to argue, and Christian lowered his chin, meeting her gaze evenly.

She fell silent.

The hair on the back of Christian's neck rose. He paused, eyes narrowing, the downpour hammering against the roof and ground in deafening sheets.

A shot cracked through the storm.

He turned instantly, lunged, and drove the group to the ground just as another round ripped through the space where they'd been standing. Water exploded off the gravel. The sound of the rain masked the direction of the gunfire, echoing off buildings, cars, metal.

"Move." He grabbed Amka and hauled her toward the front tire of her SUV. She tried to speak but didn't get the chance. He put her on her ass, one hand firm on the back of her neck as he pushed her face down to her legs. "Knees. Stay low."

Amka folded without resistance, rain soaking her hair, water running in streams over her shoulders.

May scrambled toward the rear tire, dragging Wyland with her. He slipped once in the mud, and she pulled harder, gritting her teeth. Another shot shattered the rear window of the vehicle. Glass scattered over the pavement, slick and invisible. The next shot hit the tavern's window.

Christian didn't flinch. He crouched, yanked his phone from his back pocket, and called without even checking the screen.

His brother grumbled in answer. "What the hell? It's two in the morning."

"Shots fired at Sam's Tavern. Sniper across the street."

"I'm coming," Brock answered. The line went dead.

Christian stowed the phone and pulled the weapon from beneath his jacket.

"You're carrying a gun?" May shouted from her crouch, voice nearly lost in the roar of the rain.

"I always carry a gun," he said.

Wyland fumbled in his coat and came up with a soaked Ruger. "Ditto, buddy."

May reached over and yanked it from his hand. "You've been drinking."

Christian didn't comment. He was already scanning. There was no cover—nothing but broken remains of the storage building, two half-exposed vehicles, and a town that had gone eerily still except for the downpour. Moonlight barely cut through the clouds now, just flashes in between cracks.

The rain was unrelenting. Cold. Hard. Every breath was wet air and sound.

Christian moved like the chaos didn't touch him. He positioned himself past the front tire, calculating angles in his head. This was his element, like it or not. Water rolled down his face and soaked into his collar. He didn't blink. Didn't speak. Just listened.

Another shot fired. Close. Maybe hit the alley next to the tavern.

He held up a hand, flat, steady. No one moved. He'd decide when. He'd decide how.

Nobody was dying tonight.

He lifted his head just enough to see over the hood. Rain hit him sideways, cold and needle-sharp, blurring his vision and slicking his hands. The storm had worsened. The wind shoved at the vehicles, and water flowed in muddy rivers along the curb. The dark was absolute, broken only by the occasional flicker from the floodlight above Sam's back entrance.

Another shot cracked, closer this time, and sparked against the wet asphalt.

Christian dropped back behind the Jeep. He wasn't guessing anymore. The shooter perched on the roof of the old cineplex across the street, Moosejaw Cinemas, where Tuesday tickets cost three bucks and the popcorn tasted like lighter fluid. The last movie had probably ended around eleven and the patrons were long gone. Now the theater was just dark windows and peeling paint, but the building had the elevation and cover a shooter would want.

He shifted up again and fired three shots, fast and clean. They hit the siding just above the ticket booth awning. Right where they should.

Silence followed.

He turned toward Amka, who hadn't moved. She sat curled against the front tire, rain soaking through her clothes. Her knees were up, her face down. "You okay?" he asked.

"No," she said, voice muffled. Then she looked up. "Is he gone?"

"Not yet. Don't move."

Wyland sneezed, wet and loud.

May tightened her grip on him. "What should we do?"

Christian checked the math. "Is anybody hit inside?" he yelled.

"No," Daisy called out. "We're all behind the bar now."

He extended his hand to May. "You keep Wyland down as close to that tire as you can. Give me the Ruger."

May passed it to him, wet and slippery. It was double-action and already chambered. He checked anyway. Six rounds. Compact frame, short barrel, nothing fancy.

He handed the gun to Amka. "Position the weapon on the hood. Keep your head and shoulders down. Aim straight up at the roof of the Moosejaw. Make sure you aim up there and keep down. Got it?"

She nodded. Her hair was soaked, plastered to her cheeks. Her hands shook as she took the pistol, but she held it like she'd used one before.

"Whatever you do, don't aim lower," Christian said.

"What are you going to do?" she asked.

"Run across the street. You're covering me."

Her eyes widened. "Christian, that's not—"

"Amka." His tone stopped her cold.

She swallowed. "Okay. And…if I miss?"

"You don't have to hit anything but the building, baby. You're just providing cover."

She swallowed. "Okay." She turned on her knees, staying under the cover of the hood, and positioned herself with care. The Ruger rested against the metal, angled up. Her arms braced. The gun trembled slightly, but her aim was true. "Tell me when," she whispered.

Christian inhaled, gaze fixed on the theater roof. He took a deep breath, glancing at her and then reaching over and covering her hands with his, nudging the barrel up half an inch. The angle had to be right. The last thing he needed was a bullet in the ribs from the only person trying to help.

"I can do this," she whispered.

"I know." He slid forward to the front of the Jeep, boots sloshing through water pooling in the dip beside the curb. The hood rattled under the rain, sheet after sheet pouring over it. "Fire slow. Count it out. One. Two. Three. You have six bullets. Use them all."

"Okay," Amka whispered.

"Now."

She fired.

He moved.

Rain came sideways, sharp and cold, battering his face as he broke cover. He sprinted across the open street, not looking back. Another shot. Then another. Her timing was good. Each one gave him a second more.

He hit the far sidewalk, turned, and slammed his back against the building. The concrete was wet and cold, but it gave him cover.

Two more rounds. Then nothing.

She ducked.

He rounded the corner, jumped for the fire escape, and caught the lowest rung. The metal was slick, so he tightened his grip and kept climbing. He passed the second floor, and then the third, rolling onto the roof and staying low.

Wind ripped across the building. Rain came harder up here, straight across from what felt like every direction. He crawled toward the far corner. No movement. But this was the spot. It was the only place that gave a straight shot across the intersection.

He found the shell casings by touch before he saw them. Still warm. Just a few. No scatter. The shooter had control. That told him something.

Too late, though. He was already gone.

A truck engine roared down the street. Lights cut through the storm.

Christian looked over the edge.

Brock's truck skidded into view, tires kicking up water. Doors flew open. Brock went right, behind cover. Ophelia moved left, gun drawn, sweeping.

"It's clear," Christian called down.

Ophelia ran around the SUV, crouching as she must've checked on everyone.

Christian didn't wait. "Make sure they're all right," he said. "I'm going after him." He took the wet stairs down the back, jumped the last two rungs, and hit the ground hard. Gravel shifted under his boots. The wind shoved him sideways.

He pulled out his phone. The screen lit, and he thumbed on the flashlight. Maybe his brothers had been correct in forcing him to get the phone. It was coming in handy. His gaze caught on a boot scuff in the wet dirt, and then bark torn from the low shrub beside the walkway. Weight had come through here, moving fast.

He followed it.

No theory. No instinct. Just movement, one sign after another, through the back lots behind the native association and the library.

He angled into the storm, tracking the trail toward the edge of town.

Toward the school.

The trail cut behind a tool shed and through a gap in a rusted chain-link fence. Christian followed, every step careful and measured. The rain made it harder. The storm pushed leaves flat, erased weight, and filled shallow prints until everything blurred. But not all of it. He caught where a boot had dragged through soft earth, clipped the edge of a concrete footing, and left a faint smear on wet metal.

He dropped to a crouch beside a narrow line of crushed grass. The shooter had gone through there fast, off balance, maybe trying to keep from slipping. That told him something. Probably not military. Could've been, but didn't feel like it. No retreat plan. No sign of a lookout. No suppression shots on exit. The guy's plan had been to just run and disappear.

Christian's plan would involve pain. A lot of it.

He passed the edge of the old playground with its metal swings rattling hard in the wind, plastic slide shaking with every gust, and cut across the mulch, already half-flooded. The shooter had gone straight through. Christian followed the broken path to the far fence, hopped it, and landed low in a crouch.

The trees opened just enough to show the logging road

ahead. A well-used cutout near a tributary of the river with an excellent fishing hole. Everyone knew about it and used it often. Ruts, tire tracks, animal signs—all of it churning in the mud. No clean boot prints anymore. Just chaos in every direction.

Christian stopped at the edge, lifted his head, and breathed.

Not just air. Information.

His brain ran through it like it used to back in Afghanistan. After a raid. After the target had gone to ground. It wasn't magic. It was training. Repetition. Sweat. Sand. Death.

He scanned the dark.

The shooter could've gone anywhere now, and the storm had masked the engine of his vehicle.

Yet, Christian didn't move. He listened. Watched. Felt. There were things his body caught before his brain did. A pattern in the silence. A direction in the wind. A small, instinctive pull that something was off just east of the split in the road.

He didn't know who the shooter was, but he was going to find him.

And when he did, he wasn't going to ask questions first.

But the bigger question burned hotter than the rest. Who had the bastard been aiming at? Out of all the possibilities, only one of them had been inside a fireball yesterday. One of them wasn't supposed to still be walking.

Did somebody want Amka dead?

CHAPTER 12

Amka refilled Christian's coffee. Her hand trembled with the pot, and she didn't try to steady it. The pour came fast, too much, coffee sloshing up the sides of the mug. She set the pot down hard in the center of the table. The glass clacked loud enough to quiet the rain for half a second.

"You need to sit down." He kicked out the empty chair beside him with his boot. The wooden legs scraped across the floor, uneven and loud. Amka nodded, her brain feeling fuzzy, and lowered herself into the seat. Her coat was soaked through. Her hair stuck to her cheek in strands she didn't bother to move.

The table was crowded with Christian on her right and May on her left, elbows pulled in tight. Wyland sat across from her, posture stiff, the usual slump gone. His hands were flat on the table, next to the mug he hadn't lifted once.

Amka glanced at the now covered up tavern window. The sniper had hit both her building and her vehicle.

Brock leaned against the bar behind them, arms crossed, notebook in one hand. He'd stopped writing a while ago. His eyes remained fixed on the group, watching without blinking. He looked competent and rather pissed.

Ophelia perched on a stool next to him, sipping from a mug of black coffee. Her left leg swung slightly, toes not touching the floor. Her gaze moved between Amka and Brock.

Rain hammered the roof. No rhythm. Just assault.

Christian turned his head, zeroing in on Amka. "Where is Dutch? I thought he was staying the night in your back room."

Amka's fingers curled around her mug, trying to pull something from the heat. It didn't help. "Ace was in earlier." She didn't want to get his brothers mad at him, but she wasn't up to lying right now. "He drank too much, got into it with a couple of tourists, and then drank some more. I cut him off early, but he has no problem rounding the bar and pouring his own." She'd been too busy to stop him. "Dutch drove him home and said he'd just stay there."

Christian exhaled. "Damn it, Brock. We need to do something about him."

"I know." Brock didn't move from the bar. "Let's deal with one problem at a time. Everyone is okay, and you've given me the series of events until the shooting stopped. C, it's your turn to talk. What did you find?"

"I tracked him to Blue's fishing hole. He had a vehicle and could be anywhere by now. The landing area in front of the fishing hole's a wreck with tire tracks everywhere. All flooded out."

Brock pushed off from the bar and took a slow step toward the table. "So we have a fire in the storage building owned by Amka and Wyland, and now we have a shooter who aimed at the four of you, including Amka and Wyland. Let's start with Amka. Considering you were in the building when it blew, you were probably the target."

None of this made a bit of sense. Amka stared down at the coffee. She didn't flinch and had absolutely no idea what to say.

Christian leaned in a little, bringing the scent of wild rain with him. "Amka." He used that low voice that somehow smashed right through her.

She raised her head. "I have no idea who'd want to hurt me."

"You sure?"

She just couldn't figure it out. "I'm positive."

"You can't think of any reason someone'd come after you?" Brock asked.

"None." Her voice cracked a little on the word, and she dropped her hands into her lap.

Ophelia's blue gaze remained sharp. "What about Jarod?" She placed her mug on the bar, keeping her eyes locked on Amka. Her hair stuck to her face in damp waves, but she didn't brush it away.

Amka admired that. Ophelia Spilazi was a woman comfortable in her own skin. "Jarod is in Anchorage, and there's no reason he'd try to hurt me. Not one." That was the truth.

Christian's jaw clenched.

Brock blinked. Once. Then again. "You're still engaged?"

Amka shifted in her chair, and her stomach rolled. The coffee didn't help. Nothing would. "Why wouldn't we be?"

Ophelia reached for her mug again, somehow seeming to watch everyone at once.

"I heard you had a bit of a scuffle earlier today," Brock said. "That you pushed Jarod."

There it was. Everyone in Knife's Edge knew everything. There were no secrets in the small town, and no doubt news of that simple argument had already reached the mountain folks.

May reached under the table and found Amka's hand. Gave it a firm squeeze.

Amka didn't look at her. She wasn't going to tell them the truth. Not about Jarod. Not about the fight. If they knew, they'd try to help. Try to fix it. Someone would talk, someone would overstep, and Flossy would end up in cuffs. Amka could see it happening already. "Of course we're still engaged," she said. "We just had a minor argument. That happens to people in a relationship."

The word tasted bitter in her mouth. *Relationship.* She nearly choked on it. The idea of being in anything with Jarod made her want to vomit.

Christian turned to May. His voice dropped. "Is there anyone who'd want you dead, Doc?"

Amka glanced sideways.

May had gone pale in the glow from the fire Christian had built in the stone hearth. "No."

Christian's gaze narrowed. What did he see?

Amka looked straight at May now. "May?"

May shook her head, too fast. "Nobody wants me dead. Nobody would shoot at me."

Brock cocked his head. "You know, Doc? We've had doctors rotate through this town like crazy for years, doing their time for their scholarships and then getting the hell out. Not you. You're an excellent doctor, and you signed a three-year contract. I wasn't here, but I'm wondering if anybody asked you why."

May's chin firmed. "The signing bonus was helpful, and I actually like it here, Sheriff. There's nothing more to it than that."

Brock had the same look in his eyes as his brother.

Amka tried to concentrate. Was May hiding something?

May turned to Wyland. "What about you, Wy? I mean, it was your storage building and you were right out there in the bullets. Does anybody want you dead?"

Wyland snorted. "Huh? Just my kid. He wants to inherit everything and change it." He paused, the joke hanging limp, and then exhaled. His shoulders settled. "I'm kidding. Of course Sheldon wouldn't hurt anybody."

"Are you sure?" Brock had the same easy tone, but the question landed hard. "I assume he's your only living heir."

Wyland frowned. "Seriously, Brock. Come on. Sheldon didn't shoot at us from across the street." He shook his head, jaw tightening.

If Amka remembered right, Sheldon was a good shot. He'd grown up hunting, like the rest of the town. They all could shoot, so that wasn't exactly a strike against him. "He did seem to be interested in the insurance claim for the storage building." She winced. "I'm sorry, Wyland. I'm sure Sheldon would never want to hurt you." She should've kept her mouth shut.

Wyland winked. "It's been a long day and night, girly. Don't worry about it." He looked over his shoulder at Brock. "My guess is that it was somebody local, because the tourists don't know about that fishing hole where Christian tracked the shooter."

"Maybe," Christian said. "With that stupid social media game going on, a lot of those influencers, whatever that is, have asked for tours around town. Surely the Blue's fishing hole interested a couple of them."

That was probably true. Had anybody told Christian about that video of him saving her? She wasn't going to. For now, nobody had questioned him yet. "What about you?"

"Why would anybody shoot at me?" Christian asked, eyebrows raised.

"You're kind of grumpy," Amka muttered. The feeling hit her like a slap. She froze. "Oh man, I'm sorry. That came out of nowhere."

"It's okay." He smiled. Not with a polite pull at the corners of his full mouth. It started in the eyes. His lips tipped upward, slow and uncertain, like the motion had to push through rust.

She stared, caught. When was the last time she'd seen Christian Osprey smile?

High school?

Even then, it had never fully formed. It didn't now either. His mouth curved, but not all the way, as if he wasn't quite sure how. Her heart ached. She'd love to teach him to smile again. What? No. That wasn't going to happen.

She looked at his eyes. The left was green. The right, black. Both locked on her. Both alert. Focused.

Alive.

Outside, the wind shifted. The fire popped. Someone's boot scraped across the floor.

It was impressive how he'd tracked the shooter all the way through town to that fishing hole. Through the drilling rain. Through the suffocating dark. Through probably bad memories. How many people in the world could actually do that? Not many. Not under pressure. Not with that kind of clarity. Amka wasn't even sure how he had seen the tracks in that mess of mud and floodwater. But he had. And he'd followed them like the storm wasn't even there.

Brock cleared his throat.

Amka jolted. Had she been staring at Christian? Heat filled her face.

"Amka? I'm going to assume you were the target, but Wyland, you need to be careful as well," Brock said.

Wyland ran a gnarled hand through his wet gray hair. "I'll stay sober and armed, Sheriff."

"Amka, I think you should come stay with Brock and me," Ophelia added. "At least until Jarod gets home. We have plenty of room."

"Thank you. I can take care of myself," Amka said. She had two guns and knew how to shoot.

Ophelia looked like she wanted to argue, but her mouth pressed into a hard line. The coffee in her hand had stopped steaming.

May tugged gently on Amka's sleeve. "Come stay with me."

Amka looked at her friend. "What if someone's trying to shoot me? The last thing I want is for you to get hurt."

"Then we'll shoot back," May said. Her hair was up in a

crooked ponytail now, still wet, drying in uneven curls around her ears. Her eyes were clear, stubborn.

"You're a good friend. But no," Amka said.

"I've got her," Christian said. His voice rumbled low and steady.

A shiver passed through Amka. Not from the cold. Not from the rain. Something in his voice—the tone didn't seek permission. "I don't need a bodyguard."

"Too bad. You've got one," Christian muttered. He glanced at his brother. The firelight caught the side of Brock's face, showing that strong Osprey bone structure. "At first light, I'll bring her over to your place, Brock," Christian said. "Ophelia can keep an eye on her while we check out what's left of that truck trail, although I don't have a lot of hope."

"I don't need to be watched," Amka said. Her spine locked straight as the words came out.

Christian swung his attention to her. "The fuck you don't."

Her mouth opened, stunned. She had never heard Christian Osprey swear. Or if he had, never at her.

His eyes glittered now. Not soft. Not gentle. Protective and sharp-edged. "I've given you the plan."

Brock's dark brows pulled low. "No offense, but I am the sheriff here."

Christian shifted in his chair, still holding Amka's gaze. "I might've forgotten to tell you. I just took a job with the Alaska Wildlife Troopers."

Amka blinked. The words didn't register right away. Christian didn't say things like that. He didn't make announcements. He sure the heck didn't sign up for a career.

Brock stilled. His surprise broke through the usual blankness in his face. "No shit?"

"Yeah," Christian said, lifting one shoulder. "Dutch is planning to retire and wants someone to take over the territory. I'm a civilian consultant for now. Training's in July. I think I have to take a test next week, too."

Brock clapped him on the back. The sound cracked across the table. "That's fantastic. You're perfect for that job, Christian." He was still looking at his brother, like he was seeing him differently. "You're the kind of guy who just steps out of the woods and people don't even know you were standing there. Like the trees made space for you. Ghosts. Seriously—perfect."

"Thanks." Christian pushed away from the table, chair legs scraping hard. There wasn't anything relaxed about the movement. The conversation had closed around him, and Amka felt it. Felt the space he left behind get colder by degrees.

Her coffee had gone cold in her hands.

"Let's go, Amka," Christian said. He wasn't asking.

CHAPTER 13

The rain hadn't let up. It came harder now, bringing spring in with a vengeance and not a breeze. The wipers slammed across the windshield, fast, loud, unrelenting. Visibility was garbage. The wind whistled through the shattered back window.

Christian drove her SUV up the river road like he could see fine. No music, no talking. Just engine noise and rain.

Amka curled into herself in the passenger seat with the heat on full blast. Her boots were soaked, and her coat dripped where it bunched at her sides. She couldn't get warm. The vents blew hot against her legs, but her hands still felt like ice. "Thank you." Had she ever been this exhausted? The man kept saving her, though. "For what you did earlier."

He grunted.

Of course.

He drove past the turnoff to her house.

"Hey," she said. "You missed my driveway."

"No, I didn't."

She sat up straighter. "Christian?"

His hands stayed locked on the wheel. His eyes never left the road. Trees leaned in from both sides, wind snapping their tops.

She tried to concentrate. "Where are we going?"

"I have a place."

The words sat between them. No more, no less.

She stared at him. His hands looked too big for the wheel. "What do you mean, you have a place?" So much for her thought that he didn't have a home and bunked out wherever. Maybe he was more together than she'd thought. "Christian?"

Nothing.

The dark outside got thicker. The cab of the SUV shrank. Her pulse crawled up the back of her throat. "Christian."

Still no response.

Fear hit like a wave, then anger rode in behind it, sharper, cleaner. "Answer me," she snapped, her voice high and sharp.

He looked at her. Just a glance. "You're safe."

"That is *so* not good enough," she said. "I'm tired of the grunting and the quiet, the whatever. When I ask you a question, I want an answer, considering you're driving my car and taking me somewhere I don't know. Where are we going?"

"I told you. I have a place." He turned his gaze back to the road.

She might actually punch him. "I want to go to my house," she said through gritted teeth.

"No."

No? Just no? Fury actually heated her. Finally. She clenched her hand into a fist.

"I wouldn't," he said calmly.

Her eyes narrowed. Her hand was tucked against the door. Out of sight. "How did you know?" Maybe everybody wanted to punch him and he was just guessing.

"We're almost there," he said. "Just hold on."

Then he cut the headlights.

She flinched. The dark closed in like a sealed room. Rain

drilled the metal roof, and nothing but black lay ahead. "What in the world are you doing turning off the lights? There's a storm out there."

"I know the way and want to make sure we're not followed."

She stared at the windshield. No road, no lights, just movement and shape. "You can see in this?"

"My vision's better than most."

She turned toward him, her heartbeat echoing in her head. "Better naturally, or did the military give you something new?"

Even in the dark, she caught the edge of a smile. Barely there. "I just have good eyesight, and I know this road. Just relax and enjoy the silence."

Was that a hint for her to shut up? "Why'd you turn off the lights?"

"Just in case. I don't feel anyone out there. No sign we were followed. But nobody knows this mountain like I do."

Probably true. She didn't question that part.

He moved through sharp turns with no warning, no corrections. She tried to anticipate them but couldn't. She gripped her knee instead of the door. The movement of the SUV felt more intimate without light—closer, quieter, full of tension she didn't want to name.

Eventually, he pulled under a dense wall of trees and cut the engine.

She didn't speak. The storm didn't allow for silence, and yet, the world seemed too quiet. Somehow.

He stepped out and softly shut his door.

She followed into the cool air. Rain caught her neck and slid down her spine. She shut the door and laid her hand on the hood, trailing her fingers to the front to orient herself. "Where are we?" Wind shoved her hair forward.

"This way," he said.

She hadn't seen him approach. He just appeared close

enough that she felt him before she saw him. His hand found hers.

Warm. Rough. Intentional.

Not threatening. But heat spiraled and landed in her abdomen anyway.

His grip stayed firm as he led her into the storm. Her steps followed, automatic, through soaked grass or gravel. She couldn't tell. Then the boards underfoot changed everything.

A porch.

He let go of her hand.

She didn't move right away.

"Step up," he said.

She walked up three stairs, her boots hitting wet wood. Then he opened the door, and she slowly followed him inside. The scent hit first—cedar, fresh rain, and Christian Osprey. Earth and heat and something that lived in the wild.

He shut the door behind her, bolted it, and flicked on the light.

An overhead light warmed a small cabin somewhere in the middle of nowhere. A bed sat against the far wall. Straight ahead appeared a bathroom and to its right, a narrow kitchenette. Between the kitchen and bed, a worn leather chair and sofa faced a small TV on a shelf next to a stone fireplace. The other wall was all windows. Big enough to jump out. Egress? Definitely.

She frowned. "What is this place?"

"It's mine," he said. "I built it. I come here once in a while if the weather turns bad, or if I'm not staying with one of my brothers."

She looked around. This was a freaking surprise. "You built a cabin?"

"Yeah." He crossed the room to the fireplace. He knelt and lit the logs already stacked in place. "Nobody knows it exists, so you're safe here."

She gulped. The air was warm, but her skin buzzed. "Your brothers don't know?"

"Nope."

Wow. That made her one of one person. She didn't want to feel special about that, but she did. Not that it changed anything. "I can't just stay out here with you, Christian."

"I know. But I need sleep, and I can't watch your place all night. So we're staying here."

The sofa didn't look long enough for him to stretch out. The bed was big—king-sized, and definitely built for someone his height. Right now, she was just too tired to argue with him. "All right. I'll take the sofa."

"Nope. You're taking the bed."

Her head jerked up. "I'm not sleeping in your bed while you sleep on that sofa. You don't fit."

He didn't argue. "We'll share the bed, then. I won't touch you. I promise."

Something about the way he said it landed wrong. Yeah, that hurt a little. "Fine."

"Poaching's never been my thing."

"Poaching?"

He looked over his shoulder. "You're engaged."

Right. That.

The ring stayed behind at the bar because she took it off to work. Though she always meant to put it back on, she usually forgot.

"You're still soaking wet." He looked her over. "You need something warm." There was one small dresser by the bed, and he opened the drawers, pulling out a faded black T-shirt and thick gray socks before turning and tossing them to her. "The bathroom's well stocked. Use whatever you need."

Almost in a dream, she caught the clothes and then walked into the bathroom, shutting the door. *Well stocked* may have been an overstatement. The small room held a shower, toilet, and sink in a small cabinet.

She opened one of the two drawers to find unopened toothbrushes and toothpaste. Okay, no hair ties. Why would he have hair ties? She changed into his T-shirt and socks, carefully hanging her wet clothing on the one bar for towels. She felt vulnerable and small in his shirt, but at least she felt a bit warmer. She took one of the towels and dried her hair best she could, leaving it hanging around her face.

She looked in the mirror and then winced before wiping under her eyes to get rid of the mascara that had smeared. She was pale, and she looked lost. The bruise on her cheekbone from the explosion was turning a lighter purple now. It had been a rough few days.

Tears filled her eyes, and she instantly batted them back. There was no need to cry.

She walked out of the room to find Christian bare-chested, wearing long, dark sweats.

Holy crap. His chest was even more muscled and cut than she had imagined, and he had an actual six-pack, like a real one. Not overly defined, but more natural.

Her mouth watered.

A tattoo of an osprey looked like it was flying over his left shoulder, with its talons extended and its beak sharp.

It was beautiful work.

She swallowed.

"Get in the bed," he said, no expression on his face.

"You're kind of bossy," she muttered, walking around to the other side, pulling down the covers, and slipping inside.

"When I need to be." He flicked off the lights and slid in next to her, his big body indenting the bed until she rolled toward him.

"Sorry." She pushed herself away.

The fire crackled across the room while the storm raged outside, lending a breathless intimacy to the cabin. Her heart fluttered in her chest. This felt unreal. She was in bed with Christian Osprey, and his body was even better than she'd imagined.

Not that she had imagined it. Okay. She'd imagined it more than once.

They both stayed quiet for a moment.

"You're going to have to sleep, darlin'," he said.

Did he just call her *darlin'*? Hadn't he called her *baby* the other day? Her nipples peaked. Just from his low voice. "I'm trying." But she couldn't get warm. She shivered.

"Damn it." He rolled toward her and yanked her against him, her back to his front, his powerful body wrapping around her completely.

Desire flooded her. She shivered again.

"You'll warm up. I'll let go once you do." He wrapped an arm around her waist, bending his elbow at her stomach and extending his forearm up along her chest to her collarbone. His hand settled just below her neck.

Man, he was big.

She shivered against him, acutely aware of the hardness of his chest pressed into her back. She felt small. Delicate. Desire coiled low in her stomach. "Um."

"I know," he murmured in her ear. "You're engaged. I'm just warming you up."

She hated that she was engaged. She liked that he was warming her up. "Christian," she murmured.

"No." His mouth stayed close to her ear, and his heated breath brushed her earlobe.

She shivered again and nearly groaned from the feeling of him behind her. Holding her. All strength and heat and honed muscle. They lay together, her back against his chest, his arm a solid band holding her in place. Neither moved. The fire snapped and shifted across the room. Time crawled. Her thoughts didn't.

When had she last felt safe and protected? She sure wouldn't feel like this with Jarod Teller in the bed with her.

"Why?" Christian asked, voice quiet, grip firm. Was he reading her mind?

She didn't need clarification. She knew exactly what he meant. "What do you mean?"

"Don't play dumb."

She stared into the dark. The shadows moved more than the answers.

"You don't love him."

She tried not to move against his hard body, but hers wanted to explore. Now. "How do you know?"

"I've watched you for years. You're not in love with Jarod."

Holy crap. What did he mean? He'd been watching her? For actual years? "Why do you care?" she whispered.

He said nothing.

She waited. Nothing came except a warning in the back of her head. "I might be ready to settle down," she muttered. "I want kids. I want a marriage. Why can't that be it?"

"You deserve more."

Three words. Honest. Unflinching.

Yeah. She did.

But she couldn't tell him the truth. Couldn't risk it. If Christian knew, if he went after Jarod and didn't get what he needed —if that video still made it to the press—Flossy would end up in jail, and Christian might, too. He could get himself thrown out of the wildlife troopers before he even got started. She didn't know how she knew he'd fight for her, try to protect her, but she did. Deep down.

The risk wasn't worth it.

Her throat tightened.

He held her like he'd keep holding her. "Let me help you."

"You can't," she answered, no hesitation.

He turned her and pressed her into the mattress, rolling over her with full weight and control.

She gasped. He was hard. Her body responded before her mind could catch up. She widened her legs without meaning to. Her pulse kicked. Every part of her screamed to reach for him.

"I can," he said. His voice stayed low, calm. "I have skills, Amka. Tell me what you need me to do."

Her voice felt raw. "What? Skills? What are you saying?" The breath heated in her lungs.

"Whatever you need. No questions asked. Tell me."

Holy crap on a cracker. She couldn't deal with this. "I don't need anything," she managed.

"Tell me why you're engaged to him."

"Because I am. It's what I want."

He didn't move. Didn't blink. Just looked at her as the firelight caressed his rugged face, dancing over hollows and shadows. Over hard cut bones and tight skin. "You're lying."

"I'm not." She said it fast. Too fast.

He dropped his head. Their noses nearly touched. "I think you are."

"I said I'm not."

Then he kissed her.

No warning. Just heat and pressure and those firm lips on her mouth. The kiss hit hard. She gasped into it, heart thudding, mind blank. For one second, she froze. Then her mouth moved. She kissed him back.

His hand slid into her hair and held her there, allowing her no space to move. The kiss deepened. He kissed with hunger and control, frustration folded into every motion. He didn't push. He took. Deliberate. Sure. Focusing on her like nothing else existed.

Her body reacted first—hips arching, breath catching, skin hot.

He broke the kiss slowly, pulling back an inch at a time. His hand stayed in her hair. His breath touched her lips. "Tell me the truth."

Her mouth opened. No words came out. She stared at him. Her body still burned from one kiss.

He hadn't even taken off his clothes.

She hated how much she wanted him. Hated how fast it unraveled her. "It's what I want," she said again. Not true. Not even close. But it was something.

His jaw twitched. Just once. His eyes stayed locked on hers. Anger flickered there. Not rage. Not possessiveness. Just a clean, sharp frustration she hadn't seen from him before.

He rolled off her.

Not away. Not distant. He shifted to his side and pulled her with him, curling her back into his chest, locking an arm around her ribs. "Go to sleep." His hand stayed flat against her abdomen. "I'll give you tonight," he said, voice in her ear. "But not forever. You'll tell me the truth." The calm, absolute confidence in his low tone conveyed a threat much clearer than if he'd shouted.

She shivered again, not from cold this time, and in response, he held her closer.

CHAPTER 14

Amka awoke with a jolt and sat up in the bed. Where was she? Blinking, she looked around the small cabin. Oh, yeah. She'd slept with Christian. Who actually owned a home like he might settle down. Shocking. Yes.

She glanced at the empty space where he'd been and then pressed her hand to his pillow, finding it now cold. How long had he cradled her the night before? The daylight made the cabin feel even more bare, but the fire in the hearth gave it just enough warmth to tempt her into leaving the cozy bed.

Sliding out, she headed straight to the bathroom, where she used the facilities, brushed her teeth, and put on her now very wrinkled clothes. Her jeans were stiff from drying overnight and felt a little grimy, but they'd do for now. She tamed her long dark hair the best she could with her hands and then stepped back out into the main room.

What time was it? She'd left her purse and phone in the SUV the night before. Keeping her boots in her hand so she wouldn't track more mud through the place, she crossed the room and opened the front door to see Christian's broad back. He sat on the porch steps, his shoulders back and his gaze fixed somewhere in the trees with a creek bubbling by to the side of the cabin. This morning, he wore jeans and a short-sleeved T-shirt, regardless of the chill in the air. The rain had finally stopped, but the air felt wet, and the bulbous clouds above them promised another storm. Soon.

The trees in every direction dripped more water, while scurrying throughout the forest echoed from small animals seeking food. The larger animals were silent.

"Good morning," he said without turning around.

"Hi." She paused at the doorway and then stepped onto the porch. Taking a deep breath, she squared her shoulders and walked over to sit beside him.

"I borrowed your SUV and grabbed breakfast." He handed her a closed Styrofoam container and a fork.

Oh yeah. He didn't own a vehicle. But he did have a home. Was there a chance he'd stick around? Her stomach growled. She put the boots next to her and reached for it, flipping the lid open to reveal scrambled eggs, bacon, and sausage from the Green Plate. "When did you go to town?"

"An hour or so ago. Tika hung out for a bit and then took off to explore again."

She took a bite and nearly groaned at the still warm and cheesy taste. It was kind of him to get her breakfast. "What time is it?"

"Just after seven."

She jolted. "I have to get to the tavern."

"I already talked to Daisy," he said. "She has things covered for the morning and said she hired help for the day. In addition, the hardware store actually had a window the size of the tavern one that should be installed by now."

Should his making arrangements like that irritate Amka? She let the fork hang in her hand for a second, not answering right away. The steam from the food curled up into the air between them. He hadn't looked at her yet. "You're kind of taking over."

The porch boards creaked beneath them, the sound quiet but constant. "If I were taking over, you wouldn't be engaged."

So they were back to that topic? She dug into the eggs, trying not to notice the hard, impossibly solid body next to her—the same one that had held her all night without saying a word. Her fork scraped the bottom of the container. "This is weird," she muttered.

"Agreed."

She kept eating, silence stretching between them. Not uncomfortable exactly, but not easy either. Something hung between them, and she didn't know what to do with it. "Why?" she finally asked, throwing his own word from the night before back at him. Why was he taking such an interest in her life?

He didn't pretend to misunderstand. Didn't flinch. He just kept staring at the trees like the answer might be carved into the bark somewhere. The side of his face looked as rugged and distant as the mountains around them. "I don't know."

"Christian, that's not good enough."

"I'm aware." He turned then, his focus locking on her. That sharp, mismatched gaze cut through her usual defenses like they weren't even there. Her face heated. "There's something about you."

"Yeah?" She stabbed at the last bite of egg and shoved it in her mouth, chewing slow. "Like what?"

He didn't answer right away.

She didn't push, not sure she wanted to hear the truth from him. If he could figure it out.

Nothing about her felt mysterious. In her late twenties, she managed the local bar and had never once left the state where she grew up. Work filled her days and kept her body strong. Long black hair framed her face, and her eyes matched the hue perfectly. She had decent cheekbones and skin. Not flawless, but defined enough to draw a second glance from people paying attention.

She understood exactly what she looked like. Attractive but not the kind of woman strangers noticed across a room. She didn't care. Numbers made sense, and so did people. She could stretch inventory, calm a fight before it started, and outwork anyone behind her bar. In addition, she could quilt like the best of them after a couple glasses of wine.

"You've traveled the world, C." Then she coughed. "I mean, Christian." Only his brothers called him C. She remembered him beating the heck out of a football player from another town who called him that back during a high school game.

"You can call me C."

Holy crap. Her entire body tingled. A year ago? She would've been doodling his name all over the receipts at the bar. Now? Now she was engaged to an asshat and might still end up going to prison. But she had to understand. Just this once. Her voice came out low, nearly lost under the sound of water dripping off branches. "I don't know what you've done exactly, but I imagine you've met a lot of women."

He reached to his side, picked up a to-go cup, and offered it to her.

She stared at it.

"I got you a chai latte," he said. "From Hitty's." He'd gone to both the Green Plate and Hitty's for her?

Her fingers closed around the cup before she thought twice. Still warm. Still fragrant. She took a big drink without hesitation. "Perfect," she said.

Hitty had the best coffee and ice cream on the planet, as far as she was concerned. Not that Amka had much to compare it to since she hadn't exactly made a habit of leaving the state, let alone the country. But Hitty's had to be among the best out there.

He watched her drink, expression unreadable.

"You know how I take my drink. You know what I like. So why the interest?" Her voice sharpened. "Or do you just collect wounded animals?"

His mouth curved, just barely. "Are you wounded?"

She cursed herself internally. Why had she said that out loud? "Well, someone tried to blow me up," she said, lifting an eyebrow. "Last night somebody shot in my direction, although I'm not entirely convinced they aimed at me."

"That's not what you meant by wounded."

Now he was perceptive? She dragged a hand through her unruly hair. "You're worried about me? Is that why you've gone into overprotective beast mode?"

His lips twitched again. "Beast mode? That's a new one."

She stared out at the trees, letting the quiet stretch.

Christian was just the type of guy to rescue wounded animals, and no doubt, he wanted to help her. Somehow sensed she needed it. Even if he admitted he had some kind of interest in her—and that would be an ego boost—what were they supposed to do about it?

He hadn't said anything like that, anyway. Not really. Christian didn't strike her as the type to flirt just to pass time. Maybe he had a compulsion to fix broken things. Maybe he thought she was one of them.

She wasn't broken and didn't need rescuing. Yet, sleeping in his arms had been the first decent rest she'd gotten in way too long. That wasn't nothing.

"You're in a mess," he said finally. "I don't understand it, but I want to help you out." He looked out at the drenched woods.

Yeah. That's what she figured. He'd help anybody he thought to be in danger. It wasn't about her at all. She wasn't the most worldly woman, but she knew enough to spot danger when it came wrapped in quiet comfort. Men like Christian didn't stick. They didn't belong in town life or behind tavern counters. And they sure didn't fall for women who could balance the books, handle a bar brawl, and still patch a quilt at the end of a night.

She turned toward him, closing the lid of the Styrofoam container. If she needed to scare him off, she knew how. Probably too well. "Listen, Christian. If you want to make a go of it with me, you just say the word. But I'm telling you right now. I want home, hearth, and babies, and I want them now."

He didn't blink. Didn't even twitch. That surprised her.

She smiled, slow and deliberate. "I'm not lying to you." And she wasn't. Not technically. She did want home, hearth, and babies. Just not with Jarod. God, definitely not with Jarod. But she wasn't about to say that out loud. This wasn't about Jarod. This was about watching Christian take the hit and flinch.

Only he didn't.

That irritated her a little. She sipped her chai again, finding it still nicely warm. "Christian," she said, drawing his name out a little, "you'd be an interesting life. Chaotic. Loud. Probably plenty wild."

He gave nothing back.

"But let's be honest," she went on, "you have zero intention of settling down. I've never pictured you that way." She set the cup down on the porch deck. "And when I found out you took that AWT job? It tracked."

The AWT flew into nowhere, found poachers, tracked down traffickers, shut it all down and vanished like ghosts. The few she'd met didn't have homes. Or families. No PTA meetings or minivans. Just boots, planes, and the next mission.

"So here's the deal," she said. "Either make a plan with me and give me a bunch of babies, or butt out of my life." She watched him now, waiting, keeping her expression calm and pleasant. Like she'd just offered him a sandwich. It was the only way to get him to back off, and he definitely would.

His gaze dropped to her mouth, and darn if her lips didn't

start tingling like he'd touched them. "What if I say yes?" he asked.

She snorted. Couldn't help it. "Then I'd fall off this seat in a dead faint."

That earned her the smallest hint of a smile, but it didn't go anywhere. Yeah, a woman could get addicted to that almost smile. "You're not looking to settle down, Christian. Don't lie."

He narrowed his eyes. "You playing games, baby?"

Baby? Seriously? He'd called her that at the fire, but she'd been focused on survival. Now she focused on him. That endearment should not make her go gooey inside. "No. Are you?"

His gaze lifted, locked with hers. Steady. "Don't ever play games with me, Amka. I don't lose, and I don't take prisoners."

What did that mean? Her mouth dried out immediately. She'd wanted to push him off balance, but now she wasn't so sure who'd lost their footing. "I'm not playing." She sipped her latte again to stall. "I need you to back off."

"Too tempting?"

"Yeah." The word left before she could soften it.

He felt so solid next to her. "So you really want the whole marriage, babies, family thing?"

"Of course I do." Her spine straightened. "Don't you? Someday?"

He leaned back slowly, jaw tight, eyes unreadable. "Never thought about it."

Yeah. That's what she figured. She took another long drink. The latte had cooled a bit but still held a punch of power with caffeine and sugar. "Well," she said, keeping her voice light, "I've appreciated the overprotective caveman act. Really. But I've got to get to work."

His head tilted, as if waiting for her to finish.

"Don't worry about me. I've got a Glock and a shotgun beneath the bar. If anyone threatens me, I won't hesitate."

"All right." He stood, making the porch creak in protest. "Put on your boots. I'll take you."

She blinked. "You're not going to fight me on that?"

"Nope."

She leaned back, trying to mask her surprise. That had actually worked? Apparently so. But as she slid on her boots, she couldn't help feeling the tiniest sense of sadness deep inside. What if he had said yes?

CHAPTER 15

Christian walked with Amka inside the tavern, her SUV parked out front with the board he'd inserted in the broken window protecting the back seat. Ace sat at the bar, shoveling in what looked like breakfast casserole. Christian gave him a nod. Ace returned it with a slow lift of his chin.

His brother's eyes looked a little bloodshot, but his shoulders stayed squared, and his gaze tracked sharp. He'd keep an eye on her. That was enough for now.

Christian stepped back out onto the street, heading south toward the sheriff's office. Mountain Man's Garage had already confirmed they'd ordered a replacement for Amka's busted back window, and it wouldn't take long to install once it came in. Just a cracked pane of glass, but it still crawled under his skin. The woman could've been shot.

She wanted a house. Kids. Some version of calm. Maybe that was why she'd agreed to marry Jarod? Perhaps Christian's gut feeling there was off because he wanted her. That much, he could admit to himself. But he wasn't the settling down kind.

There had to be someone better for such a sweetheart like Amka. Someone who could give her a decent life.

The thought made his ears itch.

He didn't want a wife. Never had. No woman deserved that kind of mess. But still, Amka deserved someone solid. Someone who could actually stay.

Problem was, Christian couldn't think of anyone good enough.

A green AWT rig rounded the corner, tires crunching gravel, and pulled to a stop. Dutch rolled down the window. He must've grabbed the rig from where he stored it in the garage of Flossy's B&B. "Sorry I'm late," Dutch said, grinning. "Flossy fed me."

"No problem." Christian pulled the door open and climbed in. The interior still smelled like coffee and gear oil. "Got your message last night. Guess I'm officially on the job?" Surprise filtered through him at the anticipation pulling at him. He actually wanted this job.

"Yeah, if you don't mind." Dutch checked his mirrors. "Since that one victim who disappeared was wearing an EVE logo on his sweatshirt when your brother found him, I figured we'd head out to EVE today and see if they can ID the other two victims we found. It's a long shot, I know. We've emailed those crazy scientists, but they're slow getting back to us."

"They've always been a mystery to this town," Christian muttered. "You think we're getting in?"

"We should. Damian's head of security now. I called ahead. He said he'd meet us."

Christian nodded, settling deeper into the seat as Dutch flipped a U-turn and aimed for the river road. "It's been a couple weeks since I've seen him." He'd been meaning to check up on his too-serious brother for a few days.

Dutch kept one hand on the wheel, his tone casual. "How you holding up after getting shot at?"

"I'm fine." Christian glanced out the window, tracking the blur of pine trees. "No bad dreams. Nothing. But I'd sure like to know who pulled the trigger."

"You think Amka was the target?"

Christian exhaled slowly. "Either Amka or Wyland Friday would be my guess as the target. Both attacks seem to circle back to them."

"She's gonna need cover," Dutch said, eyes forward. "You planning to provide that?"

The question hit harder than it should have. Christian didn't answer right away. Not because he didn't know, but because he wasn't ready to say it out loud. He didn't need to start unloading feelings like a damn teenager.

His phone buzzed in his jacket pocket, and he flinched, still not used to carrying the thing.

Dutch gave him a look. "You all right?"

"Yeah." Christian pulled the phone out, clenching his jaw. "Just not used to feeling this reachable." He lifted the phone to his ear. "What?"

"That is not how you answer the phone." Damian's voice rolled smoothly through the line.

Christian lifted one eyebrow. "Why are you calling me? We're on our way out to meet you."

"I understand that, but it's about to rain again, and I'd rather not spend time meeting in the parking lot," Damian replied. "You won't like it in this facility, and I'd rather not put you through our security and elevator system."

Christian relaxed. Damian had always seen through all of them. Every brother. Probably why he'd gone into intelligence. He'd also gone out of his way to keep Christian comfortable, and that building, with its underground levels, tight halls, and forest of radio towers, would set his stomach on edge. "I appreciate that," Christian said, not seeing the need to lie to his brother. "You coming into town?"

Dutch glanced over and pulled the truck to the side of the road.

"No, I can't right now. I'm in the middle of five different things," Damian said. "But I did look at the email Dutch sent. I don't recognize either of the victims—the woman or the man. I ran a full search of our records. They did not work here."

Christian popped his neck. "Would you tell us if they did?"

"I've got no reason to lie," Damian said, voice smooth as ever. "If I knew who they were, I'd say it. I also got my hands on the autopsy reports from Anchorage."

Christian frowned, glanced at the screen, then pressed the speaker button. "You're on with Dutch now. How'd you get ahold of those?"

Dutch turned his head toward the phone, brows drawing tight. "Please don't say anything sketchy."

"I'm the security director of EVE," Damian said flatly. "No condescension intended, just fact. I can access pretty much anything."

Dutch shook his head. "What are you even doing out there, anyway? That place is weird."

Damian chuckled. "Why not? It's close to home. They offered me a job. After years in the service, I could use the paycheck. Plus, I've always been curious about the place."

Christian shifted, a slow awareness pricking at the back of his neck. "You need backup?"

"No," Damian said. "If I do, I'll call you. I promise. In fact, I'll try to get into town for the next chowder day at Sam's Tavern."

"Absolutely," Christian said, more than happy to spend time at Amka's, even if it was getting harder and harder to believe anything she said about Jarod. Holding her all night had felt like torture and a blessing rolled into one. He hadn't slept that well in years, but waking up with her soft curves pressed against him had nearly wrecked him.

Another night like that? He wouldn't survive it. Not without touching her.

And that kiss...that one kiss had almost blown his head off. She sure as hell didn't kiss like a woman engaged to another man. In love with another man. Christian would never forget the sweet taste of her. He wanted another one. Now. He cleared his throat. "Damian? Since you're so good with records, think you could run a deep dive on Jarod Teller for me?"

Dutch nodded. "I think that's a good idea. Just in case. You've got access to sources we don't."

"You think he shot at Amka?" Damian asked.

Christian stayed quiet for a beat. "You already know about that? The shooting just happened last night."

"Please. It's Knife's Edge. You think I don't have people there?"

Christian narrowed his eyes. "Who are your sources?" He thought through options. "Which one of our brothers did you talk to?"

"Neither," Damian said, clearly amused. "Like I said, I've got my sources."

Christian didn't like that. Not even a little. "All right," he said finally. "I guess there's no reason for us to come out there now. But Damian, if you're in trouble, you'll call me."

A long pause stretched over the line. "If I *know* I'm in trouble, I'll call," Damian said.

Christian didn't like that answer, either. "Don't make me infiltrate that place."

"I actually wouldn't mind," Damian replied. "I just installed new security, and it wouldn't hurt to see if you could get through it."

That might actually be fun. "Not right now," Christian said. "I have too much on my plate. But maybe in a couple weeks."

"We could even pay you. Even though you're consulting with the AWT, I don't think there's a conflict there," Damian said.

Dutch leaned his head back against the headrest. "How'd you know that? We haven't told anyone yet."

"Practically speaking? It's Knife's Edge," Damian drawled.

The line went dead.

Dutch turned to face Christian. "What do you think your brother's doing at that facility?"

"I don't know," Christian said. But a warning ticked through his brain like a countdown. "I think I'm going to have to find out."

"Not today," Dutch muttered. "Today, we take these photos around town and see if anyone recognizes the two victims. Then maybe we grab lunch at the Green Plate."

Christian slipped the phone back into his pocket. "No, let's go to Sam's Tavern. I could use a burger."

Amusement flickered in Dutch's eyes. "Whatever you say."

Damn it. He had to get that woman out of his head.

Mud clung to his boots like glue. Rain lashed his face in sharp little needles. Every breath felt like it might be his last. Cold burned down deep, right into his chest.

Rough marks raked his torso, right through his shirt, through skin. Blood and rain mixed into something tacky and hot on his body. He didn't stop to check. He couldn't. Not now.

Branches slapped his cheeks. He didn't dodge them anymore. Just kept running, stumbling forward on raw instinct. No idea how long he'd been out here. No sense of time. Just pain, terror, and the stupid hope he could still make it.

What had he been thinking?

Alaska wasn't supposed to be like this. He came up here for a guy's weekend. Some kind of fun. He'd gotten cheap plane tickets and told his boss back in Phoenix he'd be off-grid for a while. His wife had begged him not to go, but he'd needed time to himself. Marriage wasn't like he thought it'd be, and his wife wasn't the sweetheart everyone thought. He missed being the fun guy.

No one expected him back soon.

Which meant no one would come looking.

He slipped again, his boots sliding sideways in the muck. Trees loomed on either side of him, dark and wet and whispering. The forest pressed in like it wanted to bury him. Hide the mess. No one would ever find the body.

Another crack of a branch behind him shot his adrenaline even higher.

Closer this time.

He nearly pissed himself.

Grunting, he picked up speed, arms pumping, lungs on fire. A flash of silver caught his attention from up ahead, some sort of a wet glint through the trees. The river. He'd heard the rush of water earlier. He could smell it now. Wet rock and glacial runoff.

If he could make it, maybe the current would carry him far enough away. Maybe the bastard behind him wouldn't follow him into the water.

Another branch snapped. This time the sound was just behind him.

He veered right, punching through the undergrowth. A root caught his ankle and he slammed forward into the mud. The impact knocked the air from his lungs. He bit his tongue trying not to scream.

He rolled to his side, coughing up dirt and blood. Pain spiked in his wrist. Had he broken it?

Get. Up.

He clawed at the ground, his fingers slipping in wet pine needles. Finally, he pushed himself to his knees. Behind him, the wind whistled.

He couldn't stop shaking. Whether it was the cold, the adrenaline, or both, he didn't know.

Voices in his head started up. His dad telling him to get a real job. His boss laughing at the idea of him surviving in the woods. His new wife crying that he had to leave her to find himself. He told her he'd go up north, find some clarity and make a decision.

Well, he found something.

The sound of rushing water grew louder. He was close. Ten yards, maybe less. He forced his legs to move, staggering forward.

Then came the crash.

A wall of force slammed into his back. He flew through the air like a ragdoll, hit hard and slid. His mouth filled with the metallic taste of blood. Something cracked. His shoulder maybe.

He couldn't move his arm. His whole left side screamed.

Mud soaked into every inch of him. His ribs ached. His breath came in short, ragged gasps.

Behind him, somebody moved. Slowly. Deliberately.

He pressed his palms to the earth, trying to get up. His right hand found a rock slick with blood. He couldn't tell if it was his. He lifted his head. The river was right there. Ten feet. Five. He could hear the burble over stone, steady and cold. If he could just get in and let the water take him—

Too late.

A weight dropped on his back, crushing him into the mud. All the air fled his lungs. His ribs popped. Not broken yet. But close.

He screamed into the ground. Muffled, pointless.

His legs kicked once. Twice. Then stopped.

The cold didn't hurt anymore. That scared him most. Because the cold was the only thing that kept him feeling alive. The storm above howled louder. Trees thrashed. Rain started to beat down.

No one heard.

He twisted his head just enough to see the river.

So close. A few more steps.

Please, he thought. But he didn't know who he was pleading to. God. The river. Himself.

His mouth worked but no words came. His body refused to move. There came a sudden flash of sharp pain, and finally, the darkness took him.

CHAPTER 16

Amka handed a full tray of coffees to Nixi, who balanced it easily and swung it up onto her shoulder. Daisy had been smart to hire the woman. "You're a great help. Would you like a job while you're in town?" She could use the extra hands. More tourists kept showing up every day, and she was running behind by the time she opened the doors.

"Yes," Nixi said, bouncing a little. Her purple hair stuck up on one side, like she'd rolled out of bed and just gone with it. "I'd love that, if you don't mind. I could use the extra cash while I do this influencer gig. I'm not slated to leave for another week."

Relief burst through Amka's still aching body. "Yeah, it'd be great. I can pay you in cash."

"Perfect," Nixi said, her grin wide, both blue eyes lit. She turned and headed toward the back like she already belonged there, her slim hips swaying without trying.

Daisy walked in from the kitchen. "I like her."

"Ditto." Amka grabbed the coffee carafe and walked down to refill Ace's cup. She leaned over the bar and rested her chin on her hand. "You don't have to watch me all day just because Christian asked you to."

Ace shrugged. "I don't have anything else going on. Plus, the food's good, and the ambiance is better." He nodded toward the bottles behind her. "How about a bit of Kahlua in this coffee?"

"How about no," she said. "You start with Kahlua, and next thing I know, you're fighting tourists on my floor, and I'm dragging you out the door."

His gaze sharpened. Both eyes were the same pale green as Christian's one green eye. "All right, then how about we have a little chat? What's going on between you and my brother?"

"Nothing." She leaned back. "He's decided I need protecting, and apparently nothing sways him."

Ace jerked his head and grinned. "Ain't that the truth. Believe me, I know." He looked around the tavern. "Where's your fiancé, anyway?"

"Still in Anchorage." As far as she knew, anyway. She glanced toward the windows. The morning plane hadn't come in yet, and she hoped it stayed grounded. One more day of peace wouldn't hurt. She looked down at her bare hand. Why put on the ring?

"You gonna tell Jarod you stayed out with Christian last night?"

She blinked once. Then again. "You knew I stayed with Christian?"

"I knew he took you home. Figured he stayed there with you."

She gave a noncommittal shrug. "Huh." So Ace actually didn't know about Christian's cabin. That was kind of funny.

Ace stretched his neck. "Amka, if you're playing games with Christian, I'd stop. Like right now."

A slight chill wandered down her back. "He said he doesn't play games."

"He doesn't."

Now she shivered. "I'm not playing games. He's the one who insists that I need cover." That was enough discussion about the man who wouldn't leave her mind. She cleared her throat. "So, Ace, I've been thinking."

"Oh yeah?" He leaned back on his stool. His long gray T-shirt stretched over broad shoulders and a frame that matched his brothers'. Around town, it was common knowledge he stood one inch taller than the other three Osprey brothers at a proud six foot six. He liked reminding them every chance he got.

She didn't think one inch made much difference, considering they all towered over her, but she liked that he still had a sense of humor about it. "Yeah. I've got some money I need to invest. What do you think about starting a new company?"

"A new company?" His eyebrows lifted. "Tell me more."

How carefully did she need to tread here? "At some point, you're going to have to fly again. I've known you my whole life, and you've always loved the air more than the ground or sea. I don't know what happened exactly, but I do know you're not meant to stay grounded."

Ace didn't reply right away.

"Let's be honest," she continued. "The other small commuters around here suck. One of them had to crash-land on a glacier last week."

He snorted, but his eyes stayed on her now, sharp and measuring.

"I'm not just looking to park my money," she said. "I want to help someone get back to doing what they're meant to do. For the safety of Knife's Edge, too. You know some of the others don't take care of their planes."

He winced. Anger flickered in his eyes and burned deeper. "It's a travesty they're still in the air."

"I know," she said, leaning in a little. "So…what if we started an LLC?"

He tilted his head.

"I've got the money right now," she continued. "You could put in whatever you have. The town still uses your plane, but it's technically yours, so that could count as your collateral."

He didn't interrupt. That was a good sign.

Her heart rate increased. Was she getting to him? She'd protect her money and maybe help him out. Somebody needed to do it. "I've been thinking about building something next door where the old storage building used to sit. We could put an office in front, but Wyland and I could still use the back half for storage. We could even build an additional rental for new businesses. Knife's Edge is growing. We could use the income."

"I don't know." He glanced again at the bottles of alcohol.

She reached out and put her hand over his. His skin felt warm. "It's time you did something again. I need a place to invest, and this makes sense to me." The idea had come out of nowhere, but now that it lived in her head, it felt solid. "We'll come up with a name. How about *Ace's Flying Company?*"

He rolled his eyes. "I don't think so."

"We'll figure it out. We've already got one plane. Maybe later we get a second and bring in another pilot." She paused as she mentally ran through plans. "We could do daily runs between towns. Mail, freight, people. Then take on charters for hunters, fishermen, mountain climbers, and tourists. You know how many people ask about backcountry flights and can't find one that's safe?"

His face had gone still. "If I invested like that," he said slowly, "I'd have to fly."

The statement emerged like a confession.

She wasn't sure if he'd been to see Smitty yet, but that could wait. Right now, she needed him to sign on so her money had a safe landing place. "I can meet with the bank. I could leverage Sam's Tavern and also use the cash I've saved."

He cocked his head. "Shouldn't you run big plans like this by your fiancé? I mean you no offense, but I don't want to be business partners with Jarod Teller."

"No. This would be my enterprise, only. I promise that Jarod won't be involved in the slightest." Her voice stayed steady. "We can make this work. I know we can."

Ace stayed quiet for several moments, studying her. No doubt seeing more than she wanted him to about her personal life. But unlike his brother, he didn't probe. Finally, he nodded once. "All right. It's a deal." He reached out and clasped her hand.

She barely kept from squealing as they shook on it. This wasn't just a distraction or an excuse. It was a solid business move. Sure, this would tie up every dollar she had so Jarod couldn't get near it, but the plan also had real potential. She could actually turn a profit, and Ace might find his way back into the air.

Numbers started flying through her head about the amount she could afford to put down, what she could leverage, and how fast they could get the permits in place. Then she turned toward the kitchen with its door ajar. "Daisy? You can come out now. I know you're listening."

Daisy stepped out, eyes wide, trying way too hard to look innocent. "What?"

"Oh shut up. You heard everything." Amka made sure the coffee appeared fresh in the pot. "Will you please draw up the papers?"

"Absolutely," Daisy said, already glancing around. "We're not busy. I can head back to my office and do it now."

Ace turned to look at the far corner behind the bar and tilted his head. "Is that your diploma on the wall?"

Daisey tossed her notepad on the bar. "Yeah. That corner's my office."

"Go for it," Amka said. "I appreciate it."

Daisy smiled wide and took a few steps, then paused. "Oh, and your will and prenup are ready."

Amka's stomach sank just a little.

Daisy glanced sideways at Ace. "Oops. Sorry. I should've whispered that."

"No, it's okay," Amka said quickly. But truthfully, she kind of wished she had whispered it. Maybe having her attorney work ten feet from the drink taps wasn't the best setup after all.

"I'll get on it." Daisy moved around the bar, already humming to herself.

Ace watched her go, before focusing back on Amka. "Prenup?"

"It just makes sense." Amka kept her tone even. "I'm a smart businesswoman."

Ace lifted his chin. "You're not wrong. I think you just talked me into a business I don't even want."

"Too late," Amka said cheerfully, just as the front door opened.

Two Alaska State Troopers walked in, both in full uniform.

She straightened as they took seats at the bar, trying to keep her steps casual as she walked down to meet them. "Hi. Welcome to Sam's. Can I get you anything to eat?"

"Coffee," they both said.

"I'm Trooper Paige Johnson," said the woman who appeared to be in her forties in excellent shape. She had sharp light-green eyes and dark red hair pulled back into a no-nonsense bun. She removed her hat and set it on the bar. "And this is Trooper Jeb Pontevo," she added with a nod toward her partner, a man who looked to be in his late sixties, if not older, with cold brown eyes and a square jaw that hadn't softened with age. "He's our expert in arson. You're Amka?"

"Yeah," Amka said carefully. Why did she feel like she'd done something wrong?

"We'd like to talk to you about the fire," Trooper Johnson said. "And the shooting last night."

They'd arrived faster than expected. She hadn't even heard the plane. "Of course. I'll tell you anything I can. But the sheriff's on it, and there are two AWT officers in town. Sort of. One's in training."

"That's fine," Johnson replied. "We like to do our own digging."

"As do I." A woman who'd been nursing a soda by the door moved off her stool and walked toward them, tossing a business card across the bar. "I'm Helene Stanford from Northside Insurance. We hold the policy on the building that was burned down."

Johnson arched one eyebrow. "Someone made an insurance claim already? That was quick." She turned back toward Amka, her eyes glittering.

Helene nodded. "Yes. A Sheldon Friday called it in already. I interviewed him earlier today."

Stupid Sheldon. Amka stared at the insurance adjuster for a moment. "I remember you from a couple of years ago. You were the adjuster for the motel that burned as well, right?"

"Yes." Helene leaned against the bar. She had delicate features and pale skin that looked luminous with her dark hair. She had to be in her mid-twenties? Maybe a bit older? "That was owned by your fiancé, correct?"

The troopers both straightened.

"Yes," Amka said, sighing. "All right. Why don't you take a seat, and I'll answer all of your questions at once?" Yeah, this might not look too good. "But you all need to know right now that I didn't see the explosive device, but I heard it blow. I did smell an accelerant and watched the fire spread quickly, but I have no idea who would've done something like this."

Not one of them appeared like they believed her. Just fantastic.

CHAPTER 17

The tequila burned down Amka's throat, sharp and fast, and she set the empty shot glass on the counter with a dull thud.

May snorted, shaking her head. "Seriously. As your doctor, I have to advise against shooting booze."

Amka slid her a look. "As my friend?"

"You drink, girl." May cupped her hands around her cheerful red mug.

The liquor had burned nice. After three hours of answering the same ten questions from the suspicious troopers and insurance agent, Amka still had a headache carved into the side of her skull. Her ribs ached, deep and low, the bruises stiffening every time she moved. Now she was at the bar with her doctor, drinking tequila like it might fix something.

The tavern sat mostly empty, lit low, in a quiet night. One table in the back still had coasters on it, damp with ringed ghosts. The jukebox twinkled but held its silence. A couple stools stood crooked near the end of the bar, nobody claiming them. The air carried the mix of lemon cleaner, old wood, and bourbon—the open-bottle kind, not the high-shelf stuff.

Ace had slumped into the leather chair by the fireplace hours ago. Bottle of bourbon gone. He'd drained the whole thing and hadn't moved since. His chin was tipped down, eyes closed, arms limp at his sides like the fight had gone clean out of him. So much for him being a bodyguard tonight.

Amka kept one eye on him. "You think he's breathing?"

May looked over, her brow pulling. "His chest is still moving. He passed out again."

"That was a full bottle," Amka said, quieter this time.

"Yeah, it was." May's forehead wrinkled and something passed through her eyes, but she turned back to her mug of coffee and drank deep.

Daisy rinsed a couple glasses at the sink, somehow tapping out a song with her foot at the same time. "It's a pity. That's one fine looking man, but his liver is taking a beating."

Amka leaned toward her, one hand pressed to the edge of the bar for balance. "Do you mind watching the place for about an hour? Then close on up?"

Daisy didn't look up. "Not at all. Where you going?"

"I have a raging headache," Amka said, still watching Ace. But she also had a plan. Possibly a stupid one.

May straightened up, slow. "Do you want me to drive you home?"

Well, Amka couldn't drive. Not like this. Besides, she had an idea. "I can't drive, and I'd love a ride home." That hadn't been her first shot of the night. "You good, Daisy?"

"Absolutely," Daisy said, jerking her head toward the fireplace. "Let's not wake him."

Ace hadn't moved. His legs were sprawled out now, boot toe pointed at nothing. A low snore rattled from somewhere in his throat, just enough to prove he was alive.

Amka watched him for a beat longer. She really was starting to get an idea, and she didn't want him knowing a thing about it.

May shook her head. "He shouldn't have had all those drinks."

"He likes to pass out in the bar," Daisy grumbled. "Make sure you charge him."

"No worries," Amka said. "It's definitely on his tab."

Daisy dried her hands on a threadbare towel.

Amka reached for her coat and slid it on, her shoulders still stiff from either the fire or from ducking down after getting shot at. Who knew? She and May eased toward the door, pushing it open just wide enough to slip out without letting in the chilly air.

"I'm parked down the street." May scanned the dark stretch of road. "Should we be looking for snipers?"

Amka spotted Trooper Jeb down the way. "No. The troopers have been patrolling all day and night. We're safe."

The world outside remained dead quiet since the rain had stopped. Gravel, snowmelt, the soft groan of wind sliding off the mountains lent a lonely air to the night. One streetlight flickered near the end of the road, casting a long shadow across May's dark blue truck.

Amka bolted to it, pulling the passenger door open and jumping inside.

May followed at a jog, slipped in, and shut her door with a quiet thud. "Why do I have the feeling that I'm not just taking you home?"

Because the doctor was smart...and a good friend. Amka pulled the seatbelt across her chest. "I have an idea."

"What's that?" May started the truck. The engine caught on the second try, coughing once before settling into a steady idle. They pulled out onto the road with nothing but the small town and dark trees behind them.

"Let's go by Jarod's house," Amka said. "He's still in Anchorage. Maybe we can find his laptop."

May glanced over. "You think?"

"I don't know, but I have to do something."

May drove carefully. "This is probably a bad idea, but I'm totally on board with you. I have your back."

"I know," Amka murmured, then hiccupped. "I appreciate it."

May's hands tightened on the steering wheel, the dash lights giving her skin a blue glow. "Are you sure you want to do this?"

"Yeah."

"Okay." May kept driving, the headlights cutting through dark that didn't seem to end. They moved outside of town, away from the river and to the Willows, a string of run-down duplexes that looked like they were losing a long fight with the land. Half of the roofs sagged. Some windows were boarded. Gutters hung down in sad curls. One of the buildings had an actual tarp nailed across part of the siding.

Amka winced. "I hadn't realized how bad it was out here." Some of the tourists had no choice but to rent this far out. Knife's Edge really did need a new motel.

"How long has Jarod lived out here?" May asked.

"I think since the motel burned down."

They pulled up to one unit on the far edge of the lot. Grass grew wild along the curb, half-dead and patchy. A grocery cart lay tipped over near the front step. Amka got out. The quiet pressed in from all sides, thick and solid, but at least it wasn't raining.

No porch light. No signs of life.

The front door was flaking paint and patched with cardboard near the bottom. Amka tried the knob. Locked.

"You don't have a key?"

The knob felt jagged in Amka's hand. "Why would I have a key?"

"Good point," May said. "But you know, you are engaged."

Amka looked around. "Do you see a rock or anything? Maybe he has a key hidden."

They searched the front area. The lawn was more dirt than

grass, with scorched patches near the walkway. Some cracked flowerpots sat empty. No key. Just trash and silence.

"Nothing," May muttered. "Let's go round back."

Amka nodded.

They crept around the side, brushing past a collapsed fence. The backyard was worse with old cans, a broken bike frame, and something that might've once been a grill. They reached a sliding glass door to find it locked.

A window caught Amka's eye that appeared half open with its screen missing. She moved toward it. "In here." Levering up on the sill, she pushed herself through, rolled, and hit the floor hard. "Ouch." Pain clicked through her from her still healing injuries. The blinds clattered above her in protest. She reached up and yanked them back.

"You okay?" May whispered from outside, her eyes wide.

"Yeah." Amka helped May inside. The room tilted a little, or maybe that was just too much tequila.

They stood in a bedroom. She looked at bare walls, a new mattress on a low frame, and piles of laundry tossed across the floor. One dresser stood in the corner, missing a drawer and listing to the side like it had arthritis.

"This place sucks," May said, looking around. "It stinks too."

"Okay. Let's start searching."

May grabbed her arm. "Wait. Let's make sure no one's here."

Amka moved slowly into the main room. A threadbare sofa sat under a window crusted with grime. Springs poked through one arm, the cushions collapsed in the center like it had been slept on more than sat in. An old box TV sat crooked on a warped stand, screen dusty, the kind that needed a slap to work. Beside it stood a bookshelf that was completely empty. Nothing sat on it but a cracked mug and a plastic comb.

"I think most of his stuff must have burned down in the fire," she said. "He hasn't collected anything else. Maybe he really is squirreling his money away to do something with it."

The kitchen wasn't much more than a corner. Dirty dishes were stacked high in the sink, most chipped. The counters were old laminate with the pattern worn off in patches. One cupboard was missing doors entirely, revealing a mess of mismatched mugs and canned beans. Two sad wooden chairs skirted an equally rundown table. Amka wrinkled her nose from the mildew and old food smell. No wonder Jarod wanted to move in with her. "I think he should burn this place down."

"Yeah, with him in it," May said grimly.

Amka giggled and then slapped a hand over her mouth. "Sorry."

May turned and looked at her. "I'm just realizing that I should've been the voice of reason, considering you drank all night."

Amka patted her arm. "You just wanted to help. Let's search this place."

"Like where?"

"I don't know. Let's tear the sofa apart."

They did. They yanked the cushions loose and found nothing underneath but lint, a broken pen, and a handful of popcorn kernels. May flipped the whole frame, and Amka peered inside with a flashlight app, but found nothing but dust, a chewed-up receipt, and one sock.

They moved on. The dresser was mostly empty with just one drawer holding old T-shirts and a warped paperback wedged sideways. Amka leaned under the bed and brought out a bright lacy red bra.

May's eyebrows rose. "I'm hoping that's not yours."

"No. Gross." Amka threw it back under the old mattress. Jarod could sleep with whomever he wanted. She leaned down to see just more laundry, stiff with age. A cardboard box in the closet held a few receipts, an expired condom, and a cheap flashlight without batteries. Nothing digital. Nothing useful.

Amka's stomach dipped. "His laptop isn't here."

"Are you sure he has a video?"

"Yes," Amka said. "I'm absolutely positive. When he blackmailed me, he showed it to me on his phone."

May dusted off her hands. "He must've taken his laptop and obviously his phone with him."

How could Amka protect Flossy? "Maybe he's already given that to somebody. Or it's all digital on his phone."

May exhaled. "We need to get our hands on his devices."

"How are we going to do that?" Amka groaned. This was her only chance to search his place.

May shrugged. "I don't know, but we can come up with a plan." She paused. "If he could get injured somehow, you could bring him into my office. While I'm looking at him, you could go through his phone. And his computer."

Amka hiccupped again. "Injured? What am I going to do? Hit him with my car?"

May looked at her. "Sometimes you gotta do what you gotta do."

"I'm not sure my doctor's supposed to be recommending a hit and run."

"Well, I didn't say you should kill him," May muttered.

A sound clunked through the wall—metal on metal, maybe something dropped.

They both froze.

"Do you know who lives there?" May whispered.

"I have no clue," Amka whispered. "I bet a couple of the tourists in town for the derby or for that influencer contest had to rent out here. Poor folks."

May started moving back toward the bedroom. "We better get out of here."

Amka followed and pushed herself through the window. She hit the ground hard, wet earth slick beneath her hands, pain firing through both knees. The cold soaked through her jeans instantly, and she bit down a curse. Mud smeared up her arms as she tried to scramble up, heart pounding.

May followed with less drama, landing soft on her feet like she did this sort of thing more often than she should.

"Can I ask what you two are doing?" The deep voice came right out of the darkness.

Amka yelped and backed straight into May. They both went down hard onto the wet ground.

Mud squelched up the back of Amka's coat and seeped instantly into her jeans, cold and gritty. A flashlight beam sliced through the dark, landing full force in her face. She threw a hand up to block it, blinking fast. "Hey."

"Sorry." Dutch stepped in closer. His boots squashed into the mud with the sound of soaked paper. His brow was furrowed deep, flashlight still trained on them like he wasn't sure if they were kids, burglars, or both. "What the hell's going on?"

"Her fiancé lives here," May blurted, already scrambling up. She grabbed Amka's arm and hauled her up with her. Amka's hands were shaking, legs soaked, hair stuck to her neck.

"Then why are you coming out the window?" Dutch asked, not moving.

Amka narrowed her eyes. "What are you doing out here, anyway?"

"I was looking around," Dutch said calmly. "Like I normally do when we have folks rent one of these units. We're having a drug problem, in case you hadn't heard. For now, what's going on here?"

"Drugs?" Amka asked, her breath still ragged, "with the folks next door?"

"Maybe," Dutch said. "But again, why are you breaking and entering?"

May wiped a smudge of dirt off her cheek. "She's not. Her fiancé lives here and she forgot her key."

"Yeah," Amka added weakly.

Dutch's gaze narrowed.

The moon hung low, a pale, sharp-edged sliver cutting through the cloud cover. Crickets chirped along the tree line, the sound brittle and constant.

Dutch clicked the light off. "I get the feeling you're not telling me the truth."

Because she wasn't.

"Come on," May said quickly. She slid her arm through Amka's. "We have to get going. Dutch, it was good seeing you."

They turned fast and marched off, shoes squishing through the muck, breath fogging in the air between them.

"We're not done with this," he said quietly after them.

"Darn it," May hissed. "Do you think he'll tell Jarod?"

Amka stumbled and then regained her footing. "Oh God, I hope not."

May glanced over. "You really might have to hit Jarod with your car."

CHAPTER 18

Anger boiled low in Christian's gut as he sat on Amka's front porch, jaw locked tight, hands stiff on his knees. The wood beneath him creaked whenever he shifted, dry and splintered in the night air. A moth batted against the porch light overhead, thumping softly with every pass. The rest of the area lay in silence, and nothing moved except shadows and his own blood pressure.

Headlights bobbed through the dark, weaving slightly before straightening out. May's truck came to a stop at the base of the drive and cut its engine, leaving only the ticking of the cooling block and a stretch of cold quiet.

The women didn't move, both staring out at him through the glass.

It took Amka several long seconds to climb down from the cab. The porch light illuminated her face, which had been smeared with mud. Her thick hair had pulled loose of its band, and a new bruise darkened her chin. "No. I'm fine. I'll talk to you tomorrow," she told May, shutting the truck door and walking toward him.

Christian stood. "Where the fuck have you been?"

She paused at the bottom step. "None of your fucking business."

He ticked his head to the side. "That's where you're wrong. I left Ace on you at the bar. That means you stay within Ace's sight."

She lifted both hands, half challenge, half defense, muddy fingers curled, chin tilted. "I don't need a keeper, Christian. And if I did, it certainly wouldn't be you. Ace had a lot to drink and fell asleep. That's not my fault."

"Yeah? Well, he's on his way to see May."

"Why?"

"Because I beat the shit out of him."

Her jaw dropped a little as she peered closer at him. "Wait a minute...are you going to have a black eye?"

"Yeah, and probably a split lip. I didn't say he didn't fight back. He had one job, and instead, he got drunk." Christian's knuckles were raw and caked with drying blood. He flexed his fingers, regretting it.

Amka looked like she'd crawled out of a ditch. She started to march past him, her nose in the air.

He clenched his jaw but didn't stop her.

Then she paused and gently took his palm, sliding to the side so the moonlight showed his hand. Hers was small, warm despite the mud caked on her skin. "How bad are your knuckles?"

Her soft touch might kill him. "They're fine."

She sighed. "You need ice, you moron."

The word didn't even sting. Not coming from her. She stomped inside and he followed, barely leashing his temper with both hands. "Why are you covered in mud?"

"Because I fell in it," she snapped, moving into the kitchen and yanking open the freezer. The door thudded hard against the side. She turned around with a bag of frozen peas and gently placed it on his hand. That gentleness did something to him, and his chest ached. Hard.

She angled her head to look up at his face. "Your lip's not going to split. It's just a little bruised. You want something for that eye?"

"No," he growled.

"Fine," she muttered. "I'm going to go take a shower."

The image hit him instantly—her, naked, steam curling around her body, water trailing down her thighs—and it nearly buckled his knees. He looked away and tried to focus elsewhere. The dent in her fridge. The mud on her floor. Anything. "I'm not messing around here," he said. "Where were you?"

"It's none of your business." She turned back, hands on her hips, chin lifted. Still breathing hard. Obviously spoiling for a fight. Wanting one. "We made it entirely clear that you don't want a relationship. So why are you butting into my life?"

He didn't answer right away since he was too busy staring at her mouth and the flash of fury in her eyes. The temper suited her. "Because you need a keeper," he said, voice lower now. "And in case you forgot, you're already in a relationship. I told you. I don't poach." It was weak. It was a lie. They both knew it. But it was all he had.

His phone buzzed in his pocket. She looked like she wanted to kick him. Hard. He lifted the stupid thing to his ear. "What?"

"Hey, it's Dutch. I just got a call. A couple of kids out four-wheeling near Rascal Mountain under the moonlight found a body with its eyes scratched out."

Christian's pulse ticked up. "Wonderful."

"Where are you?"

"I'm at Amka's. Trying to figure out why she's covered in mud."

Dutch remained silent for a moment. "What's going on with you two?"

"Nothing," Christian said curtly, although it was a fair question to ask.

"She's covered in mud because she fell out of Jarod Teller's window. Along with the doctor."

Well, that made no sense. "I think she's been drinking."

Dutch chuckled. "Yeah, I smelled tequila on her earlier. Meet me at the turnoff to Plumber Creek in ten minutes."

Christian shot the stubborn woman a hard look. "I'm going to need twenty."

"All right. Make it fifteen." Dutch clicked off.

Christian cocked his head. "Why were you seen crawling out of Jarod's window?"

She looked at the phone in his hand. "That was Dutch? What a tattletale. It's none of your business what I was doing. Maybe I forgot my key. Jarod's my fiancé. Right?"

None of this made a lick of sense. Her hair was matted with mud, her clothes soaked and clinging. She looked like she'd wrestled a bear. Her eyes still sparked with fight, and yet all he wanted to do was get her out of those muddy clothes, dry her off, and figure out what was breaking loose behind those unreadable looks she kept giving him.

Worse yet, he couldn't stop worrying about her. She wasn't his to worry about. But there was a part of him that wanted, really badly, to change that. And that part was getting stronger. Louder. More reckless. "Get your shit. I'm taking you to my place."

"No," she said flatly.

One defiant word. Just one. That was it. He ducked his head and tossed her over his shoulder.

"Hey," she squawked, squirming.

He didn't have the right to plant his hand on her ass, so he didn't. But he was starting to think he wanted that right, so he snatched her purse off the counter, stomped out of the house, and headed toward her SUV that he'd driven from the bar after he'd fought with his brother.

"What are you doing?" she snapped over his shoulder.

He didn't answer and instead plunked her into the front seat and fastened her seatbelt before she could stop him. He slammed her door and walked around to the driver's side. "You shouldn't leave your keys in the rig," he muttered, sliding behind the wheel. Though truth be told, it had made it easier for him to borrow it.

"Why? It's Knife's Edge. Somebody steals it, I'll know who they are." She crossed her arms. "Sometimes people need to borrow it, like you just did." She flipped her hair away from her face. "I'm not going to your place."

He started the engine and then backed down the driveway. "You are. Because nobody knows it's there, and it's the only place I know you'll be safe while I go deal with something with Dutch." He glanced at her after that. She was curled against the door like a pissed-off cat. Still muddy. Still beautiful. "Then we need to have a serious talk."

She crossed her arms, looking huffy and cute. Too damn cute. "I'm not talking to you about anything, Christian. Right now, you're kidnapping me."

There was a bit of truth to that statement. Even if he did just want to keep her safe. He kept telling himself he didn't have the right. But someone had to do it. If she stayed by herself, she could get shot. Or worse. "When's Jarod back in town?"

"I don't know," she snapped.

"Isn't that something you should know? Since he's your fiancé?"

She huffed and looked out the window.

What was going on?

He could see the way her jaw flexed, how her shoulders tensed just enough. Was she afraid of Jarod? She didn't act like it. She wasn't afraid of much, including him. So why was she marrying someone she didn't even seem to like? Or maybe the problem was simpler and meaner. Maybe Christian just didn't want her to want Jarod.

She ignored him as they drove.

He flipped off the lights. Once he got further away from her place and followed the path in the dark, he didn't sense anybody following them. No headlights in the distance. No dust on the road behind. But he wasn't taking any chances. Not with her.

She sat in the passenger seat, arms still folded, face turned toward the window like she'd rather be anywhere else. Her leg bounced once, then stilled. Mud cracked and flaked off her sleeve with every movement.

When they reached his place, he looked over at her. "Are you going to walk nicely inside or do you want another ride over my shoulder?"

"Screw you." She released her seatbelt, opened the door, and slammed it harder than he had earlier.

His lips twitched despite himself. She really was cute.

He followed her inside and made sure the place was secure before dragging out the same T-shirt and socks from the other night. "Here. You can take a shower and use these. Tika is roaming around somewhere, so call out if you need him. There's a nine-millimeter CZ in that drawer, and there's a shotgun by the door. I don't think anybody followed me. In fact, I'm pretty sure of it. But shoot anybody that's not me."

She lifted her chin. "Including Ace?"

"Definitely shoot Ace if he comes by," Christian grumbled, heading toward the door. "Lock this behind me, and I'm not joking." He paused at the door and turned to level her with a look. "Amka, when I get back, we're having a talk."

"I am not accepting this." Her words slurred slightly. She crossed her arms, shifted her weight, and came right at him, looking up to his face. "I am not giving you permission to take my SUV."

He cocked his head. "You can't drive."

"You can't tell me what to do." And then she shoved him. Hard. Flat palms to his chest.

He didn't move. Man, the woman really was spoiling for a fight. He got that. In fact, he'd just had a fight with his own brother. But now wasn't the time. "I have to go. Behave yourself."

Her eyes flared. "Behave?" She clenched one muddy hand and aimed it right for his gut, wincing when she made contact.

He grabbed her wrists. "You wanna talk now?" His temper wanted to blow.

"I want you to stop acting like you own me," she snapped, yanking her arms back.

He didn't have time for this. "I'm not. I'm just trying to keep you alive."

"That isn't your job." Her eyes flashed with a desperation and fear that nearly pushed him over the edge. What was scaring her so badly? She moved to shove him again, and this time he caught her halfway and kissed her. Hard.

No warning. No room for breath.

Her fists hit his chest once and then curled into his shirt. He had no idea if she was going to slap him or climb him—and didn't care. Because every part of him wanted more. And for once, he was done pretending he didn't. Finally, he wrenched his mouth free and opened the door. "We're not finished with this. When I get back, we're having that talk." He was done with the fear in her eyes. He'd take care of the threat, and then he'd figure out what to do. "Lock the fucking door." He shut it, heading out to borrow her SUV, whether she liked it or not.

CHAPTER 19

Blood dripped down Ace's temple, warm until the rain hit it. Then his skin went cold. Everything went cold. He leaned against the door of May's office building, head tipped back, eyes on the black sky above. The streetlight buzzed over him. A flickering, busted hum. Fit the mood.

He deserved the pain. Christian had done him a favor. One sharp fist to the jaw, another to the temple, and suddenly things made sense. Yeah, he'd gotten drunk again. The booze cut the edge off his thoughts. He liked that part, but he didn't like that he'd let down his brother.

Now he was bleeding. Alone, and waiting for the only person in this town who could take him out of his own head without the booze.

May.

He called her before he could think too hard about it. Told her he was bleeding. Didn't bother to explain. Then he stood still and waited for her headlights to cut through the dark. When they did, he straightened. Not enough to look good. Just enough to stay upright.

She flew out of her truck, keys already in hand. Her glasses slipped down her nose since she probably had taken her contacts out for the night. "Jesus, Ace."

"You took your time," he muttered. Damn, he loved her in glasses.

"I didn't." She got the door open fast, hands shaking. Not a good sign. Not from her. "Inside. Now. I'm going to start charging you extra for the after-hours injuries."

He followed her in, boots dragging mud, blood still trickling down his face. He didn't limp. Didn't let himself.

She locked the door behind them and flicked on the lights. He ignored the brightness and then walked toward the table without needing to be told.

"Sit."

He sat.

She moved fast, grabbing gloves, antiseptic, gauze. Her hair was wet as if she'd just come from the shower. "Are you going to tell me what happened?"

"Fell."

She gave him a look that said she wasn't in the mood.

"All right. I ran into Christian's fist," he said, voice flat. "A couple times."

She paused. Not long. Just long enough to let him know she considered his words. Then, like usual, she didn't judge or ask too many questions. Yet another thing he liked about her. Then she pressed gauze to his temple, maybe a little too hard. He welcomed the pain.

Something fell off the roof outside, no doubt a tree branch from the storm. She jolted, her head turning quickly, and then she returned to her job. Red climbed into her pretty face.

"You're jumpy tonight," he said, watching her.

"I'm not."

He kept perfectly still. "You just flinched from a simple sound outside."

She kept placing adhesive strips on the cut on his jaw like she hadn't heard him.

"Did something happen tonight?"

"I'm fine."

He narrowed his gaze, watching her move. She was wound tight. Not angry. Not tired. Something else. "You want help?" he asked, quieter this time. "You look like you need it."

"I'm the doctor," she said through clenched teeth. "You're the one bleeding."

He raised both hands, palms up. Bruised knuckles, fresh cuts, skin split at the base of the thumb. "I'm good for more than you think. Do you need my help?"

She sighed. "Seriously? What is it with you Osprey brothers taking over and wanting to help? If Christian helps Amka any longer, it's going to be right into his bed."

Ace coughed. "Huh?"

She rolled her spectacular blue eyes. With that blonde hair, she looked more like a sexy cheerleader than an accomplished doctor. Her gaze hit his hands. "Don't worry about it right now. Your knuckles are bruised. Do you want ice?"

"No."

She cleaned a different gash without another word.

He watched her. Every step. Every breath. She was listening for something. Every time the building creaked, she flinched just slightly. She didn't know she was doing it.

Someone or something had her spooked.

And here he was—wounded, useless, and sitting in her light like a stray dog who knew the vet wouldn't turn him away. He liked the pain and not just because he deserved it. Because pain got her in the room with him. That made him the worst kind of a selfish bastard.

She moved to another cut near his ear. Her hand brushed his jaw. He knew she could feel the bruise there. "You should've iced this," she said.

"I wasn't aiming to fix anything. Just didn't want to stitch my own face."

"You don't need stitches. These strips will do the trick." Her breath was shallow. Her eyes kept flicking to the window.

He couldn't take it anymore. "May."

"What?"

"You scared of something?"

She didn't answer right away and just tied off the thread, cut it, and dropped the needle into the tray like she was trying to hurt the metal. "That's the thing," she said finally. "I don't get to be scared. I have to fix people. Patch them up. Get them back out there."

He let that sit a second. "Even so, I'm happy to help."

Her eyes, when she met his, were a carnelian blue in the soft light. "You can't even help yourself, Ace Osprey."

Ouch. But that didn't mean she was wrong. "Maybe I've just been waiting for the right motivation, Doc."

The flash of alarm in her expression settled through him and landed hard. Yeah. That.

Mud clung to Christian's boots like it had teeth. Each step squelched, slow and loud in the soaked undergrowth. Rain came down steady now in a relentless drizzle. Needle-fine and cold enough to sting where it touched skin.

Dutch stood ahead with his arms crossed, jaw tight, hat dripping. The beam from his flashlight cut a white path through the dark. Just off the trail, two kids stood by their four-wheelers—Ty Weaver and Kyle Denton. Juniors from the high school. Christian had seen them around school events, mostly grinning like idiots. Tonight, they weren't smiling.

Ty's face was blotchy and pale. Kyle wouldn't take his eyes off the tree line.

"They touch anything?" Christian asked.

"No," Dutch said. "They had the sense to call right away and sat tight until I got here. But they're spooked."

Christian scanned the area. "Can't blame them." He stepped into the clearing. "Why did they call you and not Brock?"

Dutch rolled his neck, looking down the river. "Kyle wants to be an AWT, so we get together whenever I'm in town to play chess. He has my number on his phone, so he called me. I guess we can call in Brock if you want."

Why wake him up? Christian angled his head to see better. The body was sprawled wrong, like it had fallen from a height or been dropped. Limbs twisted. One hand buried in the mud like it had tried to dig its way down. The man's shirt was torn open.

Christian crouched. Dutch's flashlight beam caught the face, and Christian went still. The eyes were gone. Not just closed. Not swollen. Gone. Hollow sockets stared back at him, dark and ragged at the edges. "Jesus," he muttered.

Dutch stepped up beside him, mouth a hard line. "Told you."

Blood streaked across the man's face, dried now except where the rain had diluted it into something slick and ruddy. His mouth was open like he'd been screaming. Christian didn't want to imagine what it sounded like. He stood and backed off a few paces. "No animal did that."

"No." Dutch said quietly. "We'd see prints. Scat. Tracks going in or out. This was a human."

"Someone who took their time," Christian said. He turned toward the boys. "Ty. Kyle. Either of you recognize the victim?"

Both shook their heads fast. Ty looked like he might puke.

"He just...he was just there," Kyle said. "We thought it was a tarp at first. I went closer. Then I saw his shirt. And...his face."

Ty wiped his nose on his sleeve. "Why would somebody take his eyes?"

"I don't know." Christian turned back toward the body. The

trees pressed in on all sides—thick, dripping, watching. Somewhere out there, someone had done this with their own hands. Not from a distance. Up close. Personal.

"You get a name?" Dutch asked.

Christian pulled the wallet from the guy's pocket, careful not to smear the blood soaked through the jeans. "Arizona license. Eli Warner." They finally had a name for one of the victims.

Dutch leaned in. "We have an identification? I would've bet against it. This is something, Christian. The guy must've been a tourist?"

"Maybe." Christian stood again. "Not anymore." He stood over the body, his flashlight sweeping in a slow arc across the soaked ground. Everything was mud, pine needles, and blood. The river churned behind them, loud enough to make it hard to think.

Then he saw it.

Off to the left, a shallow depression in the moss. Another just beyond it that was barely visible under the sheen of rain. But the spacing was right. The angle was right. He took a step, crouched beside it. Let the light fall at just the right angle. "Dutch," he said.

Dutch walked over, peering down. "That a print?"

"Yeah. Boot tread. Deep enough for weight, but not the victim's. He didn't get back up." Christian followed the line with his light. "There's more. It moves off into the trees."

Dutch stood silent for a second, watching him. "You up to tracking him?"

"Absolutely." Christian followed another sign, which was a broken sapling branch at thigh height that smelled fresh. Then a heel scuff in the mud, slipping right. "He came this way in a hurry, favoring the right side. Might be hurt."

Dutch exhaled, steady. "I can't leave the body or the kids. Don't like sending you alone."

Christian looked up. "Part of the reason I'm taking this job is that I can do it alone. Plus, if I wait, the rain will wash the trail out. This may be the only shot I've got."

"I'll take the body to Doc May's so she can start the prelim, and I'll make sure the kids get home." Dutch stared into the dark. "You radio if something turns. If you catch the guy, try not to kill him. We like to take them alive and to trial."

Christian nodded once. "I understand the assignment."

Dutch looked at him for a moment, then turned back toward the clearing.

Christian didn't wait. He pushed into the trees, boots heavy, light cutting through branches and wet shadow. The uneven but clear trail kept him moving. Someone had run this way.

The woods swallowed him, welcoming him home. He moved slow and low, gaze scanning the ground, flashlight aimed at his feet, not ahead. The trail was a repetition of off-center prints, displaced moss, and branches bent the wrong direction. Enough to follow if a hunter knew what to look for. Not enough for someone less stubborn.

Whoever it was had moved fast and messy. No sign of doubling back. No care to cover the trail. They weren't afraid of being followed, or they didn't think anyone would bother.

Christian wasn't sure which worried him more.

The rain had eased to a steady drizzle, which helped. The scent of wet spruce and churned mud filled the air. The trees were packed tighter now, older, the kind of woods that didn't see casual foot traffic.

He saw a print, which was clear this time. Deep heel, tread slipping right again. The runner was still favoring that side.

Christian's boots caught in a patch of thick muck. He paused, listened.

Nothing but wind in the trees.

No birds. No night calls. Just silence.

He moved on. The trail climbed a narrow ridge. At the top, the trees thinned, giving way to a run-off ditch and an old fence line. Beyond that, down the slope, he saw the dull glow of streetlights.

He stopped upon reaching the Willows. The duplexes and rundown units sat below, hunched in the dark like a row of bruises. Paint peeling, a few windows boarded over, and puddles reflecting the weak light like oil. It smelled like trash, mildew, and rot.

He crouched and swept his flashlight off. Watched. A few porch lights were on. One TV flickered blue through a broken blind. The rest of the units looked dead asleep.

But the prints led here. No question.

He traced the last few signs and found mud scraped along the gravel, and a dirty handprint smeared low on a utility pole, like the runner had stopped to catch their breath or stay upright.

And then nothing. The trail died at the edge of the lot.

Christian's gaze drifted toward the far unit. Jarod Teller's.

It was dark.

No porch light. No movement. Curtains pulled.

But Amka had been there. Just hours ago.

So had May.

The crawl in his gut got worse. He didn't like this part of town on the best night, and this wasn't one of those. The place felt wrong. Like something had been here recently and hadn't fully left.

He backed into the trees, sat on his heels, and waited. Watched until dawn arrived, and still, nobody moved. As the sun began to light the wet trees around him, he texted Brock to give Amka a ride to work, even though that meant revealing his little secret cabin. There would be questions, no doubt. He also texted Ace to watch the bar for the day. Yeah, they'd fought the night before, but something had flickered in Ace's eyes. He wouldn't screw up again.

Finally, Dutch joined Christian, pulling to a stop quietly down the road. They met near the first unit.

Dutch took a deep breath. "We'll go one by one to interview folks, and let me flash my badge. Just look scary."

That would be no problem. Just how close had Amka been to a murderer last night? Fire blasted through Christian, and he locked that shit down. Hard.

For now.

CHAPTER 20

Amka handed off another breakfast platter to Nixi. "I don't know what I'd do without you. Thanks for covering this week."

Nixi grinned, a spark in her blue eyes. "I like it here. Who knows? Maybe after I win that fifty grand, I'll come back and do some influencing. I've always wanted to write a book."

"Great idea." Amka forced a smile. Her head still throbbed at the base of her skull—last night's tequila hadn't done her any favors. "This would be a good place for that. You could pick up shifts here part-time."

"I'd like that." Nixi spun off toward the far table, plates balanced in one hand. She moved like she'd already claimed the place. She definitely had too much energy for this early, but the customers loved her.

Lucas Landom pushed away from the bar with his to-go bag already in hand.

"One of these days, you need to try something else," Amka suggested.

The tanker chief grinned. "Maybe I will. So long as it looks and tastes like a breakfast burrito." Humming, the man strode across the bar and right out the door.

Daisy stepped out of the kitchen, flushed, a damp rag in her hand, watching him go. "He's a good-looking dude, but nobody knows a lot about him."

Amka shrugged. "Maybe most writers are like that?"

"Dunno." Daisy looked back at the kitchen door. "It's hotter than sin in there."

A flicker of unease hit Amka. She turned, opened the kitchen door, and leaned inside. Rudolph stood at the grill, pink in the cheeks, humming low. He didn't look up.

"You drinking water?" she asked.

"Don't start."

She scanned the counter. The water bottle was full, unopened. Of course it was. "If that's not gone when I'm back, I'll stand here and watch you drink it."

He grunted, but she was already shutting the door.

Mumbling about the stubborn fool, she reached beneath the bar and took out two ibuprofen to suck down with her own water. Her jaw still ached from clenching it all morning. Her chest felt tight. Her legs, restless. Last night hadn't gone away. Not the kiss. Not the way Christian had looked at her after, like he'd lost control and wasn't sure he wanted it back.

He wanted her. She knew it now. Not just a maybe. Not curiosity. That kiss had said everything he hadn't. And she'd felt it. Low in her stomach. Hot between her thighs. She still felt his mouth on hers. Her body wouldn't calm down. Her skin was jumpy and her lips burned. She'd pressed her fingers there twice this morning like it might shake the memory loose. It hadn't.

She didn't want to be thinking about him. Not while she was working. Not while eggs were burning and toast needed butter. But he was in her system now. In her mouth, her skin, even her bloodstream.

While she was still engaged to a jackass. Even if she wasn't,

Christian had been more than clear that he wasn't the staying type. Sure, they could burn up the sheets, if she ever got free of Jarod, but what then?

Then she'd be left with a broken heart.

Her phone dinged and she glanced down at a reminder. Darn it. Rudolph was due for his blood pressure refill. She'd meant to check with the pharmacy yesterday and forgot. She made a mental note to call it in before lunch. The man wouldn't say a word until his heart threatened to quit on him.

The bar was finally quiet with only a handful of stragglers nursing coffee or staring into phones. Over by the pool table, the steady tap-tap-tap of a calculator filled the silence. The insurance rep in the corner booth hadn't looked up once. Helene had scraped her shiny dark hair into a too-tight ponytail and now had a pile of folders spread around her like she was planning to gut a fish with paperwork. Every once in a while she'd look up at Amka with a thoughtful glance.

Amka sighed. She did not destroy her storage building for the insurance, darn it. But who *had* planted that explosive?

Daisy stepped up beside her, wiping her hands on a rag. "Wild breakfast rush."

"Yeah. But it's slowed down since most of the locals headed out to fish."

"Reports of the new dead guy has everyone twitchy." Daisy crouched behind the bar and pulled out a pale-pink folder. "Special delivery. Prenup, will, and your LLC information, which includes an operating agreement with Ace."

Amka blinked. "That was fast."

"I had a gut feeling time mattered."

"It does." Amka flipped through the documents, hope finally zipping through her. She signed the prenuptial agreement as well as the LLC and operating agreement before reaching for the will.

Daisy raised a hand. "Hold up. I need witnesses. Nixi?" she called.

Nixi hustled their way and plunked her tray down at the bar. "You have more information on the dead body?"

"Nope. Nothing." Daisy shook her head. "Will you witness Amka signing her will?"

Nixi pulled a pen from behind her ear. "Sure."

Daisy glanced toward the end of the bar. "Amka, I don't want to use Ace since you're going into business with him. Just to keep things clean."

Ace, black coffee in hand, kept scrolling through his phone. He hadn't asked for a drink all morning, except for more coffee.

Daisy turned toward the fireplace. "Hey, blond dude. You by the fireplace."

Steve looked up from filming himself talking about fishing lures. He broke off and wandered over, his gaze alert.

"You're a witness now," Daisy said. She looked at Amka. "Okay, sign."

Amka did so and then watched as Nixi signed as a witness before tucking her purple pen on her ear beneath her purple hair.

Steve signed with a flourish and then looked over at Nixi. "Nice footage yesterday of that secret fishing hole with the hidden walk toward those waterfalls."

"Thanks." Nixi rocked on her heels, stretching her calves. "The locals are really helpful around here."

Steve snorted. "Sure, when you look like you do. I haven't had much luck with the old guys showing me hidden gems."

Amka tucked the papers back into the pink folder, pleased to almost have her affairs in order. Just in case.

Steve nudged Nixi's elbow as she hopped on one heel, a swirl of apron brushing her thigh. "Hey, what about us collaborating? I've got a dozen ideas."

Nixi spun her tray, smirking. "How many followers do you have?"

"Almost two hundred thousand," he offered with a cocked eyebrow.

"Not bad," she replied, leaning in toward him. The woman could seriously flirt. Amka should take lessons from her. "I've doubled that."

He grinned, the bar lights flickering off his pale roots. "We'd own the feed together."

She laughed, a warm sound that echoed between them.

Daisy stepped in front of the bar. "You two can collaborate later. Right now, I need pictures of your driver's licenses." She tugged her phone from the back pocket of her jeans.

The two dug out their IDs, and Daisy snapped photos. "Thanks."

Steve leaned close enough Amka smelled his woodsy cologne. "Doesn't a will need notarizing?"

"Not in Alaska. It'd help, but we don't have a notary. I'll probably become one when I get the chance." Daisy handed back the IDs. Steve tucked his into a back pocket, and Nixi brushed his arm as she grabbed her tray.

Amka motioned to Ace. He slid off his stool. Bruises and stitches lined his jaw, but his eyes caught hers. He didn't move except to reach for the pen. "Ready to sign the incorporation documents?" she asked.

"Yep." He signed and gently placed the papers on the bar. "Looks like we're in business."

Amka slowly relaxed. She hadn't been entirely sure he'd stick to the plan. Especially after he and Christian had come to blows the previous night. "Are you ready for this?"

Ace met her eyes without hesitation. "I'm in."

She let out a slow breath and turned to Daisy. "Thanks."

"No problem. I'll get you copies, but you know that Jarod has to sign the prenup as well, right?"

"Yeah." Amka didn't care. After she met with the bank, she wouldn't be financially worth much. For now, anyway. Real hope stirred in her chest about her new venture. Maybe Christian had knocked some sense into Ace the night before. She glanced at the stitches above his eye, the bruising along his jaw. "Sorry about that," she murmured.

Daisy snorted. "No doubt he deserved it." She tucked the file folders beneath the bar and moved to collect dirty dishes from over by the dart boards.

"I did deserve it," Ace said easily. "Was my brother bruised at all?"

"Yeah. His knuckles looked bruised, and I think he's due for a solid shiner. But I haven't seen him since yesterday." It had surprised her when Brock had picked her up from Christian's cabin that morning. And Brock had seemed genuinely surprised to discover that his brother had built a cabin.

He'd stood for a long moment, looking up at it like he was calculating sniper angles. "Perfect defensive positioning," he'd muttered.

She hadn't thought of that. Apparently defensive positions mattered to Christian. She focused back on Ace. "If you can financially meet me halfway, our new building could have a third story we could use as rental. The tourists need more places to stay."

Ace scrubbed both hands down his face, jaw tight. "I can meet you halfway financially."

"You can?" she asked, not quite hiding the surprise.

"Yeah. I don't spend money on much. Once you tell me what you're putting in, I'll match it."

She might just hug him. "Great." Her fingers tightened slightly on the counter. This had been in motion longer than anyone knew. She'd already asked the banker, Peter Rentzing, to start running the numbers months ago—right around the time Jarod had forced her into that engagement. She hadn't told a soul. But she'd had a feeling. Something in her gut had whispered that she'd find the right opportunity, and when she did, she needed to be ready. Now she had a partner. One she genuinely liked and wanted to help.

Ace sauntered off toward the far corner where the TV showed a PGA tournament somewhere warm. Palm trees, clean fairways. A fantasy.

Amka leaned down for her coat. "I'm heading to the bank," she called out. "Be back in an hour."

"Hey." Ace turned away from the television. "Wait a minute. I'm your escort."

"Ace, I think I can make it down the street on my own."

He gave her a broad, almost sunny grin. "Sure. If there's not a sniper waiting to pick you off at high noon. It's doubtful, I know, especially since the troopers have been patrolling your street continually. But I'm on Amka duty."

Amka duty? She rolled her eyes. "We have to find that sniper."

"We're working on it," Ace said grimly.

She had Osprey men around too much these days. "Fine, but that means we're holding our first corporate meeting today."

"Fine by me. Why are we going to the bank?"

It was a fair question from her new partner. "Okay. So, I've been working with the bank to secure funding for a project, and now I actually have the real estate to do it. I'd planned to mortgage the bar and my house for my future, and now we just need to wait for the insurance money. I'd like to get everything in place." And maybe get Jarod uninterested in her.

"Thinking ahead, huh? When we're at the bank, we can check how much I've got in there too," Ace said, pulling the door open with a creak. "Might surprise us."

"Maybe we should build a couple buildings," she said. "And buy another plane."

He huffed. "Let's not get cocky. I don't know if we're rolling in that kind of cash."

She arched a brow. "Let's find out." It was time she concentrated on her life and built something to last, even if she was on her own. Well, as soon as she got out of this situation with Jarod.

Now the town was buzzing with the news that two local kids found a body near Rascal Mountain. Christian had gone off alone to track the killer. She'd fought herself from calling him all morning. He wasn't hers to worry about, no matter how many times he'd kissed her.

CHAPTER 21

The warmth from the fire in Sam's Tavern finally heated Christian's feet. He might need new boots. He leaned back in his chair, legs extended, coffee in hand, sleeves rolled to the elbows. The coffee was strong tonight, just like he wanted.

Dutch sat across from him, his posture loose in that deceptive way seasoned lawmen managed when they were thinking too hard.

Christian's gaze drifted past the flames, to the bar where Amka stood behind the counter with Daisy, both laughing about something. Her hair was loose again, shiny and silky down her back. She looked lighter tonight, happy, even. The tension that had clung to her last night had disappeared.

Ace had mentioned that they'd formed a business together before he left for the night. The woman did like numbers, so perhaps that's why she seemed happy?

She wiped her hands on a towel and leaned into Daisy's side as they bent over the schedule, lips moving fast, both chuckling.

Christian's throat went tight. He didn't want to need that smile. Didn't want such beauty pulling something loose in his chest. But her joy and kindness did. And he felt that need like pressure against his ribs.

She hadn't looked at him once since he'd come in.

Fine. She didn't need to.

The front door creaked open.

Cold air swept across the floor, and two uniformed troopers stepped in, hats off, coats wet from the still-misting rain. One male in his mid-sixties and a younger female with dark red hair. True red hair. They spotted Dutch and made their way across the tavern.

"Evening," Dutch said, dragging a chair out with one boot. "Coffee's hot."

They both sat. "Evening, boys," the female said.

Dutch nodded toward Christian. "This is Christian Osprey."

"Jeb Pontevo." The older guy extended a hand. His grip was firm. "This is Paige Johnson."

The woman held out a hand and Christian shook it. "Nice to meet you."

Dutch grinned. "Christian is working with me as a consultant but will be an AWT by the end of the year. He tracked the killer of the victim we found earlier. Can't believe we finally can identify one of these victims who'd had their eyes scratched out. Poor bastards."

Christian gave a short nod. "The trail led to a dead end." He and Dutch had interviewed every person either living or renting out at that dismal place, and nobody had hit. His best guess was that the killer had stashed a vehicle there and had taken off, but the trail had definitely ended there.

"We're here for the explosion and arson case." Jeb leaned forward. "I went over the wreckage next door this afternoon. Rain didn't do us any favors, but there's no doubt. Even if the explosion happened by accident, which is nonsense, somebody wanted a fire to spread."

Christian's mouth twitched. "You don't say."

Jeb nodded, apparently missing sarcasm. "I appreciate the locals sending the fragments from the device to the lab. In looking at the site, I found four pour patterns, and the accelerant soaked into the joists and floorboards. They wanted the place gone fast and didn't care who saw the flames."

Dutch exhaled, long and quiet. "We figured as much, and I don't like that Amka was in there. Did you get a chance to canvas?"

Paige groaned. "We knocked on every door in the town and have the radio station sending out information tomorrow to talk to us if anybody knows anything. Although, I figure they would've already found you."

"True," Dutch said. "There were enough of those influencers in town with phones recording that I keep hoping someone saw something, but so far, all we have is a hero video featuring Christian."

Paige grinned, her gaze wandering Christian's face. "Yeah, I saw that."

Christian lifted a shoulder. "I heard about it from Dutch earlier, and I don't want to see it." At least Nixi hadn't included his damn name. That's all he needed. "Have you cleared the scene?" The rain and storms had obliterated any evidence, and they all knew it was arson.

Paige tapped her nails on the table. "Yeah. We secured samples of a few remaining wood pieces for the lab so we can identify the accelerant, but other than that, we didn't find anything useful."

Daisy popped up. "Hi, troopers. What can I get you?"

"Two coffees, no cream or sugar," Paige said a little forcefully.

Jeb frowned. "Come on, Paige. One sugar won't hurt."

Paige's chin stiffened. "I promised Louanne that you wouldn't have any more sugar in your coffee. Your last numbers came up pre-diabetic, you know."

Jeb rolled his eyes. "You're not afraid of my wife, are you?"

"Hell, yes." Paige leaned back in her chair. "That woman is terrifying."

Jeb sighed. "All right. A coffee with nothing good in it."

Apparently Jeb was afraid of his wife as well. "How long have you been married?" Christian asked, shocking the shit out of himself. He didn't ask personal questions. Why was he asking about marriage?

"Almost forty years," Jeb said as Daisy walked away. "My wife's a sweetheart, she is. We raised five kids with me on the road a lot, and I'm lucky." He lifted one shoulder beneath his uniform. "Except for the sugar part. I like sugar."

"Stop being a baby." Paige looked at Dutch. "About the body. Did you do the notification?"

Dutch rubbed his face. "Yeah. Talked to the wife. She wants to come up here since we won't be able to transport her husband's body to Anchorage for a couple of days. It's taking time to arrange a helicopter. She plans to accompany him when the transport happens. So sad. Though it's a good thing we installed that morgue cooler in the hospital basement a few years back."

Amka's laugh floated across the bar again—soft and warm and cutting right through Christian. Then she disappeared back into the kitchen. He stared at the mug in his hand, grip tightening slightly. The idea that somebody wanted to cut off that sound, to hurt her, spiraled a fire inside him he didn't recognize.

The door opened and Jarod Teller walked in, wearing dark jeans, a button-down shirt, and a newish-looking black leather jacket. He strolled behind the counter and poured himself a beer, his gaze moving to the dark-haired gal reading through ledgers at the end of the counter. The insurance adjuster. Christian figured she was probably pretty, but not Amka pretty.

Man, he had to get a grip on himself.

Amka walked out of the kitchen with plates in her hand, caught sight of Jarod, and lost her smile. That quickly.

Christian narrowed his gaze.

Amka walked around the bar and delivered the dishes to a table of influencers over by the dartboard. Christian figured that's what they were, considering they were all talking into their phones. Then talking into each other's phones. He couldn't quite get used to this new world.

Jarod opened the till and pulled out some bills. Just how often did he do that?

Christian didn't spend a lot of time indoors, and he was about at his limit, but someone needed to cover Amka right now. He wished he could also cover Wyland, but the old guy could take care of himself. It was still possible that the attacker wanted to hurt Wyland and not Amka, but Christian's instincts whispered otherwise. Of course, his instincts might not be on track when it came to that woman.

Jarod shut the till and paused, leaning down to lift up a pink manila folder. Pink? He flipped open the top and red filled his face, turning his ears crimson. His head jerked up.

Awareness pricked through Christian, and he placed his mug on the table.

Amka returned behind the bar and reached for a beer glass.

Jarod pivoted on her, looming over her. Her head snapped up, and fire lit her eyes.

Christian stiffened.

"What are these?" Jarod snapped, loud enough to reach across the room.

The influencers all paused, turning to watch.

Amka let out a sharp breath. Her hands framed her waist, shoulders squared. "That's not your business." She didn't lower her voice, either.

Jarod's jaw clenched. He grabbed her wrist, turning it with

enough force that the beer glass in her other hand rattled against the counter.

She placed it gently on the bar and then punched him in the gut. Jarod doubled over with a muffled oof. Shock filled Amka's eyes, and she looked down at her fist as if surprised it belonged to her.

Christian stood, muscles coiling. He made it across the bar in a heartbeat. "Let go of her wrist before I break yours and shove it down your fucking throat."

Jarod released her and stepped away, his mouth open in a quiet snarl. "Mind your fucking business."

"Problem?" Dutch stepped up behind Christian.

"No." Jarod said, looking down at Amka. "We need to talk."

Dutch cleared his throat. "I'm going to ask before the other troopers do. That was a battery. Mr. Teller? Would you like to press charges against this petite and rather well-loved bartender for punching you?"

Jarod ground his teeth together. "Of course not. Amka, let's go talk."

She nodded.

"Not a chance," Christian snarled.

Jarod's chin lowered, his brown eyes blazing. "She's my fiancée, asshole."

Christian settled. He went cold. "She ain't wearing your ring, now is she?"

Amka lifted a hand. "Daisy? Would you cover the tavern for a moment? If you need help, drag Nixi from her buddies over there. Jarod, let's talk in the back room." She'd gone pale, but her chin didn't waver.

Triumph flashed in Jarod's eyes. "Yeah. Let's do that."

Amka's gaze met Christian's. "It's okay, C. I'm fine."

Something ugly dropped into his gut. Something dark and churning. "If you need help, call out. I'll be sitting right here at the bar. Teller, if you touch her, they'll never find your body."

AMKA FOLLOWED Jarod into the back room, a place she usually found comfort. It had one comfy bed, a nice bathroom, and a bin filled with lost-and-found clothes that someone always needed. She shut the door behind them with more force than necessary and leaned back against it like she might hold the tension in the room at bay with her spine.

Jarod spun to face her, his face dark with fury. "What do you think you're doing?"

She crossed her arms. "I don't know what you mean."

He lifted the pink manila folder in his hand. "You've locked up the equity in the bar and your house. All of it. With the bank."

"I know," she said flatly. "I'm investing in a business with Ace."

Jarod's nostrils flared. "The hell you are. I need that money. Unless you want that video to go live."

Her stomach dropped, but she didn't move. "I am so tired of you. Would you really send poor Flossy to prison?"

He sneered. "You think I won't? Test me."

Amka's pulse roared in her ears. Her entire life narrowed to that tiny room, his smug face, and the fury burning through her veins. She'd felt strong earlier, felt good by signing those papers, making a plan. But Jarod always knew how to drag her back down. "You're pathetic."

He grabbed her arm, fingers tight. "We're still getting married. You keep pretending like you have a choice."

Her hand twitched, ready to slap him. The urge to call out, to scream for help, pulsed behind her tongue. But then she thought of Christian and how close he'd been to putting Jarod through a wall a minute ago. The fact that he'd offered to use his skills, whatever they were, in a way she couldn't live with. "We are not getting married. That wasn't the deal."

"Deals change." Jarod leaned in. "Don't forget or get any ideas about your stalker out there taking me out. If anything ever happens to me, that video goes live. I've got it with exactly the right person on standby."

The words hit like ice water down her back. She didn't flinch—wouldn't give him the satisfaction—but her spine locked up. Her molars ached from how tight she clenched her jaw. "Who has it?"

"You'll never know. Trust me."

Her mind spun. "What if we make a deal?"

That stopped him, just for a second. His eyebrows rose. Her voice was too steady, maybe, or maybe he didn't expect her to push back at all.

"I've got everything tied up now," she went on, heartbeat pulsing hard behind her eyes, "but once I get the buildings up, I'll be making a profit. I could lend you money for the motel."

His head tilted, his brown eyes beady. "I'm starting the motel next week. Already bought the land." His mouth curled. "Wait a minute. Did you get a construction loan?"

Her stomach knotted. "Yeah."

He exhaled and his shoulders relaxed. "Well then, we'll just use that."

"No," she snapped. "We can't. Ace and I got it together."

"Then it looks like Ace is my partner now too," he said. "The drunk won't know the difference."

Her hands curled into fists, nails digging crescent moons into her palms. "He's not a drunk," she said, even though she wasn't sure she believed it.

"Oh yeah?" Jarod's voice turned mean again. "We'll see. When we get married, all of this will be half mine."

"No, it won't," she shot back. "None of it will ever be yours."

He shoved her, his palm driving into her shoulder, hard enough to knock her into the door behind her. Pain radiated down her back, dull and mean where the bruises hadn't finished healing. "Do I need to show you the video again?"

"No," she said quietly. "I have it committed to memory." She had to get his phone and into his email somehow.

"Good." His smile curved his too thin lips. "We'll go to the bank tomorrow and get this fixed. Take the construction loan and use it on my land for the motel." He turned and strutted out the back door, disappearing into the wet black of the rainy night. The screen creaked and then slammed behind him. The silence that followed felt heavy.

Amka stood frozen, heart galloping. Then her knees buckled and she grabbed the edge of the bed table for balance. Several deep breaths. They didn't help. What in the world was she going to do?

She'd joked once—half-joked—about hitting him with her car. Dark humor in a small town went far. But she couldn't actually do it. No matter how tempting it was to end the problem with a steering wheel and a well-timed swerve.

But the idea clawed in anyway.

What if she did give him the construction loan and just walked away from the entire situation, even if that meant she'd have to pay off her bar and home again?

Would he give her the video?

Could she take that chance?

Maybe. Perhaps that was her best option. The move might put her and Ace's project on hold for a little while. Ace would be furious. But he'd understand, right? If it meant protecting someone like Flossy, and it meant keeping herself out of prison? Of course, she'd have to tell Ace the truth.

Maybe.

Then again, she'd mortgaged everything. Her house. The bar. Her last shred of peace.

She didn't know what to do.

Her body gave out, sliding down the side of the wall until

she sat on the floor, pink folder limp in her lap. Her breath sawed in and out, shallow and sharp. The air smelled like fryer oil and cheap cologne.

A soft knock broke the stillness.

She shifted to the side, stiff, blinking back the blur. "Yes?"

Daisy cracked open the door and peered down at her, brows drawn. "Christian sent me to check on you. You good?"

"I'm fine." Amka stood, legs protesting, and quickly gathered the scattered papers, tucking them into the pink folder with jerky hands.

Daisy didn't move, just leaned a shoulder against the doorframe. "I guess he was mad, huh?"

A laugh tore out of Amka that didn't feel funny. "I guess so." She brushed dust from her jeans and straightened her flannel shirt. "Let's go back to work." Because what else was there? The way things were going, she'd be working long hours for the rest of her life.

That was…if she didn't go to prison first.

CHAPTER 22

Amka finished pretending to work after about fifteen minutes of shifting things around. At least Jarod hadn't returned. No doubt he was scared of Christian. The guy wasn't a moron, but he should be scared of her. Ha. Right. Like she'd actually hurt him. She closed the cash drawer like it had personally offended her and wiped the same spot on the counter she'd already cleaned twice.

"Why don't you go on home?" Daisy didn't peer up from where she was stacking receipts.

Amka's gaze slid over to Christian across the tavern.

He had that look again. Tight shoulders, jaw clenched, hands flat on the table like they were the only thing keeping him in the building. He wasn't fidgeting. Wasn't twitching. Just sitting still like only he could. Like he was holding something in by force. His attention flicked to the front door, then back to the troopers talking shop at the table with him.

Amka didn't ask. Not now, not ever. He hadn't volunteered, and she hadn't pressed. Whatever his reason was for going cagey indoors, it was his. But she'd watched him enough the last few months, coming in, getting soup, leaving fast, to know when he hit his limit. This was it.

"Amka?" Daisy murmured. "I'm happy to close up tonight."

"Yeah, I think I will head out. Thanks, Daisy." Amka grabbed her coat off the hook, slung her purse over her shoulder, and crossed the tavern without glancing around. She watched Christian's gaze tracking her, and her heart rate sped up as she neared him, but she kept her movements casual, her boots clicking on the old floorboards, steady and unhurried.

At the fireplace, she paused. His shoulders had dropped just enough to be noticeable. His eyes, though, were the same. Focused. Heavy. Like he was balancing on the edge of something sharp.

"You headed out?" Dutch asked, lounging with his shoulders and body relaxed. Good. He needed to take it easy once in a while.

"I am. It's been a long day." She looked right at Christian, not blinking. "Do you mind walking me out? After the sniper attack the other day, I would be more comfortable."

"Absolutely." He stood like he'd been waiting for the order, already in motion before she finished the sentence. His expression didn't change, but something flickered behind his eyes. Relief, maybe.

"Thanks. I appreciate it." She turned and gave the troopers a polite smile. "You all have a good night." Yeah, maybe she wanted to think she was helping him, just this once. Even if he'd never say the words.

"Ms. Amaruq." The redheaded trooper looked up, her badge catching the light. Her voice carried without raising. "We need to speak with you again about the explosion and ensuing fire next door. Only two people stand to gain from the destruction. You and Wyland Friday."

The weight in the room shifted. Everyone seemed to pause, definitely eavesdropping.

"I'd like to be included," the insurance adjuster said from her stool at the bar. She turned slowly, casual as a cobra, wine glass dangling from two fingers. Her gaze didn't move off Amka.

One of the influencers, a blonde millennial sitting next to Nixi with a microphone clipped to her coat, whispered something and then twisted in her seat to watch. The others followed, their faces suddenly lit with interest, like they'd just remembered they had followers to feed.

Christian took Amka's arm in a firm grip. Possessive. Controlled. Like the conversation was over. "Tomorrow." Without waiting for a response from the trooper, he moved them toward the door. Not fast, but without leaving space for anyone to follow.

Outside, the cold slapped Amka hard enough to burn her lungs. The wind had shifted and now carried damp smoke and thawed mud, thick and sharp. It stuck in her throat and settled low. The rain pattered down, and she barely noticed it, wiping her hair back. It'd rain for the next month. At least.

Christian stepped ahead, scanning. One hand raised, fingers loose but precise. "Hold it."

She paused on instinct, boots crunching on scattered gravel.

He took two steps forward, eyes tracking the tree line, the surrounding buildings, the shadowed edge of a truck down the way. "We're good."

"How do you know?" she asked.

"I'd feel it."

She watched his profile for a second. His mouth didn't twitch. His eyes didn't move. She didn't push because she believed him. Trusted him. The guy was as solid as the mountains around them, which is why she wouldn't question him. Plus, he kissed like a god.

Heat flared into her face. The attraction might just kill her, and she had to get a grip as they walked to her SUV. The back window was still boarded up with a piece of plywood.

He caught her glance. "Mountain Man's Garage should have a new window for you by the end of the week."

"Christian, you didn't have to—"

"No problem." He moved ahead and opened her door in a not-so-subtle command for her to get in. "I'll follow you home. I've got Brock's rig tonight."

Something in her chest unclenched as she slipped inside to sit. "Does your brother know you have his truck?"

"Probably," Christian muttered, eyes scanning the lot like he expected something to materialize out of the dark.

Amka leaned back a little, arms crossed. "I heard the Miller boys want to unload one."

Christian snorted. "Those kids ride hard. I'd spend more time fixing it than driving it." He scrubbed a hand through his dark and now wet hair, letting the rain caress down the hard angles of his face. "I guess I'll just buy a new one next time I'm in Anchorage. Or Fairbanks."

She blinked. "You can just buy a new truck?"

"Yeah. Can't you?"

Her breath caught for a second. Not now, she couldn't. Now she'd mortgaged her life to the hilt, and she might give all of that to Jarod to protect Flossy. One problem at a time, however. "You don't have to follow me home," she said, pulling the door halfway closed.

"Someone's got to keep watch."

Her shoulders tensed, and for a second she almost let her head fall to the steering wheel. "Christian, you can't sit outside my place all night."

He stepped closer, his presence brushing against her like pressure—not touch, just weight. Heat. "Who says I'm going to sit?"

She rolled her eyes, mostly because her mouth wanted to do something stupid, like smile. Or worse yet, lick that rain right off his face. "Come on. I don't know why you've appointed yourself my protection detail."

"Because you need it." He shut her door for her. Firm, sure.

Her pulse ticked hard in her throat.

Through the glass, she could still see his face, backlit by the tavern's outside lights. Her gaze dropped, uninvited, to his mouth. He'd kissed her twice, much better than the dreams she'd had about him. Reality was better when it came to Christian Osprey.

Did she want a third kiss?

Yes. But not here. Not with her life still on fire.

She blew out a breath and started the engine. The fan kicked up with a weak wheeze. Dust, and maybe the faint trace of motor oil from somewhere under the dash. Still, it was familiar. "Whatever," she muttered, more to herself than him.

She pulled onto the road and noted the headlights catching movement behind her. Brock's truck fell in close. It was entirely possible that Christian hadn't asked permission to borrow it. Probably hadn't even said a word. That made her smile before she could stop it.

Not because it was right.

Because it was so him.

She turned on the radio for some background noise. Her mind was already spinning faster than the beat with too many problems stacking on top of each other with no room to breathe.

What was she going to do about Jarod?

She really would give him everything. Just wipe the slate clean and let him win if he'd promise to destroy the video. But no. That wasn't safe. She'd have to see it be deleted, and she'd need some sort of guarantee that other copies were destroyed, if there were some. She owed that to Flossy, who'd been there her whole life.

Flossy, who had stepped in with grace and kindness after the plane went down and the world flipped inside out. Her parents, both gone, in a single crash right after her eighteenth birthday. It had taken her years to be able to fly again. Years to uncurl her hands from the armrest without shaking.

No wonder Ace couldn't get up in a plane.

She pressed the gas harder without realizing it and then turned down the river road. The drop was steep and familiar, but not with this much speed. Her headlights caught movement up ahead. A deer. Off to the side.

She tapped the brakes.

Nothing.

She pushed again.

Still nothing.

Oh, God. She couldn't stop. "Come on," she whispered, pressing the pedal harder. It sank uselessly.

The car picked up speed, its tires humming louder. The road dropped more sharply ahead into tight turns, no shoulder, and no forgiveness. She could already feel gravity fighting her grip.

Her phone buzzed in the seat next to her. She reached into her purse, fingers fumbling and clicked the screen without looking.

Christian's voice came through, low and tight. "Slow the hell down. You almost hit a deer."

"I can't," she bit out, her voice sharp as panic careened through her.

"What do you mean you can't?"

She slammed the brake again, right to the floor. "The brakes aren't working."

Silence. A half second. Maybe less. But it sped her panic up higher until her ears heated. "All right. Can you put the car into park? Your seatbelt's on, isn't it?"

"Of course my seatbelt's on." She grabbed it, yanked it across her chest, and snapped it into place.

"I heard that," Christian muttered.

She gripped the wheel tighter. The trees blurred past faster than they should have. Her tires caught gravel along the edge and pulled her too close to the shoulder. She jerked the wheel to correct, heart pounding in her throat.

"Christian—" Her voice cracked. She didn't finish the sentence. The SUV gained speed. The wheel trembled under her grip. Her breath shortened until all she could feel was the weight of the vehicle and the speed and the steep drop ahead. Panic seized her lungs. "What do I do?"

"Put the vehicle in park."

She shoved the gear lever with all her strength. It didn't budge. "It won't go."

"Okay. Take a deep breath. Just breathe."

She tried. Inhaled sharply. Her lungs didn't want to let go of the air. Her heartbeat hammered in her ears. She jerked the wheel left, barely missing a tree, and her tires skidded sideways. "I'm going faster," she whispered.

"It's okay," Christian said calmly. Too calmly. "Twist the keys. See if you can take the key out."

Hope lit her. Her fingers scrambled for the ignition. Slipped. Scraped the metal. Blood slicked her skin and her eyes blurred. "Oh God. It's not working."

"Stay calm, baby," he said. "You're going to have to go uphill soon, but you've got two quick turns first."

"I know." She barely got the words out. Her throat was too dry. If she could just get uphill, maybe, but then what? She'd have to come down again. "I don't know what to do."

The SUV shuddered under her, its wheels lifting on the next turn. She could feel it, the right side coming up just enough to lose gravity. Shaking, she yanked the wheel to the left.

"Hold on. Drive like you're in Indy. Take the curves. Hug them. Okay?"

"Okay." She could do that. Right? Red edged in from the outside of her vision.

Another deer burst from the trees. She slammed her foot down on the brake with everything she had.

Nothing.

She jerked the wheel again in a motion of pure instinct, and the vehicle launched right.

Off the road.

Into the dark.

She flew high and landed with a hard splash in the freezing-cold river. The impact crushed her against the seatbelt as the SUV hit nose-first, metal shrieking against rocks underwater. She screamed again, but the cold ripped the breath right out of her lungs. Glass cracked and then burst. The sound of water surging into the cabin was deafening. It flooded fast, no warning, icy and ruthless.

She fought to keep her head above the rising water. Her chest heaved, teeth clattering from the sudden cold. The river was deep here. Too deep. She knew that. Locals always warned about this stretch that had an undertow that didn't let go.

The SUV was sinking nose-down, pitching toward the dark bottom. Bubbles exploded around her face. Her hands fumbled for her seatbelt and then stopped. She still had seconds. Maybe.

Christian's voice was gone. Static now.

She couldn't scream again. Couldn't spare the breath. Couldn't afford to waste a single move.

Think. Move. Survive.

She braced one hand against the roof as the water reached her chin, reached for the belt with the other, and yanked the release. It didn't budge. Her fingers shook. Her skin was going numb. She had to get out.

Now.

CHAPTER 23

Christian saw the break in the trees.
The curve should've revealed her taillights. Her SUV always rode a little high, headlights tilted just enough to bounce off the shoulder. But now, nothing.

Empty road.
No lights.
No SUV.

"Damn it." He tightened his grip on the wheel and then yanked it hard, tires skidding sideways in the loose gravel. The truck fishtailed, back end swinging before catching traction and jolting to a stop half at the embankment, half in brush.

He threw it in park, already moving. Didn't shut the door. Didn't even kill the engine. No time. His hand flew to his holster in pure muscle memory and pulled the Glock to toss under the seat before leaping out of the vehicle.

The cold hit immediately, rain and wind biting through his shirt and propelling him toward the rushing river. He hit the rocks, his boots crashing through brush, his lungs already tight.

Going on instinct, knowing exactly where they were in the river, he ducked his head and dove out and down.

The river hit like a goddamn hammer. A solid wall he had to break through. His chest locked. Lungs seized. His arms, his legs, all of him went numb so fast it felt like fire.

He fought the pain and plunged down hard. He opened his eyes. The cold stabbed straight through to his skull. Visibility was shit with mud and silt clouding everything, but he forced his vision through it like he'd been trained. Pushed past the sting, the pressure.

The water enfolded him, encasing him. Panic surged first, and then training took over. He'd been waterboarded before, and he'd been shackled in a small cage. Eons away from this place and this time, but his body remembered.

His mind was stronger.

Amka. Her sweetness in tending to the hummingbirds out back of her tavern every spring. Her absolute kindness when feeding folks down on their luck who'd never be able to pay her. Her fondness of those same old and grizzly trappers who slicked back their hair and trimmed their beards before stepping foot in her establishment. She probably didn't even know that.

Her kindness and light brought them all out of the darkness. Even him. Especially him. She was the only thing that mattered.

There. Headlights, weak and slanted, already ten feet under. The SUV's nose had dug into the riverbed. Bubbles streamed up in angry bursts. It was going fast. Too fast.

Every local knew this spot. This river didn't mess around. It dropped deep here, a cut between rocks worn by decades of runoff and bad luck. If she wasn't out in the next sixty seconds, he was pulling a body.

No.

Not happening.

His hand found the knife strapped to his boot. Steel to fingers. Good grip. He angled his body down and swam with tight, snapping kicks. Short bursts. Controlled. The current shoved him sideways. He slammed into something hard and submerged, a branch or rock or both, but he didn't stop. His ribs burned but he pushed through.

He reached the driver's side.

She was still there, dark hair floating around her too pale face pressed against the window, eyes wide and glassy. But moving. A beat behind the panic was a flicker of recognition. She saw him.

He slammed the hilt of the knife against the glass.

Once.

Twice.

Third time—crack.

The front window burst to match the back one. More water surged in like it had been waiting. She jerked back and was sucked under. He went in after her, the force of the flood nearly taking him with it.

She fought the seatbelt as her hands clawed at the buckle, twisting and pushing. No give.

He jammed the knife in and sawed the belt at her waist. One, two seconds, and the thing snapped. Then he pulled her beneath the shoulder strap.

She came free, floating into his arms. Her body was heavy with soaked clothes, her limbs sluggish, her mouth slack. But her eyes remained open. Barely.

He grabbed her around the ribs, twisted, and kicked for the exit. The glass was fully shattered. He shoved them through it, turning his body to shield her from the frame's jagged edge.

Up.

The surface was too far.

He kicked harder but couldn't feel his feet. His thighs were locking. His vision blurred from the pressure and cold.

Air. Just get to air.

They broke through.

He sucked in a ragged breath and felt her body twitch in his arms. Her face was against his neck, lips parting, her mouth freezing cold. She coughed.

Still breathing.

The river didn't stop. The current pulled them sideways, churning beneath them, freezing and ruthless. He adjusted his grip and kicked again. The rocks weren't far, but Mother Nature fought him every step.

Amka couldn't help and felt like dead weight, but that didn't matter. It was better that she wasn't fighting him or the water. He had them both.

She was alive.

His boots slid over slick rocks. He stumbled, lost traction, went under for half a second, and then exploded back up, dragging her with him. The current tried to twist them. He cursed out loud and shoved forward, planting one foot after another until they were out of the rush.

Barely.

The river spat them onto the bank.

He dropped to his knees, her weight in his lap, water streaming off both of them. He could hear the truck engine still running in the distance, muffled by trees and wind and the pounding in his ears.

She coughed violently, turning into his body.

"Amka," he said, voice raw. He leaned in close to her face as he forced himself to stand, cradling her against his chest. Water sluiced off him but not enough. His clothes weighed tons.

She didn't answer.

He cupped the back of her neck, rough hands trembling as he forced her head back. "Come on."

She coughed again and spit out half the river onto his torso.

His eyes closed for a split second. The pressure in his chest cracked and released. "Good," he muttered, stumbling toward his truck. "You're good. You stay with me."

Because she had no idea. No idea how many times he'd

watched her from across the room and known she was the only soft thing left in this frozen place. No idea she'd already saved him. And he wasn't about to let her go under now.

AMKA SURFACED to reality in flashes. Heat blared against her face, the truck's vents roaring with impressive power, but it barely registered through the cold that owned her bones. Her skin burned and froze at the same time, like her body couldn't decide which direction to go. Then the engine cut, and strong hands pulled her sideways across the seat.

Christian. She might've mumbled his name.

He lifted her out of the warm vehicle and into the drilling rain, holding her against his hard chest. His drenched shirt bunched under her palm, and she tried to push away.

He didn't let her.

The cold slapped her again, but he didn't stop. He stumbled up the steps and through the cabin door that crashed open against the wall. Then she felt him—really felt him—tearing at soaked clothes, stripping both of them down fast, efficient, like fabric was the only thing keeping her from dying. Maybe it was. She wanted to speak but her jaw barely worked. He didn't care. He was already pulling her toward the bathroom, already saving her. Again.

A faucet turned and then water fell in the shower.

He lifted her and placed her inside already billowing steam. The first thing she felt was warmth. Not the gentle, toasty kind that drifted from a fire or the slow simmer of good bourbon, but a blistering, bone-deep heat. It came in waves, scorching and overwhelming. Like she was thawing too fast.

Then came the pain.

A thousand tiny needles pricked across her skin, nerves lighting up as blood returned to the frozen parts of her body.

She couldn't move. Not because she was restrained but because she was wrapped. Encased in hard muscle, iron arms, and what she was pretty sure was the heating equivalent of a human furnace.

Christian. Her back to his front. Hot water sliding over them both.

"Let your body relax. The pain will be quick," he rumbled, his mouth above her head.

She wasn't sure she could answer even if she wanted to. Her throat burned raw from swallowing the river. Her lips were numb. But her brain? Fully functional. Maybe because awareness hit her harder than the airbag had earlier. She was naked with freaking Christian Osprey.

She might actually die. From exposure…or embarrassment. She gave a half-hearted attempt to move away, forcing her eyelids to open and see the slate rock side of the shower. Had he placed that there himself? The pain began to ebb. More awareness tingled through her. A lot more.

Her shoulders only reached his chest, which was hard and shockingly hot even though most of the spray was blasting her. Her butt rested against his thighs. She closed her eyes again as she realized what was nudging her lower back.

Was he hard?

The night flashed through her head. The river, her desperation, the hope when he arrived on the other side of the glass. When he broke it and tugged her free.

He'd saved her.

She turned, surprised he let her, and rubbed both of her still chilled hands up the hard planes of his chest. A low hum wandered through her. She glanced at the osprey's talon over his shoulder and leaned over to kiss it.

He jolted. Slightly, but enough that she noticed. "Amka."

"Yeah," she mumbled, sliding her hands up to his shoulders and digging in. Her legs still trembled, but she forced herself up on her toes to wander her mouth across his sharp and whiskered jawline. A slight pain ticked through her lips, and she didn't care. "Thank you for saving me."

He instantly grasped her shoulders and set her away from him.

She looked up, surprised, and then stopped breathing.

His eyes had gone a deep hue, both colors, and his nostrils had flared. "No."

"Yes." She was tired of half living. Tired of being scared. Life could end in a second, and right now, she had a fully aroused and hotter than Hades male in the shower with her. One she not only wanted but definitely liked. She scratched her nails down his torso and nearly moaned. God. So much muscle and strength.

He grasped her wrists, pulling her free.

Irritation clocked through her, and she jerked her head back, staring at him. "You want me." It wasn't like he was hiding his rather impressive, okay, *very* impressive, erection.

"Not like this." His tone sounded final but the red filling his handsome cheeks showed a guy fighting himself. "Not because you're grateful."

"Oh." She half laughed, feeling suddenly warmer. Much. "I'm not *that* grateful, Christian." He still held her wrists, so she stepped into him, skin to skin. "I'm tired of fighting us. This. Whatever it is."

His hold loosened.

Encouraged, she stayed right where she was. "I'm glad we're both alive. What if we weren't? What if the river had won?"

"I wouldn't have let the river win. Nothing hurts you, Amka."

Those words. She was a modern woman who owned her own business. She didn't take orders from anybody. But those words and that tone. They shot a need through her that should've shocked her. Should've warned her.

It was too late for shock or warning.

A slight shudder ran through him. She swallowed and leaned in to bite beneath his pec. "Stop fighting yourself." Giving in, she licked up to his neck, tasting salt and fresh water. His hold on her wrists tightened, and the small bite made her gasp.

He released her, moving suddenly and tangling his fingers in her wet hair, dragging her head back. "You don't know me."

Another warning? "I do." She tried to tug free and didn't move. Why that shot need through her faster than adrenaline had ever flowed, she'd never figure out. "I know you, Christian," she whispered. "You try to stay distant, and sometimes you do, but if one of your brothers needs you, you're there. If I need you, you're there. If someone in the town needs you, you're there."

"Not all of me."

Now those words did catch her. She stopped and looked up at his brutally carved face. "I know," she whispered. And she did. She saw when he'd had enough and needed to be free. To be out in the wild, where sometimes he belonged. "I like you the way you are." She'd never know where those words came from, but she meant them.

He blinked. Just once. Then he moved, his fist tightening in her hair, his other hand going to her hip and lifting her. Her butt hit the smooth rock wall and he stepped into her, his forehead lowering to hers. His eyes blazed pure fire. "You sure?"

She couldn't breathe. Somehow, she was ready for him. *Right now.* "Yes."

His mouth dropped to hers, hard and fast, while he began pushing inside her. Slow. Measured. Taking his time and letting her soften around him in increments. How was she ready for him that fast?

Holy crap. She closed her eyes and kissed him back, her knees automatically pressing against his flanks. Pain ticked through her and she murmured, so he deepened the kiss, taking her over, throwing her out of her mind.

He overwhelmed her, keeping her in place.

Finally, eons later, he was fully embedded inside her, his mouth still working hers, his strength obvious.

She moved, needing more. Wanting him. He more than filled her, and she wanted him to move now.

He did.

Not gently. Not hesitantly. Like a man who'd been holding back for too long and finally had permission to let go.

His hand stayed locked in her hair, the other gripping her hip with brutal control as he pulled back and drove in again, deep and deliberate. She gasped, her back arching against the wall. Slick rock met her spine, but all she felt was him, heat, power, and hunger.

He made no sound, but his body spoke loud enough. Every thrust was a declaration, every grind a confession. He wanted this. Her. All those times she'd caught him looking at her, watching her at the tavern, as if he wanted to be right here.

She had felt his intent.

The pace built fast. Each stroke carved her open and filled her back in, pushing her higher, stretching the tension tight, and then even tighter. Her fingers dug into his shoulders, then slid down his muscled chest. It was all she could do not to come apart right there.

"Christian," she whispered, or maybe begged. She wasn't sure. Didn't much care.

He pulled back just enough to meet her eyes, his breath ragged, his mouth damp from hers. "I've got you."

He slammed into her now, sharp and rhythmic, the kind of force that stole thought, breath, past and future. Her body curled around him, legs trembling against his hips, held aloft only by his strength and whatever the hell this thing was between them.

Pressure built, spun, twisted. She tried to hold it. Tried to make this moment last longer. But he drove her mercilessly toward the edge, each stroke hitting some secret part of her no one else had ever found.

She shattered.

The climax wasn't sweet or soft. It was fierce. A raw, burning contraction that shook her from the inside out. Her vision blacked at the edges, and her body seized around him with a cry torn from the deepest part of her. She might've said his name again. Might've sworn. Might've sobbed.

He didn't stop. He cursed low and sharp in her ear, the sound of a man fighting for control and losing. His rhythm stuttered, then locked. One final thrust. And with a guttural growl, he followed her over, hips pressed tight, his body shaking against hers like the storm hadn't stopped, just moved inside them.

Silence fell.

Not from peace, but from aftermath.

He held her there, pinned and panting, his face against her neck, his lips brushing a soft kiss against her jugular that spiraled down to her heart.

She swallowed and dropped her head, right between his neck and shoulder, her body shutting down. Still there, with the shower beating against him and the steam swallowing them both, with him holding her. She relaxed and fell right into a peaceful sleep.

CHAPTER 24

The nightmare caught Christian deep in sleep, and he stilled, eyelids slowly opening. Amka lay curled against him, her sweet butt against his groin. He listened to her breathe and settled himself, sliding from the bed and making sure to keep her covered. He snagged worn jeans from the floor and yanked them on, his skin crawling from the dream.

He had to get outside. Now.

Padding barefoot across the chilled floor, he walked outside and carefully shut the door. Fresh air and freedom smashed into him, so he made his way across the small porch to sit, resting his feet on the bottom step. One by one, he forced each muscle in his body to release. Sometimes the nightmares tightened him into a raw ball of fury, but now, he could relax. Slowly.

The rain had stopped, leaving the sky a light pink and gold as dawn arrived. Birds chirped in the distance, and water dripped from branches and eaves. He pulled in the fresh air, watching the trees, calming himself. Even so, he knew how fucked up he was right now. He had a beautiful woman with a pure heart in his bed, and he was outside, by himself.

What had he been thinking taking her like that in the shower?

He scrubbed both hands down his face, his whiskers catching his palms. He'd been too rough with her last night, and that was him exhausted after fighting the river. At full strength, or even with more than he'd had, he wasn't gentle. Didn't like it gentle. She deserved better. A lot. At least deserved a little foreplay, which normally he enjoyed. Not gentle, though. Not even close.

She deserved more than staying with a guy who had to escape outside, to get away from people, more often than not. That bed in there had gotten more use the last week than it had the entire year before. He usually slept outside. Even when the weather turned worse—turned freezing. No woman would want to live like that.

Not that she'd expressed any desire to stay with him. The other day, she'd been trying to piss him off with the talk about babies and homes. Been trying to get him to back off. She'd make adorable kids.

Out there, by himself, he could imagine a little girl with her eyes and sassy attitude. Maybe a boy with those same eyes and her ability to be kind. To care about people. They'd be lucky to have her.

What did he have to offer? The promise of safety and nothing else? He could provide that from afar. Make sure nobody hurt her or anyone she loved.

But could he watch her with another man? Definitely not Jarod. The woman had punched that jackass in the stomach the night before, and Christian hadn't had a chance to figure that one out. How angry had Jarod been? Would he have cut her brakes? If not, then who?

Christian's muscles tensed again. At least now he could be sure that the fire and then the sniper had been after her. Why did somebody want her dead? They sure as shit didn't care how it happened. Fire, bullets, and now drowning. The end result was all they were going after. Jarod Teller was the only person he could imagine wanting her dead.

But why? They weren't even married. Yet.

No *yet*. He would not accept a *yet*. Amka might deserve better than Christian, but she deserved *much* better than Jarod.

Movement sounded from inside, and he remained in place, giving her some space. No doubt she regretted the night. She was still bruised from the explosive fire, had to be injured from the car wreck, and he'd taken her up against a stone wall with all the finesse of a rutting bull. He'd be lucky if she didn't try to shoot him.

Minutes passed, and the door opened behind him. He steeled himself for the demand to take her home.

She padded out to hand him a steaming cup of coffee. "I borrowed more socks."

He glanced to the side to see a dingy pair of white-ish socks with the heels up to her calves and the tops to her knees. Her thighs were bare and sexy as any mythical siren. She had the comforter wrapped around her shoulders, and she'd pulled on one of his shirts. He accepted the coffee, masking his surprise. "Thanks."

She sat next to him, placing her coffee next to her. Then she took one edge of the bedspread and stretched it across his bare back. "Help me."

Wait—what? He obeyed, tucking them both inside the warmth.

"Thank you. It's cold out here." She cuddled closer to him, tucking the cover down her shoulder to secure beneath her thigh before retrieving her coffee. "It's pretty, though."

Most women would've been pissed at finding him gone after sex. This one was confusing the hell out of him. Not knowing what to say, he took a big drink of the coffee. She'd made it strong, just like he wanted. "Sorry," he murmured.

Her bare thigh was plastered against his. "For what?"

He cut her a look from the side of his eye. Her hair had dried around her shoulders, thick and straight. Whisker burn covered her chin from his kisses, and the sight should've made him feel bad. It didn't. A sense of possession flowed through him, and he tried to shut it down. Somehow. "For leaving the bed."

She shrugged, her small shoulder bumping his arm. "Why? You like it outside. It's nice out here, although a little chilly. The coffee helps."

Why wasn't she mad? He scanned the forest around them, making sure she was safe. Tika had dropped by for a scratch behind the ears before bounding into the forest again. The wildlife made plenty of sound, so nothing was out of place there. Except the woman sitting next to him. "I don't like being inside for long." He had to get her to stop being so nice.

"I know."

What was happening? "Doesn't that bother you?"

"No. Why would it?"

His mouth opened and then closed. "I sleep outside all the time."

"I figured that."

Oh. Okay. So she wasn't really thinking of having anything with him. Good. She didn't care where he slept. That was good. All right. Irritation clocked through him, and he shoved it down. "How are you feeling?"

"A little sore, but my head is clear. The seatbelt bruised my ribs, but other than that, I'm good." Her voice remained soft. Quiet. "Do you think someone cut my brakes?"

A fresh anger slapped him, and he kept his body calm. "Yeah. I called the Millers to get the rig out of the water, but it's going to take a few days for them to get the right equipment. Why would Jarod want you dead?"

She jolted slightly against him. "He doesn't."

"I can't think of anybody else," Christian said. If she tried to defend that jerk, he might lose his mind. "Why did you punch him last night?"

She shifted against him, both of her hands cupping the mug. "That's, ah, personal." At the statement, she ducked her head, as if she knew how stupid that sounded.

"I was inside you just a few hours ago, and you slept in my arms all night. We've gone *way* beyond personal."

She sighed and took another sip. "I know, and last night doesn't change anything. But I don't regret a second."

"Neither do I," he growled before he could stop himself. "I know we can't be, can't have anything permanent, but no way am I allowing you to marry that jackass."

"Allowing?" Her voice rose. "Sorry, buddy. One night of sex doesn't give you a say in my life."

Why not? Amka wasn't a woman who slept with a guy and then moved on. She sure wasn't someone who cheated on a man she loved. "You were tight as hell last night, and no way have you been sleeping with Jarod."

She swallowed. "That's inappropriate, so watch yourself. And again, that's personal."

"Tell me something's *personal* one more time, and you're going over my knee." He would love to see his palm print on her ass. The mental image almost had him reaching for her.

She plunked her mug down on the rough wooden porch. "I've had enough of this. It's time for me to go home."

That was it. Just it. He gently put his mug next to him and hefted her onto his lap, cradling her. Twisting one hand in her hair, he pulled back her head until she had no choice but to meet his gaze. Oh, she fought him, but she didn't have a chance. He let her struggle as long as she wanted, holding her there until she finally relented. "You done?"

The look she gave him might've shriveled another man's balls. It just aroused him. Again. She then rolled her eyes.

"Knock it off." Yeah, she sounded a bit breathless, and it wasn't just from the struggle.

He liked to explain things clearly when he could. "Here's the deal. We're not moving until you tell me what's going on with Jarod. You don't love him. I don't even think you *like* him. There's no way you want to marry him, which leads me to a couple of conclusions."

Her jaw clenched and her chin firmed in a way that tempted him to take a bite right out of it. "Which are?" Now she sounded haughty.

Amusement mixed with the irritation inside him. "Either you're afraid of him, or he has something on you. Either way, I'm going to handle it." Yeah. Last night gave him that right. The least he could do was free her from Jarod.

"You're wrong." Her voice quivered just slightly, and her gaze dropped.

He tightened his hold on her hair and pulled. She gasped and those eyelids flew wide open. Damn, she had pretty eyes. Nearly black with depth and intrigue. "We're not moving. Can stay here all day and into the night. At some point, you're gonna want to go inside. We're not."

Pink spiraled through her cheekbones, and pure stubborn lit her expression.

Ah. All right. So it was a contest of wills. Apparently it was a lesson she needed to learn.

He kept her in place and continued scanning the area for threats.

She lasted an entire hour. Truth to shit, she impressed him. That was a stubborn to the soul woman. He liked that. After an outraged huff, she spoke. "Fine, but you have to promise not to do anything."

"Nope."

She gave a half-hearted struggle, no surprise flashing across her face when he didn't let her move an inch. "You're such a jerk."

"Yep."

Her sigh held a nice amount of feminine frustration. No doubt she was planning his demise. "Let me go. I need to use the bathroom."

"Nope."

She swung and slapped his chest but couldn't get much momentum from her position.

"Careful, cutie. I hit back."

She shifted her weight, her butt tightening as if she knew just what he meant. Good. It was nice being on the same page. "Fine," she exploded. "I steadied Flossy while she shot Hank, and Jarod videoed the entire thing. He's been blackmailing me. Said we just had to be engaged to give him respectability, but now he wants all of my money. And he says he wants to get married for real."

Shock careened through Christian. Not in centuries would he have figured this one out. "You helped Flossy?" Flossy and Hank had been in love, and when the cancer became too painful, Hank had asked her to help him find relief. Christian had thought one of his brothers had helped and had been relieved when Flossy wasn't charged. Hank had been a good guardian and a strong man. He wouldn't have asked for help unless he really needed it.

"Yeah," Amka whispered. "I'm sorry, Christian."

He placed a kiss on her upturned nose. "You didn't do anything wrong." Finally, something made sense. "I'll take care of Jarod."

"You can't." Tears filled her eyes, nearly throwing him into a rage. He kept his expression calm. "Jarod made copies, and if anything happens to him, he has a friend who'll send the video to the authorities. I don't much care about me, but I can't let Flossy go to prison at her age."

Of course she was worried about Flossy and not herself. "Don't worry. This is now my problem." By the time he was done with Jarod, Christian would have all copies of the video. His phone buzzed from inside the cabin, so he stood with her in his arms and strode inside, placing her gently on her feet before grabbing the phone off the table.

She stretched her neck.

He lifted an eyebrow. "Thought you needed to use the bathroom."

She shrugged. "Nope. I lied."

Yeah, he had figured. He lifted the phone, finally relaxing now that he knew what the problem was that he needed to fix. Jarod Teller. Easy enough. "What?"

"Are you at your place?" Brock asked.

Brock didn't sound right. "Yeah. Why?" Christian tensed.

"Tell me Amka is with you."

How did Brock know that? Why did it matter? "Affirmative. Why?" Christian stressed the word this time.

"Because Jarod Teller's body was just found in his truck. In Amka's driveway. You both need to come in. Now."

CHAPTER 25

They'd been driving in silence for ten minutes until Amka couldn't take it any longer. "What else did Brock say?" She settled into the passenger seat of Brock's truck. No doubt the sheriff wanted it back.

Christian's hands appeared loose on the steering wheel. His very talented hands. "Just that Jarod's body was found close to your house."

"I need clothes," she said, glancing down.

"We'll swing by your place on the way."

Her entire body ached, and not just from plunging into the river. The aftereffects of last night still tingled across her skin. Christian had been amazing, and he'd actually looked surprised that morning when she brought him coffee. She wasn't sure what he'd expected, but she hadn't had the courage to ask.

They reached the end of her driveway, and Christian slowed the vehicle.

Amka's mouth dropped open at the sight of the yellow crime scene tape stretched across the long drive leading to her house. "More yellow tape." The tape around the burned building next to the tavern was finally gone.

Dutch walked out of the trees on the far side, his gaze sharp and serious as he moved toward the SUV, looking natural in his uniform.

She rolled down her window. "Dutch, why is there a crime scene—?" Her attention caught on a vehicle farther down the road. The front end peeked out before the turn that led up to her house. Her stomach flipped. "Oh my God. Is that Jarod's truck?" It was a battered, yellow old Datsun. No mistaking it.

"I can't really tell you anything," Dutch said, gaze shifting to Christian. "We're not on the case. I've just been asked to secure the scene until the forensics team gets here from Anchorage. Supposedly they're on the next flight."

Christian sat back. "How bad?"

"Can't talk about it. We need to separate this from your work with the AWT right now." Dutch flicked a glance at the oversized shirt covering most of Amka.

Her bare thighs chilled. "Can I go inside really quickly? I need clothes." Heat flushed into her face. She'd obviously spent the night with Christian.

Dutch winced. "I'm sorry, darlin', but you can't go inside the house."

She stilled. "Was Jarod killed in my house?"

"We don't know. His body was found in the truck." Dutch planted a hand on the door. "I'm not supposed to talk to you about this. But be smart. Tons of folks saw you punch Teller at the bar, and I also had to report finding you and the doctor falling out of the guy's crappy duplex. You really do need to go to town and speak with the troopers. This is their case, not Brock's."

Christian asked, his voice a low rumble, "No?"

"No. The troopers are in town, and I think it'd be best if outsiders handled this. Not that they're going to give Brock a choice. Now isn't the time to fight for the right to have a sheriff." Dutch sighed. "Trust me, they ain't happy about that situation."

"I don't care," Christian said. "We've always had a sheriff here and usually we've stayed out of the troopers' way."

Dutch straightened. "I agree. So let's continue doing that so we can keep Brock as your sheriff, because the town needs him."

This was too much. How could Jarod have died in his truck right in front of her house? Had he gone inside? He had never cared about boundaries, so it was possible. What if he'd been killed in her home? Amka looked over at Christian. "We should probably get going if they're waiting for us."

Christian gave Dutch a look. "I need to talk to you afterward about another attack on Amka last night. Her brakes were cut."

Dutch sucked in a breath and leaned in, his gaze scouring her. Concern glowed in his faded brown eyes. "Are you okay?"

"Yes." But was she? The world kept tilting sideways, like her center of gravity had shifted and hadn't reset.

"I'll call you," Christian said, his jaw visibly clenching.

Dutch stepped away from the truck.

Amka rolled up her window and shivered. "I can't believe somebody killed Jarod."

"We don't know that."

"We don't know what?" she asked.

Christian turned back down the road toward town. "We don't know that someone killed him. All we know is his body was found."

That was true. She looked down at her bare legs and the socks still covering her feet. "May I borrow your phone?"

"Sure." He reached into his back pocket and pulled out his cell phone, handing it to her. "I take it yours is in the bottom of the river."

"Everything. My whole purse is," she murmured. Her wallet, phone, ID, the bar keys, and even her favorite lip gloss were in that purse. It had probably washed all the way down the river by now. She looked at the phone. It was locked.

"Zero-eight-zero-two," Christian said. "My code."

She glanced over at him. "Isn't that your birthday?"

"How do you know that?"

"I don't know. I must've heard it at some point," she said, frowning. "Didn't your brothers try to throw you a party at the tavern a few years back?"

He angled his head to glance up at the somewhat blue sky. "We only lasted inside for about a half hour, and then we took off. Went snowmobiling."

She studied him, wanting to know more. How did he feel about last night? She couldn't find the right way to ask him, so she went with the next best question. "How do you know your birthday?"

The legend of how Hank found the young Osprey brothers after an avalanche in some tiny settlement in the middle of nowhere was well known. They all looked like brothers—or cousins, or something—so they were probably related. But no records had ever been found.

"The circus came through when we were kids, and Hank paid a fortune teller to give each of us a birthday. He said it mattered and that we should have something normal." Christian's mouth twitched, not quite a smile. "She said that August second should be my birthday because I was quiet, stubborn, and always watching the exits. That I was a Leo. I didn't argue."

Amka studied him. "I think that's kind of sweet." It made sense, too. Leos were known for protectiveness and strength, and that early August day occurred in the deep of summer where a man like him would be most alive in the wild and wouldn't want to be boxed in by four walls. "I get that. August is when everything starts to shift. The land, the air, and even the forest feel like they're holding quietly with calmness above an oncoming wild storm."

He glanced at her. "Storm?"

"Yeah." She'd only tapped the edges of that last night. He held back and she knew it. "There's a lot bubbling under your surface. I always suspected it but now I know."

"You don't know. A few hours together doesn't give you insight. Don't make me into something I'm not. I'm not a good guy."

Right. Because good guys didn't jump into freezing water, risk their own lives, just to save a woman who was engaged to somebody else. She'd argue later. Right now, she typed in the code and then quickly called Daisy.

"Hello?" Daisy answered with a cautious note in her voice.

"Hey, it's Amka. On Christian's phone."

"Oh wow. Why is that?"

Amka shifted her weight, acutely aware of how wrong everything felt, right down to not wearing her own jeans. "That's definitely a long story. But for now, are you at home?"

"No. I'm at the tavern. You weren't here to open it."

Amka's brain just wasn't locking in. "Thank you for doing that for me."

"Of course."

"I need a favor."

Glasses clinked. "Anytime."

Amka needed to start thinking clearly. "Is Nixi around?"

"Yeah. She's slurping coffee with a bunch of her friends. They're filming more videos. Why?"

Amka thought through the specials of the day. Rudolph could easily handle the kitchen, and if Nixi would work the tables, they should be okay. "I'll meet you in the back room of the tavern where I keep an extra change of clothes. Daisy, I need a lawyer."

∼

CHRISTIAN INSISTED on driving them the few blocks from the tavern to the sheriff's station, his eyes sweeping the rooftops. Only a few nights had passed since someone shot at them, but it already felt like years. He parked right out front and ushered them inside, covering their backs.

Inside, Brock lounged against the counter while Flossy sat behind it, alert as always. The two troopers stood near the hallway leading to the offices and interrogation room.

Flossy looked up. "Oh, Amka. I'm so sorry about Jarod." The elderly woman had run the front of the sheriff's station for years.

"Thanks," Amka said.

Brock pushed off the counter. "Christian, why don't I talk to you outside while the troopers speak with Amka?"

"No. I'm going in with her," Christian said.

"No, you're not," Jeb cut in. "We'll speak with you next."

Christian leveled them both with a cold look. "I'm fine."

Amka patted his arm. Both troopers tracked the movement.

"Come on into the conference room," Jeb said, opening the door.

"Hey, Amka," Amos called from the basement. "We have a lawyer in town now. She should be with you." Amos had been their resident weather guru for eons, and he lived in the basement, rarely venturing out.

Amka paused and raised her voice enough to reach him. "Thanks, Amos. I brought Daisy." She shivered and stepped into the conference room, aware of every inch of herself. No makeup with her hair a mess, though she'd at least brushed it out at the tavern. She sat at the table next to Daisy, across from the female trooper with the red hair. It was time to be formal, so she looked up and focused on the lead officer. "Trooper Pontevo, what happened to Jarod?"

"Amka, we met the other day. Call me Jeb." He shut the door

behind himself and walked around to sit next to his new partner. "We're friendly here."

"You can call me Paige, as well. Where were you last night?" Paige jumped right into the questioning.

Amka sighed. There was no point in dancing around it. "I was at Christian's. He has a cabin."

Paige placed her phone on the table and rattled off the names of everyone present as well as the date and time. "Sorry about that. I forgot the recording. You spent the night with Christian Osprey last night?"

Daisy shook her head. "That's irrelevant." She sounded like a badass lawyer all of a sudden.

"If he's her alibi—" Paige started.

"Alibi?" Daisy cut in. "We don't even know what happened yet. In fact, why don't you fill us in, Jeb?"

Wow. That edge in Daisy's voice could cut glass. Impressive. Amka felt her shoulders start to relax.

Jeb didn't flinch. "Jarod Teller was found in his truck, in your driveway, after being shot in the head."

Shock ripped through her. She gasped. "Somebody shot him?"

"Yep," Jeb said. "And there's no way it was self-inflicted. I could tell just from one look at the body, which has already been sent to Anchorage for an autopsy. We had a transport helicopter that brought new fire equipment to town, so the timing worked. Unfortunately, that means the body of Eli Warner stays in the cooler here a few more days. We think Jarod's truck was leaving your house based on how it was positioned. Did you see him last night?"

"No." Amka's voice dropped. "Not after the fight we had at the bar." Why did she have to fight with him in front of everyone? "He left and I worked late before heading home. My brakes were cut and I crashed into the river."

"Excuse me?" Jeb's brow wrinkled in disbelief.

She nodded. "I went into the river."

Daisy swiveled to look at her. "Are you all right?"

"Christian saved my life," Amka said. "But my rig's still at the bottom of the river. We've got to pull it out."

"Wait a minute," Paige said, leaning back and raising a hand. "This is your story? That you got in a fight with your fiancé last night. Then you were driving home, somebody cut your brakes, and you crashed into a river. Christian Osprey saved you. Then you stayed the night with him, while somebody murdered your fiancé in your driveway. That's your timeline?"

Amka swallowed hard. "It's the truth."

"What were you and Jarod fighting about?" Jeb asked.

"Money," she said without hesitation. "I mortgaged my house and the tavern to go into business with Ace Osprey. Jarod wanted the cash for his motel. I figured he had enough funds from the insurance payout for his motel."

Paige's brows drew down. "Yet another fire in town? What a coincidence, huh?"

Not a convenient one. Amka looked at Daisy, who was studying the troopers.

"How long have you been engaged?" Paige asked.

"Since New Year's." That had been when Jarod first blackmailed her.

Paige leaned forward. "I see. And yet you stayed the night with Christian Osprey last night, correct?"

Heat rushed into Amka's face. "Yes."

Paige placed elbows on the table. "Do you feel bad about cheating on him?"

So much for them all being friends.

"That's irrelevant," Daisy snapped before Amka could speak. "Stick to the facts."

"I can stick to whatever I damn well want to," Paige said without even looking at Daisy. Her focus never left Amka. "Did anybody else see you last night?"

"No," Amka answered. Her back was straight, her tone calm, but her stomach had gone cold. She felt like she was gripping the edge of something slippery, and her fingers were starting to give.

"Nobody saw you drive away?"

"I have no idea."

Jeb cocked his head. "Nobody saw you crash into the river?"

"Just Christian. He was behind me in Brock's truck, and he saved me."

Paige didn't blink. "Why was he behind you? Did you plan to meet up?"

All of this sounded so bad. Terrible. "No. He just wanted to see me home safely after everything that's been going on. That's all." Yet he probably would've watched outside her home all night. If he had, maybe Jarod would still be alive.

Paige drummed her fingers on the tabletop. "Did anybody see you at the river or going to Christian's house? In other words, can anybody verify what you're saying?"

"No." Each answer dug a little deeper, like Amka was carving her own grave, one monosyllable at a time. Her heart thudded under her ribs, steady and dull.

Paige sat back, her expression unreadable. "When was the last time you saw Jarod?"

"I already told you," Amka said, voice tight. "Last night. At the bar." Her throat was dry, her palms damp against her jeans.

Daisy's chair scraped against the floor as she leaned forward. "Stop asking her the same questions. She's not going to answer them on repeat just to make you feel like you're doing your job."

"We have to ask. This isn't making sense, and you know it, counselor," Jeb said.

Amka's fingernails dug into her palms. Her body felt heavy, like the adrenaline from the morning had drained out and left her made of lead. She glanced at Daisy, then back at the two troopers.

"So let me get this straight," Paige said, voice ice-cold. "You cheated on your fiancé, and your alibi is the man you cheated with?"

Amka didn't answer. She didn't have anything left to say that would make this look any better.

Paige turned to Jeb. "Doesn't Osprey have military experience?"

"I believe so," Jeb said quietly.

The implication settled into the room like a weight. Cold. Heavy. Final.

"Do you cheat on your fiancé often?" Paige asked, cool and direct.

Amka pressed her lips together, not seeing a reason to answer that.

Paige wasn't deterred. "Dutch found you and the doctor, who we'll talk to later, breaking and entering Jarod's home. Want to explain that?"

"I forgot my key." Amka wouldn't say more than that. She couldn't get May in trouble, too.

Paige was quiet for moments. Waiting. Amka had watched a criminal show detailing the interrogation method. If the silence stretched long enough, the interviewee usually started talking to fill the quiet.

Amka didn't.

Respect filtered through Paige's eyes before she switched topics. "Is there anybody else we should know about? Other lovers of yours? Someone who might've been jealous enough to kill Jarod?"

"No," Amka burst out.

Daisy folded her arms. "That's quite a reach."

"It's a fair question," Jeb said. "Let's not pretend it isn't. How long have you and Christian Osprey been involved?"

Amka paused. She didn't even know how to answer that. "We're not. I didn't say we were seeing each other."

"But you went home with him last night," Jeb said.

Amka needed to get out of there. Now. She wasn't ashamed of her night with Christian, and she didn't want to share the details with anybody. Especially the troopers. "Yes. We were freezing from the river, got into the truck, and went to Christian's to warm up. I stayed there. We haven't been dating."

"So it was a one-night stand?" Paige's voice was flat.

"Careful," Daisy warned.

Paige didn't blink. "Was it?"

"I don't know what it was," Amka said. Her temples ached. This was too much.

Jeb lifted his chin. "Jarod was shot. Close range. Not self-inflicted. Do you know anyone else who might've wanted him dead?"

"Neither of us wanted him dead," Amka said.

"Right," Paige said softly. "Obviously not. What about you and Jarod? There have supposedly been attempts on your life this last week. What were you and Jarod into that has you both in so much danger?"

Nothing. They weren't even together. But if Amka admitted that, she'd have to admit to the blackmail. To what she and Flossy had done. "I'm finished talking. Arrest me or let me go." She stood, and Daisy did the same.

Paige smiled. "I don't think we need to do that. Not today, anyway."

CHAPTER 26

Christian leaned against the hood of Brock's truck, arms crossed, gaze on the rooftops across the street. Morning light reflected off the windows and metal, throwing slivers of glare into his eyes, but he didn't blink. He wasn't looking for anything in particular. No scopes were aimed at them. Watching helped him think and anchored him in his body, which still felt like it hadn't caught up from the chaos of the last twelve hours.

He didn't like standing still. He didn't appreciate being exposed like this, with his back uncovered and the wrong kind of quiet pressing in. But he also wasn't ready to go inside. Not yet.

Brock stood a few feet away, boots planted, face tight. "You gonna tell me what's going on with Amka?"

Christian didn't move. "Somebody cut her brakes and she crashed into the river last night. Got her home, got her warmed up, and then you called me this morning to come down here."

Brock's chin lifted and his eyes narrowed. "Her brakes were cut?"

"I think so. She lost control on the river road because the

brakes failed completely." Christian lifted one shoulder, the smallest shrug, though anger spiraled tight in his chest. Not panic. He didn't do panic. But whatever lived beneath his skin had teeth, and it was gnawing at him now. "We'll have the Miller boys pull it out once they have the right equipment."

The SUV. It was still in the river. Who had gotten to her brakes that night? He didn't like the idea of security cameras in his town, but maybe it was time to change that thinking.

Brock's eyes flashed. "Why didn't you call me?"

Christian paused. A slight shift in weight, a slow exhale through his nose. The night before, he had forgotten all about the SUV the second he stepped into the shower with Amka. Then he'd stopped thinking entirely. "There was nothing you could do last night. The more immediate concern was getting her warm."

"You've had a thing for her, C. I know it, just because I know you. Now her fiancé is dead after she spent the night with you?"

Christian didn't flinch. Didn't offer a single word. Because there was nothing to refute. Brock knew him too well.

"Still," Brock continued, voice edged and sharp now, "you wouldn't cross that line. Not with an engaged woman. Not even for her."

Christian wasn't sure that was true anymore. Even if he hadn't known about the blackmail, that the engagement wasn't real, he would've taken her home. He would've undressed her out of wet clothes and held her until her body stopped shaking. He wouldn't have sent her away. Not even to keep his conscience clean.

Especially when she made the first move. Even he wasn't that strong. "Maybe we just slept."

"Bullshit." Brock scrubbed a rough hand through his thick, dark hair. His jaw flexed. "What aren't you telling me?"

Christian could feel the air change. Like a shift in barometric pressure before a storm. The blackmail sat like a lead weight in his chest as it was the perfect evidence against Amka. Brock was the sheriff, and that meant lines had to stay in place. Christian would protect his brother. "Nothing."

Brock's tone dropped, low and sharp as a blade. "I swear to God. You're going back to this again? We've done the secrets-before-trust routine, remember that? You want another year of radio silence between us? You want to lose this again?"

Christian's jaw flexed, a muscle twitching near his temple. That hit where it was supposed to. Direct and deep. Last year, when everything between them had fractured—when pride, grief, and too much silence had built a wall none of them could break down—that had nearly ended everything. Four brothers who loved each other but couldn't look each other in the eye.

They'd all thought one of them had helped Hank die. And no one had talked about it. They'd let silence rot what should've been unbreakable. They'd been wrong, and it had taken too long to fix it.

Brock didn't let up. "Tell me the truth. All of it. You owe me that."

Christian exhaled through his nose and looked up, a headache forming at the base of his skull. He wouldn't go distant with any of his brothers ever again. "Jarod was blackmailing Amka."

Brock gave one sharp shake of his head. "Blackmailing Amka? Come on. She's never done a thing wrong in her entire life. What in the world could Jarod have on her?"

Christian glanced toward the sheriff's station, then back at his brother. "For what happened to Hank."

The tension snapped between them like a cable pulled too tight. Brock straightened. "Flossy shot Hank."

Christian's chest hurt at the thought. "Amka was there. She helped Flossy steady the gun. I guess she found them on the way to work, and Flossy couldn't do it alone."

Brock's face went pale. His lips parted, but nothing came out. He took a step back.

"He fell into the river after. They didn't mean for him to even get wet. The entire situation happened fast, and they weren't prepared. But who would be? Apparently, Jarod caught them. Somehow. Recorded the entire thing."

Brock's eyes darkened. "He had a video of Hank dying?"

Christian's throat tightened. "Yeah. Jarod took it and used it against her. Forced her into the engagement. Said he wanted to be respectable. That's a lie. He wanted her, and I could see it. I think he would've tried to force her into an actual marriage."

Brock stared at the asphalt, breathing hard. "I can't believe this."

The wind kicked up again. Something banged in the alley behind them that sounded like loose metal, maybe a trash lid. Christian didn't turn to look.

"Jesus," Brock muttered. "So, Amka's fiancé, who was blackmailing her, was murdered the night she stayed with you. The two of you are each other's alibis. Could this get any worse?"

Christian didn't reply. There was nothing to say that would make it sound better. There was only the truth, and it was already heavy enough. The air sat dense between them, filled with heat and silence and the raw edge of too many truths laid bare. Christian let his arms drop to his sides, hands clenched into fists.

Brock eyed the sheriff's office. "Trooper Johnson asked me if I thought Amka had demolished her storage building for the insurance money."

Christian exhaled slowly, keeping his limbs loose. Then he breathed in for a seven count and out for an eleven. Calm. He would remain calm in every situation so he could act. If she was in trouble, he'd take care of it. Didn't much care how.

The door opened and Jeb stood, his uniform already wrinkled but his eyes sharp. "Christian? We'd like to speak with you now."

"We can eat outside if you want," Ace said quietly in the tavern. A cup of coffee steamed on the table next to him, untouched.

Christian shook his head. "No, I'm okay." After two hours trapped in a room with the troopers, he felt surprisingly relaxed. Probably because Amka was across the tavern, safe and working, where he could keep an eye on her.

Brock sat next to him, shoveling in his second bowl of chowder. "It is clam chowder day," he mumbled.

"Isn't it though?" Ace grinned.

Christian studied him. "You don't look shaky today."

"I'm not," Ace said. He glanced down at the coffee like it held some kind of answer. "But I see why you don't drink."

That hit Christian harder than it should have. The honesty in it. The clarity. Was Ace finally leveling out? Finally pulling himself together?

"Was the questioning helpful at all?" Ace asked.

Christian lifted a shoulder. "No. They're fishing and don't have anything, so they don't know where to look. They're going to try to keep Jarod's death quiet for now, and they might actually pull it off since they flew his body to Anchorage already."

"In Knife's Edge?" Brock snorted. "Ha." He ripped open a bag of saltines and dumped them into the bowl, the wrappers crackling like gunfire in the quiet lull between lunch rushes.

"Maybe it's possible," Ace said. "We're the only ones who know. We're not going to talk. Neither are the troopers. And it's not like Teller had a decent job in town. People might not notice he's gone for a while."

"Yeah," Christian muttered, not wanting to hear the asshole's name again. He still couldn't get the image of Amka punching him in the stomach out of his head.

The door opened, and Christian looked up. Damian strode inside, the subtle energy in the room shifting as soon as he crossed the threshold. Today, he was dressed down in black slacks and a white button-down, sleeves rolled to the elbows. He moved through the bar like he belonged there and pulled out a chair.

Christian nodded. "D."

"C," Damian said smoothly. He raised a single finger in Amka's direction, and she winked at him before disappearing into the kitchen. Christian tensed. His fingers curled around the edge of the table as his shoulders locked down, but he didn't move. Not until she came back out carrying a steaming bowl of chowder.

She walked straight over. "Here you go, Damian. What do you want to drink?"

"Just water," he said.

Christian finally breathed again. She needed to stay within sight.

"Thanks," Damian said.

Amka gave Damian a polite smile, then looked around the bar, her brow furrowing. "Has anybody seen Nixi? I thought she was working the floor."

"Yeah, she was just here," Brock said, lifting his chin. "Huh. Maybe she took a break."

"Maybe," Amka murmured. She looked pale, the kind of pale that didn't come from bad lighting but from running too hard for too long. The woman had been through enough the last week to break most people.

Christian leaned in slightly. "You need to rest a bit yourself."

She gave a half laugh and scanned the bar again, like if she kept looking, she'd find more minutes in the day. "I don't have time."

"Make time." His tone was low but final. His brothers all looked at him, and he ignored their expressions and didn't move, just kept his gaze on her. He could tell she wasn't up to fighting him, at least not right now.

"Fine," she said finally, voice clipped. She turned to walk back toward the register, but her posture had slumped, and her eyes had squinted as if she was fighting a headache.

"Christian, what is going on between you two?" Damian straightened. "I came to town because I heard Jarod Teller got his head blown in, but there's obviously more to the story than I heard."

Christian's head snapped toward him.

Brock leaned over the table. "How do you know that? I thought we were keeping it quiet."

Damian slowly turned his head. His black hair was growing out, and he looked more like Christian than the other brothers with the same cold composure, the same stillness. But where Christian was all silence and action, Damian was calculation and precision. His deep green eyes cut across the room, pausing on Amka, and then focused back to Christian. "I run security for one of the most insulated facilities in the world. Do you honestly think I don't notice when a forensic team out of Anchorage reroutes to Knife's Edge in the middle of the week?"

"Good point," Brock muttered, taking a long drink of his coffee.

Damian kept his gaze on Christian. "What's going on, or rather, when did it start?"

Christian didn't flinch. "Last night."

"Well. She's a sweetheart." Damian sat back. "Not great timing with her fiancé getting shot in the head."

"No," Brock said. "Definitely not."

Damian turned to Brock. "Since there've been attacks on both her and Jarod, do you think it has something to do with whatever was going on between them?"

Christian answered before Brock could. "No." His voice was sharp, final, and cold enough to stop that line of questioning where it stood.

"Well," Damian said calmly, "maybe she knew something she didn't know she knew. If that makes any sense." He glanced up with a small smile as Amka set a glass of water in front of him. "Thanks, Amka."

"Anytime." She didn't look at Christian. Her tone was polite, but she pivoted smoothly and walked back toward the bar without hesitation.

Christian tracked her retreat with a muscle tightening in his jaw. He didn't say anything.

"Take it easy," Ace said, leaning toward him. "She's within sight."

Christian didn't respond.

"I hope she knows what she's gotten into," Damian grumbled, wolfing down the chowder like he'd skipped breakfast.

"She hasn't gotten into anything," Christian said, tone clipped. "This thing between us is short lived." The words clutched something hard in his gut.

Ace barked out a laugh, Brock snorted, and a grin quirked one side of Damian's mouth.

"Shut up," Christian said. "She's the type who needs a house, kids, a stable life. One in town."

Brock nodded. "So give her that."

"Right. While I'm gone half the time, out in the wilds," Christian said. "That's not exactly fair to her."

"Too much of you at once is probably overwhelming anyway," Damian said easily, tearing apart a sourdough roll.

Christian shot him a look but didn't argue. He knew who he was.

"In the meantime, what's the plan?" Damian asked, setting his spoon down.

Christian leaned back in his chair. "What do you mean?"

"I mean, do you have one?" Damian's eyes narrowed just slightly. "Obviously someone's targeting her. I hadn't realized you and Amka had started something up."

"We haven't," Christian said. The words came too fast.

Damian raised an eyebrow. "Protested a little hard there."

"Whatever," Christian muttered.

"Do you want her safe or not?" Damian asked.

Why did he have to drill down on it every damn time? "Yes," Christian snapped.

"I figured," Damian said, completely unfazed. "Which is why I'm asking—what's the plan?"

"I was just going to stay by her side until we figure out who's trying to hurt her," Christian said. He knew how primitive and reactive he sounded. "But you're right. The fact that Jarod's dead does lend weight to the idea that it's all connected."

Ace stretched his shoulder in a habit he had picked up after the plane crash. Probably didn't even know he did it. "We could take shifts watching her."

"I've got her," Christian said without hesitation.

Brock and Damian shared a look. It lasted a beat too long.

Christian didn't move, but his voice dropped. "Knock it off."

Brock smirked. "How good's your intel, Damian?"

"Pretty good. One shot. No weapon found at the scene. His laptop and phone have not been recovered from either his place or the truck—which is weird." Damian's tone was all business now. "Somebody cleaned it up fast."

Christian needed to know if Jarod had gone in Amka's house. "Did he die in the truck?"

"I don't know," Damian answered. "I'll get the report once the forensic team finishes. Probably before the troopers do." He wiped his mouth with a napkin, folded it once and set it on the table. "I'll share the information when it arrives."

"Good," Christian said, glancing across the room.

The troopers sat at a booth, working their way through

bowls of chowder while chatting with the insurance adjuster. She listened intently, but no way were they telling her about Jarod. However, they were all interested in that explosion and fire.

"The fire's interesting," Damian said. "Apparently, there's talk she might've set it herself."

Brock coughed. "Amka? She would never do something like that."

"They don't know that," Christian said, jaw tight.

Damian drank his water. "Somebody tell me why Amka was engaged to that jackass in the first place."

Christian didn't move.

"I obviously don't know the full truth," Damian said, looking between the brothers.

Christian had already walked Brock and Ace through it earlier that morning, so he gave Damian the short version—Hank, the recording, Jarod's threat, and the blackmail-turned-engagement that followed.

Damian frowned, one brow arching. "Huh. Not sure how I feel about that."

"What do you mean?" Christian asked, voice lower now.

"Losing Hank like that," Damian said. "It still grates. I don't blame Flossy or Amka, but I don't like that there's a video of Hank dying floating out there."

The idea made Christian want to punch somebody. "Ditto."

"We've got to find that footage," Brock said, fingers tapping the side of his coffee cup. "Fast." He grimaced. "The fact that Jarod's laptop and phone are missing doesn't look good for Amka if the troopers learn about the blackmail."

"I'll use EVE's resources," Damian said. "Our tools can track digital movement, even off-grid. But if Teller was telling the truth, and someone else has the video? They'll upload it. Sooner rather than later."

CHAPTER 27

Behind the bar, Amka checked through a list of supplies she'd need for the coming week. Now that the plane route occurred at least every other day, she didn't have to plan so far ahead. She read the paper again, fighting to stay focused. Jarod was dead. While she didn't want to be selfish, what did that mean for her? Sure, she didn't believe he deserved to be murdered. But what about the video?

Who had it and when would they either upload it to a social media site or turn it over to the DA in Anchorage?

Should she give Flossy a heads-up? She didn't want to alarm the elderly woman, but she also wouldn't want to be surprised by this.

Of course, that might be the least of Amka's worries. The troopers obviously considered her a suspect in Jarod's death, and she couldn't fault them. They'd personally witnessed her punch him the night of his death.

Her focus kept shifting from Jarod to the night with Christian. It had been incredible, but he hadn't exactly waxed poetic that morning. However, he was living a much more stable life than she'd known. Maybe he'd stick around town, not that he'd mentioned building his life with another person. Oh, he wanted her. Maybe even liked her. Although, she was crazy to be thinking about the future right now. About romance. Her life was a disaster.

Lucas nursed a beer at the far end of bar, his fingers flying over his laptop. It was nice to see him writing and not putting out fires. She checked to make sure he didn't need a refill. Not yet.

Helene Stanford walked up from her chair by the dartboards, briefcase over her shoulder and her dark hair up in an intricate braid. She sat on a stool and plunked her case on the one next to her. "I was hoping we could chat now that the lunch rush has ebbed."

Amka forced a smile for the insurance adjuster. "Of course." At this point, she should start charging the woman rent. "Where are you staying?"

Helene drew out a legal pad from her case. "I secured a room at Flossy's BnB, so I was fortunate. Got the last one for the week." She smiled, her gaze remaining serious. "I've been hanging out here as well as Friday's grocery store. Just watching you all while waiting for the forensic reports about the fire, which could be weeks out." She glanced around, pausing at seeing the four Osprey brothers speaking quietly at their table by the fireplace. "The local sights aren't bad, either."

Amka could attest to that. "This is also a great place to catch up on the local gossip."

"Yes." Helene tapped her pen on the paper. "The town is abuzz, and that group of influencers just add to the rumors. From what I can tell, folks around here don't think you and Jarod Teller make a good couple. You don't make sense to most of the people who seem to know you."

"I don't know what to say about that." It was so weird to hear Helene speak about Jarod in present tense. Frankly, it was a miracle that Dutch and the state troopers had been able to keep a lid on the murder. They were probably trying to get past the week while the influencers were in town.

Helene just studied her. "Don't you think it's an odd coincidence that your fiancé's motel and your storage building both burned down? With the insurance payout, Mr. Teller will be able to build a luxury hotel instead of the rather ramshackle one that was there, and you'll be able to build something much nicer than the storage building. Property values have just increased in Knife's Edge, and more people are visiting. Plenty of tourists. Did you set your fire, Amka?"

"Of course not." By the looks of it across the room, Christian had just shifted in his chair. He'd been inside more than an hour, and that was probably his record for the tavern. Now she knew he could stay inside his cabin for a night. Well, most of a night. Both times she'd stayed with him, he'd been gone long before she'd awakened. She didn't have an excuse this time to get him outside, but considering he was sitting with his brothers and not the troopers this time, he probably didn't need help.

Helene cleared her throat.

Amka jumped, tearing her focus away from Christian. She had to stop thinking of him in that shower. Who knew sex could be that wild. And freaking amazing? She swallowed.

"Are you all right? You're flushed," Helene said.

"I'm fine. The idea of being accused of arson is insulting." And terrifying.

Helene sat back, today looking official in a black blazer with a white T-shirt over jeans. Her lipstick was a pretty light pink that most women couldn't carry off. "I'm just doing my job and don't mean to cause you any concern, but I have to investigate. In addition, my boss has asked me to look into the motel fire again. Do you know where Mr. Teller is right now?"

Being autopsied in Anchorage. "I don't," Amka lied. "But he

often takes off on fishing or camping trips, so it's not a surprise."

"Can you call him? I'd really like to speak with you two together."

"Already tried." She might as well keep lying. "He must be out of service range, which is usually the case around here." Amka's palms began to sweat. "I'll let you know as soon as I hear from him, and I can give his number to you as well."

Helene scribbled a couple of notes that were impossible to read from Amka's position. "I already have it in my files but thought you'd know of his whereabouts." She looked up. "The obvious crime would be that the two of you successfully burned down his motel for insurance money and then tried it again with your storage building."

"But the motel burned because of faulty wiring," Amka protested.

Helene made another notation. "Maybe not."

Amka didn't have any knowledge about the motel fire. "Jarod and I weren't even dating at that time."

"So you say." Helene zeroed in. "You know the better story?"

"I have no idea."

The woman pursed her pink lips. "What if that anger was real? The whole town saw you punch him right here in your tavern. I believe a few of the influencers even posted about it and how wild it can get here in Alaska."

Amka placed her list on the ledge beneath the bar. "I don't follow."

"What if the two of you have one of those psycho, dark romance type relationships?"

Amka frowned. "What are you saying?"

"What if you burned down his motel because you were pissed, and what if he decided to return the favor and burn down your building? You're not working together and are actually in some sociopathic but sexy fetish? That involves fire?"

Amka's mouth dropped open.

Helene pressed on. "I ran my theory by the two Alaska state troopers, and they were very interested in it. I think I'm on to something."

Amka couldn't breathe. That was insane.

Nixi came in from the kitchen, her purple hair curled into spirals of purple and now pink. "Sorry I'm late. I told Daisy I'd be here a while ago, but I got caught up videoing the basin of Tomalley Falls. It's gorgeous." She paused right by Amka and looked around the tavern. The color slid from her face and she wavered.

"Nixi?" Amka grasped her arm. "What's wrong?"

Nixi turned and headed through the doorway to the small bedroom instead of the kitchen.

Amka looked wildly around, only seeing the Osprey brothers and the influencers. She turned and followed her, ignoring Helene's sputtering. Upon reaching the back room, she paused in the doorway. "Are you all right?"

Nixi sank onto the bed, her purple hair too bright against her now pale skin. "Sorry. I haven't eaten, and sometimes when my blood sugar gets low, I lose control of my limbs." Her hand shook when she raised it to her face. "I feel like a dork."

The door burst open and Steve Coltrap hurried in. "I'm sorry, I know I shouldn't be here, but I saw you almost go down. Nixi, what's wrong?" He sat next to her and patted her hand.

Now there was a man who could share his emotions.

Nixi coughed out. "I'm an idiot who forgot to eat."

Steve slipped an arm over her shoulder. "You can't sacrifice health for this business, no matter how successful you are. Let's go back out there, sit by the fire to warm up, and get you some protein." With his blond hair, he looked like a young attorney. A hot one.

Apparently Nixi thought so, too. She leaned into him. "I'm so glad we found each other on this trip. I know you're in the middle of that live video with those guys from New York. Go back and do that, and I'll meet up with you later. Right now, I think I'll jump over to the Green Plate. I heard they have homemade chicken noodle soup today."

"It's fantastic soup," Amka agreed, concern filtering through her. "I hope we haven't been overworking you."

"No." Nixi waved the thought away. "I just forgot to eat." She pushed to her feet and nudged Steve back the way he'd come. "I'll go out the back door." She winced. "Please keep this totally embarrassing moment between us. I don't want any of the other influencers to see me losing it. That actually might make for a good post."

Steve grimaced. "You're not wrong. Okay. I'll go cover for you. How about we meet up tomorrow morning for a sunrise post? We could catch some spectacular footage."

Nixi stretched up on her calves. "That'd be great. I think you have a great eye for posts. You're going to grow fast."

Steve patted her arm, his lips curving. "Thanks. I'm definitely seeing the draw of this kind of lifestyle." He turned to Amka. "If you change your mind about that interview, let me know. I'd love to reveal your identity. The woman the hot-bodied Alaskan rescued."

Amka paused. "Now that you bring it up, why hasn't anybody identified us? All of you know our names by now."

Nixi snorted.

Steve flushed. "Let's just say that Alaskan threatened death, and nobody thought he was joking." He pushed open the door and returned to the bar.

Amka studied Nixi's still pale features. "Christian threatened *everybody*?"

Nixi walked across the cozy room, her normally graceful movements stilted. "Boy, did he. I wouldn't post his name, or yours, for any amount of prize money." She opened the door and looked over her shoulder. "I'm sorry about this. I'll be back to work tomorrow."

"No worries." Amka wanted to remain in that room and not deal with the insurance adjuster. Or try to keep herself from gaping at Christian like an awkward teenager lusting after the hot and mysterious guy in class. But she had to be a grown up. The fact that he'd protected her from more publicity she didn't want only made more butterflies wing through her abdomen. Enough of that. Smoothing back her hair, she moved back into the bar and found Helene waiting for her.

Just great.

While Amka couldn't seem to banish these feelings about Christian, she didn't have to allow any additional stress into her life. "I'm done talking to you without a lawyer," she said to Helene.

The woman sat back. "I'm not a cop."

"I don't care." It was too bad Daisy had the afternoon off. "I'm done." She forced a smile. "Can I get you a drink?"

Helene huffed out a breath. "Fine. I'll take a mimosa."

So the woman wasn't going to leave the tavern. Just fantastic. Amka poured the champagne and orange juice, sliding the glass across the bar.

The door opened and a young blonde woman with wide brown eyes walked inside, a green puffer coat encasing her. Definitely a tourist. Locals considered the spring weather a new heatwave. Visitors found it downright cold. "Hi." She moved toward the bar. "Um, a nice lady named Flossy told me I could find the sheriff here." She looked around the tavern. "Does your sheriff drink during the day?"

Not since he'd accepted the sheriff job. "Just coffee." Amka lifted her head and cocked it toward the woman. The four Osprey brothers had paused their discussion when the door had opened, so she kept her gaze on Brock.

He kicked back his chair and stood, heading her way,

looking Alaskan tough in jeans and a dark T-shirt with his badge clipped at his belt. It had taken a nagging Flossy to get him to wear it, and it looked natural on him.

Christian followed, unsurprisingly. He'd been eyeing the door for a while.

"Hi," Brock said to the woman.

"You're the sheriff?" She stuck her hands in her thick jacket.

Brock sighed. "That's what they tell me."

The woman blinked, looked at him, at Christian, then back to Brock. "Um, okay."

Yeah, they were something to see. Tall, dark, dangerous and more than a little harshly handsome.

"Can I help you with something?" Brock asked.

"I'm gone." Christian nodded at Amka and walked outside.

That's it? *I'm gone?* Amka barely kept from rolling her eyes.

The blonde brushed hair out of her eyes. "Hi. I'm Lorrie Warner? My husband was, ah—" Tears gathered in her eyes.

"Yeah." Brock gently took her arm. "Eli Warner. We've been expecting you. I'm so sorry for your loss."

"Thank you." She turned slightly and looked around the tavern as if wanting to escape the conversation. Poor woman. Her shoulders slumped. "What now?"

Brock led her to the door. "Let's go down to the station so I can get your statement, and then we'll figure out where to go from there. We're a couple days away from having the right helicopter to get his body to Anchorage for an autopsy."

She exhaled. "I don't have to, um, identify, um, him?"

"We can use a picture for that," Brock said, escorting her out.

Amka's heart hurt for the woman.

Steve moved up, his brow wrinkled as he placed his phone on the bar. His blue eyes had darkened. "I have bad news."

She looked down to see a video identifying both Christian and her at the storage building fire along with news of the shooting the other night as well as Eli Warner's death. The flirty influencer, a brunette Amka had only seen once, mentioned that Christian was currently unattached and had three just as sexy Alaskan badass brothers. Oh, they weren't going to like that. At all. She peered closer. "This already has five hundred thousand views."

Steve pressed his lips together. "And thousands of comments. Many proposing marriage to Christian, or to any brother he may have. Or any cousin or even young grandpa." He reclaimed his phone. "Are you going to tell them?"

"No," she breathed. "Are you?"

"Oh, hell no. I like my head on my shoulders and not rolling across the floor."

Good point. Although there was one Osprey brother she was going to find after work. They needed to talk.

CHAPTER 28

Amka took a drink of water around midnight, scanning the tavern to make sure everyone was good. She'd managed by herself the entire night and was suddenly grateful for both Daisy and Nixi. She didn't want to go back to doing everything herself, but she'd just mortgaged both of her assets. Although, now that Jarod had died, she could change that and just use the insurance money and part of the equity in the tavern only…if she didn't go to prison.

They were doing a good job keeping Jarod's death a secret, but she didn't know how long that would last. This was Knife's Edge, after all.

The door opened and fresh rain blew in, followed by Christian.

His black hair curled around his ears from the rain, and his dark green T-shirt showed spots from the downpour. In the dim light, the brutally carved planes of his face made him look dangerous. Wilder than the storm outside.

Her heartbeat increased rapidly, and her lungs felt like they'd turned inside out and heated. Liquid dampened her thighs, and her nipples sharpened. Thank goodness she'd worn a bra today.

Sometimes she just slapped a couple of nip covers on, but those weren't a match for Christian Osprey.

The bar had quieted when he'd walked in. Yeah, he had presence.

Dutch pivoted off his stool, clapped Christian on the arm, and headed outside. He'd been on protective detail all night and had entertained her with stories about his time with the AWT. The door slowly swung shut.

Christian looked over at her, scanning her face. A muscle ticked in his jaw. She must appear as exhausted as she felt.

"Everybody out. Tavern's closed." He set his stance but didn't raise his voice.

The people around the two remaining tables instantly stood, with the influencers downing their drinks quickly.

Amka's mouth gaped open, and her brain scrambled. What the heck was he doing? Finally, she shook herself out of the odd daze. "Christian—"

One look from him froze the words in her throat. Just a flicker of that gaze with no expression on his face. No real movement from his body. But she stopped talking and just stared. She might've short-circuited a little. Her body flushed hot and not just from temper, but she watched as everyone left cash on their tables and then edged around Christian to exit. He kept his focus on her, but she had no doubt if anybody made a wrong move, he'd see it. Take them out.

Silence fell. Somehow charged.

She cleared her throat and walked to the other side of the bar to bus the tables.

"Leave them."

"No." Finally, with her back turned toward him, she found her voice as she collected the empty beer mugs on her tray. She'd never leave a mess in the bar.

To her surprise, he moved to the other table and collected the various glasses to take into the kitchen.

She followed and then loaded the dishwasher as he took a dishrag and cleanser out without saying a word. What in the world was happening right now? Starting the washer, she emerged in the bar to see him finish wiping down the last table. "What are you doing?"

He returned to the bar and barely had to lean over it to drape the rag over the faucet. "Helping."

She was almost too tired to get angry. Almost. "You can't just come in here and order everyone to leave."

He slowly turned to look at the quiet and vacant interior before focusing back on her. "I just did."

"Don't you *ever* do that again."

Something broke through his impassive eyes. Something that glittered with darkness. "Then don't drive yourself so hard you look like you're ready to pass out."

What a nice description of how she looked. She threw up both hands. "Just leave, okay? I don't need you bossing me around." Even if she kind of, very deep down, liked it. Liked the feeling of being protected. "Got it?"

"How you getting home? And if you tell me you borrowed Smitty's piece of shit second rig that's all of a sudden parked right outside, you're not going to be happy with my response."

"I'm *already* not happy with you," she spat. Her SUV was currently at the bottom of the river, so she'd borrowed the only vehicle in town she could get in trade for two bowls of soup. She figured Dutch would follow her home, anyway. That so wasn't true. She knew that Christian would be covering her since Dutch had all evening. Ace had taken his turn after lunch through dinnertime. She probably had the best trained bodyguards in all of Alaska, and she hadn't hired one of them. "I know we take care of our own in Knife's Edge, which is why I've not only accepted around-the-clock protection but truly appreciate it. However, I'm drawing the line when it comes to everything else. Stop bossing me around."

He planted both hands on the bar. "Then you're going to hate my next statement."

What if he said she was staying with him? She didn't want him taking over her life. Her body desperately wanted to stay with him. "What's your statement?"

"I want you to go out and stay at EVE until we figure out who's after you and why."

If he had said he wanted her to grow tusks and become an elephant, she would've been less surprised. Knife's Edge and the EVE facility existed peacefully with very little interaction. Once in a while, the people who worked and lived there came into town, but it didn't happen that often. Nobody from town, as far as she knew, had ever stayed the night out there. "Are you insane?" It'd take hours to drive into work every day.

"No. Damian has already okayed it. Your pass will cover your living quarters and the cafeteria, but you won't have access to the facility."

Part of her was intrigued by the idea of staying at EVE, but not within those parameters. "So what exactly am I supposed to do all day hiding out there?"

"I don't know. Knit?" Whatever flared in her eyes must've given him a warning. "Or plan your world domination with Ace? You must have a lot to do to prepare for your businesses. I'm sure the internet connectivity is phenomenal out there."

She didn't want to run and hide. Sure, she understood that Christian and everyone protecting her were well-trained and had skills she probably couldn't imagine. She always thought she was a practical woman, and the rational avenue to take would be to hide out. But for how long? "If I leave, we'll never find this guy. You know that." She couldn't think of one person who wanted her dead—especially since Jarod was now gone. Not that she had truly believed he wanted her dead. It didn't make sense. "We can't let him go into hiding, too."

"Are you saying you want to be bait?" How could Christian

sound so threatening without the inflection changing in his deep tone?

A shocking desire to appease him rocked through her. What the heck? She was learning all sorts of unimpressive characteristics about herself tonight. "I'm the guy's target. We all agree on that at this point. So why go into hiding? So will he until I return."

"We'll find him first." Christian turned toward the doorway, revealing the weapon tucked into the back of his waist. "Our best theory is that Jarod got into something dangerous, resulting in attacks on you before his death. The shooter might be done, or he might think you have information from Jarod. Either way, we're conducting a deep dive on Jarod's life. Did you know he flew to Anchorage at least once a week last year when the planes were operating? He's done the same this spring."

"No. I didn't pay any attention to him last year, and this spring, I was just happy when he was gone." She hadn't cared one whit what he was doing outside of town.

Christian's eyelids dropped to half-mast. "Why didn't you come to me?"

Why would she have? "Jarod has an accomplice, and there wasn't anything you could do about that."

"That's where you're wrong. I would've taken care of it."

She shivered. "Nobody can fix that situation." Especially when there was no solution, no matter what Christian said. Plus, what if he had just gone and tortured Jarod to get her off the hook? She wouldn't have wanted that on his shoulders when he was still dealing with his time in the service. "I try not to burden my friends with my problems."

"Is that what we are? *Friends*?" That half-mast look made him appear like a full-bred wolf contemplating dinner.

"How would you define us, Christian?" she snapped.

He inhaled slowly as if trying to check his own temper. "At

the moment? You as a brat and me as a man losing his patience. Fast."

"You are in a rotten mood."

He nodded. Once. Shortly. "I'm in a horrendous mood."

Now he was agreeing with her? "Why?"

His chin lifted. "Why? Well, how about this. There's some psycho killer out there ripping out the eyes of victims, and the wife of one of those poor saps identified his body earlier and was too upset to talk to me about it. That's professionally. Personally? The best scenario for the woman I'm fucking is that someone we don't know uploads a video that'll put you and Flossy in prison. The worst scenario is that someone keeps trying to kill you, and I'm not fast enough next time to protect you. That'd make a guy a might cranky."

"The woman you're fucking?" Her voice shook as fire blew through her.

"Yes."

Oh, he wanted to get shot. "You mean fucked. The woman you *fucked*. Once. For two seconds in the shower." All right. It had been a lot longer than two seconds. "Past tense. Over. Not ongoing." She'd never sworn this much in her life. "You used the wrong damn word."

Now those lids flicked open. Green and black eyes narrowing, he turned and reached for her. "Let's remedy that then."

His hands were firm on her biceps as he lifted her. She yelped and bent her knees, raising her legs to keep from hitting the counter. He planted her ass on the bar, none too gently, stepped between her thighs, and kissed her.

Hard.

His mouth crushed hers like he meant to rewrite the conversation in tongue. She tasted frustration, fury, and that feral edge that had always made Christian dangerous in all the right ways. Her hands came up to push, but she didn't. Couldn't. His grip was iron, but the heat beneath it was the real trap.

"You don't get to ignore reality," she breathed when he broke away, their foreheads nearly touching. "We're not ending this argument with more sex."

"No," he growled, voice low and gravel-thick. "There's no argument." He slipped his hands under her thighs and yanked her closer, sliding her butt to the end of the bar, where her legs hung over. Then he flattened one palm over her chest and pushed.

She fell back onto the heavy wood. Her breath caught; his didn't. He leaned over her, his cock hard beneath his jeans and against her core. Demanding. She might've whimpered.

He dipped his head, kissed her throat and then went lower, ripping open the buttons of her flannel. He tore her bra in two, and his heated mouth found her breasts. First one and then the other, his tongue lashed. "Tell me to stop."

She didn't. Couldn't.

Fire zinged through her too delicious to ignore. She didn't know her body could do this. That she could feel like this.

He licked down her abdomen and then nipped her hipbone. Then he hooked his fingers in the edge of her jeans and panties and dragged them down with the precision of a strategic battle plan. "You were right about one thing," he muttered against the inside of her thigh, breath hot, voice deadly sure. "Our time in the shower was way too short. I didn't nearly get to indulge myself enough."

Her fingers threaded into his hair just as his mouth found her, and the words she meant to say came out as a whimper swallowed by a moan.

This couldn't be happening. Christian Osprey had his mouth on her clit. His tongue. His fingers. He gave a soft hum of pure male satisfaction that nearly shot her right off the bar. In response, he clamped both hands on her thighs, holding her open for him.

She gasped, hips jerking. He didn't ease up. Just flicked his tongue, slow and devastating, then pressed in deep enough to have her crying out, just once, sharp and breathless.

Then he stopped.

Not all the way. Just backed off, let her hover on the edge while his breath ghosted over her soaked skin.

"No," she choked, half a plea, half a curse.

He chuckled darkly against her. "Not yet."

And then he was back—tongue stroking, curling, relentless. Her vision blurred. She braced on her elbows, every nerve a live wire. Heat coiled low, tight, unbearable—

And again, he pulled back.

"Christian," she snapped, furious, desperate.

"You'll come," he murmured, kissing her inner thigh like he hadn't just tortured her within an inch of her sanity. "When I say."

She would've cursed him, but he was already on her again, tongue rougher now, purposeful. Her orgasm built too fast, too strong, and just as it crested—

Gone.

He licked a lazy path lower, ignoring the way she trembled, ruined and wild.

Her head fell back with a thud. "You bastard."

He grinned against tender flesh. "Say it again." Then he latched on—mouth hot, tongue firm, sucking her clit like he meant to leave a mark.

She lost it.

The orgasm hit fast and mean, yanking her under before she had a chance to brace. Her thighs trembled and tried to clamp around his head, but he held her still. Her hips bucked, wild and unforgiving, not caring that she probably caused bruises on her butt. She couldn't get a breath in and just gasped as a noise tore out of her throat, rough and real and helpless.

Her back arched. Then she fell flat against the bar, one arm flailing out for balance she didn't have, the other gripping his hair like a lifeline.

And still, he didn't stop.

"Christian." It came out wrecked. Barely a whisper.

He held her there, mouth dragging every last aftershock out of her, lips relentless, tongue merciless. It was too much. Way too much. Her muscles spasmed again, her legs twitching, and all she could do was take it. Shake through it. Pray he'd stop before she blacked out.

When he finally pulled back, her body was drenched, twitching, useless.

Christian rose slowly, licking his bottom lip like he'd just finished dessert and was considering seconds. One strong hand banded across the front of her throat and pulled her into a seated position.

Her hair flew around her face and sparks spiraled throughout her abdomen.

He stepped back, his gaze on fire, and slowly removed his belt.

CHAPTER 29

The belt hit the floor with a hard metallic clink.

He was past restraint now. Way past patience.

But when he looked at her, spread out on the bar, thighs still trembling, hair wild, eyes dazed like she couldn't remember her own name, something inside him shifted.

Possessive didn't cover it.

She was half-dressed. Nothing below the waist. Her upper half stole his breath with her torn bra and open flannel clinging to her skin. One sleeve had slipped off her shoulder, revealing a fresh mark he'd left there earlier. She looked ruined and radiant. Her lips were parted, eyes dark and glassy, her chest rising and falling too fast.

She looked like surrender and defiance wrapped in fire.

His hands curled into fists for a second. Not because he was angry. Because it was too much. Because she undid something in him, and he didn't know how to survive it without sinking his body into hers.

He stepped in before she could slide off the bar and lifted her, closing his arms around her back and under her thighs.

She gasped, her fingers gripping his shoulders, nails biting into his skin. "Christian—"

"I've got you." His voice sounded raw. "Always."

She didn't question it. Didn't try to fight as he carried her deeper into the tavern. Her body settled into his without hesitation, her cheek brushing against his chest.

The wooden floor creaked loudly from his heavy boots, and his senses stayed sharp. He was aware of everything—the faint creak of the rafters, the wind cutting through broken panes, the settling pop of old wood. The danger hadn't passed. It had just taken a step back to let him forget, for one minute, what they were walking through.

But he wouldn't forget.

He shifted her in his arms as he neared the heavy table in the far corner. It was scarred and old, gouges along the top, bolted to the floor. Solid. A survivor. It would hold.

He lowered her gently, giving her a second to find her balance. She was unsteady but didn't fall. Her hands gripped the table edge, her head bowed, breath coming in shallow gasps from her first orgasm of the night.

He wasn't finished.

He turned her and bent her forward, over the table, with both hands on her hips. Her palms flattened against the wood. Her back arched. That beautiful ass rose into view, bare and flushed. Her legs parted slightly, already inviting him in again.

He stared for a moment. Memorized every inch of her like he wouldn't get another chance. The flannel had bunched up at her waist. The torn bra had mostly fallen off. She was laid out for him, vulnerable but not weak. Never weak.

He shoved the flannel out of the way and reached down, sliding his hand along her spine as she let out a shaky breath. "Mine," he muttered.

She turned her head slightly and looked at him over her

shoulder. Her eyes were heavy, still dazed, but focused on him like there was no one else in the world.

"Say it," he growled.

"Yours," she whispered, her voice cracked and certain.

That was all he needed.

He gripped her hips, angled himself, and slammed into her in one hard, deep thrust.

She moaned his name, her voice catching, her head falling forward. Her hair spilled across the table in a mess of silk.

The sound she made landed deep in his chest. Not just arousal. Something stronger. Something that dug under his ribs and stayed there.

He locked both hands on her hips and started moving. Relentless. Not sloppy. Not gentle. Just pure intent. Every thrust was a promise, a mark, a vow that no one else would ever have this. No one would see her like this, hear her like this. Not while he was breathing. The thoughts ran through his head, and he didn't fight them. Not right now. Later.

She took all of him. Back arched. Hips lifting to meet him. Her breath broke apart, and her body felt slick and furnace hot around his cock.

He leaned in, his chest brushing her back, his lips near her ear. "You'll stay safe. Say it."

She gasped, her voice thin. "I will. I promise."

That undid him in a way nothing else ever had.

He drove deeper, arms wrapping around her, anchoring her against him. He could feel every breath she took. Every tremble. She was real. She was here. A perfect package of beauty, brains, and kindness so pure it stole his breath. Every time.

Each muscle in his body stayed keyed in, his hearing picking up every creak and shift outside the room. The wind had changed again. Something metal rattled on the roof. No danger coming for them. For now.

She clenched around him, her body pulsing hard, and he felt her teeter on the edge.

He didn't let up. Not now.

Her hands gripped the table hard. She jerked once, her whole body seizing around him. Her orgasm tore through her, raw and shaking, and her cry hit him like shrapnel. Her body clenched around him, so tight he might never get free. Was just fine with that.

Only then did he let go.

He came inside her, a deep sound pulled from his gut. His grip didn't ease, not until he was spent, still buried in her, chest against her back.

The table creaked under their weight. Her body sagged, breath uneven, arms trembling. He stayed inside her, forehead pressed to the back of her neck, heart still hammering like he could smell danger coming. Because it was.

And he'd do anything, obliterate any line, to keep her safe. Some people respected him, and some people feared him. Not one of them had any idea what he could do, what he would do, to protect someone he loved. He slowly withdrew from her, nearly seeing stars when her internal walls gripped him on the way out.

Love?

As was his nature, he accepted the thought because it held truth. Most men in love became softer. Kinder. Easier. That wasn't in his nature. Protecting and defending was. Even if he had to be the ice-cold weapon they'd trained.

So be it.

AFTER A LONG-ASS DAY working as a consultant to the AWT, Christian finally relaxed when he walked into the tavern, the previous evening still with him. He'd taken Amka three more times during the night at his place, where he much preferred she stay the entire day. She had, of course, argued with him until he brought her into town. He'd had Ace waiting, and he'd been on Amka duty all day.

Christian hoped they'd found time to plan their enterprises while he and Dutch had canvassed most of the area with pictures of the two unknown and now eyeless victims. He'd done his best to describe the third victim who had disappeared, but finally, he stepped into town to see Dutch and Brock sitting with Ace by the fireplace. Nixi was bustling around, handing out drinks.

Everything in him went stone cold, and then immediately warmed, when Amka walked through the door from the kitchen, delivering plates of burgers to people talking into their phones at a long table. Why didn't they just talk to each other? Christian clocked everyone's position in under a second and noted Eli Warner's widow sitting at a table, talking with one of those influencers.

The blond guy. Steve somebody.

Christian lifted an eyebrow and looked over at Dutch, who shrugged. Interesting. Christian gave Steve a look, and the man paled slightly. Good. Only an asshole would take advantage of the vulnerable widow. Christian kicked back a chair once he reached the table. "I got nothing all day."

"Ditto." Dutch scrubbed both hands down his well-worn face. "Nobody recognized the two victims. I had three pukers."

"I had one lady pass out," Christian grumbled, "Maybe we should have an artist render pictures of what they looked like before they had their eyes gouged out."

Dutch nodded thoughtfully. "You know, that ain't a bad idea."

Brock snorted. "You guys couldn't think of that to start with?"

Ace rolled his eyes, which were shockingly clear. "Amka was

safe all day. I saw no threats, although that Steve guy over there flirted with her a few times, and the stupid insurance adjuster kept bugging her until I snapped at the woman. She stormed out."

"Thanks," Christian said. He'd have to get the scoop on that later. He jerked his head toward the two at the table. "Please tell me that poor widow isn't giving an—"

"She is," Dutch grunted. "I told the social media jackass to leave her alone, but she said she didn't mind giving an interview. I think she's pretty lonely. She doesn't seem to have any other family back home, from what I got when I interviewed her, and considering her husband was just brutally murdered and had his eyes cut out, I didn't argue with her."

Brock sighed. "We'll keep an eye on her and make sure she gets to Anchorage when the body goes."

Christian couldn't imagine losing more people he cared about. His gaze drifted to Amka, where she joked with a couple of fishermen by the pool table and then took their empty dishes back into the kitchen.

She looked over her shoulder, saw him, and winked.

He sat back, stunned.

She had to be sore. He hadn't gone easy on her last night, and frankly, it had been the best night of his entire life. She still had enough sass in her to challenge him. Publicly. Damn, he liked that.

"Did she just wink at you?" Ace put down his coffee mug.

Heat shockingly filtered into Christian's face. "No."

"Yes, she did," Brock said, cutting him a look. "What's up?"

He'd never lied to his brothers, and he was done lying to himself. "She's under my protection," Christian said. "I'm not good for her long term, or for being close to her, but nobody harms her. Ever."

Silence fell like somebody had dropped a thirty-pound

boulder in the middle of their table. All three men were usually phenomenal at hiding their expressions. Not right now. Shock covered their faces. Christian felt an odd, grim sense of pleasure at that.

"Well, all right," Brock said. "Just so you know, I think that you are good for her, but you'll have to figure that out yourself."

Ace nudged him hard with an elbow. At least it looked hard. "Seriously, now that you're all in love and planning your future, you think we all should, Brock?"

"Yeah," Brock said, snagging a french fry off Dutch's plate. "I definitely think that. I don't want to be the only one who's happy."

"I didn't say I was going to be happy," Christian said. "I said that I can't let her be hurt. That's as far as I can go with her. She's a settle down type and I'm just not."

Ace chuckled. "This is going to be fun. By the way, have you told her that she's safe for life now?"

Christian leaned back further in his chair. "Well. No."

Dutch threw his head back and laughed. "Oh, you're not wrong, Ace. I'm sticking around town for a bit. This is going to be a lot of fun." He glanced at his watch. "However, right now, I've got to go. There are a couple more people up in Blue Creek who weren't home earlier. I don't think we're going to find anything on these two vics, but we've got to do the job."

"You want me to do it?" Christian asked.

"Nah," Dutch said, already pushing up from his seat. "One of the ladies said she'd bake me a pie if I waited till later. I like pie."

Who didn't?

Dutch stood and then paused. "Wait a minute. Did you get hold of Damian?"

"I did," Christian said. "I texted him the pictures again to look at, and he said he has no idea who those two victims are." He was starting to worry that they'd never identify them. How sad would that be? To die and have nobody that cared? At least he had his brothers. And Amka. She'd care.

"What do you think?" Brock asked.

Christian scratched a mosquito bite on his arm. "I think Damian's holding something back. I don't know what or why, but he's not telling me everything."

Ace stood and tossed a twenty on the table. "I hate him working at that place. He's not just there to provide security. We all agree on that, right?"

Brock nodded grimly. "Yeah, we agree on that. But we also agree that Damian's the smartest person we've ever met, and he's well-trained. He knows what he's doing."

"Not without backup, he doesn't," Christian snapped. "He talked about me trying to infiltrate the facility and test how good his measures are. I think I should do it. I mean actually do it and find out what's going on." He looked at his brothers. "You two in?"

"Absolutely," Ace said.

Brock blew out air. "Yeah, I definitely am. It could cause some problems with the sheriff position, but if I get canned or arrested, Ophelia can take over. She'd be a better sheriff than I am anyway."

"Okay," Christian said. "As soon as we figure out who's trying to hurt Amka and kill them—"

Dutch cleared his throat.

"I mean arrest them," Christian said half-heartedly. "We'll figure out what's up with Damian." He looked at Ace. "I feel like we're pretty solid with you right now. Have you been seeing Smitty?"

"Maybe," Ace said. "Don't want to talk about it."

Fair enough. Christian didn't push.

"Come on, Dutch. I'll walk you out," Ace said. "I promised Doc May I'd come by so she could check the shoulder I put out last week."

"That Doc May, she's a pretty one," Dutch murmured, his voice trailing off as they walked across the tavern and then out the door.

Brock watched them go. "You think he has a hard-on for the doctor?"

"I don't know. He does get hurt a lot," Christian murmured thoughtfully. "I thought he was just being a moron, but maybe he has ulterior motives." He could respect that. Definitely. Christian's gaze returned to watch Amka by the bar.

"Can I give you a little advice?" Brock asked.

Christian cocked his head. "Always."

"You might want to let her in on your plan about keeping her safe from a distance but not being in her life. I find they like to know what you're thinking."

Christian folded his arms. "I haven't formulated the entire plan yet."

Brock chuckled again and pulled Dutch's deserted plate toward him to finish the fries. "Like I said, this is definitely going to be fun." His phone buzzed. He lifted it to his ear. "Yeah. Thanks. Gotcha." He clicked off and looked up. "The Miller boys finished pulling Amka's rig from the river earlier while you guys were out scouting."

"That was the mechanic?" Christian asked.

"Yeah. The brakes were cut."

Fury tasted like ashes. "Of course." He'd figured. Still, hearing the truth confirmed settled hard in his gut. "I still can't figure why anybody would want to kill her."

"Jarod had to have been into something dangerous, and somehow she's involved," Brock said. "I don't have a lot of pull outside of here, but Dutch does. He should have the background on that idiot soon. I need to ask Amka what she wants to do with the body once the coroner in Anchorage releases it. Officially, she was his fiancée."

Just then, the doors opened and both Alaska state troopers walked inside, moving immediately toward Amka.

Christian didn't think. He stood and walked toward her. "What's going on?"

"We need to bring you in for formal questioning, Amka," Jeb said. "We're sorry, but we now have an even better motive for you to have killed Jarod Teller. Let's go. Now."

CHAPTER 30

The room felt colder than it should've, like the walls had secrets and wanted her to hear them crack.

Amka sat stiffly in a hard-backed chair that was just slightly too low, her knees awkwardly angled. Her spine ached. Every muscle below her waist reminded her she'd barely slept last night—and exactly why.

Across the table, Jeb folded his hands. Paige didn't sit. She stood, arms crossed, leaning against the filing cabinet. Amka couldn't think of them officially since she'd gotten kind of used to them. First names was probably inappropriate, but who cared?

Christian wasn't there.

Neither was Brock.

They'd been told to wait outside, and the fury on both their faces when she was escorted in without them had scared her more than the actual interview.

"Thanks for coming down voluntarily," Jeb said, his voice doing that forced-politeness thing that made Amka's back teeth ache.

Daisy, seated next to her with a legal pad and zero humor,

didn't respond. She'd even dressed like a fancy lawyer in a light green skirt and jacket set with gold jewelry, her thick hair up in a tight bun. "She's here briefly. Keep that in mind."

"We're going to walk through a few things," Paige said. "Officially, you're not under arrest."

Yet. The word wasn't said, but Amka heard it anyway.

Jeb cleared his throat. "We don't have autopsy results yet, but I saw Teller's body, and he was shot in the head by close range. In that truck in your driveway."

Amka's stomach dropped.

"But that wasn't the only trauma." Jeb crossed his arms. "I observed lacerations and scratches on Teller's arms and torso. Defensive wounds. From a fight, we believe."

Amka's mind blanked completely.

"We're not saying it was you," Paige said.

"We're saying we haven't ruled you out," Jeb added, too casually.

"I didn't scratch him. You all saw us in the bar. We argued, and I may have, um, punched him lightly in the stomach. That didn't even slow his stride." She swallowed and stopped talking when Daisy shifted her weight.

Paige took the seat next to her partner, her face softening and looking more at home with the smattering of freckles across her nose. Her red hair was down around her shoulders. "Let me help you, Amka. Did he attack you? Did you have to shoot him to defend yourself?"

Amka's mouth dropped open. "I didn't shoot Jarod." He had nearly attacked her a few times, but not the night of his death. "You already know that I spent the night with Christian."

Jeb sadly shook his head. "We know that's what you and your lover said. It's possible you killed Jarod and went to Christian's. He might be innocent, but if we charge you, he goes down too. He'll never be an Alaska Wildlife Trooper, at best. At worst, he's going to prison."

Paige planted a hand over a manila file. Her nails were a pretty pink. It was an odd thing for Amka to notice. "I don't think Christian would survive in a jail cell, do you?"

Amka slowly shook her head. Christian needed the outdoors.

Daisy held out a hand. "Stop trying to terrify my client. She didn't kill Jarod and neither did Christian. You're fishing, and I'm getting bored." She tapped her pen on her so far clean legal pad. "Somebody has tried to kill my client three times. You know this. We believe it had something to do with Jarod's life, maybe his many trips to Anchorage, and we'd truly appreciate it if you'd do your jobs and find out what."

Paige sighed heavily and looked at her partner as if at the end of her rope.

Jeb's chin lowered, giving him the look of a pissed off Doberman. "We have a couple of theories about that. First, what if Amka was setting the explosive and accelerant in the storage unit to catch Jarod there later? We noted that he often spent time at the bar, behind the bar, pouring drinks. Perhaps you got caught in your own trap?"

Amka couldn't comprehend. "You think I nearly got myself blown up or burned up on purpose?"

"No. We think it was an accident. The fire wasn't supposed to happen until later when Jarod was in the building." Paige nodded, her voice cajoling. "We've confirmed with Wyland and Sheldon that they wouldn't have needed to enter the building for another week, which you knew because you know their restocking schedule."

Sure, she did. They owned a storage building together. "I did not set that fire."

Daisy tilted her head. The heat was frizzing her hair a little, but she still appeared powerful. "Do you think Amka shot at herself somehow from a sniper's position?"

Jeb slowly smiled. "No. We think that Jarod was going after some payback for the fire."

This was freaking insane.

Daisy chuckled. "Wow. You two should write thrillers along with our tanker chief. This is ridiculous. So with your current theory, did Amka cut her own brakes? Or did Jarod cut them as another play in a weird game between them?"

"You catch on fast," Paige said, her voice dripping with sarcasm now. "We're not sure. Could go either way. Maybe Jarod cut the brakes and then a very furious Amka murdered him an hour later. Or perhaps she cut the brakes to give herself an alibi for the murder."

Wow. Amka looked at Daisy. "I can't even understand any of this."

Daisy's eyes narrowed. "Me neither."

Paige coughed into her hand. "Sorry about that. Spring allergies. Where is Jarod's phone and laptop? We've been told he had both, and yet we can't find either one."

"I have no idea," Amka said. If she did, she'd be erasing the video.

Daisy crossed her arms. "We're about done with this questioning. You have more. What is it?"

What could it possibly be? There couldn't be any more.

Jeb tapped the folder again. "Do you know about the life insurance policy Jarod took out two weeks ago?"

She stopped breathing. "What?"

Jeb nodded. "He listed you as the sole beneficiary. One million dollars, payable upon death."

She stared at him. "What?" How in any world did that make sense? Jarod didn't even like her. "You're lying."

Paige shook her head. "No, we're not." She pulled out a stapled stack of papers to hand to Daisy.

Daisy flipped through them. "Yep. One million."

"I have no idea," Amka whispered. The room tilted slightly. "He never told me."

"Sure," Paige muttered.

Daisy sat up straighter. "Are you implying that my client, who has a visible alibi for the night in question, had motive based on a policy she didn't even know existed?"

"We're saying everything's on the table," Jeb replied. "Jarod was killed. Amka stands to benefit. That's motive."

Amka gripped the edge of the chair. "No. He never even mentioned insurance."

"You can deny it all you want," Paige said. "But that policy was active. You're the named recipient."

Amka's world tilted around her.

Daisy leaned forward, calm and cutting. "Out of curiosity, has anyone checked for life insurance policies on my client?"

Jeb raised an eyebrow. Paige didn't move.

"Well?" Daisy pressed. "If you're following the money, then follow it both ways."

Paige exhaled and pulled out another stack of papers. "There's a policy," she said. "It was filed the same day with the beneficiary listed as Jarod Teller."

"How much is the payout?" Daisy asked, her voice flat.

Paige hesitated. "One million."

Amka's body went cold.

That policy had never been mentioned. Never signed. Never discussed. She couldn't imagine why he'd—

Wait a minute. Why would he do that? Bile roiled around in her stomach. Had Jarod planned to kill her for the money? Had he been that evil? Why take out both policies? Just to look innocent? He was a jerk, but she hadn't imagined he was that cruel. "He took it out without telling me," she whispered.

"Sure, he did," Paige said. "We have your signature on yours."

"No you don't. I never signed that." Amka pulled Daisy's notepad toward herself, reached for a pen, and signed her name three times. Then she pushed away from the table. "This is my signature. Feel free to compare them. I'm done." She stood.

Jeb slid the notebook toward himself. "Signatures can be changed, but we'll send this to the lab to compare. Might have to ask the FBI for help."

Amka's legs trembled. She had to get out of there. "Either arrest me or I'm leaving."

Paige also stood. "In that case, you're under the arrest for the murder of Jarod Teller. Put your hands behind your back." She moved in with the handcuffs. "You have the right to remain silent. The—"

Amka wavered as the room morphed and Paige's voice muffled into something unintelligible. Was she going to prison?

TWO HOURS AFTER BEING ARRESTED, the metal chair bit into Amka's thighs. Cold, unrelenting. Her palms rested on her jeans, but her fingers wouldn't stop twitching. Across the table, the wheeled-in computer monitor crackled to life, cords looping down like snakes. A grainy video feed showed Judge Bobb Kerrick in his cluttered office, half-buried in paperwork. Fallon Price, the Anchorage ADA, leaned in from his square, the glow from his screen casting hard shadows across his face.

Daisy sat to Amka's left, jaw set, one heel tapping steadily under the table. She hadn't spoken much since they'd arrested Amka. Just squeezed her arm and told her to breathe.

The troopers had wanted to take her to Anchorage for processing, and Christian had lost his mind, with Brock not far behind him in the fury stage. Thank goodness Dutch had arrived and calmed everyone down. He'd processed Amka himself and then had set up an immediate virtual arraignment.

Amos, the weather guru who lived in the basement of the sheriff's office, had managed to hook them all up so they could do this. Amka stared blankly at the squares in the computer monitor.

Prosecutor Fallon didn't even wait for the judge to ask. "We're requesting bail be denied, Your Honor, and we'd like to secure Ms. Amaruq in the Alaska Correctional Facility in Anchorage until trial. She is a clear flight risk with motive, opportunity, and no credible alibi."

Amka's breath snagged in her throat.

Daisy's head whipped around. "Excuse me?"

Fallon didn't blink. "Ms. Amaruq was seen punching Jarod Teller in the stomach the night he died. We have multiple witnesses at the tavern who can verify that. He was found dead in her driveway hours later from single gunshot wound to the head. There are scratches down his torso that suggest a physical struggle before he was killed."

Amka's vision tunneled for a second. Her stomach turned over. She couldn't spend months in the Anchorage prison waiting for a trial. What was she going to do?

Daisy's voice sharpened. "Are you saying she scratched him to death?"

"I'm saying she had motive." Fallon held up a file. "A million-dollar life insurance policy. Ms. Amaruq is the sole beneficiary. That policy was filed two weeks ago by the victim, and she never mentioned it."

"Because she didn't know about it," Daisy shot back. "She had zero knowledge about any life insurance policies, which means Jarod purchased them both, which doesn't lead to any good conclusions about him. If he broke the law in this manner, who knows what else he was into, or who might've wanted him dead. You're reaching by charging my client."

Fallon's expression didn't change. "They were engaged."

Daisy didn't flinch. "That isn't exactly probable cause, and you know it."

Amka wanted to crawl out of her skin. The walls felt too

close. The lights too sharp. She could hear the buzz of the camera overhead and the faint whir of the old HVAC system grinding away. The room smelled like stress and bleach. Her fingers went numb.

The judge cleared his throat, clearly over the back-and-forth. "Ms. Amaruq, do you have an affirmative defense?"

Amka opened her mouth. Nothing came out.

Daisy stepped in. "My client does have an alibi. She was with Christian Osprey that night. She had a car accident on the way home and plunged into the river. Christian rescued her and took her home to warm up. They were together all night."

Fallon leaned forward. "It's not quite that innocent, judge. Christian Osprey is a man she was having a secret relationship with, while still engaged to the victim. A man who's also a person of interest. That's not an alibi, Your Honor. That's a co-conspirator."

Amka's chest went tight. Her throat burned. She'd known this would be bad, but not like this. "I would never kill anybody, and neither would Christian," she whispered. Not now that he was out of the military, anyway.

Daisy put a hand on her arm, firm. "Amka, I've got this."

Fallon lifted an eyebrow. "That's an interesting claim, Ms. Amaruq. But without proof, we can only go on what we know. Which is this: Jarod Teller named you as his beneficiary, and now he's dead in your driveway. Shot in the head. You were engaged to him, and now you're sleeping with a man who may be fabricating an alibi on your behalf. None of this looks good."

Daisy jumped in. "That's enough, Fallon."

"Bail should be denied," Fallon snapped.

"No," Daisy said. "There shouldn't be any bail. My client has no criminal history, owns a business in town, and has nowhere to run."

Judge Kerrick rubbed his temple. The screen wavered slightly. "We don't have a murder weapon. We don't have DNA.

We don't have fingerprints. Just the punch, the body location, the policy."

"Which is already a hell of a lot," Fallon muttered.

The judge exhaled. "Bail is set at fifty thousand. Ms. Amaruq is to remain within Knife's Edge and check in daily with one of the three troopers in town. I believe we have two Alaska State Troopers and one Alaska Wildlife Trooper in Knife's Edge currently?"

"Affirmative, Judge," Fallon said.

The judge banged the gavel. "It is so ordered. Any further developments and we'll reconvene immediately."

The screen faded into gray.

Amka didn't move.

Daisy stood and nudged her shoulder. "Come on. You're getting out."

Amka rose on stiff legs. In the hallway, Christian and Brock stood like sentinels, both furious.

Amos called out from the basement. "This is bullshit. Amka wouldn't kill anybody."

Amka paused. She'd never, in her entire life, heard Amos swear. "Thanks, Amos."

Christian looked like he wanted to tear a hole through the nearest wall. "You okay?" he asked.

She wanted to pour herself right into his chest and let him shield her from the world. But the troopers were watching. "Yes."

Daisy patted her arm. "They're going to put you in a cell, and we'll run to the bank. Don't worry. Christian and I will figure this out."

Christian nodded. "I have the fifty grand right now. We'll take care of it."

Paige slowly smiled, her trooper hat tilting slightly. "Well now. Isn't that sweet?"

CHAPTER 31

The tavern was too warm tonight. After being let out on bail, Amka had returned to work. Where the heck else would she go? She found comfort in her bar. So far, word had not gotten out that she'd been arrested or that Jarod had even been murdered. It was crazy how many secrets could actually be kept in Knife's Edge. She'd had no clue.

Right now, she would just be grateful she could spend more time in this tavern that she loved so much. Christian had almost kidnapped her and taken her to EVE, but she'd protested, as had the troopers. She was supposed to stay in Knife's Edge. So she'd come to work while Christian had headed out to interview the last few citizens about the eyeless victims. Dutch had offered to go, but he'd looked exhausted, so Christian had insisted he'd take care of it.

He really did protect his friends. Amka wiped a forearm across her brow and shoved the door to the kitchen closed with her hip. Her legs ached. Not just from her stressful day, but from what Christian had done to her last night and this morning and maybe one more time after that. That man had no off switch. She felt immensely grateful for that fact.

She moved behind the bar, her muscles slow to cooperate, and grabbed the lemon bucket to refill the slices. The bar crowd was light but strange tonight. The kind of strange that upped her anxiety.

On Amka duty, Dutch sat in the far corner with a view of both doors, filling out reports and mumbling to himself.

The door creaked open, bringing with it a gust of cold air and the doctor. May had her blonde hair scraped back in a bun so tight it tugged her eyes wider. Her scrubs were wrinkled and there was a smudge of something, not blood, but close, on the sleeve of her hoodie. Her shoulders slumped, and her shoes scuffed softly as she made her way to the bar.

"I need a shot," May muttered, voice rough. "Something that will make me forget what a shattered femur looks like. I had to send the Japley kid to Anchorage for surgery. She flipped over a four-wheeler."

Without hesitation, Amka poured a double shot of rye and set it down without a word.

May took it in one go, hissed through her teeth, and blinked twice. "Okay. That helped."

"You want food?" Amka asked.

"Later. Maybe. Depends on if my stomach forgives me." May rubbed her temples. "You look like you got hit by a truck."

Amka snorted. "Feel like it. A very attractive, heavily armed one." She really wanted to act normal and share gossip with her friend. To pretend for a moment that she wasn't out on bail for an actual murder charge. "As in a hot bodied loner with an attitude."

May cracked a tired grin. "Seriously?" She leaned in, her voice dropping. "You and Christian? Finally?"

"You expected it to happen?" Amka whispered back.

May shrugged narrow shoulders. "It's the way he watches you when he's in here. Like he has a bead on you at every second. I was hoping you'd both turn around and see each other." She wiped a hand down her face. "I'm a romantic, you know."

Amka hadn't known that. "Then I'll give you all the details when we don't have to whisper. For now, would you like another drink?" She could give the doctor a ride home in May's truck and return it tomorrow.

"Yes. A double." May leaned on the bar like she didn't care if anyone saw her unraveling.

Amka fetched her a glass of water, a double shot of rye, and then busied herself wiping the same spot on the bar until her hand cramped.

So folks in town had noticed the tension between Christian and her. She'd wondered. Now her mind wouldn't stop spinning about him. How he'd held her last night like she was something he'd never expected to find. How he'd kissed her like he was starving. How he'd whispered her name like it meant something. Real. Solid. Permanent.

And now?

If he'd finished looking for a killer taking eyeballs, he was now back out in the woods with Brock, chasing leads on Jarod's murder and trying to stay three steps ahead of whatever was coming next—while the state troopers attempted to tie her to Jarod's death. She hated that her chest hurt when she thought about Christian. She hadn't signed up for this. Not the feelings. Not the what-ifs.

She tossed the rag in the sink and moved into the kitchen, noting how pristine it looked after Rudolph had shut it down for the night. The chef was a genius at not only food preparation but cleaning. He never missed a spot. So she paused at seeing a folded up piece of paper by the back door.

A note? She hurried and picked it up, wondering if it was Rudolph's. If she should call and ask before opening it. Not that the old chef had any secrets. The paper was off-white. Heavier than standard. She unfolded it and read:

The town will hate you when the truth comes out. You're a killer, and Flossy deserves to hang. Have $50k in a plain bag by Friday when I send more instructions. You and Jarod send the money, and I won't tell a soul. You have plenty, and he has insurance money.

HER STOMACH LURCHED. The paper shook in her hand. Now somebody new was blackmailing her? As well as Jarod? It was shocking that the secret of his death still held.

She folded the note twice and walked back into the bar to shove it beneath the stack of invoices under the register, then placed a battered menu on top. No one saw. Her pulse galloped and she fought the urge to throw up.

"You good?" May asked.

Not even close. Amka almost reached for the note but paused at seeing the stress lines extending out from May's eyes. "The broken bone was a rough one?"

May looked down at her hands. "Yeah. I had a few rough ones today, but I can't talk about the other ones. Margie Japley already posted on Instagram about her femur. I texted her a copy of the x-rays and she squealed, she was so happy." May shook her head. "Kids."

Amka wouldn't burden her about her earlier arrest or the blackmail note right now. May had apparently dealt with enough today. "I've got you, May. You drink all you want tonight." She poured another and then turned back to the taps and double checked the pressure on one. Her throat tightened. The walls of the tavern pressed in. She thought she was done being scared. She thought with Jarod gone, the nightmare would slow down.

Apparently not.

May cleared her throat again. "You okay?"

Amka pasted on a smile. "Yeah. You?"

May raised an eyebrow but didn't push. "Why don't you sit down and dish on Christian? You look like you could use a break. It seems like you're listing to one side."

"This is my sexy limp," Amka muttered, reaching for a tray. "I'll gossip later."

May snorted, and Amka walked over to an odd grouping by the pool table that included the widow, the insurance adjuster, and two influencers. The widow—Lorrie, that was her name—looked up and offered a faint smile.

Helene didn't. The insurance adjuster looked two drinks past tolerable and not slowing down. "I'd like another martini, which makes it easier to warn you that my report states that I'm suspicious either you or your fiancé started the fire in the storage building. Mainly because Mr. Teller is avoiding talking to me about it. I'm thinking that we should reopen the investigation into the motel fire." She hiccupped.

Jarod wouldn't talk to anybody ever again. "Neither Jarod nor I set that fire," Amka said.

Helene popped her last olive in her mouth and handed over her empty glass. "Any idea where he is?"

Amka tried to force a smile. "He's still off-grid. He can disappear for weeks when he wants time with nature."

Steve snorted, too loudly. "Oh, that's real convenient. Maybe he did set those fires. He's purposefully not answering your calls, Helene. It's so obvious."

"Knife's Edge doesn't exactly have cell towers every ten feet," Amka said dryly.

Lorrie, her blonde hair up in a ponytail, cradled her glass like it held answers. "You're not worried about him? I mean, there's a killer in those woods." Her voice cracked on the last.

Amka's heart hurt for the young widow. "I'm sure Jarod is fine. He likes taking off and camping by himself." His body was in Anchorage and not even close. "I don't think he's anywhere near town."

A sigh escaped the widow before she could say more. She blinked again, then pointed vaguely at her wineglass. "Can I have more of this? It's the only thing keeping me upright. I want to just go see my husband, even if he's in a freezer, but the sheriff won't let me."

No doubt seeing the man without his eyes would be traumatic. Amka hesitated. "How would you like some food instead?" She wasn't Rudolph, but she could throw together a sandwich for the woman.

"She's fine," Steve said, already reaching across her to nudge the wine closer. "We've got her. I'll make sure she gets back to Flossy's in one piece."

"You're on your third drink, too," Amka said, eyeing him.

He smiled. "I function great on three drinks."

"I'll be fine," Lorrie murmured, already halfway through the glass. "Really. Just…I don't want to feel things tonight. Eli was a great man, and I miss him."

Nixi finally looked up, resting her chin on her fist. "I'll make sure she gets to Flossy's safely."

Amka hadn't realized Flossy had an open room. More likely she'd somehow made room for the poor widow. "Thanks, Nixi." She forced a smile. "I'll bring another round and some pretzels for you all."

Nixi nodded, her concerned gaze on Lorrie.

Steve leaned in. "Helene? We should do a collab. Something about insurance and the wilderness. What do you think?"

Amka turned toward the bar, the weight of too many secrets pressing between her shoulder blades. Jarod was dead. Helene was looking in all the wrong directions. The widow was unraveling. And somewhere out there, someone still thought they had fifty grand coming.

And her heart? Her heart was in the woods with a man who barely knew what to do with it.

She had to talk to somebody about the blackmail note, so

naturally, she grabbed her phone and texted Christian: NEED TO TALK. TONIGHT. ALONE. IMPORTANT. No emojis. Just the truth.

The reply came fast. I'LL BE THERE BY MIDNIGHT. DON'T LEAVE THE BAR.

No "baby." No "sweetheart." Just orders. Protective, infuriating orders that she both hated and kind of wanted. He wouldn't be so bossy if he didn't care. Of course, he was all rough and little diamond. But his actions spoke loudly. He'd saved her a few times now, risking his own life each time. That mattered. She dropped the phone and went back to slicing lemons, hand steady now. Of course, her gaze kept sliding to the end of the bar. Her thoughts to what he'd done to her on that burnished wood. She'd blushed the entire time she'd bleached and cleaned it earlier.

And he was coming back at midnight.

CHAPTER 32

Amka reached for the lemon bucket again and realized, too late, it was already full. She tried to remember filling it. Her brain felt like it had a time delay, like she was working underwater.

She leaned on the bar for a second. Just a second. Her legs buzzed. Her shoulders felt like lead. Her whole body was one big, throbbing mess.

Dutch now slept in his chair by the fire, his chin down, his breath even.

Across the room, Steve told some loud story about a bear and an airhorn. Helene pretended to laugh, but her glass was empty again. Unless she waved, Amka wasn't refilling it. Lorrie had gone quiet, her eyes dim, and May…May was fully asleep on the bar, arms tucked under her head, a doctor puddle in rumpled scrubs.

Amka glanced at the clock. Christian would be back shortly, and she had every intention of closing down when he arrived.

A tray clattered onto the bar beside her.

"I'll help," Nixi said, her purple hair spiked up and her blue eyes surprisingly clear. "You look wrecked."

Amka looked over at her, startled. "What?"

"You're toast. I can see it all over you." Nixi motioned to the tables. "Let me bus. I could use some exercise, and I'm tired of listening to Steve hit on all three of us. The guy is seriously lonely, and that's just an ick for me."

Amka opened her mouth to brush off the help, but the words didn't come. Her throat tightened. She bit back the refusal and gave a slow nod. "Thanks," she said. "Yeah. I appreciate the help."

Nixi gave her a small smile, already moving through the bar like she owned the place. Efficient. Graceful. Like she wasn't wearing the same boots she'd worn to cross three rivers that week, if her last post was to be believed.

Amka grabbed a rag and started wiping down the bar again —an actual dirty spot this time. "Didn't peg you as the dishwashing type."

"I'm not," Nixi said, stacking glasses. "But I've had enough tequila and tragic Instagram DMs for one night. Felt like time to be human again."

Amka snorted. "That bad?"

Nixi shrugged. "Worse. Some guy sent me a picture of his kneecap and asked if it looked infected."

"Why?"

"Apparently, I mentioned in a post that I once dated a paramedic. That's all it takes now."

Amka shook her head, still smiling. "How'd you get into all that, anyway? The followers. The hiking. The selfies with yaks or whatever."

Nixi paused, her tray half full. "You want the honest version?"

"Absolutely."

Nixi exhaled a laugh and leaned her hip against a barstool. "All right. I had a fiancé. Classiest and smartest guy I ever met, with broad shoulders and a stamina that wouldn't quit. He wasn't ready for, well, us, and he broke my heart. Right in two."

"I'm sorry. The dumbass. He couldn't be that smart if he let you go."

"Right? The cliché burns more than the betrayal. I left town with nothing but a credit card and a backpack and figured I'd just…keep moving."

Amka grinned. "And become famous?"

"I didn't try to. I posted a video of me screaming into the Grand Canyon. People liked it."

Amka laughed. The sensation felt strange in her chest. "That's it? You screamed into a canyon and it went viral?"

Nixi's eyes sparkled, and in her capri jeans and blue flannel, she looked like a sprite. "People love a meltdown. Especially when it's well-lit."

They worked in silence for a bit, stacking chairs, clearing dishes, wiping tables. It felt weirdly good to be doing something without thinking, without plotting, without fearing every shadow that moved. Just her and Nixi. Motion and heat and dish soap.

"Do you like it?" Amka asked eventually. "The life, I mean."

"I like the parts where I'm on top of a mountain," Nixi said. "Not so much the part where people think that makes me whole."

Amka understood that all too well. The way people looked at her behind the bar and assumed she was fine. She could pull a perfect pint and smile while her world crumbled in the walk-in freezer. "You're good at this," she said quietly, nodding at the now-pristine tables.

Nixi rolled her neck. "I'm good at surviving. The rest I make up as I go."

They carried the last trays of dishes into the kitchen. The space was silent, clean, still smelling faintly of garlic and heat. It should have seemed peaceful.

But Amka felt the weight in her chest returning. There was a note by the register saying someone thought she was a killer.

That Flossy deserved to hang. That fifty grand had to appear by Friday. She didn't even know who she could trust anymore.

Except, maybe Nixi.

Nixi stood by the dish pit, sleeves rolled up. She looked like she belonged there. Not glamorous. Not curated. Just...real.

"Hey, thanks again," Amka said, pushing open the kitchen door. She might as well collect the dishes from the drunk trio joking loudly about insurance and influencers.

Nixi looked over her shoulder and grinned. "Anytime. Seriously. It feels good to help someone who's not trying to get me to sponsor their beard oil." She stepped toward the sink.

Amka moved into the bar, pausing when a loud, sharp metallic pop echoed from the kitchen. She froze. "Nixi?"

An explosion hit with a ferocious bang. A white-hot flash blew beneath the door. A roar like a collapsing roof thundered. The entire kitchen rocked with sound as dishes must've shattered.

Amka shoved at the door, fighting a heated current. The fire alarm screamed. "Nixi!" she yelled.

No response.

Just the crackle of fire.

And a single, broken sound—something between a gasp and a groan—from inside the smoke.

THE BLAST HIT JUST as Christian reached the front door of the tavern.

A bone-deep whump of pressure punched the front windows of the structure, followed by the sharp crack of glass.

His gut clenched so hard he gasped. Amka.

He didn't wait. He ran.

The door slammed open as he charged inside, adrenaline already surging through his veins. The tavern was chaos with smoke in the air, chairs tipped, a few people shouting. A wineglass rolled across the floor and shattered against a stool.

The scent of smoke wasn't campfire. It was industrial, with scorched insulation, burning oil, something chemical and wrong. He scanned the room out of habit, making sure nobody else was on the ground. No visible casualties, yet.

Behind the bar, Amka was trying to get through the kitchen door, shoulder down, shoving against it like sheer willpower could move it.

"Get back," he barked, vaulting the bar in one clean move.

She turned, ash streaking her face. Her eyes met his, wild and terrified. "Nixi's still in there."

There wasn't time to argue. He wrapped an arm around her waist, lifted her up, and planted her on the bar in one smooth motion. "Get over there and stay down. In case there's another explosion."

She didn't argue. She swiveled around and dropped behind the bar like she'd done it a thousand times. Her eyes tracked him the whole way.

Dutch came up like a freight train, boots pounding. His nostrils flared at the smoke as he leaned down and grabbed the red fire extinguisher. "Let me go first."

"I'll get the girl, you take the fire." Christian shoved open the kitchen door, bracing against the wave of heat and thick black smoke that poured out. The stench was of fire, scorched oil, and melted plastic. Heat pressed against him like a solid force. Breathing hurt.

"Nixi!" he roared into the chaos, eyes already watering.

A faint cough answered, thin and desperate.

He dropped low and entered. Muscle memory took over. *Breathe through the shirt. Stay under the smoke line. Count your steps.*

The kitchen was wrecked. Fire danced along the stainless steel counters, eating through a stack of takeout boxes. Grease sizzled in a broken fryer. Light fixtures popped and flickered. Visibility was trash. The heat had teeth. Glass crunched beneath his boots. He kept his head down, sweeping the floor with one hand. The coughing came again. Closer now.

He found her against the industrial fridge, curled in on herself, face smeared with soot and blood. One of her arms was pinned awkwardly behind her. Her flannel shirt had burn marks on one sleeve, and her lips were cracked.

"I've got you," he said, scooping her up in a controlled lift, careful with her neck. She didn't weigh much.

Her lips moved, barely audible. Her eyelids fluttered open, unfocused.

Dutch stormed in behind him, fire extinguisher blasting foam, cutting through the flames. The sound was deafening in the tight space. White mist overtook red.

Christian turned and carried Nixi back through the smoke, past the boiling metal, and into the main bar. He laid her on the floor behind the bar, away from the worst of the heat. The fire wasn't spreading, but they'd need to evacuate into the cold soon. "May?"

The doctor was already vaulting a stool, hair messy, face pale but focused. "Clear space," she ordered, dropping to her knees. "I need a towel. Water."

Amka shoved both into her hands seconds later. Her own shook, but her grip didn't falter. Her gaze never left Nixi's face.

Nixi coughed again, lungs rattling. Her eyes shot open, frantic, lost. She gasped and reached for Christian's sleeve. "Пожар. Всё горит. Он сказал не подходить…"

Amka leaned over. "Is that Russian?"

Christian gripped Nixi's shoulder gently, his thumb finding the warm skin at her collarbone. "Yeah," he murmured, the translation automatic. He'd learned the language in the service, buried it, but it came roaring back. "She's saying everything's burning. That the fire's coming closer."

May's face darkened. "She's inhaled something. Possibly concussed. We need to get her out of here. Now."

Christian lifted her again. Nixi whimpered, coughed, but didn't resist.

Amka stood, shaken but solid. "Take her. I'll wait for Lucas and the fire truck."

"No. You're with us," Christian ordered.

Dutch came out of the kitchen, extinguisher hissing in his grip, his face streaked with soot. "Fire's down," he said. "Decent explosion. I'll call Brock and the troopers, and I'll close the place down."

"Thanks." Christian carried Nixi outside and toward the doctor's truck with May and Amka running beside him. Cold air hit them as they moved. The contrast slapped the sweat from his skin and cleared the smoke from his throat.

Nixi's fingers curled into his jacket, just barely. She coughed once more, then her eyes opened a sliver. "Не оставляй меня," she whispered.

Don't leave me. Christian interpreted her words instantly. "I'm right here," he said. "I'm not going anywhere."

She rasped out one more word, her voice thinner than air. "Damian."

Then she went completely limp in his arms and her eyelids fluttered shut.

CHAPTER 33

Christian stood in the hallway, arms braced on either side of the doorframe, staring into the clinic room like he could will the machines to do their damn jobs when too often they'd failed in his life. In clinics and hospitals a million miles away from this one, in dirt and sand, blood and eventual death. But he was here now. Home in Alaska.

Nixi remained unconscious, a pale figure swallowed by hospital sheets and shadows. Oxygen cannula in place. Bandages on her arm. A burn on her neck just starting to blister. The monitor beeped steadily, showing normal vitals, but quiet. Too quiet.

He hated that sound. It was a false comfort. Machines could lie. He'd seen them do it before—steady vitals until they flatlined in the middle of a breath.

Amka sat outside the exam room, blanket draped around her shoulders like armor. One knee bounced. She appeared calm but a tear tipped over onto her face.

Christian's jaw locked.

Someone had just tried to kill her. Again.

He clenched his fists and exhaled through his nose. He

wanted names. Faces. A reason. But mostly, he wanted blood. Whoever had planted that device, whoever had set that fire—they hadn't missed by much. If Amka hadn't shut the door from the kitchen when she went into the bar, she'd be dead.

He forced the thought down. Buried it like a live wire.

May stepped out of Nixi's room, chart in hand. Her scrubs were clean now, hair pulled back. Professional. Controlled. Not the woman passed out at the bar two hours ago. "She's stable," May said, her voice clinical and direct. "The smoke inhalation isn't critical, but she's hypoxic. There's swelling in her airways. She needs to stay here under oxygen and observation. I've set her fractured radius. I'll sedate her if she starts to panic again."

Christian exhaled. "How long?"

"At least overnight. Maybe longer. I'll know more after the next scan and blood gas. We've started fluids. She's going to be weak for a while."

He looked over her shoulder at Nixi's still form. "She said Damian's name."

"And she spoke Russian. Just who the heck is this woman?" May asked.

Christian slowly shrugged, the tension pulling tight between his shoulders.

May tucked the chart against her chest. "You need to take Amka home."

His gaze snapped to her.

"She's not burned. Not concussed. But her cortisol is off the charts and her blood pressure is riding a spike that's going to crash sooner than later." May's voice didn't waver. "You keep her upright any longer, she's going to fall on her face. If you want her safe, get her horizontal with a blanket and water."

"Got it."

May turned back into Nixi's room. "Take my rig tonight, because I'm staying here. I'll call if anything changes."

The outside door opened and Steve the influencer guy

helped Lorrie Warner inside. The widow leaned heavily against him, and she'd gone stark pale.

May hurried toward them. "What's happened?"

Steven handed the woman over. "We were by the pool tables when something exploded in the kitchen, and a mug fell off one of the shelves above us and hit her on the head. She seemed fine, but then she passed out after we finished helping Dutch lock up."

May put her arm over the woman's shoulders. "Come on back to an examination room. Let's take a look at you, um—"

"Lorrie," the woman whispered. "I came up here to identify my husband's body. I just want to take him home."

Christian stepped back, dug out his phone, and moved toward the far wall of the hallway. He scrolled to Damian's name to call.

One ring. Two. Voicemail.

He hung up. Tried again. Same result.

Christian didn't curse. Didn't pace. Just stared at the wall while heat started crawling back up his spine. If Damian was embedded, the radio silence could be anything—mission blackout, comms interference, or just his usual ghost routine.

Still, Christian hated the silence.

He'd do anything to protect his brothers. But what did Damian need in this situation? Christian had sensed something in Nixi's voice just before she passed out. Panic. Recognition. The way she'd said Damian's name, like it wasn't just a word. Like it was a warning…or a need.

Christian moved back into her room and took a picture with his phone. Not a close-up, just enough. Nixi's face, half turned on the pillow, the oxygen line stark against her pale skin. He moved around and got a better shot of her entire face. Even so pale, with bruises already forming, she was lovely. Damian's type? Or Damian's enemy? Or someone he once worked with?

Christian sent the picture to his brother with a message:

EXPLOSION. NAME IS NIXI. SHE'S ALIVE. SPOKE RUSSIAN AND SAID YOUR NAME RIGHT BEFORE SHE PASSED OUT. YOU KNOW HER?

He hit send.

Still nothing.

Christian scrubbed a hand down his face, then turned to find Amka sitting, arms tight around her ribs like she was holding herself together by force of will alone. He crossed the hall. "You're done here," he said softly.

Her chin lifted, defiant.

May's voice echoed in his head. *You want her safe, get her horizontal.* "I'm not asking," he added.

Amka's lips pressed into a line, but she didn't argue. Didn't snap back like she might've on another day. She stood without a word, blanket slipping off her shoulders, and walked with him through the exit, quiet and steady until they reached the cold night air.

Then she leaned into him. Not much. Just enough to tell him she needed the contact but wouldn't admit it out loud. He gave in to his own needs and turned, lifting her against his chest. Right where he wanted her.

He didn't look back. Nixi was safe for now. Damian would call when he could. But Amka was still breathing beside Christian. And she was his priority.

Everything else could burn.

Tika showed up like a storm.

Amka was halfway through peeling off her smoke-wrecked sweater in Christian's living room when the front door blew open and the wolf-dog barreled in, all muscle and mud and eyes that didn't match.

"Oh my," she muttered, just in time to catch him before he launched all hundred pounds of himself onto the couch.

"Hey," Christian protested, moving for the animal.

Amka held up a hand as she and the animal landed on the sofa. "No. He's fine. Let him be."

Tika barked once, sharp and proud, then dropped to her lap with a huff. His fur was damp, his paws filthy, and he smelled like pine needles and the wind. She ran her hands along his sides anyway, checking for wounds. Nothing but brambles.

"You didn't call him home," she said.

"I don't need to. He comes home when he's ready."

She looked up at Christian. He was leaning against the doorframe, arms crossed, eyes shadowed but steady. That hit her strange. She stared at him, then at the dog sprawled over her legs, then back again. She saw them both. "You're the same," she said. "You and him."

Christian raised an eyebrow. "Because we have different colored eyes and growl?"

"No," she said. "Because you don't belong in a cage, and God help anyone who threatens what you care about."

Christian didn't respond. But his mouth twitched like maybe he wanted to.

"And the eyes," she added, softer. "People look at both of you and only see the wild."

He almost smiled again. "You saying I need obedience training?"

The idea made her laugh, and at the feeling, her entire body relaxed. Finally. "No. I'm saying I get it. Would never cage either of you." She went with her heart and said what she thought. It was all she had, and she'd give it to him. "Thought you should know that."

The silence that followed wasn't awkward. Just real. Like something had settled between them.

Then she remembered. She sat up straighter, nearly pushing Tika off her lap. "I needed to show you something earlier."

He tensed. "What?"

"Somebody left a note by the back door. I didn't recognize the handwriting."

"Where is it?"

She should've shoved it in her pocket. "I put it under the invoices and forgot all about it after the explosion."

His mouth firmed. "What did it say?"

"The note said that the town would hate me if they found out about Hank, that Flossy should be in prison, and that I need to give them fifty thousand dollars for their confidentiality. No. That Jarod and I need to have fifty grand. That he has insurance money and I own the tavern." She gulped. "Somebody is blackmailing me. Again. But also Jarod. Is this someone new, or could it be the person he trusted to have the video?"

Christian's face didn't change, but she saw the shift in him. The way he pulled inward, calculating. Fierce. Before he could speak, his phone buzzed from his back pocket. A quick expression of annoyance darkened his handsome face before he pulled it out. "What?"

The man really didn't like the phone, now did he?

"Doing what?" He remained still in that way he had. "From credit cards? Yeah? What about video?" He listened again. "Canvas? Yeah. I guess it's worth a shot. Thanks for tonight. You were on it." He clicked off.

Amka tilted her head.

"Background from Jarod's credit cards came in. All of those trips to Anchorage? He stayed at the Wallace Motel most every time, and he ate meals out. With somebody. This was all last year, so it's doubtful we'll find any CCTV, but Dutch has a couple of troopers hitting the motel and each of the restaurants to see if we can find who Jarod ate with."

That didn't sound helpful. "Nothing else?"

Christian studied her. "He spent a lot of time at a couple of strip clubs."

She rolled her eyes. "I couldn't care less. I'd just like to know if the person trying to kill me thinks I know something about Jarod, because I don't." Frustration crawled with pinpricks beneath her skin. It wasn't fair. "We're no closer figuring out who wants me dead, or who has the video of Hank's death." Her entire life was at risk from both situations.

"I know." Christian eyed the window as energy rolled off him.

She looked out at the darkness. "You can go, C. I'm safe here. Nobody knows where we are." This place was probably the safest place in Alaska right now. "Go. Take Tika if you want."

He clenched his jaw so hard a muscle rippled near his cheekbone. "I'm not leaving you."

Sweet. The dangerous man had such a sweet side. He'd probably be insulted if she told him that. So she stood. "When you sleep outside, where do you go?"

He didn't answer. Just stood there looking at her, a glitter in his eyes. A deep one.

"Christian?"

"There's a ridge up behind the cabin. Protected from the wind with views in every direction. Set into the hill."

So nobody could surprise him. From any direction. "It sounds nice." She dropped the blanket and walked over to him, taking his hand. He let her. "Do you have to sleep alone out there?"

His chin slowly lifted. "You are not sleeping outside just because I have issues."

"It isn't raining, and the stars are out. Why wouldn't I want to sleep outside?" She'd grown up in Alaska, for goodness sakes. "I've camped out beneath the northern lights so many times I can't count them. Why do you feel badly about sleeping in nature?"

"Because I have to. When there isn't a choice, it's a weakness."

Wow. When he decided to be truthful and possibly vulnerable, he went all in. She tightened her grip on his hand, which was so much bigger than hers. Warmer, too. "Look at it like a strength. The entire world is trying to get back to nature, and you live easily there. I can't imagine anybody not wanting to sleep outside on a night like this. I'd like to sleep with you." Beneath the millions of stars they could see in Alaska.

"You've been in two explosions in less than a week, and your body has to hurt. You need a bed."

"I need you." Apparently he wasn't the only one being vulnerable tonight. "Where you're comfortable. I assume you have a sleeping bag?"

"Of course."

She looked down at the wolf-pup, who was staring at her like he was also following the conversation. Somehow. "Then let's all sleep outside. Yeah, I hurt. But nature can heal. You know it, our people have always known it, and I feel it deep inside." She'd always embraced her Inuit culture, and the pulse of Alaska sang through her often. "Please."

He straightened. "All right. But if you get cold or uncomfortable, you will tell me. Got it?"

"Yeah." She felt like she'd won a huge battle. "Show me your spot, Christian."

CHAPTER 34

The morning air tasted like wet moss and new leaves. Cold, clean, and just sharp enough to keep him still. The sky hadn't gone blue yet but the dark was losing its grip, softening at the edges, turning that shade of gray that meant the sun was getting ready to climb.

A thrush called once from deep in the trees. Another answered. Somewhere downhill, a stream moved fast over rock, swollen from melt. The earth smelled like thaw and pine needles.

Christian sat at the edge of the ledge. There was no reason to move. No threat in the silence. Just a wide sweep of forest waking up.

Behind him, Amka slept curled inside the thermal sleeping bag atop a thick mat he'd dug out of his gear closet, her back tucked against the stone ledge. He'd insisted on the mat for her comfort, and truth be told, he hadn't minded. Had enjoyed holding her all night in the snug sleeping bag.

Her breath was steady, her face half-buried in the bag's hood. Tika had parked himself across her ankles and was snoring like it was a job. The animal hadn't stirred once all night. Neither had she.

Birdsong grew louder as the light shifted. Yellow-green lichen glowed on the rocks, and dew clung to the low brush like the whole world had exhaled and settled. Spring was coming fast now. He could feel it pushing up from the ground.

Nothing moved in the trees. Not yet. Still early. The kind of early he liked. Quiet. Alive. His bones knew this kind of morning. His blood settled into it without asking.

He watched the ridgeline and listened to the forest breathe.

Tika finally stirred, stretching and yawning, pushing to his feet. He padded over and sat, nudging Christian with his ear.

Christian obliged him and scratched down his head, feeling the thick fur.

Tika turned his head and looked behind him.

"I know," Christian murmured. The woman had slept outside with him all night. Not one complaint. Only a sleepy pointing out of the various constellations. She even created a couple of new ones for him. For fun. He'd never met anybody, besides his family, who accepted him just as he was. But what did that give her? He glanced over his shoulder to see her thick hair tumbled out of the bag. Protection, for sure. Love. Yeah, he could probably do that. He wasn't sure about romance but could probably ask Brock for advice. He seemed romantic. Sometimes.

Tika yawned again and then eased away, climbing down the rocky trail and disappearing into the forest. Maybe to hunt or just explore.

Amka mumbled something behind him and he turned, watching her come awake. She was even more beautiful than the sunrise now coloring the sky pink. "Hi." Did she sound shy?

"Hi." He moved to her. "You okay?"

"A little cold." She flapped open the bag in obvious invitation.

Well, all right. He slid back inside and enclosed them, spooning her with her sweet ass against his groin. Instantly, his cock went rock hard.

She giggled. Not laughed. Not chuckled. But actually giggled, sounding young and free. Had he ever heard her giggle before? His heart thumped. Hard. "Are you sore from sleeping on the ground?"

"Nope." She wriggled her butt. "This mat you forced up here makes this as luxurious as a real hotel bed. Like one from a fancy hotel in Anchorage." She wriggled again. The brat was doing that on purpose.

He'd been a perfect gentleman all night, and Hank would've been proud. "Your body is way too sore for what I want to do with it." He might as well be honest with her.

She turned in his arms, her hip sliding across his erection. From the spark of wickedness in her eyes, she meant the torturous touch. "Like I said, I'm not sore." She rolled her hips against him again, playful and sure, and that smile—half-mischief, half-invitation—cut clean through his good intentions.

Well, all right. He was just done fighting them.

He kissed her, taking over slowly, until her teasing quieted, lips parting under his. His hand slid under the sleeping bag, up beneath her shirt, across the warm skin of her stomach. She sucked in a breath.

"You okay?" he asked, voice low against her mouth.

"I'm perfect," she murmured, breath hitching. "Touch me."

God help him. He was trying.

His hand slipped under her shirt, rough palm to bare skin. She sucked in a breath, hips shifting just enough to tell him she wanted more. He rubbed his thumb over her nipple—slow, light—and felt her body tighten against his.

She didn't say anything, didn't need to. The way she moved said it all.

He dragged his mouth along her neck, tasting sweat and salt and her. Her shirt was in his way, so he shoved the material up. She lifted her arms, sleepy and sure, and he yanked the shirt off and tossed the fabric aside. Somewhere. Who cared?

He looked down, unable to help himself. Her hair was wild, eyes half-lidded, chest rising fast. She looked unreal. He leaned in and took one nipple between his lips. Sucked. She groaned, low in her throat, and her nails dug into his back.

That sound she made. Yeah, he could live there.

His hand moved again. Down her stomach. Into her yoga pants. She opened for him like she'd been waiting all night.

Warm. Slick. Already there.

His breath caught in his chest. "Still good?"

She nodded fast, then wrapped her leg around his and pulled him closer. "Yes. Christian, yes."

He slid a finger inside. She clenched around him, hips grinding slow. He added another, worked her open, kissed her again just to keep from losing it.

"God, you feel good," he muttered against her mouth.

"Then don't stop."

Not a chance in hell.

He shifted down and kissed her breast, slow and reverent, then the other, and felt her fingers grip his shoulders tight. She was hot silk and heat, already wet. He groaned into her skin, and her hips lifted, her breath catching.

"More," she whispered.

So he gave her more. "One of these days, I'm gonna make you beg." Not this morning. Not when her body had to be hurting from the explosions, and not while he wanted to show her that he could be gentle. Not often. But sometimes.

He used two fingers now, working gently, circling with his thumb, listening for her sounds, the way her thighs tightened and her breath got shallower. She was unraveling under his hand, and Christ, it was the most beautiful thing he'd ever seen.

Watching her face, he felt every pulse and tremor, and didn't stop until her body arched and she came apart in his arms, trembling against him, her breath a broken whisper of his name. He kissed her as she came down, deep and slow, his hand still resting between her legs, holding the heat of her.

When she opened her eyes again, they were clear and full of something he wasn't sure he deserved.

"You sure?" he asked, voice rough now.

"Yeah." She smiled, slow and certain, shimmying out of her pants. "I want you. Now."

He kissed her again, her jaw, her throat, her shoulder. Then he rolled on top of her, careful not to crush her. Slowly, taking his time, he slid inside her, inch by inch, and she gasped his name like a prayer.

Everything else disappeared.

The sleeping bag, the ledge, the chill in the air were gone. There was only Amka wrapped around him, clinging to him, moving with him like this was always meant to happen. And maybe it was.

When she dug her nails into his ass, he started to pound. Hot and fast, hammering into her as if he never wanted to be free. Her gasps spurred him on.

Fire rushed through him, down his spine, blasting into his cock. He switched his angle, pounding against her clit, and she went over. Hard. She arched against him, the cords in her neck stretching, her mouth forming his name.

Her internal walls grabbed him so hard his vision went black. The climax ripped through him, taking everything he wanted to be, giving it all to her. Panting, overcome, he stayed inside her as she quieted.

"Definitely not too sore," she murmured with a half laugh.

He didn't deserve her. Didn't care. It was too late for them both to find another path. Christian rested his cheek against her hair and listened to the world breathe. For just a moment of peace.

They had this brief reprieve for now but would have to get off the mountain soon. She needed to check back in with Doc May as well as the troopers, and he needed to cut off the head of whoever wanted to hurt her.

But they had a few minutes. So he leaned down and kissed her again. Harder this time. He had only so much gentle in him. By the quickening of her breath, she was just fine with that.

Hopefully she understood how far he'd go to keep her safe now. There were no limits.

None.

CHRISTIAN STOOD near the sink in the small examination room, arms crossed, boots planted, watching Amka sit on the paper-lined table in jeans and a thick white sweater. They'd stopped by her place for clothing on the way in, since the forensic team from Anchorage had cleared the scene. They'd actually done a good job cleaning up after themselves.

Amka swung one foot, a healthy flush on her face. He'd put that there. He tried not to smile.

Doc May clicked through her tablet with one hand and aimed a pulse ox at Amka's finger with the other. Her pink scrubs were wrinkled, her blonde hair shoved into a bun that had started to slide sideways. "You're stable. Blood pressure's a little low, but not dangerous. No signs of delayed shock. No coughing, so your lungs stayed clear. That's good."

"I'm feeling fine," Amka said.

May smiled. "Still had to check. Headaches?"

"Only when Christian won't stop watching me."

Christian didn't blink. "Get used to it."

That flush went full-on crimson red in her cheeks, and he watched, fascinated.

May snorted without looking up from her screen. "Don't make me kick you out of here, Christian."

Christian gave Amka a look.

She looked back like she was weighing how hard she could kick him with one boot. "May, how's Nixi?" she asked.

"Still out, last I checked." May glanced at the clock on the wall. "She woke up briefly around four, so I gave her more fluids and pain meds. Nixi was resting easy when I walked by a few moments ago."

The front door slammed open.

Heavy boots. Fast steps. Heading their way.

Christian turned toward the hallway just as Damian appeared in the doorway. No perfectly pressed slacks. No Armani suit jacket. Just jeans worn at the knees, T-shirt stretched and inside out at the collar. Hair a mess. No fancy watch or matching belt. Just wild eyes and too much urgency for a guy who normally tied his shoes with military precision.

Christian stared at him, stunned. His brother looked unhinged.

"Where is she?" Damian barked.

Christian stepped out into the hallway, putting himself between Damian and the exam room. "Who?"

"Nixi. Where is she?"

Christian didn't ask more. "This way." He just turned and walked, Damian fast behind him to the last door on the left. He pushed it open.

The bed was empty. Blankets had been shoved to the side on the bed and the IV unplugged. A hospital bracelet, torn off not cut, sat on the tray.

No Nixi.

Christian's gut dropped. He looked around the room fast.

The bathroom door lay open, and the window appeared mostly shut. "May said she was here this morning."

"She's supposed to be here," Damian snapped. His voice cracked around the edges now. "Where the hell is she?"

Footsteps pinged behind them.

Doc May came in. "Amka ran down to the restroom. I had to give her a tetanus shot and she hates needles." May's eyes went wide, and her tablet nearly slipped from her hand. "What? No. Nixi was here sleeping. Her arm is broken, she can't—" Her voice cut out. She strode to the bed, looked at the unplugged equipment, then the bracelet on the tray. "I didn't hear a thing."

Christian turned to her. "She walk out or was she taken?"

"She shouldn't be walking at all due to her condition. She has a fractured radius, and there are two layers of gauze covering her burns. Additionally, the IV medications are still metabolizing in her system. If she got up and left, I'll eat my stethoscope," May said.

Damian's jaw snapped shut. "Oh, you don't know her. I'd bet my life that brat ignored the pain and walked right out of here."

Christian looked at Damian, whose green eyes burned a deep fire. "Who is she?"

"Stella," Damian said, his teeth audibly grinding.

"Your ex-wife?" Christian had never been so shocked in his entire life.

Damian's chin lifted with a look most people would run from. "We didn't exactly get divorced."

What the fuck?

CHAPTER 35

Amka stepped out of the restroom and paused, adjusting to the cooler air in the hallway. The hospital lights were too bright, but her headache had dulled to something manageable. It had settled into a soft throb behind her temples. Man, she hated needles. Why did she have to have another tetanus shot, anyway? She rolled her shoulders, and the soreness in her body made itself known. A deep, even ache stretched across her thighs and down her back, earned the good way.

Something had changed with Christian that morning on the ridge. With them both. She didn't want to let him go. At the thought, she paused. She'd probably been in love with him for months. Her chest heated.

If he thought he was getting away from her, he'd lost his mind.

She walked slowly at first, letting her body settle. Thank goodness she'd been able to get some of her own clothing. Her home had still smelled like chemicals, but they'd at least cleaned up. She hoped Jarod hadn't been killed there, and Christian said he didn't see any evidence that he had. She had grabbed fresh clothes and an overnight kit.

Now, as she made her way down the quiet hallway, she thought about Lorrie Warner.

The woman had been knocked down during the chaos at the tavern. Amka had barely gotten a look at her before Christian had pulled her away from the fire, but someone had said Lorrie had taken a mug to the head. One of Amka's mugs that decorated the place had fallen from a shelf. That detail wouldn't let go. Lorrie's husband was dead, and Amka had no idea whether the woman had even had a chance to grieve properly.

May had mentioned that Lorrie had stayed overnight.

The least Amka could do was look in on her. She turned left at the end of the hall and stopped outside Room 3. The door was slightly ajar. The light inside was dim. She hesitated and then quietly walked in, not wanting to awaken the young widow if she'd found sleep.

What Amka saw didn't fit.

Lorrie was sitting up in the hospital bed. Her blonde hair was down, loose across the pillow. The blanket was pulled to her waist. Her expression was soft, even peaceful. Steve was leaning over her. His hand cupped her face. He was kissing her.

Not on the cheek. Not her forehead.

Mouth to mouth. Close. Long. Intimate.

Amka didn't move. What the heck? Was Steve taking advantage of the poor woman? She was about to intercede when Lorrie lifted her hand and touched his chest. There was nothing hesitant about it. No confusion, no distress. She looked at him the way a woman looks at a man she wants.

What was happening? This didn't make any sense.

Steve leaned back and chuckled, his blond hair catching the light from the bathroom. "I can't believe it worked. This was insane, and we did it. Fucking Eli. Damn, he was hard to kill."

Amka gasped.

Steve turned at the sound, eyes catching hers. The smile

dropped from his face in a blink. "You weren't supposed to hear that," he said, too calm. He grabbed her by the arm and yanked hard, pulling her fully into the room, quietly shutting the door behind her. He shoved her onto the bed, where she fell, her mouth opening to scream.

"Stop," he hissed, yanking a gun out of his jacket pocket to point at her. A matte-black pistol.

Amka pushed herself off the bed, her gaze shifting between them. "What did you do?" She looked at Lorrie, whose eyes had gone wide. "Lorrie?"

Lorrie plucked a loose string on the white blanket covering her. "Eli was mean. A total jerk. Steve and I have been in love for years, and he thought, well, we should be together." Tears filled her eyes. "They're business partners, and Steve is so much better at it than Eli is. He should run the construction company. We should do it together."

Amka tried to make sense of the entire situation. "You're an influencer." She would not look at the gun. Instead, she tried to make eye contact with Steve. "You have tons of followers."

He smirked. "Yeah, I've done that for fun for a while. When I saw the contest, I came up with the plan."

The plan to brutally murder Lorrie's husband? Amka slowly shook her head. "I don't understand."

Lorrie preened. "See? Steve is super smart. He went to all of those small towns and did the interviews and everything. He might even win the fifty grand. Can you believe it? He talked Eli into meeting him up here for a boys' week."

Steve snorted. "I figured this hick town in the middle of nowhere would be a good place to take care of the problem." He shrugged. "I thought I had him that first night, nearly nailed him through the window of the tavern."

Amka gaped. So he'd aimed inside the tavern and not at her on the street? "You were the sniper?"

"Yeah." Steve's chest filled. "I'm a pretty good shot."

This made no sense. "So you weren't shooting at me?"

"No. Why would I shoot at you?" Steve frowned.

Amka couldn't breathe. He was a crappy shot, then. Didn't come close to taking out the guys inside the tavern, even with the window open. "Why did you cut my brake line and plant those explosions?"

He looked at her blankly.

Lorrie coughed. "That wasn't Steve. He's a good guy, Amka. He didn't try to hurt you."

A good guy? Amka's stomach lurched. If she screamed, Christian would come running, but Steve would just shoot him. Or her. Or both of them. What should she do? She gulped, trying to keep him talking. Christian would come looking for her soon and hopefully hear them. "So you killed your friend out in the forest and gouged out his eyes?"

Steve winced. "Yeah. It was totally gross, to be honest. But once I was here, I heard about those other deaths, and I figured why not? Everyone would think he was just another victim." His face fell. "But now you know everything, and I'm sorry, that can't happen."

Amka looked at Lorrie. "Why didn't you just get a divorce?"

Lorrie looked down at her hands. "Eli had money. It was his before we got married, so it'd be his if we got divorced. Our community property isn't much. So now his money is ours. We plan to do really good stuff with it. I promise."

"Don't give me that innocent act," Amka spat. "You're a stone-cold bitch, Lorrie. A killer."

The woman paled.

"Actually, I'm the killer," Steve hissed. "You're about to know that. If you scream, I'll shoot you and everyone who even thinks of coming through that door." He gestured with the gun toward the window. "Go to the window and open it. Quietly. No screaming. No sudden moves. We're getting out of here, and you're going first."

She shook her head. "I'm giving you one warning. You do not want to do this. Christian will find you, and he'll destroy you."

Steve just stepped closer, gun steady. "You're going out that window."

She turned toward it. Her body was shaking. Not visibly, but she felt it. Deep in her legs, in her spine. If she let Steve get her outside, he'd kill her. No question. Her hand touched the sill.

Steve moved behind her, close. Too close.

She took a breath. There was only one way out of this. Then she turned, fast and low, and drove her shoulder into his gut.

He grunted, staggered back, the gun jerking upward as she grabbed for his wrist. She locked both hands on Steve's arm, trying to wrestle the weapon free. He shoved her hard. They went down together, tangled, his knee hitting her side.

The gun scraped across the floor.

She went for it.

He grabbed her ankle.

She kicked, connected with something soft, and crawled for the gun, trying to scream but her voice went hoarse out of panic. Her breath burst out of her.

His hand caught her shirt and yanked her back. Her nails scraped the tile. She twisted, elbowing him hard in the ribs. He swore. They rolled, her back hitting the wall, his weight pressing down.

She reached up, found his face, and raked her nails down his cheek. He hissed and shoved her head to the side, fingers digging into her jaw. Her hand shot out, found the base of the IV stand. She gripped it and swung, tears clogging her eyes, panic heating her breath.

It connected.

He fell sideways, stunned for a second, just enough for her to scramble free. They both reached for the gun, hands connecting, scrambling.

The weapon fired.

The sound was deafening. She felt the pressure in her ears before the pain hit. The window cracked. Lorrie screamed.

Steve wrenched the gun free, backed up on his knees, and aimed it at Amka's head.

⁓

CHRISTIAN STARED AT HIS BROTHER. "You're not divorced?"

"No," Damian said.

A gun discharged down the hallway.

Christian's blood iced.

Then it surged.

"Amka," he breathed. He ran, a panic taking over. One he didn't recognize and hadn't felt before. His boots slammed against the tile, and he hit the hallway corner hard, the sound of a woman screaming curling inside his ears. High. Panicked. Lorrie?

Going on instinct, he followed the sound and kicked open the door to the third and last room in the small hospital. He saw Steve first, kneeling, pointing a gun at Amka, breath heaving like he'd just run ten miles. Blood along his face. Eyes wild.

Then Amka.

She was on her back against the far wall. Her shirt was torn at the shoulder, her lip split, and her chest rose fast and shallow. But she was breathing, her eyes wide.

That was all Christian needed to see.

He hit Steve full force, shoulder down, fists already moving. The two of them crashed against the wall, the gun skidding across the floor. Christian drove a punch into Steve's ribs, then another, higher, into the neck.

Steve tried to fight back. He got one hit in—glancing, sloppy. Christian didn't care. He was inside his own head now, where it was quiet and efficient. Where every movement had a goal.

Take him down.

He slammed Steve to the ground and drove his knee into the man's chest, pinning him.

Damian flew in behind him and kicked the gun out of reach.

Steve screamed. Christian moved off the asshole.

"You good?" Damian asked, yanking Steve onto his feet. Something popped in Steve's arm. The guy cried out, his face going stark white.

Christian didn't answer. He was already edging toward Amka. "Hey," he said, voice hoarse, controlled only by force of will. "Amka. You with me?"

She blinked slowly, lips parted. Blood had run from the corner of her mouth, down her chin. Her right hand trembled slightly where it gripped the floor. But her eyes were clear. Alert. "I'm okay," she whispered.

"Bullshit," he breathed, brushing her hair back from her face. "You're bleeding."

"So are you," she said, her voice rough.

He realized then that he was. His knuckles were split open from hitting Steve. Didn't matter. He helped her sit up carefully, one arm bracing her back. She winced but stayed conscious.

Behind them, Lorrie started sobbing. Damian barked something Christian didn't catch, and the woman stopped.

Amka shuddered. "Steve and Lorrie are lovers. They planned to kill her husband. Steve shot at Eli that night outside the tavern, and then Steve killed the poor guy in the forest and cut out his eyes to look like the other victims. But Steve didn't set the explosives or cut my brake lines."

What the hell? Christian grasped her arms, his brain trying to make sense of the situation. The sniper was Steve? And the asshole had been aiming for those tourists inside the tavern? Christian should've looked at all angles of this. "Are you hurt?"

"No." Amka sniffed. "He told me to go to the window, so I had to try for the gun. I couldn't let him get me outside."

"You were smart. And brave." Christian pressed a kiss to her temple, though all he wanted to do was break Steve's neck.

Damian shoved Steve against the wall as May came into view, her eyes wide. "I texted Brock. He'll come down and arrest these assholes."

Christian helped Amka out of the room. "You scared me," he said.

"I scared myself," she murmured. "But I wasn't going out that window."

He didn't smile. Not yet. Not until she was checked out again. Not until he saw her in clean clothes and could hold her without shaking. "May? Would you take a look at her, please?"

"Of course." May moved on ahead. "Come down to the examination room. Um, again."

As they left the room, Christian glanced at Steve, who had crumpled against the wall. He was lucky he still breathed. Christian didn't say a word—just stared him in the eye with a promise of death if Christian ever got the chance.

Steve looked away first.

CHAPTER 36

The tavern still smelled like burnt wood and bleach.

Amka sat at the far table near the back window, a warm bowl of chicken soup from the Green Plate in front of her, but her appetite hadn't caught up yet. Daisy had brought the soup in a thermos from the café and now busied herself with cleaning soot off the bar. They'd closed for the week, but Amka wasn't up to figuring out how badly the kitchen was damaged right now.

Lucas had come by to survey the place, muttering the entire time that he'd moved to Alaska to get away from fire and would never miss a town meeting again. That somebody else could take over as tanker chief. His jaw tight, he'd told Amka he'd be back soon for an in-depth investigation.

Poor guy. All he wanted to do was write his darn book.

Christian sat to Amka's right, one arm resting along the back of her chair like he'd planted himself there permanently. Damian sat across from them, shoulders stiff, eyes constantly scanning the room like a threat might come through the door at any second.

Nobody spoke for a while. The soup cooled.

Christian looked at Damian. "Time for you to catch us up. We knew you were briefly married to a woman named Stella for a job in Intelligence, and that you got divorced, but you'd never talk about it."

Amka studied the brothers. No doubt Christian had never forced his brother to talk. That wasn't his style.

Damian ran a rough hand through his thick black hair. "Yeah, Stella and I married for a job. It was a shitshow and I can't tell you much about it. But we never got divorced. I've been looking for her for years, and now that I'm out, I planned to find her. I had no clue she was in town."

This was too weird.

"You married a purple haired pixie-like twenty year old?" Christian shook his head.

Damian barked out a laugh. "She's a master at disguises. Stella is thirty and her natural hair color is platinum blonde. Think Russian starlet." He tugged out his phone to text. "I'm asking Dutch to put out a BOLO on her, but they'll never find her. She's that good."

Christian narrowed his gaze. "You seem okay with this. That she was in town and now she's gone."

Damian smiled, and there was no humor in the look. More like anticipation. "Yeah, but she was here for a reason, so I'm sure I'll see her soon. Can't wait." He rolled his neck. "We have more immediate concerns, don't you think?"

Amka stirred her soup and kept her voice even. "Yeah. Whoever keeps trying to kill me, besides Steve, has to think I know something about Jarod. Right?"

"Right," Christian said. "I can't think of any other reason. Brock texted earlier with news about the canvassing in Anchorage. A bartender there kind of remembers Jarod often hanging out with a woman last summer, but he can't remember much about her. She might've been blonde...or brunette."

"That's not helpful," Amka sighed. She hadn't wanted to

know anything about Jarod. "Whoever has the video must be starting to wonder about Jarod's whereabouts. Nobody in town has really asked yet, because he so often took off, but even they will soon." She'd already given the scary note to Christian, and he figured it had to be from the person that Jarod trusted. Maybe she should just pay up. Her heart hurt. How was she going to protect Flossy? The sweet woman could not go to prison.

Christian's phone buzzed. He checked the screen, eyes narrowing. "Dutch." He stepped away from the table, pacing toward the front window as he answered. "Yeah?"

Amka eyed him, knowing he wanted to be outside. Out hunting for whoever was trying to hurt her. "I initially didn't want to date your brother because I didn't want to have to take care of a man."

Damian snorted. "Seriously? Sweetheart, you don't read people very well."

"I know." She let an embarrassed grin slip. "Since we've been, well, whatever we've been doing, he's rescued me from an explosion, bullets, a freezing river, and a psycho with a gun by putting himself in danger each time. He paid my bail, and he's kept me safe for more nights than I can count." Sure, she probably could count them, but why?

Damian watched his brother for a moment. "I don't think he's the easiest of guys, but he'll definitely take care of you. That probably goes both ways."

"I know, and I'm happy to make sure he gets outside and doesn't force himself into society. I accept him as he is, and I like him." More than that. Way more. "But he doesn't exactly seem like he wants to get serious, you know?" She hadn't been joking about wanting kids.

Damian's mouth twitched. "He's serious, Amka. Believe me." He glanced at her, his eyes a burning green in the tavern. "He's not great with words, but he'll stick. I hope you slap him upside the head if you need."

That was sweet. Osprey sweet. "You think I'll have to?"

"Yes." Damian took a sip of the soup. "He's also thickheaded and doesn't realize what a good mate he'd be. You might have to smack him a few times."

She could do that. Her stomach grumbling, she forced a sip of soup, but it tasted like salt and metal now. Her lip was still swollen, and she could feel the tight scab forming just inside where she'd bit down too hard during the fight. Every muscle in her body ached. Her ribs throbbed. It had been a seriously rough week.

Christian's voice cut across the room. Sharper now. "You're what?" he said into the phone. He turned around slowly, lowering the phone from his ear. Then he retook his seat, irritation rolling off him along with that heat he always seemed to provide.

"What is it?" Damian asked.

"Dutch says he's off chasing a lead on the eyeless victims. He's going quiet for a while—no cell, no updates, no backup."

"And?" Damian prompted.

Christian scrubbed a hand down his face. "I've been pulled off as a consultant on the case."

The words didn't register at first. "What?" Amka asked.

"There are charges pending against you," Christian said. "And possibly against me. Dutch didn't give details, but he said his boss said I'm out of it until the situation is resolved."

That sucked. "I'm so sorry, Christian," she breathed.

"Not your fault," Christian said. "I just don't like Dutch going at it alone."

"He's been a lone wolf his whole life," Damian said. "Plus, I've been keeping track of the investigation through various avenues, and there are no leads. Not good ones. The first murder occurred months ago, and there's nothing. My guess is that it'll take a while to break. Probably several more months."

Christian stretched his neck. "Hopefully not more victims."

Amka shivered. "Word's gotten around about the deaths, so everyone knows to be careful. But the tourists don't listen."

"It's just so odd that nobody can identify the victims," Damian muttered. "Now that we know Steve killed Eli Warner, all of the victims are unidentified again."

The front door opened with a jingle that was too cheerful for the mood inside.

Wyland Friday walked in first, his boots dragging slightly. His gray hair was fuzzy around his head, and his whiskers rampant across his worn face. Sheldon followed, a white-paper-wrapped bouquet in his hand.

Amka stood without thinking. Her body didn't want to move quickly, but she made it work. She approached them both. "Our kitchen is out, but I could get you both a drink if you'd like."

Wyland awkwardly patted her shoulder with his beefy hand. "We just wanted to check on you. Make sure you're okay." The old guy's eyes softened. "Maybe you should take a vacation?"

It wasn't a horrible idea, but her problems would still be there when she returned.

Sheldon smiled, looking nice today in dark jeans and a blue sweater that brought out his eyes. He'd combed his hair back, too. "The explosion was bad enough, but it's all around town about the influencer jerk who tried to kill you. I thought you could use something better to focus on." He held out the flowers.

Amka blinked. "You brought me flowers."

"Yeah." Sheldon cleared his throat. "I figured nobody else would. Thought it might help."

She stepped forward, took the bouquet from his hands, and gave a small nod. "Thank you."

Sheldon smiled. "You bet. I'm hoping when you feel better we could take in a movie? There has to be a good one coming to town soon."

She was saved from answering when Daisy came over and took the flowers. "I'll get water."

Amka turned back toward the table. "Thank you for checking on me. Are you sure I can't get you a drink?"

Wyland hunched his shoulders in his black flannel shirt. "No, thanks. We've got inventory to do. If you need us, you call." He nodded at the Osprey brothers and then shuffled to the door. It seemed like people aged during the Alaskan winters and showed it in the spring. Amka should probably take Wyland soup during the colder days once her kitchen was back up and running.

Sheldon hesitated. "We'll talk soon. Call if you need anything." He turned just as Helene Stanford walked inside, rolling a small suitcase.

"Oh, good. You're all here." She reached into a wide bag over her arm and brought out two envelopes, one for Amka and the other for Wyland. "Northside Insurance has preliminarily denied your insurance claim upon the belief that either Amka Amaruq or Jarod Teller planted the device that caused the storage building fire." She shuffled the bag onto her shoulder. "I'm headed back to Anchorage. If Jarod Teller decides to show up for an interview, you have my contact information."

Wyland looked down at the envelope. "Where is Jarod?"

Amka shook her head. "I don't know. I'm so sorry about this, Wyland. I promise we didn't destroy that building."

Wyland opened the door and walked outside.

Sheldon's face turned a motley red. "Find that idiot, would you? The insurance money is ours." He followed his father outside.

"Come eat your soup," Daisy ordered, carrying the flowers in a mason jar back to place in the center of the table. "Listen to your lawyer." She paused, taking the envelope. "I know Nixi left the hospital, and I thought we'd hear from her." She pulled her phone out of her back pocket to show to Amka. "Her entire account has been deleted. Gone. I can't even find one picture of her on here."

Now that was impressive. "Maybe she just wanted to go off-grid." Amka wasn't going to blow her cover. Or whatever she was doing. Although, man, she was curious.

"I guess." Daisy pushed her wild hair away from her face. "Before I forget, as your attorney, I received notice of a pretrial conference in a week. We'll meet tomorrow and I'll tell you the steps. Plus, I have copies of your business documents and last will and testament." She nudged Amka into the chair. "Eat your soup." She turned and headed back to the bar.

"Will?" Christian asked.

Amka shrugged. "Figured I needed one." She picked up her spoon and sampled the soup. It tasted better this time.

"Nothing is going to happen to you. Period," Christian said.

Damian's phone buzzed, and he read the screen. "Finally. I have the ME's report on Jarod's autopsy." He scrolled for a moment. "Jarod was shot. Single gunshot wound to the head, close range. Entry just above the right brow. No exit wound. The bullet lodged in the rear cranial cavity. The medical examiner said it's still intact and was removed for ballistics. They haven't matched it to a weapon yet."

Amka's pulse kicked. She didn't say anything.

"He was still in the driver's seat," Damian added. "He had defensive injuries from scratches and contusions. There was a struggle. From what they can tell, it was quick, and he died right there. His body wasn't moved."

Christian's mouth was a hard line. "Murder weapon?"

"Small caliber. They'll know more after testing, but it wasn't something heavy. Point-blank, no hesitation."

Amka gripped the edge of the table. "So someone got in the truck with him."

"Looks that way."

Christian slowly worked through the evidence. "And Amka's house?"

"They found no evidence of an altercation of any type inside the house," Damian said. "The forensics cleared it. If Jarod was ever in there, it was just him and whatever personal effects were left behind. Nothing ties the murder to your house, Amka."

She breathed out, but it didn't help. "So he died in his truck, in my driveway." The strongest urge overtook her, and for once, she didn't fight it. She stood, moved in front of Christian, and dropped onto his lap, needing safety. The feeling of protection.

Surprise flashed across his rugged face for the briefest of seconds. He frowned but cradled her, shifting her into a more comfortable position.

She could see Damian grin from the corner of her eye. Sure, Christian might need some taking care of, but not like she'd thought. Everybody needed tending. He seemed to look out for everyone around him, and she hadn't seen that. Now she did. Giving in to all of her feelings, she leaned up and kissed him beneath the ear.

He stiffened.

She grinned. Couldn't help it. Maybe he would fight her on getting serious. Or dating. Or whatever the kids were calling it these days.

He tugged back her head to look into her eyes. "Does anybody know you created a will?"

What an odd question. "I don't know. It wasn't a huge secret." Although she hadn't wanted Jarod to know. "Why?"

Christian studied her face for a moment. "The storage building. What was the arrangement with it before you drafted a will?"

She scrunched up her face. "Oh. Huh. Wyland and I had an

informal agreement that if one of us sold or died or something, that the other would get the building. Real estate hasn't been worth much here until just recently. I'm sure he has a will now, too. Maybe?"

Christian stood suddenly, placing her back in his very warm chair. "Stay here with Damian. I'm going to talk to Wyland." He strode across the room and opened the door just as Brock and the two Alaska state troopers walked in.

"We need to talk," Brock said.

"Later." Christian moved past him and out into the spring day.

Jeb removed his trooper hat and shook his head. "He gets odder every day." He turned and zeroed in on Amka. "We're here to investigate the second bombing of one of your properties, Ms. Amaruq."

Just wonderful.

CHAPTER 37

Christian drove the truck out of town. He was so off right now. Not the usual calm man they all knew. He couldn't keep a thought. Was this what it was like to really care about a woman? Somebody wanted her dead, and that just pissed him off.

He hadn't been able to find Sheldon Friday. Somehow the jackass had managed to take off between his leaving the tavern and Christian heading into the grocery store. It had taken Christian five minutes just to find Wyland in the back doing inventory, and another to figure out Sheldon had left.

Just how badly did Sheldon want that insurance money?

Beside him, Amka had the window cracked, her elbow resting on the ledge, dark hair caught by the wind. She hadn't said much since they left town, just a quiet thanks when he handed her the to-go coffee Daisy had shoved into his hand.

Christian kept one hand on the wheel and the other resting loosely on his thigh. He'd borrowed Brock's truck again, the beast rumbling reliably along the river road. Yeah, he should get his own rig once things calmed down. He wanted to go to Anchorage and choose, then he could drive it home.

Maybe Amka would come with him.

No. He had to stop thinking like that. Yeah, he wanted her. Probably loved her. And she was a sweetheart to sleep under the stars with him. But no woman would want that life for years. For decades. She deserved so much better.

She was quiet next to him. The kind of quiet he liked. Damn it.

The sky had finally opened into something close to blue, and the trees lining the bank shimmered in the sunlight, the new leaves catching every ounce of it. Spring had taken hold with green pushing up through the last brittle remnants of snow. It smelled like thawed earth and cold water and something alive.

He adjusted his grip on the steering wheel. "I don't want you to get the wrong idea." He sounded like a dumbass.

Amka turned her head, one brow lifting just enough to be amused. "Which would be?"

He blew out a long breath. "You're staying at my place, and I want that. But I also don't want you thinking it means something I can't give. I'm not good at whatever this is."

She was quiet for a second. Then, "You mean relationships?"

He gave a tight nod. "Yeah." The truck rolled along a bend, and the river glinted beside them, swollen, fast, and loud over the rocks. He kept his eyes ahead. "I care about you. That's not the problem."

"Then what is?"

He hesitated. "I'm not a settling-down type. You've seen how I live. And you deserve more than half a man who sleeps on a ridge because he doesn't know what to do with four walls."

Amka sipped her coffee, her tone remaining thoughtful. "You think I don't already know that about you?"

He glanced at her. She didn't look hurt. Just contemplative. "This is temporary."

She added, "You think I want some guy who comes home at five every night and talks about tax brackets? I like you how you are. You don't have to sell me a version of yourself that doesn't exist."

"I'm trying to let you down easy here." He might have to be an actual jackass.

She snorted. "No."

He paused. "Excuse me?"

"I said, no. I'm not allowing you to let me down at all. I've decided I want this, and you're not going to play the wounded but heroic hero by making choices for my own good." The woman actually sounded amused...and slightly bored.

"Don't piss me off, Amka."

Now she full-on laughed. "*The Hulk* is one of my favorite movies." When his ears started to heat, somehow she noticed. "Fine. We'll talk about it at a later date. For now, we have enough on our plates."

The knot in his chest loosened just enough that he could breathe again. He rubbed the back of his neck. "Exactly. I don't like you being in the middle of this mess. Someone's trying to kill you. Someone's blackmailing you. Maybe the same person. Maybe not. I don't like how it's circling you."

"I don't like it either," she said. "But we'll figure it out."

"I've been trying," he said, frustration flaring. "None of it fits. Jarod gets shot in your driveway. There's a blackmail note targeting both of you. Somebody bombs your tavern twice. Steve kills Eli in the woods and leaves his body to rot. And somehow, none of this connects clean."

She sipped more coffee.

Her cabin came into view just ahead, tucked beneath the trees. Somehow, she'd talked him into taking her home to get more clothing before heading out to his place. He slowed the truck out of instinct, eyes sweeping the surrounding woods. No sign of anyone. Nothing out of place. But that didn't ease the tension riding in his spine.

Amka leaned forward and looked at her house as they passed

it toward the end of the drive. "You still think I shouldn't have come here?"

"I don't like how calm you are about it," he said bluntly. "Your house was cleared, yeah, but Jarod still died out there in that truck. Someone came to your property, shot him point-blank, and left. That should rattle you more."

"It does," she said simply. "But I'm used to losing people. My grief doesn't scream."

He parked and killed the engine. "You ready to go inside?"

"Yep." She didn't look over to the side where Jarod's truck had been. The troopers had it towed the day before.

They walked up to the front together, and the woods around them whispered with the wind. Birds chirped like nothing had happened here. Like no one had bled, or died, or killed.

She opened her door and moved inside. Christian followed her, his mind calculating where Sheldon might've gone.

The cottage smelled faintly of must and something floral beneath it, like old soap or dried lavender trying to hold the place together.

The living room opened straight from the front door, cozy but compact, with worn hardwood floors and a low wood-beamed ceiling that made the space feel like it belonged in another time. A faded rug lay between a wide old armchair and a comfortable looking couch. One of the couch cushions was askew, and a folded throw blanket had been shoved hastily to the far end. Against the far wall stood a cast iron wood stove with a small pile of split logs beside it, the ash pan still half full.

To the right, the kitchen took over the back half of the room without any walls separating it. A pine counter stretched across as a partial divider, with three mismatched stools tucked beneath it. The counter had water rings and a dark gouge near the edge—probably from a dropped knife or someone getting too enthusiastic with a can opener. The stove was clean, and the fridge was covered in handwritten notes.

Christian stood in the middle of the room, unmoving, his shoulders still tight. Her stillness caught his attention, and he partially turned. "Amka?"

She blinked once and then again, staring at a simple green knit hat on the counter. "Christian. I think I know—"

The blast of a gun discharge caught his attention right before pain burst through his chest. He pitched forward, smashing into Amka and the counter, and the world went dark.

AMKA WENT DOWN HARD, flailing under Christian. Warmth pooled over her arm. Red warmth. "Christian?" A buzzing filled her ears. Was he shot? Slight movement sounded, and a shadow crossed her vision. Pain burst through her head, and she slumped unconscious.

Amka drifted. Sound fractured. What had hit her head?

The weight on her shifted. She tried to hold on, tried to grip Christian, but her fingers wouldn't work. Nothing did. Her body had turned traitor. Blood soaked her shirt—his, not hers—and it was warm and awful and everywhere.

Christian.

She wanted to scream but couldn't shape the breath. Her lips barely parted. Her vision pulsed white around the edges. A face came close, too close, and she turned her head instinctively, but pain lanced her skull like a nail driving through the base of it. Her neck refused to support her. She gagged.

Then everything tilted.

Her body was hoisted awkwardly, dragged or carried, she couldn't tell. Her head lolled to the side, and she caught a glimpse of light flashing past the window. The interior of the house was gone. Her cheek scraped against something cold and rough—someone's jacket maybe—before she was dumped hard against what felt like vinyl. A truck seat. A door slammed.

An engine rumbled to life.

Moving. They were moving.

She was being taken.

Her eyes cracked open, barely slits, just long enough to catch the blur of trees sliding by in streaks of dark and green. Her head lolled, vision doubling. The buzz in her ears got louder. Christian's face filled her mind. The sound of the shot. The heat of his blood. His body dropping onto hers like he was trying to shield her even in death.

No. No, he couldn't be dead.

She had to fight. Had to stay awake. Get help. She tried to move. Her muscles didn't listen. Her right hand twitched, fingers curling weakly around air.

The vehicle stopped.

A door yanked open. Rough hands gripped her shoulders. She moaned, barely audible. Then her body was dragged again, this time across gravel. Pebbles jabbed at her ribs. Her knee hit something sharp, and she winced.

Another car door opened. She was lifted, shoved inside. This time the air smelled different. Greasy. Like fast food and gasoline. Her temple bumped the window. Stars exploded behind her eyes.

She thought she might throw up.

Someone swore. Something metal clicked.

The car rocked as someone climbed into the driver's seat. The engine revved, and the vehicle accelerated fast, throwing her against the seat. Her head rolled. The pressure behind her eyes pushed outward.

Christian.

She tried to focus. The pain in her head increased like a shriek. Then everything zipped out again, swallowed by a wave of black.

∽

CHRISTIAN CAME to flat on his stomach, one cheek pressed into the cold floor. The copper tang of blood filled his mouth. He pushed up to hands and knees, gritting his teeth. The sharp pain in his shoulder lit his vision white, but he didn't stop.

His hand came away wet. The blood was his.

He looked toward the door. It stood wide open, wind curling inside. Amka was gone. He swore. Loud and raw. His vision wavered when he shoved himself to his feet. He stumbled to the kitchen counter and grabbed a towel, pressed it hard to the hole just under his collarbone. The bullet had passed through muscle. He was lucky. If it had gone half an inch lower, his lung would be done.

But luck didn't matter now.

He yanked his phone free and called Brock.

"Hey—" Brock started.

"Got shot, and somebody took Amka from her house. I'm fine. They're in your truck. Call Damian and Ace, get everyone looking, and I'm going tracking." He clicked off and grabbed gauze and duct tape from the nearest drawer. Slapped them over the worst of it. The world tilted again. He gripped the counter to steady himself before heading outside.

Outside, the morning had turned quiet again, the kind of quiet that didn't sit right.

He had to find her. God. How had he let himself get fucking shot? Was he that turned around about her that he'd forgot his own damn focus? He followed the prints down the porch steps. Blood smeared the edge of the wood. Not his. Amka's. A streak where someone had dragged her across the dirt.

The scuff marks led to where Brock's truck had been parked. Fresh tire tracks bit deep into the gravel, kicking up from the sudden acceleration.

He followed on foot, moving fast despite the fire in his shoulder.

The truck had gone north, toward the old fire road. A

shortcut toward the valley. A good two miles of winding dirt before it met worn asphalt. He ran the distance. His chest burned, and he tasted blood again, but he didn't stop. Couldn't stop.

The tracks finally veered off. Just before the switchback, they curved behind a stand of alders and stopped. Brock's truck was there. Christian quickly searched it and found nothing but a bit of blood on the passenger seat. Amka's. Had to be.

A second set of tires showed. Narrower, more aggressive pattern. SUV, maybe. Possibly a light pickup with off-road grip. The angle said she'd been moved fast. No blood on the ground now. Probably moved her to the second vehicle unconscious.

Christian pressed a hand to the earth where the tread turned. Still damp. Still fresh. They'd moved fast. He stood, chest burning. His shirt clung to him, soaked through on one side, the duct-taped gauze useless now. The pain in his torso flared again, sharp and biting. He ignored it.

He turned in a slow circle, scanning the tree line.

Then he cupped his hands around his mouth and let out a sharp, rising whistle.

Waited.

The wind moved through the branches. A raven called overhead. Nothing else.

He whistled again. Louder this time. A raw edge clung to the sound.

Silence held for three long seconds.

Then, crashing brush to the east. Four-legged movement.

Tika burst from the trees at a dead sprint, tongue lolling, fur bristled. His mismatched eyes locked on Christian, and he didn't stop until he reached him. He skidded to a halt, nose down, breath coming fast.

Christian dropped to one knee again and gripped the thick ruff of fur. "Good boy," he muttered, the tightness in his throat burning worse than the hole in his chest. "We've got her trail. Let's finish this."

Tika turned and sniffed the dirt, pacing the edge of the second set of treads.

Christian followed, scanning the ground.

There was a drag mark. Slight. A vehicle had trampled the pine needles. No blood now, but the direction was clear.

He moved fast, boots churning mud, gaze on the disturbed path. He couldn't believe he'd tried to brush her off, and she'd laughed at him.

Knowing they belonged together.

And he'd fucked it up. Had let himself be shot and her be taken. She had to be all right. He needed to tell her everything— especially how he felt about her.

Tika ran beside him, nose low, tail straight behind him. They cut into the old logging road, the tires having spun deep here. Water had pooled in the ruts, and rocks jutted up in scattered clumps. The vehicle was still moving fast. Maybe thirty, thirty-five. Too fast for rough terrain.

He followed the track into thicker forest, branches scraping his arms. The sky had clouded again, light dimming. But the trail was solid.

He kept going. Pain shot down his arm. His knees ached. Sweat stung his eyes. None of it mattered.

She was out there.

He would find her.

"I'm coming for you," he said aloud, voice rough.

Tika growled and pressed ahead again.

Christian followed, boots steady in the mud. He would track them until the road gave out. Until his legs did. Or until he lost too much blood.

His vision wavered and he blinked several times to focus.

He had to find her.

CHAPTER 38

Amka slowly came to, her head aching and her nose hurting. Why did her nose hurt? She tasted blood. Wait a minute. Blood.

Christian.

She gasped, opening her eyes. He'd been shot.

The room came into focus and she tried to move but couldn't. Where was she? Wait a minute. She looked down, noting she slumped on a ratty old wooden chair. She was in Jarod's apartment. In his small and dingy living room in the Willows.

The couch was across from her. Ugly green, ripped open at one corner, stuffing leaking out like it'd given up. A crusted plate sat on the armrest. She couldn't move her hands, which were tied behind her to the chair. Wood bit into her wrists. Before she and May had broken into the place, she'd only been here once to try to talk him out of the fake engagement, and he'd grabbed her and tried to kiss her. She'd kicked him and ran outside to her car, careful not to be alone with him again.

Light caught her eye, and she turned to see a filthy window.

She smelled old pizza, feet, and something moldy. The carpet, what little showed, was worn to the threads.

The fake-wooden kitchen door was shut. The bathroom, too. Her pulse pounded against the rope. She tugged once and just caused pain up her arms.

The kitchen door was shut, and she couldn't see into the one bathroom.

"Oh. Finally." Helene Stanford walked in from the bedroom, this time wearing jeans and a sweatshirt, her black hair up in a ponytail. "Sorry about your nose. I kind of dropped you a couple of times." Her dark gaze narrowed. "You're heavier than you look."

Amka lifted her chin, her hands tied behind her back and to the chair. It was a cheaper wooden chair. Could she damage it? Right now, her head felt like mush. "I don't understand." Why would the insurance adjuster kidnap her?

Helene drew out a matching chair from the dinged oak wood table. "What's there to understand? We're going to wait right here until Jarod decides to come get his fiancée. Do you think I don't know what happened?"

Amka slowly twisted her fingers and winced as rope bit into her skin. "What exactly do you think happened?" Who was this woman?

"I saw how he looks at you. He wants you. Thought he could just drop me like I don't matter? Like all the time we spent in Anchorage doesn't matter? Our plan is going perfectly, and he just takes off?" Her eyes flickered. "I don't think so."

Amka noted the woman's bag and the rolling suitcase in the corner with a laptop perched on it. That was Jarod's. The insurance adjuster had been keeping his laptop? "You're his friend who has the video."

Helene drew back, her jaw clenching. "Friend? His *friend*?" She leaned forward now. "No, honey. I'm his soul mate. You're our ticket to a decent life."

Amka tried to add up the numbers. "The life insurance policies? You sold those to him?"

"Yeah, and I signed your name on yours. His was just to make it look like you both took those out. Guess who was going to have a rough hike later this summer?" Red tinged Helene's cheeks. "That was the plan, and then he took off. We had a little fight because I saw how much he wanted you. I'm sure that would've changed once he had you. But then, he's off pouting. Or whatever. So, he can come and get you…or I'll end you for him."

Amka frowned. "What's your plan here? That Jarod comes back and then, what?"

Helene slowly shrugged. "I think he just needs to see how much I love him. Then we'll go on with our plan."

The plan to kill Amka and get the life insurance of a million dollars? "Bad plan." Especially since Jarod was dead. Very much so. "Wait a minute. Just how crazy are you?"

"I'm not. Love does that to a girl." Helene flattened her hands on her jeans. "I'm sure Jarod is keeping track of news from town, and when you go missing, he'll come find you. And me. We'll settle everything."

Nausea rolled through Amka's stomach. "What would you do for love?"

Helene sniffed. "Everything."

"Did you set those explosives in my storage building and kitchen?"

"Yep." Helene arched an eyebrow. "You're surprisingly resilient. Cut your brake lines, too."

Amka struggled against the ropes. "Why? You know I don't even want Jarod. Obviously you know about the blackmail."

"Extortion," Helene corrected. "He had to be engaged to you for folks to believe you'd take out insurance policies on each other. But he really thinks he wants you. He won't once he sees how far I'll go to have him." Her voice cracked on the end.

What would the woman do if she discovered Jarod was dead? Amka tried to focus. "Did you kill Christian?" He couldn't be dead. It wasn't possible. The man was larger than life. Strong. Deadly. Hers.

"Dunno. He sure wasn't moving when I dragged your ass out of there. I've never smashed anybody in the head before and was worried I hit you too hard with the gun. But you seem okay. For now, that is." She sounded more thoughtful than psychotic, which was terrifying.

Where was that gun she'd referenced?

Could Amka keep her talking? For how long? Jarod wasn't ever coming back. "You met Jarod after his motel burned down. You were the adjuster, right?"

"Yep. Fell for him right then and there." Helene brushed a strand of her dark hair away from her face. "He burned down the motel himself. You know that, right?" When Amka shook her head, Helene's smile widened. "See? He trusted me with the truth. I gave him that payout in an instant, knowing we'd be together forever. But he wanted more money. Wanted you. Thought he could get both."

Amka tried to work her hands free. Where was that gun? She could try to break the chair, but that'd give Helene time to reach the gun. "The video? It's on the computer?"

Helene lifted her head, looking down her nose. "Yeah. On Jarod's computer, my phone, and his phone. Which he should be checking since I've left him fifty messages, including the one about meeting him at his place with his meal ticket." She cocked her head. "I suppose it might be in the cloud, too? I've never understood how the whole cloud thing works."

Amka's hands were screaming now, the rope grinding her skin raw. Her circulation had vanished long ago. The legs of the chair wobbled every time she shifted. Her fingers were wet—blood or sweat, she didn't know. Maybe both.

Tears gathered in Helene's eyes. She sniffed again. "Maybe I should just kill you and leave your body for him to find. That would be a show of love, right?"

Amka's mouth opened and then closed. She could feel the dried blood on her upper lip from falling on her nose. "No. Definitely not."

"I don't know." Helene looked down at her hands. "I guess it could be an offering." Her shoulders hunched.

"Did you try to blackmail me?"

Helene wiped her nose on her sleeve. "Yeah, I left both notes for you. The first one about the explosion and fire was so Jarod didn't get pissed. He didn't know I'd rigged that to kill you. He wasn't ready to kill you, but I was, so I learned how to create the device from an internet video. The weird note got Jarod off my back. Well, at least he wasn't sure I'd done it. I'm a good liar."

Amka thought about who could've been hurt. What a horrible woman. "How long have you been in town, anyway?"

"A few weeks. I've been staying here. Well, until I officially showed up, and then I did get a room at Flossy's."

Amka needed to find that gun. "You left the blackmail note after Jarod disappeared?"

"Of course." Helene preened. "The note was a wake-up call for my man. I figured it would get him mad and he'd try to find me. I just don't understand why he's left me. It doesn't make sense."

The woman was unraveling. Amka had to move and now.

She took a breath that barely made it past the pressure in her chest and twisted, leaping up and slamming the side of the chair against the wall. Wood splintered. Pain shot up her arms as the impact jarred every bone from elbow to spine. The chair didn't break. Not yet.

Helene frowned. "That was stupid. You're just going to hurt yourself."

Amka did it again. Harder.

The backrest cracked. Her shoulder burned white-hot. She

gritted her teeth and threw herself against the wall one more time. The chair exploded behind her. Jagged legs snapped, and she hit the floor in a tangle of broken wood and rope. Her wrists were still bound, but the chair was gone.

Helene shrieked and dove for the bag by the suitcase.

"No—" Amka tried to crawl, but her right leg buckled under her, the thigh muscle seizing from the fall.

Helene ripped a gun out of the bag.

"Don't," Amka gasped, her voice shredded.

Helene turned, weapon in both hands now, her eyes wild. "You think you can just take everything from me?" she panted. "You think you matter more?"

Amka scrambled forward. Her wrists howled in pain. She got her knees under her and lunged out of pure instinct and desperation.

Helene fired.

The shot cracked into the wall, wood dust raining down.

Amka slammed into her. The two women hit the floor in a heap, and the gun slid across the fake wooden floor to hit the front door. Amka tried to twist her hands free of the rope, Helene clawing at her face.

"You ruined everything!" Helene screamed.

Amka drove her shoulder into Helene's gut. The woman grunted and elbowed Amka hard in the jaw. Lights burst behind her eyes.

They rolled.

Helene landed on top, fists raining down. Amka raised her arms, still bound, trying to deflect the blows. She caught a punch across the cheekbone, and the world tilted.

She fought through it, leaning up to slam her forehead into Helene's nose.

Helene howled, blood pouring from her nostrils. She recoiled just enough.

Amka bucked hard, shoving her off.

They both scrambled for the gun, and Helene got there first. She grabbed it and turned, already firing.

The gun kicked in Helene's hand, the sound tearing through Amka's skull. She flinched, breath caught in her throat, waiting for the impact—

It never came.

The front door exploded inward.

Christian.

He didn't pause. Didn't shout. Just moved, fast and precise and kicked the gun out of Helene's hand. Tika hit the woman, snarling, his massive body slamming into her side. She screamed and went down hard with the wolf-pup pouncing on top of her chest, his teeth bared.

Amka pushed herself upright, breath scraping raw in her throat. Her cheek stung. Her wrists burned. Everything inside her shook, but she was still here. Still breathing. Her hands were still tied, but she dragged herself back, wedging into the space between the ratty couch and the coffee table. "Christian?" He was standing? There? How?

Tires shrieked outside. More boots. More noise. It barely registered.

Christian reached her, crouching. "Amka? Talk to me."

Even now, he was giving orders.

Brock stormed in, gun drawn, eyes wild. "Clear?"

Christian didn't look up. "Got her," he said, voice all steel.

Brock's gaze swept the room, locking on Amka for a half second. His jaw ticked. He didn't speak again, just moved toward Helene.

Damian slid in behind him, along with Ace.

Amka finally sagged, her body trying to melt into the floor. "How did you find me?" Her shoulders ached from where Helene had sat on her, and the rope at her wrists had rubbed her raw.

"Tracked you. Tika and me."

Oh yeah. He could track anybody. Her face throbbed from the last punch, but everything still worked. Mostly.

Christian leaned in closer, those dual-colored eyes concerned. "Baby? Tell me you're okay."

Baby. He'd called her that before. She smiled.

Panic sizzled across his face. He dropped beside her and took her face in his hands like he was afraid to break her. "I've got you. You're okay now." His voice was rough. Warmer than anything she'd ever heard.

She couldn't see well. "Weren't we just in this situation? Seriously?" She was so over explosions and people pointing guns at her. "I need a vacation."

Something flickered in his eyes. Humor. Relief. Rage. She couldn't name the sentiment. But the sight grounded her. Behind him, boots pounded again. Troopers shouting. Brock cuffed Helene as Ace watched dispassionately and Tika sat quietly to the side.

Where had Damian gone?

Amka swallowed down the lump in her throat. "I'm glad you're here," she whispered to Christian right before she passed out.

Cold.

CHAPTER 39

Christian sat in the hospital chair, hard plastic digging into his back, his gut clenching. His hands were braced on his thighs, stiff from holding still too long, the wound in his shoulder screaming. Didn't matter. He kept his eyes on Amka.

He almost lost her. Couldn't lose her. Ever.

She was propped up in the hospital bed, bruised, stitched, and stubborn. An oxygen monitor clipped to her finger beeped steady and soft, almost in rhythm with the slight tremble in her hands. She kept her voice calm and even as she finished walking the troopers through the entire ordeal. Her tone didn't shake, but her fingers did.

Doc May moved quietly behind her, checking vitals, peering at her pupils with a small light, the hem of her green scrubs looking worn over her white tennis shoes. Her blonde hair was piled up in what had probably started as a neat bun hours ago. She didn't say much. Just nodded, made a note on a chart, moved to the next thing. Focused. Controlled. Probably pissed.

May hadn't stopped glaring at Christian since she'd walked in and realized his shoulder was bleeding through the half-assed duct-tape job he'd done hours earlier. He hadn't let her touch him. Not yet. Not until Amka was cleared.

"...And she fired the gun, but I'd already slammed into her," Amka finished, her voice raw. "Then Christian and Tika came in." She looked toward him then, gaze landing on his shoulder with something soft in her expression. "He saved me once again."

Paige, sharp in her uniform and perfectly gelled bun, jotted a few final notes. Jeb stood beside her, hat in hand, mouth twitching slightly as he chewed over something. Paige snapped the notebook closed. "It's a strong statement, and we believe you. But it doesn't change what we're seeing in Jarod Teller's case."

Amka's jaw twitched. "He's dead. What more do you need?"

Jeb shifted his stance. "We know that. But Helene Stanford was clearly waiting for him to show. That doesn't track with her being the shooter. He was a bad guy, Amka. If you killed him in self-defense, let us help you."

Christian stiffened. "You're saying you still think she did it?"

"Yes," Jeb said. "Even more so now. But it was probably in self-defense. The prosecuting attorney agreed and charged her. This isn't going away."

Christian started to rise, already ready to snap, but Doc May turned then—fast, sharp—and cut the air with one hand. "Hold it," she said, her voice clipped. She moved around the bed with that deceptively graceful doctor glide and pointed a finger at Christian. "Sit. Down."

He opened his mouth.

"I said sit," she snapped. "You're still bleeding through gauze held together with actual duct tape. This is not a movie, and you're not Rambo. But I'm finishing with my patient before I deal with your nonsense." She turned back to Amka. "You were charged?"

Amka nodded, her gaze intense on the doctor. "Yes, and it's okay. I didn't kill him, and I'm willing to go to trial to prove it."

May took a step back. "Amka—"

"No," Amka said. "I've got this."

Warning ticked down Christian's spine. What had Amka said right before he'd been shot? When she looked at that green hat on the counter?

May turned, her jaw set, desperation in her eyes. "I shot Jarod."

"No," Amka protested.

May held up a hand, looking at the troopers. "I dropped by Amka's house that night to return the hat that she left when she stayed over last week. She never leaves her door locked, so I just dropped it on the counter. When I was leaving, Jarod was there, and he was drunk." Tears filled the doctor's eyes. "He dragged me into his truck, tried to take off my clothes, we fought, and I grabbed the gun from under his seat. I pointed it at him, trying to get out, and he lunged. I shot."

"That's not true," Amka said. "It's not."

Shock ricocheted through Christian. "Both of you stop talking right now." He needed to call Daisy.

May shook her head. "The gun is in my office here. Bottom drawer." She pushed strands of hair away from her face. "I'd appreciate it if we could keep this as quiet as possible. I moved out here for privacy."

Shit.

Paige exited the room and returned with a Glock in a plastic bag. Did the trooper just keep those in her pockets? "Dr. Smirnov, we're going to have to arrest you."

May looked at Christian. "You can right after I stitch him up. I'm the only doctor here. Come on, Christian."

"No. You can do it here," he said.

She sighed. "Fine. Let me get supplies." Jeb followed her from the room and they both returned very quickly.

Christian helped her remove his shirt.

"I can't believe this," she muttered, poking him with her gloved hands. "You're lucky the bullet went all the way through. I'm giving you a local whether you like it or not."

Christian looked at the distress on Amka's face.

She cleared her throat. "That explains why you were doing shots at the bar. That isn't like you."

May sighed. "Yeah. It was self-defense, but I still killed a man."

Amka shook her head. "You didn't have to confess."

Christian barely kept from shaking his head. The woman had planned to actually go to trial to protect her friend? She needed a damn keeper. Good thing it looked like he'd live through the night, even though May seemed to be stabbing him rather strongly with the needle as she patched him up. "It's going to be okay, Amka." He'd make sure of it. Somehow.

May finished and ripped off the gloves. "I'll call Daisy. Hopefully I can be out on bail later today because we don't have another doctor." She patted his shoulder. "I did a good job here. Don't screw it up and rip out my stitches. Any chance I could get you to stay in the hospital?"

"No," Christian said shortly. "However, we'll wait here for you to get released on bail."

"Thanks." May moved and then tripped, nearly going down.

Christian caught her, surprised by the feel of metal in his hand.

May winked and stood. "All right, troopers. Let's do this." They all three left the room.

Christian looked down at his hand.

"What's that?" Amka whispered.

"A phone. Best guess? Jarod's phone." The doc must've taken it after shooting him. Damian had taken both the laptop and Helene's phone right before the troopers had arrived earlier. With his resources at EVE, he should be able to find the video of

Hank's death on each device as well as the cloud—and delete them.

Amka prodded her swollen nose. "We have to help her. Jarod tried to attack me a couple of times, so I could testify he was like that."

Anger cut through Christian and he shoved it away. "That's the kind of thing you're gonna want to tell me from now on, sweetheart."

A pretty blush wandered across her face. She liked endearments. Good to know. "Why would I do that?" Her chin rose.

"Because I love you. Want you forever." He stood and crossed to her, not caring how badly his shoulder and front of his clavicle felt. He'd almost lost her, and that couldn't happen again. He hadn't planned to find love, but he had, and now he'd figure it out. "I'm not sure how we're gonna do it, but there's no way I can let you go. Not now. Not ever." He leaned down and kissed her. "Think you have enough room in your life for an AWT and wolf-husky mix?"

"Yeah," she said softly, "I have more than room. You two are my life."

CHAPTER 40

T*hree weeks later*

AMKA SETTLED into the chair at the campfire, her gaze on the river creek running along the edge of Christian's property. Tika stretched out next to her, snoring rhythmically.

Movement sounded behind her, and Christian dropped a blanket over her, picked her up, sat in her chair, and planted her on his lap. "Sun's going down. It's going to get cold."

She snuggled into him, her nose in his neck. "Is your shoulder okay?"

"It's fine. Nothing to worry about."

Worrying about him was now her right, and she kind of loved it. She cuddled deeper beneath the blanket. "Are you taking care of me?"

"Always. That's my job."

She shut her eyes for a moment. They'd take care of each other, but she truly enjoyed the feeling of shelter. "This might sound off-kilter, but I think Tika might be getting a cold. He's snoring like crazy." Did wolves get colds? Most animals could, so it made sense. "I wonder if we should take him to the vet."

Christian stretched his long legs out to the fire. "He'll be fine. Even if it is a cold, he'll shake it. Don't worry." He kissed the top of her head. "Are you sure you're okay moving in here at my place? There's plenty of room to expand my house. I mean, our house."

"Sure. I like it here."

"I'm having plans drawn up and have an idea for a bedroom that can be both inside and outside with the right hydraulics." His low voice rumbled across her skin. "We could close it up for bad weather and keep it open for good. Put it against the rock."

Amusement slid through her. "For a good defensive position?"

"Of course."

She kissed his neck. "Sounds good. However, I assume hydraulics cost a lot. Since I cleared the mortgage on my place, I can contribute once I sell my house. Also, a new insurance adjuster is looking at the storage unit fire, and since Helene admitted to setting it, we should get that money soon."

"Don't need money." He shrugged. "A buddy from the Navy took all of my income and invested it really well since I didn't spend it on anything but this land and a few supplies. Take your money and start those businesses with Ace. It'll be good for both of you."

How sweet was that? She leaned back to study his face. In the firelight, he looked rugged and untamed. Totally sexy. "Also, and this is weird, it looks like I actually get the million dollars from Jarod's insurance policy that he took out just to look like we were both on the same page with the life insurance." She swallowed. "I won't want that money and would like to donate it to Knife's Edge Native Association." She held her breath.

"I like that." His gaze warmed. "Excellent idea."

Her body calmed. It figured that Christian wouldn't care less about money. However, he loved his brothers. "Don't you think we should tell Ace that Doc May was charged with Jarod's murder?" May's arraignment had gone just like Amka's, via Zoom, and so far, nobody in town even knew about it. May was out on bail for the time being, working as their only doctor. Apparently Daisy had painted a dire image of what would happen to the town if they didn't have a doctor for any length of time.

"Not today. Maybe those two should figure it out together?" Was that amusement in Christian's voice? Seemed like it.

Amka narrowed her eyes. "Don't tell me that the mysterious, wounded, and badass Christian Osprey is a matchmaker."

"Say that again and I'll spank you." While he sounded lazy and amused, he probably wasn't kidding.

"I'm comfortable right now. I'll say it again later." She rested her head against his good shoulder, listening to his heartbeat. "I like that you're no longer fighting us and thinking I could do better."

He shifted her slightly. "You probably could do better, but it's too late for that. You're in my heart, and I'm determined to be in yours. We'll just have to figure it out." His broad and strong body remained relaxed around her, as if once the decision had been made, he was totally at peace with it.

She tilted her head to better see his eyes. "You've been in mine for months. I love you, Christian. You're better than anybody else in the world for me, and I hope you someday realize that."

"Sure." He kissed her nose, something passing through his eyes. He liked being told he was loved. She'd have to do that every day. "Doesn't matter. You're with me." He frowned. "It's going to be hell leaving you this summer for AWT training. Like I need training." His jaw clenched.

She ran her palm along the stubble, smiling when his jaw

relaxed. "It'll go fast, and you'll make an amazing Alaska Wildlife Trooper. It's the perfect job for you." In fact, he was already back on the case with Dutch, although they didn't have any leads yet. Dutch's lead hadn't panned out. That was something she'd worry about another day, and she liked the idea of Christian and Dutch working together. "I'm glad you're going that avenue." He needed a purpose to be happy, and he liked protecting and defending. It made sense.

"As am I."

She played with a button on his dark flannel. There was nothing like a mountain man who looked good in flannel. "Have you heard from Damian?"

"Yep. He successfully deleted every copy of the video showing Hank's death, even from the cloud. However, he hasn't found his wife." Christian flashed a smile. A real one. "That's going to be fun to watch. I've never seen D so ruffled."

"I guess." Amka really wanted to find Nixi and get to know her better. How fascinating. The woman was practically a spy. Or actually one. "I scrolled through social media, and not only are all of her posts gone, so is the one about you carrying me out of that fire. It's completely gone." What kind of connections did it take to really get something off the internet? Like completely?

Christian stared at the fire. "She came to town for a reason, and Damian is the only one I can see. So she'll be back."

"I hope so."

Christian tangled his fingers in her hair and drew back her head, taking her mouth. He kissed her deep and full, sending sparks of fire to her core. Throughout her entire body. Then he released her. "I love you, Amka. Want to share a name. I'll get a ring and all that, but I wanted you to know."

She blinked. "Are you asking me to marry you?"

He kissed her again. "I'll do it with a ring. I'm more just telling you that it's happening. Probably later this summer."

Happiness filled her along with amusement. Maybe a little exasperation. "The proposal is happening later this summer?"

"No. The wedding."

She paused. Then chuckled. "What am I going to do with you?"

"Live happily ever after with me and my wolf-husky snoring mutt."

Yeah. That sounded just about perfect.

~

Keep up with the crew in Alaska with Ace's book, Burn of Summer!

~

If you enjoyed the Alaska wilderness, give Idaho a try with the Anna Albertini Files. Here's a quick excerpt from Anna's newest release, Habeas Corpus:

Two elderly women walked inside the store, chattering happily about finding the perfect wedding gift for somebody named Allison as they shook snow off their coats on the mat. I stopped walking and hovered, not wanting to startle them. In unison, they silenced and looked at me. The tallest one screamed and laboriously pulled a humungous silver-barreled revolver out of her wide crocheted purse.

I froze. "Whoa."

Her hand shook on the obviously heavy weapon. She was about my height and slender beneath her black wool coat, the long sleeves partially covering her hands. "Don't move."

"I'm not." I took a deep breath. "That's the biggest handgun I've ever seen." I wasn't a *Dirty Harry* fan, but I was fairly certain I saw him wielding one of those on a commercial for an old movie.

She nodded vigorously, her faded green eyes wide and curled white hair bobbing. "It is. It's a Smith & Wesson 500 revolver. I borrowed it from my grandson, George."

I had absolutely no idea why George would need that much firepower. "Is your grandson here?" I wouldn't mind a voice of reason.

She snorted. "No. He's working. Today is a workday for most folks your age. But not you. You robbed this place."

My head dropped to note the disaster of stains, now including blood, on my wool coat. "I didn't rob anybody." Holding my hands up, I let the bloody tissues float to the floor. Except one. That one remained stuck to my injured right wrist. "The Cupid gang came in and robbed us. They tied us up, and I just got free."

"Help me," Lisa called out.

The armed woman swung her gun down the hallway. "Who's that? Is this a trap?"

I sighed. "No. That's Lisa. She owns the place. I'm Anna Albertini. What's your name?"

The second woman, who had to be in her late seventies, narrowed her gaze. She was under five feet tall with short, white hair, dressed in an overflowing gray coat that nearly brushed her ankles. "Albertini? Like Elda?"

Hope burst through me. "Yes. Elda is my nonna."

She pulled a cell phone from her right pocket and pressed a button.

"Hello," Nonna answered.

"Hi, Elda, it's Martha," the older woman said. "Tricia has a gun pointed at a woman who says she's your granddaughter, but she's at the antique store covered in what looks like paint, ink, dirt, and blood."

Nonna sighed. "That *is* most likely my Anna."

I nodded wildly. "Hi, Nonna. It is me, and we were just robbed by the Cupid gang."

"Again?" Anger coated Nonna's words. "Tricia? You turn that gun away from my granddaughter, or I'm bringing my spoon to the barn raising this spring. Don't think I won't do it."

All three of us winced. Nonna was well known for keeping a wooden spoon in her purse to clap people's heads.

Tricia slowly lowered her shaking arms and sighed in relief. "Sorry about that. Can't be too careful, you know?"

I finally breathed. "I know. Do you mind calling the police?"

ACKNOWLEDGMENTS

Thank you to everyone who helped bring *Thaw of Spring* to life. The snow may have melted, but the danger hasn't. This time it's rain, mud, and secrets blooming beneath the surface—and as always, it took a team to shape the chaos into a story. If I've missed anyone, blame the fog, caffeine withdrawal, or the characters refusing to follow directions.

To Big Tone: you don't brainstorm plot twists or proofread pages, but you do keep me sane when the deadlines hit and the words stop flowing. You're the voice of calm in the storm and the one who reminds me to close the laptop and go live a little. I'd be lost without you.

Karlina and Gabe, you're the steady heartbeat of my world. This writing life might be full of fictional drama, but you two keep the real stuff grounded and full of love. Thank you for being my constants.

To Caitlin Blasdell, my brilliant agent and trusted navigator. Thank you for steering my career through deadlines, contracts, and everything in between. You keep the business side from feeling like a black hole and make sure the stories stay at the center.

A huge thank-you to Stacey Tardif for making room in your editing schedule for this one. You came in with fresh eyes, sharp instincts, and a killer sense of what needed tightening. Your edits made the story smoother, stronger, and more alive. I'm so glad you joined the chaos.

And to Jennifer Eschrich at Tantor Media, thank you for

breathing life into these characters through audio. Your professionalism, insight, and easy collaboration made this process a joy. I couldn't have asked for a better partner to bring these voices into readers' ears.

Big thanks to Anissa Beatty, who leads the Rebecca's Rebels street team, and thank you to my incredible Beta Readers—Gabi Brocklesby, Heather Frost, Joan Lai, Madison Fairbanks, and Leanna Feazel—thank you for your sharp eyes, honest feedback, and unwavering support. You help me spot the plot holes before the characters fall through them, and you cheer like crazy when it all comes together. You make this whole journey brighter.

Endless thanks to Kathleen Sweeney and the creative wizards at Book Brush. You turned spring in Alaska into something moody, mysterious, and beautiful. I throw concepts at you like confetti, and you somehow always turn them into something stunning.

Thanks also to Writerspace, for helping connect these wild Alaskan stories to the readers who love danger, romance, and a little mud on the boots. Your support continues to mean the world.

To my family—Gail and Jim English, Kathy and Herbie Zanetti, Debbie and Travis Smith, Stephanie and Don West, Jessica and Jonah Namson, Cathie and Bruce Bailey, and Chelli and Jason Younker—you are my rock-solid foundation. Your support never wavers, even when I'm mumbling to myself about fictional people doing terrible things. I love you all more than words (and that's saying something).

READING ORDER

I know a lot of you like the exact reading order for a series, so here's the exact reading order as of the release of this book, although if you read most novels out of order, it's okay.

GRIMM BARGAINS

1. One Cursed Rose
2. One Dark Kiss
3. One Shattered Crown

KNIFE'S EDGE, ALASKA SERIES

1. Dead of Winter
2. Thaw of Spring
3. Burn of Summer

DARK PROTECTORS

1. Fated
2. Claimed

3. Tempted Novella
4. Hunted
5. Consumed
6. Provoked
7. Twisted Novella
8. Shadowed
9. Tamed Novella
10. Marked
11. Wicked Ride
12. Wicked Edge
13. Wicked Burn
14. Talen Novella
15. Wicked Kiss
16. Wicked Bite
17. Teased novella
18. Tricked novella
19. Tangled novella
20. Vampire's Faith (**A great entry point for series.**)
21. Demon's Mercy
22. Vengeance novella
23. Alpha's Promise
24. Hero's Haven
25. Vixen novella
26. Guardian's Grace
27. Vampire novella
28. Rebel's Karma
29. Immortal's Honor
30. A Vampire's Kiss novella
31. Garrett's Destiny
32. Warrior's Hope
33. A Vampire's Mate novella
34. Prince of Darkness
35. Eye of the Cat
36. Heart of the Hunter

STOPE PACKS (wolf shifters)

1. Wolf
2. Alpha
3. Shifter
4. Predator
5. Enforcer

LAUREL SNOW SERIES

1. You Can Run
2. You Can Hide
3. You Can Die
4. You Can Kill
5. You Can Scream

DEEP OPS SERIES

1. Hidden
2. Taken Novella
3. Fallen
4. Shaken (in Pivot Anthology)
5. Broken
6. Driven
7. Unforgiven
8. Frostbitten
9. Unforgotten

THE ANNA ALBERTINI FILES

1. Disorderly Conduct
2. Bailed Out
3. Adverse Possession
4. Holiday Rescue novella

5. Santa's Subpoena
6. Holiday Rogue novella
7. Tessa's Trust
8. Holiday Rebel novella
9. Habeas Corpus
10. Celtic Justice

SIN BROTHERS/BLOOD BROTHERS

1. Forgotten Sins
2. Sweet Revenge
3. Blind Faith
4. Total Surrender
5. Deadly Silence
6. Lethal Lies
7. Twisted Truths

SCORPIUS SYNDROME SERIES

Scorpius Syndrome/The Brigade Novellas

1. Scorpius Rising
2. Blaze Erupting
3. Power Surging - TBA
4. Hunter Advancing - TBA

Scorpius Syndrome NOVELS

1. Mercury Striking
2. Shadow Falling
3. Justice Ascending
4. Storm Gathering
5. Winter Igniting
6. Knight Awakening

MONTANA MAVERICK SERIES

1. Against the Wall
2. Under the Covers
3. Rising Assets
4. Over the Top
5. Holding the Reins

Redemption, WY

1. Rescue Cowboy Style (Novella in the Lone Wolf Anthology)
2. Rescue Hero Style (Novella in the Peril Anthology)
3. Rescue Rancher Style (Novella in the Cowboy Anthology)
4. Book # 1 launch - subscribe to my newsletter for more information about the new series.

ABOUT THE AUTHOR

New York Times, USA Today, Publisher's Weekly, Wall Street Journal and Amazon #1 bestselling author Rebecca Zanetti has published more than ninety novels and novellas, which have been translated into several languages, with millions of copies sold worldwide. Her books have received Publisher's Weekly, Library Journal, and Kirkus starred reviews, favorable Washington Post and New York Times Book Reviews, and have been included in Amazon best books of the year.

Rebecca has ridden in a locked Chevy trunk, has asked the unfortunate delivery guy to release her from a set of handcuffs, and has discovered the best silver mine shafts in which to bury a body…all in the name of research. Honest. Find Rebecca at: www.RebeccaZanetti.com

Printed in Dunstable, United Kingdom